THE POPPY DICHOTOMY

War on two fronts

Richard Cave

RC Creative Solutions

*Dedicated to my mum, who has always been there
to support me in my creative endeavours,*

The only easy day was yesterday.

CONTENTS

FOREWORD

To those men and women whom in secret and great danger protect our peace on a daily basis, we are to never know their efforts, the only measure is that we are free to live our lives without fear or tyranny.

PREFACE

All characters appearing in this work are fictitious.
Any resemblance to real persons, living
or dead, is purely coincidental
This is historical fiction,

CHAPTER 1

Poppy

The grey concrete housing estate loomed over the neighbourhood like a forgotten relic of a bygone era, its once-proud facade now marred by the scars of neglect and decay. Broken windows adorned with graffiti tags cast jagged shadows against the weathered walls. At the same time, litter danced in the breeze like confetti at a desolate celebration.

Broken pipes leaked steadily, their rhythmic drips echoing through the empty corridors, adding to the symphony of decay that permeated the air. Water stains snaked down the sides of the buildings like tears shed for the forgotten souls who once called this place home.

Broken garage doors creaked in protest as they hung precariously from their hinges, their rusted frames a testament to years of abandonment and disrepair. Vandalised cars, their windows smashed and tyres deflated, stood as silent witnesses to the rampant disregard for property and life.

Amid this urban wasteland, a lone fox darted across the atrium, its sleek form a fleeting glimpse of life amidst the desolation. The early morning sun struggled to penetrate the thick veil of gloom over the estate, its feeble rays casting a pale glow on the concrete jungle below.

But despite the darkness that shrouded the estate, there was an eerie sense of finality in the air, as if the buildings themselves were resigned to their fate, standing as silent sentinels of a world forgotten.

The morning unfurled its discordant symphony with the clink of milk bottles and the ceaseless hum of traffic outside the imposing brutalist architecture. The sun, a brazen intruder, cast its unwelcome rays upon the chintz curtains, defiantly closed to shield the room from the impoliteness of the sunlit day outside.

In the bedroom, the atmosphere was draped in the soft glow of early morning. An alarm clock, an unwelcome harbinger of reality, pierced the cocoon of warmth at precisely 0600. A hand emerged, slapping the snooze button as the bed's occupant burrowed deeper into the sanctuary of sheets, where the allure of sleep lingered like a siren's call.

The incessant banging on the bedroom door abruptly shattered the morning's tranquillity. "Bugger off, Danny. I'm asleep," barked Daphne Wills, a woman of fifty, her voice slicing through the air with a resolute force. Her son, Danny Wills, a determined eighteen-year-old, stood outside, unyielding. "Mum, you'll be late for work. You're going to miss the bus."

"I am fine. I am up," asserted Daphne, her words tinged with the reluctance of abandoning the sanctuary of dreams.
"Like I believe you. Come on, or I will come in. Your tea is getting cold," persisted Danny.
"I will be up in a moment."
The door swung open abruptly, revealing Danny's impatience. He entered, forcefully pulling back the curtains, ushering the dawn into the room. The ambience, a throwback to the 1960s, was adorned with an icon of the Virgin Mary and a Cross above the bed, showcasing Daphne's devout Christian identity. A reasonable person and a nurse, she wore her values like armour.

"Mum, you're seriously going to be late," urged Danny, a

reminder of the impending chaos outside.

Simultaneously, the alarm clock resumed its relentless buzzing. Daphne, reluctantly emerging from the cocoon of sleep, reached out to silence it again. Unfazed, Danny walked over, relegating the alarm to a corner, where it continued its persistent drone.

The covers pulled back, revealing Daphne's bleary eye. "My darling child, I should have given you away at birth. Forgive me, dear Lord."

Danny pointed to the neatly ironed nurse's uniform on the landing, ignoring her melodramatic plea. "Get up. Tea's getting cold, and I've ironed your uniform."

Daphne relented, albeit begrudgingly. "I'll be down in a minute."

"You better," Danny replied, walking into her eyeline. He, too, donned nursing scrubs, a stark contrast to his British-born effeminacy.

With an HCA badge bearing his name, he leaned in, kissing his mother on the forehead.

"My sweet boy," Daphne murmured with a smile.

"Enough of that. Stop procrastinating and get up," Danny commanded, the persistent buzz of the alarm underscoring the impending chaos awaiting them outside the sanctity of their home.

***

The traffic stretched endlessly down the road, a sluggish serpent inching forward with painful deliberation. The morning sun, an unforgiving brilliance, cast blinding rays on the beleaguered drivers. Backlighting the tendrils and wisps of exhaust fumes in front, the sun painted an ethereal picture of morning commotion.

Amidst this automotive queue, the traffic lights presided over the roadworks, imposing an ephemeral pause on the chaos of trapped vehicles. At the helm of a Biege Volvo estate car sat Derek, a seasoned 67-year-old. Clad in driving gloves, a hat, and yellow-tinted glasses, he emanated impatience—an individual shackled by time's relentless ticking.

Derek's Beige Volvo estate, impeccably maintained and freshly waxed from the weekend prior, mirrored his personality. Beige, droll, and reliable, it exuded simplicity, devoid of outrageous nuances or a flair for the dramatic. Much like Derek, the car embraced straightforward shapes—angular and concise.

Derek himself was a reflection of his vehicle—unassuming and dependable. However, an unseen force had unshackled his temper on this particular day. The culprit: a relentless ticking clock, ticking away precious seconds.

Whatever stirred his agitation held paramount importance, a sentiment lost on the indifferent and selfish drivers surrounding him, who exhibited no inclination to learn, understand, or care about his pressing concerns.

Radio Four played softly in his car, the mellow ballad and legato strings providing a counterpoint to the morning aggravation. Derek's fingers tapped in rhythm, subconsciously responding to the frustrating tableau around him.

As the traffic lights shifted to green, a reckless driver abruptly cut him off, catalysing Derek's visible agitation. "For

GOODNESS SAKES, hurry up!" he bellowed, his exasperation echoing within the confines of his vehicle. However, fate seemed to conspire against him. When he reached the green light, it had transformed into an infuriating red. Derek's frustration erupted in a symphony of shouts and rhythmic slaps upon the steering wheel.

Equipped with a satellite navigation system, Derek's vehicle added to the auditory chaos with its mechanical drone. "Take the next left. Take the next left," it repeated, oblivious to Derek's mounting irritation. "I know, you stupid bloody cow!" he retorted, the tangible edge of annoyance in his voice.

The electronic navigator persisted, "When convenient, make a U-turn. When convenient, make a U-turn."

In frustration, Derek's hand swiped at the GPS, sending it tumbling off its mount and lodged beneath his seat. Leaning to retrieve it, he was serenaded by the impatient chorus of horns from the car behind him. When Derek finally looked up, he realised the traffic light had betrayed him again, shifting back to green.

Attempting to move forward, Derek's car betrayed him again, sputtering to a stall. "WILL YOU JUST Fu..." his expletive hung in the air, a testament to the absurdity of his morning ordeal.

***

Daphne's apartment, a relic of time etched in worn linoleum and dim light, unfolded with the symphony of everyday sounds. Old furniture, worn but well-loved, occupied the room, each piece telling a story of days gone by. A coffee table, its surface inset with colourful tiles, stood proudly in the centre of the room, a relic from a bygone era. Nearby, a gas fire. Above the fireplace hung a Goya painting of the Blue Girl, her enigmatic gaze captivating all who dared to meet her eyes. It was a prized possession, adding a touch of sophistication to the otherwise quaint surroundings.

Despite the vintage decor, a small flat-screen TV stood out as the lone modern appliance in the room, a testament to the passage of time. Yet even this modern contraption seemed to blend seamlessly into the muted colour scheme of the room.

Every inch of the space was meticulously arranged, with lace doilies adorning the side tables and porcelain dolls gracing the surfaces of the furniture. Nicknacks and souvenir plates adorned the walls, each a cherished memento of days gone by. Each step she took, accompanied by the familiar tap of her shoes, resonated with the echoes of countless journeys. In her grasp, the hessian shopping bag swayed gently, a silent witness to the routine of life.

Beside her, a force of urban vitality named Danny guided her forward, a dance of family woven into the fabric of their shared existence. The worn-out hallway held stories in its weary walls, whispered through the worn soles of their shoes.

Approaching the stairs, Danny, a contemporary knight with the city's flair, unfurled a coat for Daphne. His ensemble spoke of urban chic — a robust puffy jacket, the glimpse of an iPhone from his pocket, and Beats headphones draped casually. A bike helmet adorned his head, a utilitarian crown for the daily urban quest.

"Mum, your bag," he offered, a simple gesture underscored by a shared smile, a language moulded through the silent conversations of countless days. Daphne, cloaked in the shield of her coat, turned towards the door, ready to embrace the world beyond.

"If you did your driving lessons, you would have a car and drive me to work," she teased maternally, a timeless plea resonating with the undertones of adulthood. Danny, ever the impatient youth, responded with urgency.

"Mum, you're going to miss the bus."

Their banter painted the air as they stepped into the harsh sunlight. Danny, the urban navigator, claimed his symbol of autonomy — an expensive mountain bike. A final door check: Outside, the estate sprawled, its ambience shifting into a darker, more ominous tone. The concrete, once a blank canvas, now bore the stains of iron and salt, a testament to the harsh realities of the urban environment. Dust from worn brake shoes, a gritty residue of ceaseless motion, lay scattered across the once pristine landscape. The transition from the haven of Homelife to the exterior mirrored the stark contrast between the familiar and the unknown, each footfall resonating with the heartbeat of a city pulsating with life and challenges. A shared smile was exchanged once more, and he descended the stairs with the ease of a seasoned city dweller.

The crossbar of his bike rested on his shoulder, each step a rhythmic testament to the fluidity of urban life. Meanwhile, Daphne Descended in the working lift, the vertical journey marking the beginning of their separate trajectories, united by the unspoken family bonds against the backdrop of the rough housing estate. Their shared world blended routine and the tacit understanding that defined their urban saga.

The door, a threshold bridging the tranquil sanctuary of Homelife to the perils of a vibrant, bustling city, swung open. Stepping from the comfort of chintz and faded seventies-style pictures, surrounded by humble chipboard furniture adorned with faux woodgrain and the touch of nylon carpet underfoot, the world beyond unfolded.

***

The morning sun painted the main road with a golden hue as Derek manoeuvred his Volvo through the urban bustle, trailing a slow-moving bus. Ahead, at a weathered bus stop, Daphne gestured urgently, beckoning the driver to halt. The bus groaned to a sudden stop, interrupting the flow of traffic to the rear.

The metallic voice of the satellite navigation system echoed within the confines of Derek's Volvo, a persistent reminder of the ticking clock and the relentless pursuit of a destination.

"Five minutes from destination," it droned mechanically, the words repeating like a metronome measuring the dwindling time. The car, a cocoon of impatience, hurtled forward with Derek at the helm, each passing second intensifying the urgency of his quest.

Distracted by the robotic directions, Derek's eyes caught sight of the sat nav dangling awkwardly beneath the seat, a manifestation of technology gone awry. Time slipping away, frustration etched lines on his face, he impulsively overtook the stationary bus, oblivious to the imminent intersection where Danny was poised to join the flow.

The Volvo whizzed by, narrowly avoiding Danny, who, with nimble dexterity, swerved to dodge a potential collision. Reacting to the close call, Danny smacked the roof of Derek's car, a silent reprimand. The Volvo, seemingly indifferent to the disruption, sped away, leaving behind the echo of a hurried horn.

After exhaling a measured breath, Danny resumed his bicycle journey, seamlessly blending into the city's machination. The clash of vehicles became a transient episode in the intricate dance of the waking metropolis.

From inside the bus, Within the confined space, Daphne navigated the familiar routine of securing her passage. The exchange at the driver's window, marked by the clinking of coins, unfolded as a daily transaction emblematic of urban life. Engaged in this mundane yet essential act, the bus driver, attuned to the bustling city outside, observed the near miss involving a confident young man.

"Oh, that was close. Is that your young Danny, Daphne?" inquired the driver.

Daphne, a touch of maternal pride evident in her demeanour, affirmed the identity of the audacious cyclist and shared a wistful desire.

"Yes, it is. If only he would get a car, we could go to work together," she mused.

Their banter had a familiar rhythm; the bus driver responded with a hint of flirtation, a testament to the camaraderie they had cultivated through daily exchanges.

"And what, miss, our morning rendezvous, Miss Daphne?" he rejoined.

Embracing the lighthearted moment, Daphne made her way to her seat. Her fingers traced the contours of the cross pendant hanging from her necklace, a quiet gesture that held significance. The driver caught her gaze in the rearview mirror, their connection lingering as the bus resumed its journey. It was about to carry its eclectic mix of passengers and their untold stories through the bustling cityscape.

As the bus engine surged in pitch, a crescendo of mechanical life, the unmistakable whoosh of the air brake filled the air, signalling the imminent departure—the vehicle set in motion with a sudden lurch, navigating the urban sprawl.

While navigating the familiar ritual of the bus ride, Daphne sought out her customary seat. Her practised movements brought her to the chosen spot, a brief pause before the adventure of the commute unfolded. As she settled into the worn upholstery, her routine gaze found its way to the driver, a playful twinkle in her eye.

A flirtatious dance, unspoken but understood, played out

between Daphne and the driver. She bit gently on her bottom lip, a subtle expression of coquetry, only to avert her eyes in a momentary self-consciousness. Now in motion, the bus carried with it the hum of the city. With her secret indulgence, Daphne immersed herself in the daily machinations of urban life.

**

The sleek beige Volvo glided into the suburban cul-de-sac, its boxy form a stark contrast against the backdrop of well-maintained 1970s houses. With an abrupt halt, it reversed swiftly into a driveway. Derek, the man behind the wheel, unleashed a frustrated honk, and a beat later, the horn sounded again in agitation.

Sally, a woman of around 25 engrossed in her mobile phone, emerged from the house, the stylish yet understated homes framing the backdrop for the unfolding family drama. Derek, his impatience palpable, engaged the parking brake and exited the vehicle, his demeanour reflecting growing anxiety. Still absorbed in her phone call, Sally casually took her place in the rear of the car.

Derek's eyes shifted between Sally, the house, and the phone in her hand. Frustration manifested in rhythmic slaps on the car roof, followed by a leaning motion into the car, punctuated by assertive horn presses.

"Sally, what is your mother doing in there? We need to hurry," he urged, the impatience echoed in the prolonged beep of the horn. Sally, seemingly unperturbed, responded without diverting her attention.

"You know how Judy is, always late," she remarked.

"It's only Dad, your Grandad, dying. Come on, JUDY, HURRY UP!" Derek's urgency heightened.

Judy, seemingly indifferent to the situation, eventually emerged, taking her time to lock up the house. In sheer frustration, Derek stormed towards her, seized her arm, and led her to the car. He pushed her into the passenger seat, and by the time she had shut the door and was about to fasten her seatbelt, Derek was already in motion.

The Volvo surged forward, slicing through the morning air with urgency. Inside the speeding vehicle, tension hung thick, accentuated by the clash of generations. Judy, at 65, grappled with the seatbelt, a simple yet profound act amidst the turmoil.

"Hang on, I've not got my belt on! What's got into you?" she exclaimed, her voice slightly strained.

Derek, the driving force behind the wheel, intensely met her gaze. "Judy, when I rang and said Dad was dying, I wasn't taking the piss."

The weight of mortality lingered in the air, an unspoken truth that Judy, seemingly unmoved, challenged. "Does it make a difference if we are there or not?"

Sally, a witness to this familial turmoil, couldn't remain silent. "Mum! Uncle Derek is right. That's a bit mean. He is your Dad."

As the car hurtled forward, Derek, the embodiment of frustration, couldn't contain his exasperation. "Derek, slow down," Judy implored.

"I can't believe you are my sister. At times, you can be a bit of a cow." Sharp and unfiltered words echoed in the confined space, leaving an uncomfortable silence in their wake. The road stretched ahead, a metaphorical journey mirroring the emotional tumult within the speeding Volvo.

"Your sat nav is broken, Uncle Derek."

***

The midday sun cast harsh shadows on the quiet street outside the estate, where Danny navigated the concrete jungle on his high-end mountain bike. A sudden awareness tingled down his spine as he rounded the corner, revealing an unexpected encounter with the local gang. Early risers, they were, riding on menacing BMX and mountain bikes.

Quick thinking propelled Danny behind a truck, his pulse quickening. Gripping the tailgate, he seized the opportunity for a burst of speed, aiming to slip past the gang unnoticed. Fate, however, had a different plan, and the truck slammed to a stop. With predatory eyes fixed on Danny's expensive mountain bike, the gang spotted him.

The Bike Gang Leader, a figure of intimidation, barked, "You better stop and give us that bike, nursey."

Danny, fueled by adrenaline, sprinted ahead. The gang, undeterred, gave chase, their menacing presence growing closer. Approaching a crossroads, the terrain offered a slight downhill advantage. A risky decision loomed for Danny – face the gang or attempt a daring escape.

Without hesitation, he opted for the latter. The junction approached, and Danny leapt over the crossroads with unyielding determination. In the daring move, he cut in front of the same Volvo from earlier, provoking an abrupt brake that disrupted the gang's pursuit. Their threats echoed as Danny pedalled away, leaving the gang behind.

His destination emerged on the horizon – Fair Oaks Retirement Home. The pursuit, a thrilling race against time, propelled Danny toward an uncertain sanctuary. The asphalt beneath his wheels hummed with the rhythm of escape, weaving a tale of danger and determination in the heart of the mundane suburbs.

***

The Fair Oaks Retirement Home, an austere haven for the elderly, stood as a stoic sentinel against the backdrop of the overcast English sky. The Edwardian building, once a grand house, had been repurposed to cater to the needs of its aged inhabitants. Its red brick exterior, adorned with climbing ivy, exuded an old-world charm.

A green lawn stretched in front, offering a serene welcome to both residents and visitors. The gravel car park, modest in size, hinted at the intimate nature of this refuge. Enclosed by a high wooden fence, the exterior bore a corporate-looking sign proudly displaying the home's name. The transformation from a private residence to a place of care was subtle yet discernible.

A closer inspection revealed the subtle markers of its purpose. The locks on the door hinted at the need for security and safety. A concrete ramp, discreetly hidden by strategically placed plant pots, offered accessibility. Behind the curtains, a glimpse into the interior unveiled scenes of residents navigating their daily lives with canes and walkers.

All windows were shut, preserving a sense of privacy and containment. A small sign displaying the establishment's opening hours was a practical touch amid the quiet.

The tranquillity of the location was complemented by the interplay of fragrances—whiffs of the sweet garden mingling with clinical scents of antiseptic and the ever-present aroma of cabbage wafting from the kitchen's extractor fans.

The Fair Oaks Retirement Home, in its unassuming exterior, concealed the stories and experiences of those within. It stood as a testament to the passage of time and the gentle embrace offered to those in the later chapters of their lives. A black ambulance, discreet yet laden with solemnity, occupied the entrance. Two men dressed in dark suits orchestrated the entrance with a gurney, a silent harbinger of the weightiness of the day's events.

Derek's arrival shattered the tranquillity. His Volvo, hastily brought to a stop, screeched, betraying the urgency on his face. Abandoning the car without bothering to shut the door properly, he hurried toward the entrance, his eyes locked onto the private ambulance.

Adjacent to the entrance, a bike rack whispered of a younger presence. Danny's mountain bike, a relic of youthful energy, leaned against it—a silent contradiction amid the sombre proceedings.

Derek's voice, heavy with regret, broke the quiet air. "Judy, we are too late, too bloody late."

Judy, following Derek's hurried steps, approached with scepticism. "Could have been for somebody else."

"What, two on the same day? Do the funeral people do a buy one, get one free deal?"

Derek's sentimentality clashed with the gravity of the moment.

Unfazed by her brother's outburst, Judy reached the entrance. With a gesture toward the door, she teased him, "Are you going to go in or what?"

Sally, the younger generation trailing behind, lifted her eyes from her phone and greeted with the disheartening news. "Great, no bloody signal either. Wonder if they have wifi?"

The air outside the retirement home crackled with unspoken tension, the private ambulance standing as a silent witness to the tragedies within. The family, gripped by scepticism and despair, stepped into the dim porchway, leaving the quiet bike rack as a lone testament to the presence of life amid the encroaching shadows of mortality.

***

The care home hallway exuded an atmosphere of quiet dignity, a sanctuary amidst the chaos of the outside world. The plush carpet, soft underfoot, stretched out before visitors, its comforting embrace offering solace to weary souls. Plastic flowers, their vibrant hues a stark contrast against the muted tones of the hallway, adorned vases strategically along the corridor.

A grand set of wooden stairs stood at the heart of the hallway, a testament to exquisite craftsmanship marred only by the utilitarian addition of an ugly stair lift bolted on, a necessary compromise in an ageing institution. Despite this intrusion, the stairs retained an air of elegance, their sweeping curves and intricate details speaking to a bygone era of opulence and refinement.

Framed pictures adorned the walls, capturing moments of joy and camaraderie, a reminder of happier times that once filled these halls. Cluttered with announcements and updates, notice boards added a touch of functionality to the otherwise decorative space.

Near the empty reception desk, a board with flickering lights stood sentinel, its purpose long forgotten but its presence a reassuring constant in the ever-changing landscape of the care home. The mahogany wood panels and furniture exuded an aura of tradition and prestige, harking back to an era where respect and craftsmanship were revered above all else.

Leaded windows lined the walls, casting intricate patterns of light and shadow across the carpet, their presence like a protective net enveloping the hallway in a cocoon of warmth and security. The Axminster design of the rug, a nod to a bygone era of elegance, mingled seamlessly with the shadows, creating a tapestry of light and dark that danced across the floor.

Plastic covers adorned the doorways, a practical solution to prevent scuffs and scratches from marring the pristine surfaces. Red lanyards hung in the corners, their purpose unknown, but their presence was a silent reminder of the lives that once filled these halls.

The Fair Oaks Home Main Entrance Corridor stretched before Daphne, clad in her blue scrub uniform, nitrile blue gloves, and disposable apron. With delicate care, she navigated the wheelchair carrying an elderly, vacant patient suffering from dementia down the corridor towards the entrance. The door buzzer resonated, signalling the arrival of visitors.
Outside, Derek, accompanied by Sally and Judy, exuded a calm demeanour, yet impatience etched across Derek's face. The elderly patient in the wheelchair remained still, donning an oxygen mask—a silent spectator to the unfolding scene.

Continuing her careful navigation, Daphne spoke aloud to the unresponsive patient, Geoffrey. Her words, resignation and quiet frustration, floated in the air.
"Here, Geoffrey, another impatient, demanding family here... they must wait. I don't want to jolt you about... vultures circling the dead... only here for Christmas and Birthdays... to satisfy their guilt.

The persistent door buzzer and Derek's impatient banging provided a dissonant backdrop. Daphne, unfazed, continued her soliloquy.
"He will just have to wait."
Derek's voice, impatient and insistent, cut through the corridor.
"OPEN THE BLOODY DOOR!"
Daphne, undeterred, responded to the unseen Derek.
"I don't know what the hurry is. Johnny is dead. Why the rush? He is with the Lord God now."
She brought the wheelchair to a halt, pulling out a photo

pass. She swiped the pass, approaching the door and allowing Derek's impatient entry.

"I suppose you are here for Jonathan Hodges."

"COURSE I BLOODY AM," Derek snapped, frustration evident. "Been waiting outside for too long."

"He is not going anywhere. There is no rush."

"I want to say goodbye to my father."

"You were too late. He has already passed. You missed the Doctor. If you follow me to the family room, I will get you the certificate. It's peaceful there while we prepare him."

Derek, however, had reached his limit. Ignoring the nurse, he made a determined beeline for the stairs, heading to his father's room.

Judy, attempting to smooth the situation, apologised.

"Sorry about that. He is headstrong and loved his father."

Daphne observed Derek's departure and offered a wry, unwanted, but valid comment.

"He is far ruder than his father, bless the Lord."

***

Outside the room of Wing Commander Andrew Bryce, Danny hesitated before the whiteboard bearing the official designation. A distinct RAF cap badge adorned the board, emphasising the gravity and history of the occupant within. Danny knocked gently, awaiting permission, and slowly pushed the door open.

"Danny, is it?" came the aged yet firm voice from within.

"Yes, sir. May I come in?" Danny responded with a respectful tone.

"Of course, do come in."

At the seasoned age of 97, Andy sat on the bed adorned in blue pyjamas and slippers. An electric wheelchair rested quietly in the corner, bearing silent testament to the passage of time. The room exuded a neat, tidy air, surrounded by a trove of RAF memorabilia. A black and white photo featuring Andy and two friends graced the nightstand.

Danny entered without formality, sitting on the edge of the bed. Without uttering a word, he gently clasped Andy's hand, silently acknowledging the shared grief he was to impart.

"It's Johnny, isn't it?" Andy spoke, his eyes reflecting a deep understanding.

Danny looked into Andy's eyes, affirming the loss. Johnny was gone.

"Well, he liked always to be first," Andy remarked wistfully. He then placed his other hand on Danny's, a silent gesture of comfort and solidarity.

"Would you stay for a while? I am on my own now," Andy requested, his gaze momentarily shifting towards the neatly hung blazer, medals, and grey flannel trousers in the corner. He knew Johnny was ill and had prepped for the worst by having his uniform ready to go; they had hung far longer than expected, a reminder of Johnny's wayward tenacity.

"Anything for you, sir. Anything," Danny replied, his commitment echoing in the quiet room, where the weight of memories and the passage of time seemed to converge.

***

In the dimly lit room number 16, the lifeless body of Johnathon Hodges, aged 99, lay on the bed, surrounded by a family less empathetic than practical. Sally and Judy, seemingly unaffected by the solemnity, were focused on the room's contents. Sally rifled through Johnathon's possessions on the dresser. At the same time, Judy, dismissive of the body, continued her quest for an elusive will.

Daphne, the caregiver, stood by the window, her discontent evident. Derek, on the other hand, sat on a chair, his eyes moist, gazing at his deceased father.

Seemingly unburdened by sentimentality, Judy remarked, "Dad didn't have much here, just a few knick-knacks and a photo of Mum. I know he had a will, but I can't find it. That damned gold poppy as well."

Derek, wiping his eyes, countered, "You know, Judy, he wasn't one for keeping anything. Mum was the hoarder. The only things he cared about were his shotguns and boots. His stuffed animals had to be thrown out before moving here."

Daphne, perturbed, interjected, "Do you not want to wait for the undertakers to remove him first? This feels very wrong, almost rude." She was getting frustrated, pulling on her rubber gloves and then adjusting the thin plastic apron. She badly wanted to remove the sheet over Johnny's face, not so much for his dignity but for her sake,

With a touch of hypocrisy, Derek declared, "He was a countryman. Death to him was another day, a part of life, a next step. He wouldn't want us to waste time sobbing."

Maintaining her professional composure, Daphne commented on the unusual circumstances, "Well, he is your father, but this is a bit out of the ordinary. The undertakers will be here in a minute. For the record, I find this a bit... wrong and very unchristian."

As Daphne pulled out a necklace with a cross on the end and mumbled the Lord's Prayer, Sally, the granddaughter, voiced her concern, "Mum, there is nothing here. I think the staff want to clean up. It's a bit creepy you going through his stuff while he is still in here."

Judy dismissed Sally's unease, stating, "Sal, stop being a fuss. He would not care; he's gone. Trust me, your Granddad hated a fuss. Anyhow, he must have left something behind. Need something for the service. Plus, I am trying to find Mum's gold brooch shaped like a poppy."

Sally, attempting to connect with her late grandfather, asked about war memorabilia, "Anything from the war? His medals or something?"

Judy delved into the dresser drawers, and Sally joined her, offering assistance, "Oh, Mum, let me give you a hand."

Knowing his father's history, Derek debunked any notions of wartime heroics: "You won't find any medals. He never served. Spent the entire war working at McLeod Lodge. You know Mum was embarrassed about it... Think he was ashamed as he never spoke about the war."

After reminiscing about her father's past, Judy revealed, "I know he was in the home guard. Think they took pity on him on account of his asthma."

Daphne, his nurse of many years, always a beacon of truth, refuted the claim, "He never had asthma. Fit as a fiddle. Bit of arthritis, that's it."

Disillusioned with the lack of meaningful possessions, Derek remarked, "What a way to go. All this time on the planet, and all you have to show for it is a set of pyjamas and false teeth. Is there a suit we can bury him in?"

Sally, defending her grandfather's legacy, chided Derek, "Dad, that's mean. He must have done something. He worked at the Lodge for ages before you sold his house to pay for this grim place..."

Daphne interjected with exasperation, "I have only been at his beck and call for the last ten years. He had no asthma, only a bit of gout. I have no idea where you got that from. It seems like you never really knew your father. God bless his soul." The rubbing of the cross and her looking at the ceiling,

Offened by the accusation, Derek retorted, "How dare you..."

Seemingly unaffected by the unfolding tension, Judy continued her quest for family secrets: "Mum and dad never spoke about the war. They never saw much of it, being in the countryside. I suspect they had a right old time of it. It's not like the people in London are getting blown up. It probably explains why he left his village. Sorry, nurse Delilah, whoever you are, he did have asthma. It's why he could not serve."

Daphne, unwilling to let misinformation prevail, reiterated, "So you say, so you say. In case you've forgotten, Fairoaks was his home and family, too. I cared for him, he cared for us... so I dare, and Daphne is written on my badge."

As Daphne expressed her frustration, Derek, realising the strain on her, walked over to her, gently holding her elbows, "Judy, come on. Dad's lying here. Have some respect. He loved Mum to bits."

Sally, intrigued by the mention of a scandal, prodded, "Scandal in our family. Pray do tell, Mum."

Derek, now concerned about the impact of their gossiping on the nurse, scolded, "Sally! You're upsetting the staff. Sorry Daphne "

Undeterred by her brother's admonitions, Judy continued rifling through drawers, divulging the big family secret: "He left the village with Mum due to something about him not going off to fight in the war. He had to join the home guard, and there was a ruckus. My brother and I do not have happy memories of the village."

***

The room hung heavy with the awkwardness of grief when an unexpected disruption shattered the sombre atmosphere. The entrance of an elderly man in an electric wheelchair, adorned in a blazer, WW2 medals, and an RAF officer's cap, sent a ripple of astonishment through the room. The Union Jack he forcefully threw over the lifeless body intensified the shock, leaving the family startled and the health care assistant attempting to intervene.

"Andy, come outside for some fresh air, and I need a vape. Why did you do that?" Daphne Wills, the caregiver, scolded, trying to defuse the tension.

"You disrespectful bunch. He deserves a military funeral," Andy, the intruder, barked, his voice resonating with authority.

Sensing the need to maintain peace, the undertakers solemnly entered the room, providing a buffer between the aggrieved family and the unexpected visitor. Despite Daphne's attempts to redirect Andy, he stood his ground, vehemently defending his intrusion.

"Bloody families, don't you have respect for us old people? Going through his things, especially what he did for you all. Good old Scallywag was Johnny. Deserves a good send-off. Known him since school; he was a good friend, my best friend," Andy continued, his words a rebuke to the family's perceived disrespect.

The chaos escalated when Danny, the health care assistant, rushed into the room, his expression a mix of shock and apology. "Mum, sorry, he just slipped by, and I could not stop him."

Stoic in their duty, the undertakers subtly shifted the Union Jack to the side as the family members, startled and disrupted, began to disperse. Derek and Judy, the deceased's children, exchanged one last glance with their father, the weight of their emotions visible in their eyes. Seemingly detached from the moment's solemnity, Sally resumed her phone engagement. At the same time, Danny sought solace in a comforting hug with his distressed mother.

The intrusion had left an indelible mark on the room, a clash between generations and perceptions of respect. Their expressions are unchanged; the undertakers moved with a sense of practised solemnity, acknowledging the complexities of grief and familial dynamics. The Union Jack, once thrown haphazardly over the body, now lay to the side, a symbol of conflicting sentiments and the clash between military honour and familial discord. Ironically, the flag was upside down, a sign of distress for the military.

***

The care home garden unfolded like a hidden oasis, tucked away from the bustling streets beyond its walls. A riot of colours greeted the eye as vibrant blooms swayed gently in the breeze, their petals brushing against one another in a delicate dance. Tall, swaying trees provided shade from the relentless sun, their branches reaching skyward as if in silent supplication.

Beneath the canopy of greenery, well-tended flower beds burst with life; each bloom is a testament to the care and dedication of the gardeners who tended to them. Roses, dahlias, and daisies mingled in a harmonious tapestry of hues, their fragrant perfume hanging heavy in the air.

In the courtyard, beneath the sprawling branches of ancient trees, a series of benches were thoughtfully arranged, offering inviting spots for residents and visitors alike to rest and reflect. Each bench bore the weathered marks of countless seasons, its wooden slats smoothed by the passage of time and innumerable moments of contemplation. Some benches were positioned in secluded alcoves, providing quiet corners for reflection. In contrast, others stood proudly in the courtyard's centre, offering panoramic views of the surrounding garden.

A brick BBQ, weathered and worn from disuse, stood as a silent sentinel in one corner of the courtyard, its grill adorned with a layer of rust that spoke of summers long past. Nearby, several tables stood ready for use, their surfaces marked with faint traces of previous gatherings. In the warmer months, these tables would come alive with activity as residents and staff gathered to enjoy al fresco meals, basking in the sun's warmth and their companions' company.

A ritual of solace unfolded in the secluded enclave of the garden smoking area. The air hung thick with the aromatic clouds of tobacco and the subtle bitterness of nostalgia. Andy, stationed in his wheelchair, his silhouette softened by wisps of smoke from his pipe, exuded a seasoned air of resilience.

Derek and Judy, the children, shared a moment of shared anxiety as they both ignited their cigarettes. The flame danced at the tips of their respective smokes, casting intermittent shadows on their faces, etching the lines of concern that time had etched. The garden, usually a place for serenity, now bore witness to the palpable tension between the siblings.

In the backdrop of this familial tableau, Daphne, the enigmatic nurse, withdrew to a secluded corner, evading the watchful eyes of the family. A subtle act unfolded as she delved into her pocket, retrieving a gleaming solid gold poppy brooch. Her gaze lingered on the precious artefact, silently acknowledging its significance. With a deft motion, she concealed it again, the secret weighing heavy in her pocket.

Danny, perceptive in his observance, caught sight of his mum looking at something and placing it in her pocket.

Derek extended a hand, a hesitant greeting breaking through the fragrant air. "Hello, Sir, my name is Derek. I was Dad's, sorry, Johnny's son. Not met you."

Andy, a frail figure weathered by time and memories, responded with a nod, his eyes scanning Derek's features. ".You look like your dad when he was younger. You, young lady, look a lot like your mum. She was a pretty thing as well." A little twinkle in his eye as the bowl of his pipe flared cherry red.

Caught between grief and curiosity, Derek asked, "You knew Dad when he was younger?"

"Of course," Andy replied, a hint of nostalgia in his voice. "We were friends together. We shared a tin bath as nippers. He left the village later due to some unpleasantness."

Derek's brow furrowed, seeking clarification. "Unpleasantness? What was that?" He looks across at Judy, who shrugs.

"Him being an outright coward," Andy stated matter-of-factly, sending shockwaves through Derek's emotional landscape.

"That is my dad you are talking about; how dare you!" Derek's indignation flared, a protective son rising to defend his father's honour.

Sensing the tension, Judy chimed in with her brand of confrontation. "He's been dead a couple of hours, and you call yourself his friend."

"No, no, no, you misunderstand me," Andy interjected, a trace of regret in his eyes. "We were like brothers. I will explain why I called him a coward and the most honourable man I knew. I grew up with Johnny at the farm. When we were nippers, we even shared a bath." He sits back and smiles.

The air thickened with anticipation, a complex tapestry of emotions weaving through the garden. As Andy prepared to unravel the enigma of Johnny's past, the benches became a stage for a narrative that promised revelation and reconciliation, a legacy intertwined with layers of camaraderie and perhaps unspoken valour. Whatever it was, it had to start at the beginning. The eddies and swirls of the tobacco smoke dancing in the light brought air to this mystery.

CHAPTER 2

1932 Wiltshire

The English countryside unfolded beneath the vast expanse of the sky, a canvas painted with childhood innocence. The year was 1932, when children roamed freely in the fields, immersed in the sweet symphony of their carefree laughter. The melody of "The Sun Has Got His Hat On" by Ambrose & his Orchestra echoed through the air, a nostalgic tune encapsulating the era. A Windup gramophone is playing in the long grass.

A group of young boys, their shoulders adorned with stripped branches, engaged in a spirited game of war. Deep in Wiltshire's heart, the field witnessed their imaginative play. Some toppled over, feigning death, while others orchestrated pew-pew sounds, lost in the magic of their collective imagination as they pointed their imaginary guns at each other.

The biplane's unexpected arrival shattered the English countryside's tranquillity, injecting excitement into the children's hearts. Like little warriors, they brandished branches as makeshift weapons, their imaginations transforming the peaceful field into a battleground.
With their determined aim, the children directed their wooden arms towards the sky, treating the passing biplane as their adversary. In a playful response, the pilot, a distant silhouette against the azure canvas, engaged in the charade. He waggled his wings, a theatrical gesture of mock defeat that mirrored the joyous rebellion below. As the mechanical hum

grew quieter and quieter in the distance

The symphony of youthful cheers erupted, carried by the wind as the children, their spirits soaring, raced back to the village. This fleeting moment, a blend of innocence and imagination, etched itself into the tapestry of their shared childhood, a memory destined to linger like the echoes of laughter across the expansive fields of Wiltshire.

As some parted, two carrying their precious gramophone and horn home, others transitioned to the village fountain and war memorial.

Nestled amidst the undulating hills of Wiltshire, the quaint village revealed itself as a timeless tapestry of history and tradition. Three interconnecting streets formed the heart of the settlement, converging at a stone fountain that stood as a silent witness to centuries of communal life. Here, villagers would gather to draw water for their households. At the same time, travellers could quench the thirst of their equine companions before continuing on their way.

The village's architecture, fashioned from sturdy grey stone and timber, exuded a rustic charm that spoke of generations past. Each building bore the weathered marks of time, its tiny windows and doors beckoning visitors with the promise of warmth and welcome. By the water pumps, hay troughs were thoughtfully arranged, catering to the needs of both man and beast alike.

At the northern end of the village, atop a gentle rise, loomed the majestic silhouette of the Norman church. Its spire pierced the sky, towering above the rooftops in silent reverence, a beacon of faith and solace for the villagers below. Traffic in the village was sparse, the rhythm of life dictated by the slow passage of time rather than the hurried pace of modernity.

With its weathered facade and welcoming hearth, the village pub served as the bustling epicentre of community life. Here, locals would gather to share stories and laughter over pints of ale, finding solace and camaraderie amidst the familiar surroundings. Nearby, a modest wooden building housed the church meeting rooms, echoing with the solemn tolling of bells and the gentle chime of the clock.

On the corner of the village square stood the village school, its sturdy walls a testament to the importance of education in the community. Here, children would gather to learn and grow, their laughter and chatter filling the air with youthful exuberance. And at the heart of it all, the village centre would come alive each week with the bustling energy of the marketplace, where farmers would gather to sell their livestock and goods, forging connections that spanned generations.

Concealed among the shadows, the children lay in ambush, fixated on Miss Rutherford's Sweet Shop and Post Office across the road.
A formidable figure emerged from the bank, a stern woman with her nose held high, exuding an air of authority. Miss Rutherford marched towards her shop, an unwavering force commanding attention.

From the side of her face, the viewpoint observed the subtle stage whispers of the children stalking her. Attempting to conceal her smile, Miss Rutherford navigated through the ambush, aware of a child's leg protruding from the hiding spot. A spot in happier times as a child she once played.

Upon reaching her shop, she unlocked the door with purpose, the catch clicking as she pushed it open. The closed sign turned to open, signalling the beginning of another day. With a sudden spin, Miss Rutherford caught two boys attempting to sneak past.

"Caught you!" she exclaimed, identifying them as Andrew William Bryce, a skinny and pale child, the runt of the litter and the only survivor of measles and Peter Smith, a porcine child, spoilt by his father, the Publican and local fixer. Gripping them by the ears, she exerted control, and their struggles met with painful resistance. They wriggled and squirmed, but her vice-like fingers were holding.

"You can stop struggling. It'll be the constable for you," she warned, invoking the consequences of thieving in the county. Accusing them of stealing sweets, she dismissed their futile resistance, demanding the whereabouts of the third culprit.

Realising the jig was up, the other children emerged from their hiding spots, shamefaced and defeated. Peter, now in tears, apologised, fearing the impending belt from his father.
Amid the chaos, Johnny Hodges, the mischievous mastermind, stepped forward. Leaning against the door frame, he exuded confidence, hands behind his back, a cocky grin on his face.

"Morning, Miss Rutherford. Fine day today," Johnny greeted, seemingly oblivious to the turmoil he had caused.

Miss Rutherford, incensed, accused Johnny of thievery and threatened to smack his legs. Johnny, ever the provocateur, denied any wrongdoing, leaving Peter to confess under limited duress.

As Miss Rutherford scolded, Johnny slowly revealed a brown paper bag filled with sweets. The shock on Miss Rutherford's face was palpable as she dropped the two boys, who promptly fled. Andy punched Peter in the arm, and Johnny ran off in the opposite direction with the spoils of war.

"I will so help me crown you, boy. Johnny Hodges, I am speaking to your father and Constable Dickens later!" Miss Rutherford vowed, her words echoing through the high street.

From the crow's perspective, looking down the street, Peter ran to the pub. Andy swiftly escaped, leaving the village to grapple with the aftermath of a childhood caper. The innocence of the English countryside collided with the stern reality of Miss Rutherford's discipline, creating a vivid tableau of a bygone era. The street, once a hubbub of small children, became quiet and stoic as the echoes faded.

***

For the village's children, Hobbs Lane was a playground of endless possibility, a canvas upon which they painted their wildest imaginings. From daring games of the army and cowboys and Indians to spirited reenactments of the beloved tales of Robin Hood, the woods echoed with the laughter and shouts of youthful exuberance.

Inspired by the adventures of their fictional hero, the children would gather around the crackling radio to listen to the serialised tales of Robin Hood, their imaginations ignited by the daring exploits of the legendary outlaw. With bows fashioned from sticks and arrows tipped with leaves, they would embark on their own quests for justice, their youthful spirits undaunted by the shadows that lurked in the depths of the woods.

Yet amidst the innocent play and carefree laughter, Hobbs Lane held secrets hidden in the tangled undergrowth and whispered in hushed tones by those who knew its dark past. Poachers and gamekeepers engaged in a timeless game of cat and mouse, their cunning and guile matched only by the ancient woods that bore witness to their age-old rivalry. In the quiet of the off-season, the woods became a battleground where wits were tested, and alliances forged, adding another layer of intrigue to the enigmatic allure of Hobbs Lane.

The late afternoon sunlight cast elongated shadows on Hobs Lane as Johnny sprinted around a corner, colliding with Constable Dickens, who was gracefully pedalling his bicycle. The clash echoed in the quiet street, leaving Johnny momentarily stunned. Realising the constable was still on the ground, Johnny returned to offer assistance.
"Sorry, Mr. Constable Dickens, let me help you up!" Johnny's apology rang sincere in the air.

Constable Dickens, a man in his mid-twenties, brushed off

the dust from his uniform, eyeing the boy with a mixture of sternness and amusement. He spared a moment to check the condition of his bicycle before addressing Johnny.

"Be careful now. I nearly came a cropper there. What are you running from?"

Johnny, trying to deflect attention, mumbled, "Nothing, it's nothing."

However, the constable wasn't one to be easily deceived. His gaze bore into Johnny as he continued his inquiry, suspecting a familiar culprit behind Johnny's haste.

"Look me in the eye. Is it that bully Peter Smith again?"

Johnny hesitated, then admitted, "No, sir. It was Peter's idea, but promise you won't tell my dad."

Intrigued, Constable Dickens observed Johnny closely. His suspicions deepened when he noticed something concealed behind the boy's back.

"What's that behind your back? That's it, show me."

Johnny reluctantly revealed a paper bag filled with sweets, offering it to Constable Dickens.
"Hmm, what do we have here?" the constable mused. "Caught red-handed, the smoking gun. Aniseed Balls! Aniseed Balls!!"

He took one out, inspecting it with playful theatrics, then popped it into his mouth. Johnny, wide-eyed, watched in shock.

"You're eating the evidence!" Johnny exclaimed.

"What evidence?" Constable Dickens retorted, a smirk playing on his lips. "Seriously, you stole the aniseed balls."

Leaning down, the constable whispered conspiratorially to Johnny, "Everyone knows the lemon drops are in easy reach on the right. I am confiscating this bag of aniseed balls as proceeds of crime, do you understand?"

A distant crack in the woodline diverted their attention. Constable Dickens called out, "Andrew William Bryce, come out! I know you've been following Johnny. Come out, seriously. You have red hair; you stand out like a sore thumb at a toe hospital. Out here, the pair of you."

Andy, Johnny's accomplice, emerged from the shadows, armed with a large stick resembling a toy rifle. He handed one to Johnny and kept another for himself.
"Here, Johnny. We may need these in prison. Brothers, right?"

Constable Dickens intervened before their imaginations could run wild. "Alright, you two are not going to prison today. You will apologise to Miss Rutherford and do chores for her. Are you seriously stealing Aniseed Balls? They are useless sweets of no use to anyone.

The lemon drops are easier to reach. I've never been caught. Here, have an aniseed ball each. I will take the bag to the station. It's going to get dark soon; best go home."

As Constable Dickens cycled away, laughing, he left behind two boys with aniseed balls in hand, the taste of mischief lingering in the air. The amateur escapade had earned them a lesson, a handful of sweets, and a shared laughter echoing through the quiet streets of Hobbs Lane.

***

The Hodges farm, nestled amidst the rolling hills of the countryside, exuded an aura of rustic charm and simple tranquillity. A modest tenant farm, it comprised a scattering of weather-worn structures that bore the indelible marks of years of toil and labour.

At the heart of the farmstead stood a stone cottage, its sturdy walls imbued with the echoes of generations past. A perpetual wisp of smoke curled lazily from its chimney into the sky. It was a comforting beacon for weary labourers toiling in the nearby fields, promising respite and sustenance.

Surrounding the cottage, a verdant garden flourished under the tender care of the farmer's wife. Rows of robust vegetables thrived in the fertile earth, their vibrant hues a testament to the nurturing hands that tended to them. Carrots, cabbages, and turnips flourished under the nurturing gaze of the sun, their leafy greens reaching skyward in silent tribute to the cycle of life and growth.

Amidst the verdant bounty, the farm cat prowled with silent grace, a vigilant guardian tasked with keeping the rodent population in check. With stealth and precision, it stalked the garden's perimeter, its amber eyes gleaming in the dappled sunlight as it carried out its silent duty.

Beyond the cottage, a pair of weather-beaten barns stood sentinel against the elements, their timeworn façades bearing the scars of countless seasons. Within their weathered walls, the rhythmic sounds of farm life echoed—a symphony of bleating goats and the gentle whickers of a cobb horse, their presence a testament to the symbiotic relationship between man and beast that defined the agricultural landscape.

In the summer heat, the ground surrounding the farmstead hardened and rutted under the relentless sun, its parched earth bearing witness to the season's trials. Yet, when the rains came, the landscape transformed, shrouded in a cloak of muddy earth that clung to boots and hooves alike, a reminder of the cyclical nature of life on the farm.

Despite its humble size and unassuming appearance, the Hodges farm pulsed with the rhythms of life, its rustic beauty a testament to the enduring spirit of those who toiled upon its hallowed grounds.

As the dusk settled over the Hodges farm cottage, Johnathon raced toward the door, clutching his makeshift toy rifle. The door creaked open, and a man emerged, a faint smile playing on his lips. Over his shoulder, he slung an accurate rifle, a trade tool. Johnathon approached eagerly, his eyes reflecting the anticipation of a valuable lesson.

The man, Frank, a weathered figure and a veteran of the last war, eyed Johnathon's inventiveness and intercepted Johnathon's toy, tossing it aside with a casual yet authoritative gesture. "C'mon, Johnny, put that toy away. It's about time you learn to use the real thing and get a rabbit for the pot."

Wide-eyed and excited, Johnathon questioned, "Yes, Dad, you mean I get to shoot it?"
Frank, a wise father, responded, "Yes, and don't tell your mother. You know how she frets. You can show me the animal tracks and plants we can eat on the way."
Andy, sheltered from machismo by his overbearing and doting mother, seized the opportunity. "Can I come too, Uncle?"

Frank gently refused, considering the farm's safety and Andy's mother's concerns, "Sorry, young'un. You know how your mother worries. Best be getting home to her."
With that, Andy pilfered John's makeshift rifle and scurried away, leaving Johnathon disappointed.

"Aw, Dad," Johnathon protested.

Frank, the pragmatic father, reassured, "You can tell him about it at Sunday school. Now, how about you find some rabbits? Mum is making one of her pies. You best wash your mouth when you get home. Smells of aniseed. Eating sweets before dinner—your mother will not like that."

They strolled down the garden path toward the field. Cradling the rifle almost too large, Johnathon focused intently on the task at hand—to find rabbits and not let his mother down. The camera captured his determined face, concentration, and desire to prove himself. The sun dipped lower, casting long shadows on the path ahead, signalling the beginning of an adventure that would unfold in the quiet fields of the farm cottage.

CHAPTER 3

Prelude to War

Andy's tale captivated the assembled audience in the present-day tranquillity of Fairoaks Retirement Home Gardens. The ceaseless chatter and puffing of cigarettes had given way to an attentive hush as the family visitors and staff hung on to the threads of Andy's narrative.

As Andy continued to recount his past, the weight of time-pressed upon him, fatigue seeping into his words. The vivid recollections of a bygone era became a haze, and confusion clouded his once-clear storytelling. A chill crept through the garden, settling in Andy's weary bones.

"It was a strange time for us all," Andy mumbled, caught in the shadows of his own memories. "I was too young to know about the great war, and it felt like it was always a long summer or winter—winter, Danny. Could you take me in, please? I am cold."
Danny Wills, a dutiful presence, responded, "Yes, Wing Commander. Let's take you back to the mess." He throws a faux playful salute,

Derek, Judy, and Sally, the attentive listeners, were left in the garden, lingering in the echo of Andy's fading words. The longing for more stories about their father, Johnny, painted expressions of anticipation on Derek and Judy's faces.

"Before you go," Derek pleaded, "may we come back and talk some more? We have no stories about Dad."

Judy, a silent observer, added her request, "Find out where Mum's poppy brooch went."

Daphne Wills, a figure of composure, interjected, "Well, you can come back tomorrow if Andy is happy with that."

Danny, with the electric wheelchair in tow, began the slow journey into the retirement home, his gaze lingering on Derek and Judy. The wheelchair creaked against the corridors, fading away from the garden's calming and cold atmosphere.

"We will lock up your father's room," Daphne assured them, her voice carrying a sense of finality, "and you can come back tomorrow to look. We also have a luggage room. You can have a look there."

Derek and Judy, joined by Sally on her phone, walked to the car park. Sally, with practical concerns, turned back to Daphne.

"Can I have the Wi-Fi password for tomorrow?" she inquired, blending the realities of the present with the mysteries of the past. The request lingered in the air, a subtle reminder that even amidst the weight of history, the contemporary world insisted on its own terms.

***

In the muted atmosphere of Andy's room, the afternoon light cast a gentle glow upon the scene. The air carried the subtle scent of aged memories, and the quiet rustle of blankets marked Danny's entrance. Andy, weathered by time and the weight of untold stories, sat propped up on his bed.

As Danny attended to Andy, adjusting the blanket with familiarity, he inquired about Andy's well-being.

"You okay, Andy? Do you want to have a Grandad Nap?" Danny offered, his concern evident in the soft cadence of his voice.

"No, just sit with me for a bit," Andy replied, his gaze fixed on the unseen horizon of recollections. "Can I be frank with you?"

Always patient and perceptive, Danny responded, "Yes if it's about Johnny's strange family."

"Strange and very rude," Andy murmured, a shadow of disapproval in his tone. "Johnny was a secretive chap, but their questions were tiresome. He showed no interest when alive; now he has... gone."

Danny pulled up a chair, a sturdy companion in the quiet room; as Andy's hand sought Danny's, a silent pact formed between them. The touch, an unspoken bridge between past and present, carried the weight of unspoken stories.

"Thanks, love," Andy expressed, his voice a whisper fading into the realm of memories. Danny, understanding the need for quiet companionship, held Andy's hand with a comforting assurance.

Danny noticed his mother's presence in the doorway in a subtle shift. She held a cross, a symbol of both solace and inquiry. Their eyes met, and without words, she mouthed the word 'tea' and mimed the delicate act of drinking from a cup. Danny nodded, acknowledging the silent request for a momentary reprieve.

The room retained its tranquillity as Andy drifted into the embrace of a momentary slumber. A tender smile played on Danny's lips, and he pondered the intricacies of Johnny's enigmatic past. Daphne puts her hand in her pocket and walks to the corridor kitchen.

***

The Volvo, an unassuming vessel containing the Hodges family, eased out of the Fair Oaks car park into the afternoon light. Behind the wheel, Derek seemed either oblivious to or defiant of the "No Exit" sign. He pressed on with a casual determination or perhaps a disregard for traffic norms, attempting to navigate a path through the narrow exit.

In the unfolding drama, the Fair Oaks minibus materialised on the scene, catching Derek off guard. The sudden appearance forced him to slam on the brakes, the vehicle shuddering to a halt. Daphne, a silent observer from the main entrance, discreetly retrieved a precious artefact from her pocket – the gleaming golden poppy brooch.

With a delicate yet purposeful gesture, she studied the intricate details of the brooch as if seeking solace or drawing strength from its silent presence. Cool against her fingertips, the metal held secrets and memories known only to her. As quickly as it emerged, the brooch vanished into the sanctuary of her pocket, its significance known to her alone.

The click of the electric kettle drew her out of her revelry as she poured two cups of tea, the steam rolling up her face and fogging the window. Her face was proud of her beautiful, caring son,

***

The vibrant neon glow of Tesco illuminated the dreary streetscape, casting an otherworldly hue upon the wet paving stones below. As the rain drizzled gently from the overcast sky, the air hung heavy with the damp chill of impending nightfall.

Despite the dampness, there was an unmistakable allure to the scene—the pulsating red and blue lights of the storefront beckoned like a siren's call, promising warmth and sustenance within. A makeshift bulletin board adorned the frontage, a patchwork of local advertisements and notices, offering a glimpse into the tapestry of community life that thrived amidst the urban sprawl.

Against the backdrop of the neon-lit facade, steel tambour shutters stood sentinel, their mechanical hum signalling the transition from day to night. Yet, amidst the facade of security, a broken CCTV camera spoke volumes—a silent testament to the fragility of law and order in the face of urban decay.

As pedestrians hurried past, the pavement beneath their feet bore the scars of neglect—pockmarked with discarded chewing gum, sweet wrappers, and other refuse that danced in the wind like forgotten spirits. The lone bin, standing sentinel at the edge of the sidewalk, stood empty and forlorn, its contents scattered by the whims of passing gusts.

In the shadow of the bustling supermarket, the walls surrounding the shop bore the unmistakable imprint of urban artistry—graffiti tags adorned the brickwork like a vibrant tapestry of rebellion and self-expression, transforming the drab concrete into a canvas of kaleidoscopic colour.

Just off his shift, Danny steered his mountain bike to a stop. Lady Gaga's beats pulsed through his headphones, creating a rhythm for the mundane evening ritual. He swiftly secured his bike outside the store, the metal lock clicking into place, and pushed through the sliding glass doors.

The store, a haven of convenience, awaited him with its aisles of neatly arranged products. Danny, on a mission, moved with a purpose. A loaf of bread, a carton of milk, and a convenience meal found their way into his basket. Yet, spontaneity seized him as he sauntered past the sweets section.

His gaze lingered on the vibrant assortment, and an impulse guided his hand to grab a packet of lemon drops and some aniseed sweets, an unexplored indulgence. The aisle's artificial glow framed his silhouette, contemplating the unknown flavours within his grasp.

As he approached the checkout counter, a young Asian boy akin in age to Danny manned the till. Their eyes met, and an unspoken connection sparked. The boy, harbouring a secret, flirted discreetly while his uncle, engrossed in a phone call, remained oblivious to the exchange. The air buzzed with a shared understanding, a fleeting moment of connection.

With goods ready for purchase, Danny reached the counter. The transaction unfolded in silence, save for the electronic beeping of the barcode scanner. As he prepared to exit, the lad at the till conveyed a silent message, mouthing, "Call me." A scrap of paper with a mobile number nestled within the bag, a clandestine invitation that lingered in the air.

Exiting the automatic doors, Danny found himself smiling. He stole a glance back, capturing the essence of a moment suspended in time before venturing into the night.

The mundane yet charged encounter added a subtle layer of intrigue to the routine, and Danny walked away, feeling the pulse of life beneath the surface of the everyday.

The echoes of Lady Gaga's music lingered in Danny's ears as he stepped out of Tesco Express, still riding high on the subtle thrill of an unexpected connection. Cloud 9, however, would soon crumble beneath the shadows that awaited him.

Approaching his mountain bike, Danny found it surrounded by the ominous figures of the gang from earlier. Among them, the leader stood next to the bike, an envious gleam in his eyes. A knot tightened in Danny's stomach, and a plea for peace slipped from his lips.
"I don't want no trouble, man, please."

The leader's eyes, dark pools of resentment, locked onto Danny. His words dripped with venom, echoing like a sinister melody.

"Too late for that, bro; you dissed me earlier and made a mockery of me and my boys."
Danny demonstrated fear in his voice, "I just want to go home to my mum."

"Too late, you bender," the leader spat, eyes narrowing with malice. The atmosphere soured with aggression. In pleading for mercy, Danny emphasised his bike's significance, a hard-earned possession. Yet, the leader, fueled by perceived slights, declared possession.

"You shouldn't be riding a man's bike; it's mine now."

The tension reached a boiling point. Held from both sides, Danny faced a menacing ultimatum. The gang leader, revelling in a twisted power play, insinuated an unwanted attraction, a vile spectacle for their amusement.

"I could be your bit of rough," he jeered, inciting laughter among his cohorts.
For his safety, Danny surrendered the bike key. His dreams of a simple journey home were shattered. As he attempted to flee, a brutal punch to the stomach halted him. The gang's cruelty escalated, the leader striking him repeatedly. In a cruel twist, a concealed knife revealed itself, plunging into Danny's side.

Armed with a baseball bat, the shopkeeper rushed to intervene, swinging at the heartless gang. Unfazed, they dispersed, leaving Danny crumpled on the pavement, blood staining his puffer jacket. The Asian lad from the till ran out, cradling Danny's head, both consumed by tears.

The street became a stage of tragedy, feathers from Danny's torn jacket drifting like mournful whispers. The shopkeeper, determined to seek justice, dialled the police. As the sirens wailed in the distance, Danny slipped into unconsciousness, his world tainted by both tears and blood, leaving behind a chilling aftermath in the cold, unforgiving night. Snow White feathers, falling and soaking blood like blotting paper, Dannys' life force spilling out onto the street.

***

The dimly lit hallway of Daphne's flat echoed with the hushed urgency of a late-night doorbell. Daphne, a mix of worry and anticipation etched on her face, was desperate to phone her Danny, who was late home. His tea sat on the kitchen table cold and congealed. The persistent ring of the doorbell disrupted the silence, prompting her to scramble towards the entrance.

As she approached the door, shadows of two figures clad in hi-vis yellow jackets loomed behind the frosted glass. An involuntary shiver ran down Daphne's spine. She fumbled with her pockets, instinctively seeking solace in the reassuring weight of a golden brooch. This piece held secrets she dared not expose. With trembling hands, she concealed the emblem within a ceramic keepsake on the hall table, her actions driven by fear.

The doorbell chimed again, accompanied by an insistent knock. Through the frosted glass, the concerned gaze of a policeman peered in, urging her to open up.

"Mrs. Daphne Wills, it's okay. It's the police. Don't be frightened. Come to the door," the police officer assured.

Daphne hesitated, her internal turmoil evident. She clutched the icon of the Virgin Mary on the wall, seeking solace in a moment of silent prayer, then mustered the courage to open the front door.

"Mrs Wills, it's about Danny," the police officer continued, his voice carrying the weight of sombre news.

"He's been stabbed," added the female officer.

A chill descended upon the hallway, freezing Daphne's features in a mask of disbelief. The police officers, bearers of grim news, maintained a sombre demeanour.

"You need to lock up the house and get your coat; he's still alive," the male officer instructed.

Daphne's eyes flickered to the ceramic keepsake on the table, a silent witness to her hidden guilt. Without a word, she grabbed her coat, a shield against the impending storm. She prepared to confront the unknown awaiting her beyond the threshold. Once more, the door is a portal from safety to the maelstrom of modern life.

***

Navigating the labyrinthine corridors of the hospital felt like a daunting task, especially when time was of the essence. Every turn seemed to lead to another seemingly endless hallway, lined with identical doors that offered no clue as to what lay beyond.

The situation's urgency only added to the sense of disorientation, each passing moment amplifying the anxiety that gnawed at the edges of consciousness. With each step, the footsteps echo reverberated against the sterile walls, a constant reminder of the race against time.

The harsh double doors swung open, their echo resonating through the sterile corridors of the hospital. Daphne, her face marred by streaming tears, stormed into the unforgiving fluorescence trailed by the two police officers who had escorted her. A determined stride carried her down the hospital corridor, eyes fixed on the nursing station.

Unyielding, she pushed through the crowd, an embodiment of maternal urgency. The two police officers flanked her, silent sentinels in the face of impending distress.
"Where is my boy?" Though strained, her voice cut through the hospital's background hum. Adorned with a trembling chain, her hand sought solace in the worn cross that dangled from it. Fingers rubbed the symbol of faith, a silent plea in the face of the unknown.

A tender touch rested on Daphne's shoulder, the female police officer's hand a gesture of comfort, a surrogate for the solace a mother might provide to her child in times of anguish. In the harsh clinical light of the hospital, the trio stood united, poised to confront the heart-wrenching reality awaiting them.

***

The dim glow of the early morning crept through the half-open curtains, casting a muted hue over the hospital room. Nestled in the uncomfortable visitor's chair, Daphne stirred from her restless slumber. Before her, in the sterile confines of the hospital bed, Danny lay still, a silent figure beneath the white sheets. His face, partially obscured by a mask, betrayed the weariness of someone who had faced the shadows of the night.

Monitoring equipment hummed softly, a mechanical lullaby weaving through the room. A sizable bandage adorned Danny's side, a testament to a recent skirmish with fate. Daphne, still holding Danny's hand in a protective grasp, had succumbed to sleep in her vigil.

The entrance of a nurse disrupted the quietude. With a gentle hand, she pulled back the curtains, ushering in the hesitant light. Daphne, roused from her dreams, blinked away the remnants of sleep.

Danny's eyes flickered open at the head of the bed, a bewildered gaze fixed on the unfamiliar ceiling. The nurse approached with practised reassurance.

"Nurse." Daphne's voice wavered between relief and trepidation.

"Danny, Danny, hello, sleepyhead," the nurse cooed, her voice a balm in the waking world.
Now fully alert, Daphne rose from her chair, a motherly urgency propelling her into action. The nurse, mindful of the fragile equilibrium of the room, addressed Danny.

"Danny, your mum is here. You're safe in the hospital. Try and stay as still as possible."
Outside the cocoon of the room, a police officer stationed as a guardian entered. His presence added a layer of formality to

the scene.

"Hello, Danny. You scared us and your mum. We need to talk about what happened," he declared.

The nurse, perceptive to the need for a moment of respite, intervened. "Woah, everyone, let him wake up. Please, give him some space."

As realisation dawned on Danny, fear flickered in his eyes. He felt the weight of their collective gaze and, in that moment, became acutely aware of the pain throbbing from his side. Grimacing, he clutched the sheets, silently acknowledging his ordeal.

"I'll wait outside. Mrs. Wills, Daphne, shall we get a cup of tea while the nurse does her thing?" The police officer gestured toward the door, a subtle invitation for a brief retreat.
"Thank you," the nurse replied, a nod of gratitude passing between them. The room, once again cloaked in a hushed tension,

***

The early morning light cast a subtle glow across Andy's room, where he lay in bed, a silent observer of the world unfolding on his television screen. The news anchor's voice resonated in the room, reporting on a grim incident that transpired the previous night.
"Who is it?" Andy's voice echoed, taut with tension.

"It's Miss Fontaine, your care manager," came the reply.

The TV, a persistent background hum, played the local news, a tapestry of events weaving into Andy's consciousness.

"Around seven last night, a local man was stabbed outside this supermarket. He is in serious and stable condition," intoned the news reader.

Another knock punctuated the news report, and Miss Fontaine entered, a figure of concern etched on her face. The urgency in the air was palpable as she rushed to silence the unfolding tragedy on the screen.

"Police have appealed for any witnesses. The stabbing has been reported as a hate crime. The man's name has not been released as of y..."

The TV blinked into silence, and Miss Fontaine turned toward Andy, her eyes carrying a weight of sad news. She settled onto the edge of Andy's bed, a gesture that mirrored the gravity of the situation.

"Andy, I am so sorry to tell you, but it's about Danny."

Andy's gaze shifted from Miss Fontaine to the dormant television, the abrupt stillness reflecting the hollowness settling in the room.

"It's him that was stabbed. I knew something was up. He's never ever late. Ever. Poor kid."

The unspoken reality hung in the air, a heavy shroud casting shadows over Andy's room. The morning light, once benign, now carried the weight of a world forever altered by a single act of violence.

A single zenith of light danced on the dust motes from the partially drawn curtains, its finger pointing directly at the picture frame of Andy and Johnathon as adults with a mysterious suited figure. The beam plays on the motto of the RAF cap badge Per Ardua Astra,

***

The pale light of day cast a muted glow over Moonraker House, a quiet facade disguising the turmoil within.

The bike gang leader sported the unmistakable style of grime house fashion, a nod to the urban culture that defined the streets he roamed. His attire, a fusion of casual comfort and streetwise edge, mirrored the aesthetic embraced by the grime scene.

Clad in loose-fitting jeans that hung low on his hips, he exuded an aura of laid-back confidence, his movements unrestricted by the confines of tight clothing. The denim, worn and faded from countless adventures on the asphalt, bore the scars of his journey through the city's gritty underbelly.

Atop his upper body, he wore a baggy top, its oversized silhouette a testament to the significant influence of grime fashion. Adorned with bold graphics and vibrant colours, the garment spoke volumes of his allegiance to the urban subculture that shaped his identity.
His choice of attire didn't stop there. An emblazoned with the logos of Akademiks, Nike, and Adidas, a tracksuit jacket added a layer of street cred to his ensemble. The iconic hood pulled over his head, adding a sense of mystery to his presence, obscuring his features in the shadows of the city's neon glow.

Completing his look was a pair of Nike Air Force 1s, their pristine white finish starkly contrasting the grime and grit of the streets. As he strode confidently through the urban jungle, the rhythmic thud of his sneakers against the pavement echoed the beat of the city's heartbeat, a testament to his arrogant ego as a true urban warrior. The proceeds of crime and aggressive shoplifting pay for all.

A shadow in a despairing world led his crew to the level where Daphne's house was nestled. With a calculated air, they surveyed the surroundings, the air thick with tension. No attempt at stealth, their reputation was the armour against interference, and the lack of police in the brutalist estate gave them free rein.

Outside the door, a small bouquet of flowers and a small teddy bear, a card was tucked in the top. The leader just kicked it across the landing; carnations and sprays land on the cold, wet concrete, the handwritten sympathy card soaked in the puddle, the ink now spreading.

"Stay out here. They're both in the hospital, so no one around. But if you see anyone, you know the score," the gang leader ordered, his authority unchallenged.

As the gang initiated their intrusion, the door yielded to their force, protesting with a creak. The leader, a sinister figure against the backdrop of despair, slinked into the house, accompanied by a couple of cohorts. Chaos ensued within as they ransacked the flat, leaving destruction in their wake. The echoes of shattering glass and splintering wood reverberated through the desolate halls.

In their ruthless pursuit, they pilfered Danny's electronics, the flickering glow of the stolen TV casting an eerie aura. Daphne's cherished jewellery, a testament to memories and sentiment, fell prey to their callous greed. The hall stands, a silent witness collapsed in their wake, the keepsake tumbling down. The gold poppy, a delicate emblem, lay abandoned on the floor, a casualty of their unchecked rampage.

The gang leader's gaze fell upon the fallen keepsake in the aftermath. A moment of unexpected contemplation seized him, and he pocketed the gold poppy, its significance lost on him. The gang vanished into the labyrinth of despair with their spoils in tow.

Amidst the ruins, a passerby, pushing a pram, beheld the shattered door. A sense of civic duty compelled her to reach for her mobile phone. As she dialled the police, she became an unwitting harbinger of justice. The broken fragments of Coleshill House, witness to an unspeakable violation, echoed the silent plea for retribution. The teddy bear is face down, sodden, and drowned.

***

Danny lay in the sterile hospital bed, a fragile figure amid the stark surroundings. The door swung open, disturbing his uneasy slumber. In rolled Andy, propelled by a motorised wheelchair, his determined entrance accompanied by the weary Miss Fontaine and a police officer. After a cursory assessment, the officer deemed the elderly man harmless and departed.

Daphne, arising from her vigil, confronted the unexpected trio.

"Miss Fontaine, what are you doing here?" she inquired, her tone a mixture of concern and irritation.

Nonchalant and unapologetic, Andy interjected, "Oh, it was me. They Could not stop me, I just wanted to check on Danny."

"Andy, you should not be here," Daphne chided.

Ignoring their protests, Andy dismissed the duo. Daphne shrugged and looked at the copper. "Shall we leave them to it? We'll be outside, alright, love."

As the women exited, Daphne stole a lingering glance back. Andy manoeuvred his wheelchair closer to Danny, an unspoken bond evident in the gentle clasp of their hands.
"He will be safe with me. Go get a cup of tea; I will look after him," Andy assured, his voice carrying a paternal reassurance. Leadership from his past had resurfaced,

The room is now private, and Danny's vulnerability surfaced after the recent ordeal. "Wing Commander, so sorry. So sorry."

Andy, undeterred, countered, "What are you being sorry for? You were robbed and assaulted. It's not your fault."

The admission weighed heavy on Danny's conscience. "But my secret is out. Everyone knows. My mum has not said anything, but she is religious, you know..."

"They said on the news it was a hate crime. Your mum thinks it was because you are black, not the other thing," Andy interjected, a hint of consolation in his voice.

Danny continued as the unspoken truth hung heavy in the air, "The police were here. It's so embarrassing, having to tell them I am..."

"Gay," Andy finished the sentence matter-of-factly.

The shame resonated in Danny's eyes as he looked away. "Yes, that."

Andy, offering a reassuring smile, quelled the self-pity. "Not your fault you are a raving poof, is it?"

The unexpected support from Andy brought a mix of emotions, and Danny, looking down in shame, whispered, "They stole my bike as well."

"Don't worry about that," Andy dismissed the concern with a wave.

"It's so hard being an outcast, Andy. Do you know what it's like to be an outcast? The colour of your skin, single mom, she does her best, but being different...gay! Can you imagine?" Danny bared his soul.

Andy's eyes reflected the weight of years. He responded, "Shame, it's not a new idea. People will surprise you."

Opening a chapter he had long kept closed, Andy spoke of a fellow villager, Johnny, and a hidden history from the war. Captivated by the revelation, Danny urged Andy to share the untold story.

Andy's gaze turned distant as he began to unveil a buried truth. "It began around 1940. We were young men then; Johnny lived at the farm opposite the village…"

CHAPTER 4

The letter

The year was 1940, and the vast fields of Wiltshire lay as a picturesque backdrop. A rifle in hand, a young man moved across the landscape with purpose. Each step exuded confidence, and the practised precision with which he handled the firearm spoke volumes. As he aimed and fired, the quiet countryside echoed with the sound of his solitary pursuit – rabbit hunting.

Returning to the farmhouse, the skilled hunter Jonathan carried a brace of rabbits, the spoils of his morning expedition. Once an instrument of precision in the field, the rifle rested atop the Welsh dresser. The fading notes of Noel Gay's music blended with the rustic aroma of the countryside. The old gramophone is in the corner, and the platter is turning.

In the farmhouse kitchen, Jonathan placed the rabbits on the table, and the scent of the outdoors filled the air. As he brewed a cup of tea, Frank, a weathered figure, entered the room, his eyes immediately drawn to the bounty.

"I'll skin them later," he grumbled, "after you make me a cup of tea. Oh, there's a letter for you."

"War Office?" Jonathan questioned as he opened the envelope, quickly scanning its contents before passing it to Frank.

Frank exclaimed excitedly, "Looks like you're off to London. I told you studying with Old Jed would pay off. Though I'm unsure how he and I will manage at the farm with you gone."

A knock disrupted the moment, and in burst Andy, a boisterous teenager, with his own news.

"You seen this? Been asked to go to London for the RAF," Andy exclaimed.

"Me too. We're on the same date," Jonathan replied.

Frank sighed, "God help us all with you two in the RAF. Hopefully, this thing with Poland will be over soon. I can't see us going to war. Especially with you two herberts flying. At least it's not the bloody Navy but the bloody Navy."

***

The architecture of the historic venue echoed the grandeur of bygone eras, with its iconic Victorian pavilion standing tall as a symbol of cricketing heritage. Its elegant facade, adorned with intricate detailing and towering spires, exuded an air of timeless sophistication, transporting spectators back to a bygone era of gentlemanly sportsmanship.

The pavilion's regal presence commanded attention, its arched windows and ornate balconies offering panoramic views of the meticulously manicured grounds below. Bathed in daylight, its iconic facade witnessed a long queue of young men adorned in smart suits. Each carried a small case, anticipation and excitement etched on their faces. Among them, Jonathan and Andy stood animated, their enthusiasm palpable. RAF sergeants and medical orderlies ushered them toward the main door, marking the beginning of their journey.

The makeshift medical office on the Ground exuded a cold and sterile aura, its barren walls and harsh fluorescent lighting casting a clinical pallor over the room. Folding chairs lined the perimeter, offering scant comfort to those awaiting their turn for examination. The air was thick with tension, palpable even amidst the antiseptic scent that permeated the space.

Within this austere environment, Jonathan found himself thrust into a battle of wills, his aspirations clashing head-on with the uncompromising mannerism of Mr Gubbins.
As Jonathan entered the room, a sense of apprehension washed over him, mingling with the nerves churning in his stomach. Mr Gubbins, a stern and imposing figure, stood at the centre of the room, his gaze piercing and unwavering. With each passing moment, the tension between them seemed to mount like a storm brewing on the horizon. Mr Gubbins, a seasoned civil servant with a reputation for his acerbic bearing, had taken an instant dislike to Jonathan,

"Right, young man, you have asthma; you can't join the RAF, Navy, or Army," declared Mr. Gubbins, a severe figure with a disapproving countenance.

Jonathan's immediate reaction was disbelief. "What? I don't have asthma!"

His protests fell on deaf ears as Mr. Gubbins, armed with medical reports and a damning police file, dissected Jonathan's aspirations. "You do; the MO has just told me. Your war is over before you begin. You wouldn't have got in anyway, with your police file. Let's look at two counts of poaching, petrol theft, arson, and affray. Yet, your examination report says you are good at maths and geography. Did you cheat?"

The young man vehemently denied any wrongdoing. "Never dream of cheating, and I was sat next to my friend who can't even read a map, let alone understand geography! But I want to be a pilot. I want to fly. Give me a chance. I want to do my bit for the war effort."

Mr. Gubbins, unyielding in his stance, dismissed Jonathan's aspirations with a curt assessment. "Slim chance of that, young man. We are going to war; we can't have asthmatic thieves and vagabonds in the officer corps. Can we? I am amazed you had the cheek to show up."

Despite Jonathan's pleas and insistence that the diagnosis was incorrect, Mr Gubbins, adopting the role of a self-proclaimed guardian angel, informed him of an alternative fate. "What you are, son, is a thief and vandal with a chronic medical condition. You'll hinder the Military; we don't need your type. Here is a warrant to go home and a letter for local defence volunteers. They're called the Home Guard. You'll have to sit the war out, let real men deal with it."

Jonathan, crushed and dejected, voiced his frustration. "This is so unfair. I want to do my bit. They will call me a bloody coward, white feathers in the letterbox. My dad told me about the cowards in the last war."

Mr Gubbins, unrelenting in his stern demeanour, offered a parting rebuke. "Yes, you should have thought of that before you left for here. Would the RAF let you fly or be near an aircraft?

As Jonathan, still grappling with the shattered remnants of his aspirations, attempted a final plea, Mr. Gubbins 'intolerance peaked.

"But I can handle a gun, and..." Jonathan's words hung in the air, desperate to salvage some dignity from the wreckage of his thwarted dreams.

Mr. Gubbins, however, was unfazed. His response was sharp and unwavering. "Get out of this office, and don't let the door hit you on the way out. Good day to you. Serve your King by being a farmer like your father. Take this letter and go home. You should be ashamed of yourself for even daring to show up. Remember my face, Mr. Hodges. Remember it."

With those cutting words, Jonathan, the would-be pilot, was ushered out of the office, clutching a letter that carried not the promise of soaring through the skies in defence of his country but rather a redirection toward a fate he hadn't envisioned — one of the farm fields and the echoes of unfulfilled aspirations. The door closed behind him, sealing the reality of his altered destiny.

With those harsh words, Jonathan left the office, carrying a letter that would redirect his path away from the dreams of flight and service to his King.
Opening the door, he was met with Andy's beaming smile.
"I am going to be a navigator! Whatever that is..."

***

The evening sun cast a moody glow upon the farm cottage, a worn structure that had weathered years of toil and hardship. Burdened by a weighty shame, Johnathon stood before the door, apprehensive about what lay beyond it. He took a reluctant step forward, each footfall echoing the toll of a dream shattered.

His father, Frank, emerged from the cottage, weathered lines etched on his face, a testament to the struggles of a life lived. As Johnathon approached, a silent exchange passed between them. The disappointment in Frank's eyes was palpable, a heavy cloak draped over a relationship strained by circumstance.

In the humble kitchen, Johnathon's dejection settled like a storm cloud. He slumped at the table, eyes cast downward, a portrait of despair. Frank, with a stern countenance, eyed his son with a mix of reproach and frustration. The belt, ominously placed on the table, hinted at the gravity of their impending conversation.

"So, your thieving and poaching have caught up with you, and you are malingering with asthma," Frank's voice cut through the heavy air, his words carrying the weight of unspoken disappointment. "And I swear you have never had it. Did you lie to the Doctor to get out of serving, you coward?"

"Dad," Johnathon began, a feeble attempt to defend himself, but Frank's words surged like a torrent.

"HOW DARE YOU CALL ME DAD after all your mother did for you, and me, me ME LOOKING AFTER YOU since her passing. God bless her. If she could see you now, sit here, a failure and a COWARD! A COWARD!!! Lying about being ill."

The accusations hung in the air, a bitter testament to fractured trust. After reeling from the verbal onslaught, Johnathon tried to clarify, "I never said anything about being ill. The Doctor just said I had it. Told you before, he didn't even examine me."

"You expect me to believe that?" Frank's tone dripped with disbelief. "Well, you must earn your keep if you want to live here. You must join the Local Volunteers while friends like Andy do a real man's job. Or you are out. How am I to show my face with my cowardly malingering son who is living at home when half the village's sons are at war?"

The weight of judgment bore down on Johnathon, his pleas for understanding falling on deaf ears. "But father, I did nothing wrong. They just walked me into an office, and then suddenly I was gone into the street."

"You expect me to believe that? I know what you did. You turned up with a story and a pretend cough to get out," Frank accused, the disappointment etched on his face.
"No, I never. Please listen to me!"

"Then you told them about your police record, and you got away Scot-free," Frank continued, unfazed by his son's protestations. "You go to your room and will be doing all the farm hours now. You are not to go to the village, ever. If you ever see Andy's mother, she may give you a piece of her tongue, too. The shame you brought down on this... This family!"
"I did nothing wrong, father, please."
"ENOUGH, YOU COWARD!" Frank's final words echoed through the cottage, sealing Johnathon's fate. The door to his room closed a symbolic barrier between the son and the father, a tangible manifestation of dreams shattered and a future uncertain.

***

In the sterile confines of the modern NHS hospital room, Andy and Danny engaged in a conversation that carried the weight of untold stories. The faint hum of medical machinery provided an incongruous backdrop to their words. With a cup of tea cradled in his weathered hands, Andy leaned forward as he recounted a chapter of history that had been etched into the fabric of their village.

A nurse entered the room, a fleeting interruption that made Andy fall into a momentary silence. His gaze lingered on her as she deftly attended to the medical equipment, changing a drip bag with a precision that hinted at the routine nature of her duties. Once the nurse left, Andy resumed his narrative, the words flowing like a steady stream.

"It was a great shame not to serve during the war," he began, the gravity of those times reflected in his eyes. "Young men had gone off, leaving their families, sometimes never to return." There was a poignant pause; the weight of unspoken sorrows hung in the air.

Sitting in the hospital bed, Danny absorbed Andy's words, sensing the depth of history that was about to unfold. "So Johnny not going was like a terrible thing," he mused, probing for understanding.

A shadow passed over Andy's face. "A rumour had gone round the village, started by a nasty piece of work at the pub. Plus, Johnny had a reputation for being difficult," he explained, the nuances of small-town judgment colouring his words.

"Difficult?" Danny questioned, his curiosity piqued.

Andy nodded, his eyes reflecting a mixture of empathy and understanding. "He had history in the village. I'll talk about that later. But if you refused to go, you could be arrested. Everyone thought he was malingering and a coward. Frank's father had served with distinction in the Great War, which made the family shame worse."

As the weight of societal judgment settled on Johnny's shoulders, Danny couldn't help but feel a surge of empathy. "Was there anything he could have done?" he asked, searching for a glimmer of hope in the narrative.

"Oh, he had to join the Home Guard," Andy responded, carrying the gravity of wartime responsibilities.

Danny, ever the wit, injected a moment of levity into the conversation. "What, like Dad's Army... don't tell him your name, Pike, haha."

A brief smile touched Andy's lips, acknowledging the humour but underlining the seriousness of the situation. "What are you on about? It was serious business," he remarked a sombre reminder that behind the banter lay a turbulent chapter of their shared history.

***

In the dimly lit village church hall, a motley crew of local volunteers stood in formation, a ragtag assembly of old, young, and infirm. Their attire was a mix of worn-out uniforms, and a sense of earnest determination filled the air, accentuated by the white LDV brassards adorning their arms. The eclectic group was on parade, a makeshift army preparing for a war that crept closer with each passing day.

The atmosphere crackled with anticipation as Captain Chiles, an authoritative figure with a weathered face, stepped forward to address the troop. His voice cut through the air, carrying both command and camaraderie.

"Right, good effort tonight. Meeting same time on Friday," Captain Chiles declared, his eyes scanning the assembled volunteers. "There's a Signaller's course in a week. Pte J Hodges is in my office after the parade. You're on it."

As the captain's words resonated in the hall, attention turned to Private Johnathon Hodges, a figure with a complex history etched on his face. His gaze met Captain Chiles, and a subtle nod acknowledged the directive. The path ahead seemed uncertain, yet there was an unspoken understanding of duty.

After the parade, Captain Chiles took Private Hodges aside, the two figures standing in the hushed aftermath of military preparations. The captain's voice held a stern command as he outlined the next course of action.

"Right, young man. You are to travel to Amesbury on the train where you will be picked up for your course," Captain Chiles directed, his eyes scrutinising Johnathon's worn uniform. "Due to the state of your uniform, you are to wear your work clothes. Pack a small case. They will give you a new uniform when you get there. Do you understand?"

Johnathon's response was concise and respectful, "Yes, sir. But

I did not volunteer for a signals course."

The captain's reply came with an edge of authority, "Do as you are damn well told and go. Spoken to your father, and he will make sure you go. Asthma or not. Clear? Stop fighting for yourself, and fight for your King."

The weight of duty settled on Johnathon's shoulders as the captain's words echoed in the quiet hall. The clash between personal desires and the call of duty marked the beginning of a journey into the unknown, where each step carried the weight of a nation at war.

***

The train compartment featured two leather benches opposite each other, with a narrow corridor adjacent to one side. Entry to the compartment was granted through a sliding door, which revealed a space tainted by the lingering odour of cigarette smoke, its walls stained yellow with time. Johnny sat alone, his cap resting on the bench, while his small leather suitcase occupied the overhead rack. He gazed out the window with solitude as his companion, where the verdant landscape unfolded before him. The train's rhythmic motion carried him through rolling hills and valleys adorned with golden fields, resembling a moving patchwork quilt.

The side door creaked open as the train rattled and clicked rapidly, introducing an unexpected guest. A man in a suit stepped in, an air of formality contrasting the casual atmosphere of the compartment. Lost in his contemplation, Johnathon initially remained oblivious to the newcomer's presence. It was considered impolite to stare at a new passenger; such behaviour was deemed inappropriate and socially unacceptable.

The man sat opposite Johnathon, his figure eclipsed by the shadowed interior of the compartment; a brief moment of silence lingered, broken only by the rhythmic symphony of the train's journey.

"Recognise me, young man?" The man questioned, his voice cutting through the ambient noise, prompting Johnathon to redirect his gaze. Confusion etched across his features, Johnathon met the stern scrutiny of this civil servant, who removed his hat, revealing a countenance marked by severity and purpose.

The atmosphere shifted, and the compartment became a stage for an unspoken tension. A silent dialogue between the two figures unfolded, framed by the fleeting scenery outside the window. The conversation remained unheard, concealed by the walls of the train carriage. But the urgency in the man's gestures and the gravity of his words were evident, creating an air of intrigue that hung palpably in the confined space.

Outside the carriage, the Wiltshire countryside continued its relentless passage, indifferent to the clandestine exchange within. A momentary pause in the journey, a confidential meeting on the rails, set against the backdrop of a nation at war. The train carried its secrets, and Johnathon, caught in the currents of fate, found himself at the crossroads of circumstance and choice. His face was shocked and confused; whatever the arrangement in this private meeting was, it was severe.

***

The Oxfordshire Village of Coleshill lay quiet under the noonday sun, its streets resonating with the hushed footsteps of a young man named Johnathon. He strolled down the high street, an air of anticipation clinging to him like the faintest mist. In his left hand, he clutched a worn suitcase, a silent companion on this unexpected journey. His right hand held a copy of The Times, its pages a refuge from the enigma unfolding before him. It had been a long ten-mile walk from Swindon, but the weather was fair; the suit felt constricting.

Johnathon's steps led him to a quaint Post Office, its entrance a threshold to uncertainty. Nervous glances darted about as he entered. The village post office exuded a sense of retro charm, its interior adorned with relics of a bygone era. A large weighing scale dominated one corner, accompanied by a meticulous array of brass weights of varying sizes. Shelves lined with tinned goods created the illusion of abundance, though the reality was far more modest. Each item was meticulously labelled with neat penmanship on paper tags.

A blackboard displayed the names of villagers awaiting parcels and their identities scrawled in chalk with a sense of anticipation. Nearby, an honesty box sat beside a small basket of fresh eggs, a testament to the community's trust. Glass jars brimming with humbugs and toffees tempted patrons from atop the counter. At the same time, a stack of unfolded newspapers awaited perusal, accompanied by a ball of string and a pair of scissors for wrapping purchases.

Behind the counter stood a bakelite telephone and a mechanical till adorned with brass inlay, its display revealing prices with a satisfying pop. Posters advocating for the war effort adorned the walls, serving as reminders of the tumultuous times. Despite the challenges of rationing, Mabel diligently maintained a tidy shop, her efforts evident in the window displays boasting vibrant blooms and a vacant glass cake cover adorned with a paper doily—a poignant reminder of a simpler time.

His eyes scanned the room like a cautious traveller in unfamiliar terrain. Behind the counter, a little old lady, the postmistress, observed him with suspicion. A sense of urgency underscored his movements as he approached her.

"Excuse me, miss? I need to speak to a Mr. Jones," Johnathon inquired, his voice laced with uncertainty. The postmistress, Mable, eyed him warily, a silent arbiter of secrets hidden within the walls of her establishment.

"Wait there, young man," she commanded, her steps purposeful as she circled the counter, reaching for the telephone. Amelia, the postmistress's niece, a small observer, gazed at Johnathon with innocent curiosity. A shy smile and a subtle wave between them painted a brief interlude of humanity amidst the unfolding drama.

As the telephone conversation commenced, the shop bell chimed, heralding the arrival of another player in this unfolding narrative. Sarah, a twenty-year-old woman, entered the Post Office, radiating a striking elegance that contrasted with the town's modest surroundings. Her eyes, sharp and inquisitive, fell upon the scene before her—a tableau of uncertainty and quiet tension.

Amelia's presence, the shared exchange of glances, and the subtle sparks between Johnathon and Sarah set the stage for a delicate dance of connections in this small Oxfordshire enclave. Sarah reached into her pocket and gave the little girl a toffee, who unwrapped it with glee and popped it in her mouth. Her eyes lit up with the sugar rush.

Yet, beneath this seemingly ordinary encounter, hidden from view, the postmistress clutched a Webley revolver, a silent arbiter ready to enforce the unspoken rules of the game.

"Stay there, you two," Mable declared, her tone cold and commanding, the revolver a shadowy secret behind the counter.

"It will be in your interest not to move, the pair of you."

"Sorry, Auntie," young Amelia chimed in, her voice a sweet melody that cut through the tension in the air. Her eyes, wide and innocent, scanned the faces of the strangers in the Post Office, finding solace in the smiles between Johnathon and Sarah. A dimpled smile adorned her cherubic face, a beacon of purity amidst the currents of uncertainty.

The postmistress, Mable, with a cautious bearing and watchful eyes, engaged the telephone exchange operator in conversation. Laced with an air of mystery, her words were a prelude to the unfolding events that hung in the balance. She spoke using veiled speech.

"Can you put me through to Mr. Jones, please? I have two packages for him," Mable inquired on the village telephone, her tone hushed as if the very walls had ears.

Johnny's gaze lingered on the enigmatic girl who appeared to be entangled in the same game as him. Uncertainty hung in the air, and he chose the silence to keep his thoughts guarded. Studying her, he noted the captivating features that framed her countenance – big oval brown eyes, brown hair cascading gracefully, high cheekbones, and a cherubic smile with a subtle dimple on her chin. She, too, was carrying a small case and holding that day's Times newspaper in her hand.

Her movements possessed a feline grace, a quiet and deliberate fluidity that intrigued him. She seemed both physically fit and unremarkably ordinary, a paradox that heightened the intrigue surrounding her.

As their eyes met, a subtle exchange occurred, and she offered a coy smile that sent a ripple of warmth through Johnny. A peculiar sensation enveloped him – a fusion of caution and an inexplicable connection. He carried the weight of prior warnings, a reminder to trust no one on this unfamiliar journey. The rules were clear, and he was resolute in adhering to them during this juncture of his life.

CHAPTER 5

Aftermath

The upper-level flats of Daphne's residence felt desolate, shrouded in police tape that blocked the entrance. Daphne, accompanied by the same Police Officer from earlier, moved toward her flat. The door was sealed with a silent promise of unwelcome revelations. Politely, the officer halted, allowing Daphne to enter the aftermath of her violated sanctuary.

Inside the hallway, the remnants of her life lay scattered, a testament to the chaos that had transpired. The professional and sympathetic constable stood back, readying her notebook to document the devastation. The door was a barrier to the chaos outside had failed, and it was seen inside this once proud and clean home.

"Take your time and watch your step. It's quite a mess," the officer advised.

Daphne surveyed the wreckage, her personal effects strewn like casualties of an unseen battle.

"It's awful, my things everywhere. Can it be tidied away?" Daphne inquired, her voice laden with hope.

"With a bit of time, Miss Wills, it'll be as if nothing happened," the officer reassured, though the statement's weight hung in the air.

Overwhelmed, Daphne sought guidance. "What do I do? Where do I start?"

The officer, stepping past her, critically examined the scene. Forensic stickers and fingerprint dust marked the violation that had taken place.

Daphne's eyes caught a keepsake on the floor. Nudging it with her foot, she discovered it empty. A sharp breath escaped her lips.

"You okay, Miss Wills? It's a lot to take in," the officer offered, attempting to refocus on the task.

Her gaze fixed on the vandalised Virgin Mary on the wall, Daphne clutched her cross, whispering a silent prayer.

"They damaged my Virgin Mary," she revealed, the pain evident in her voice.

The officer acknowledged the emotional toll but redirected the conversation to the investigation.

"Right, you need to tell me what's missing or vandalised, particularly anything valuable," she instructed.

Nodding, Daphne wrestled with the weight of her losses. "What do I tell Danny?"

The officer hesitated, recognising the challenge. "It's up to you, but I don't think he's well enough…"

Daphne's composure crumbled, tears flowing freely.

"Tell you what, love. I'll look in the kitchen and make you a nice hot cuppa before we start," the officer suggested, attempting to provide a momentary respite.

"You're a good soul, a good soul. My boy is single and needs a good girl like you," Daphne remarked, gratitude in her tearful eyes.

"Yes, Mrs. Mills, Danny is special," the officer replied, retreating into the kitchen.

As she disappeared from view, a muttered comment under her breath lingered.

"Awkward."

***

The hospital room, bathed in sterile light, welcomed the morning. An efficient and caring nurse entered to clear away the remnants of Danny's breakfast. Awake and fueled by his first meal in what felt like an eternity, Danny acknowledged the nurse's presence.

"You are feeling a bit better this morning?" the nurse inquired.

Danny, still navigating the post-breakfast haze, managed a response. "Yes, the first time I have eaten in what seems like forever."

The nurse, recognising signs of improvement, assured him, "You're looking better. I'll return later to wash you; that should make you feel even better."

Eager to present a more respectable appearance, Danny seized the opportunity. "Oh, please. My hair is so... manky. And I don't look respectable. Can I ask a favour?"
The nurse, ever professional, inquired, "Yes, what is it?"

"Well, it's a bit embarrassing," Danny admitted. "Do you have any moisturiser? The air con is playing havoc with my skin."

With a playful wink, the nurse responded, "Girl's got to look good."

"Hey, girl..." Danny playfully bantered.

"Don't worry," the nurse reassured, her light-hearted nature creating a momentary escape. Danny, influenced by the effects of morphine, couldn't help but let a hint of his natural charm shine through.

"Oh, I came out a bit there, didn't I?" he chuckled.

"We know that you run a different course. It's fine. Your mother doesn't know, does she?" the nurse shared, offering a knowing smile.

"No, and it's so bloody obvious. Everyone around here can see it," Danny admitted.

"Mums are funny," the nurse reflected. "When I married my wife last year, it took a lot of convincing. It's a phase. I am disgracing the whole of Nigeria, apparently" she smiled,

"A phase? Dorothy is my roommate, ha ha," Danny quipped.

As the banter unfolded, a knock at the door signalled Andy's arrival. In his wheelchair, Andy greeted Danny, and the nurse offered to make tea.

"You like 'em old," she playfully teased Danny.

"Shush, sister!" Danny responded, feigning embarrassment.

Thoughts of Johnny Hodges, labeled a coward in the village, lingered in Danny's mind. He sought clarification from Andy, who had alluded to Johnny's alleged misdeeds.

"You know what you were talking about with Mr. Johnny Hodges and him being a coward. I don't quite understand. Something must have happened to upset the village," Danny inquired.

Andy, positioned closer, took a deep breath, signalling the beginning of a tale with secrets and untold truths.

Andy's eyes drifted back to the summer of 1932, a time etched in memory, where the bonds of friendship and the thin line between courage and mischief were tested.

"1932, summer," Andy began with a wistful look as he recalled the events. Danny captivated, leaned in, eager to hear the tale unfold. Andy moved his electric chair forward to part his knowledge without others hearing.

"Johnny, despite his mischievous reputation, was a friend. We were just nippers, causing trouble and mischief around the village. But one day, things took a turn," Andy continued, his voice carrying the weight of nostalgia and unspoken gratitude.

"We were near the old Mill, exploring as usual. The air was thick with the scent of summer, and the sun painted everything in hues of gold. Little did we know, trouble lurked around the corner," Andy's words painted a vivid picture of innocence overshadowed by impending danger. Like that, Danny was drawn in.

***

The summer of 1932 bathed the village in a golden haze as if the essence of love and nostalgia had descended upon the landscape. Al Bowlly's crooning voice filled the air, emanating from an old gramophone serenading a young couple lost in the throes of affection. The melody, "Love Is The Sweetest Thing," casts a spell, encapsulating the innocence of a bygone era.

Heytesbury Mill stood at the heart of this idyllic scene, its waterwheel still beneath the radiant sun. A tableau of young love unfolded – a couple on a picnic, the music creating an ephemeral cocoon around them. Heytesbury Mill stood as a proud sentinel amidst the rural landscape, its weathered timbers and imposing structure a testament to centuries of industry and craftsmanship. The Mill's sturdy stone foundation rose majestically from the earth, anchored firmly in the soil as if rooted in history.

A mill pond, nestled in the embrace of summer, became a playground for the village youth. Like the tinkling of wind chimes, laughter echoed as children, including Peter, Johnathon, and Andy, played in the refreshing waters. With its silent and still wheel, the mill pond became a haven for the carefree spirits of adolescence.

In the background, Old Jed, the weathered gamekeeper, savoured his solitude in a van, accompanied only by his faithful collie named Snitch. He devoured sandwiches, engrossed in "the sporting times," a pink newspaper that whispered tales of a world beyond the village. Snitch, ever watchful, waited anxiously for a spoilt crumb to fall.

A low wall guarded the pond's edge, where teenagers embarked on daring leaps into the incredible, inky depths. Peter, the self-appointed lord of the heights, hesitated, relishing the admiration of his peers. Below, more minor children splashed and swam, finding solace in the shallows.

There was an unwritten hierarchy where you could play; older children sought the top, whilst the younger, weaker ones paddled in safety.

Nestled beneath the towering bulk of the ancient oak water wheel, the mill channel cut a sinuous path through the landscape, a silent witness to the passage of time. Its once-rushing waters now flowed more subduedly, but their depths still held a sense of mystery and allure. Known simply as "the chase" to those who frequented its banks, the channel was a place of adventure and exploration, a hidden gem at the heart of the Mill's domain. As the excellent oak water wheel turned overhead, its rhythmic cadence served as a constant reminder of the timeless dance between man and nature. The wheel was locked today, and the sluice held back the water weight.

As the sun painted the scene with hues of amber and gold, Andy and Johnathon scaled the heights, their perspective shifting as the world expanded. The older teenagers, daring and fearless, plunged into the water, their joyous shouts mingling with the summer breeze.

Like a fading echo, the music melted away, leaving behind the sounds of playful splashes and youthful camaraderie. The pond, the Mill, and the timeless melody of Love Is The Sweetest Thing bore witness to a moment suspended in the amber of memory, a snapshot of a summer that would forever linger in the hearts of those there.

The air hummed with the defiance of youth as Peter Smith, a stout and determined figure, stood at the precipice of Heytesbury Mill. The ancient sentinel mill watched over the landscape as if holding the secrets of generations. His arms crossed, a bold challenge etched on his face, Peter seemed impervious to the sceptics below. Today, it was a pirate ship, and Peter was Captain Blood.

"Hey, you're too small to come up here. Get back down," warned the older child in a feeble attempt to assert dominance.

"It's not your Mill. We can come up here anytime, and it's Captain to you," Peter retorted, unyielding in his stance. The breeze whispered through the blades of the stationary waterwheel, carrying the echoes of a dare.

Andy and Johnathon, allies in this teenage rebellion, rose behind Peter. The trio, bound by camaraderie and a shared sense of daring, stood united against the sceptics, for they were his ravenous crew.

"It's dangerous. You won't be able to reach the top of the wall," cautioned the young man, a hint of concern seeping into their bravado.

"We're jumping!" declared Peter, dismissing any notion of retreat.

"Are we?" Andy hesitated, glancing at Johnathon, whose uncertainty mirrored his own.

"I'm not. It looks too high, and you're not a good swimmer, Andy," Johnathon reasoned, a voice of caution in the face of recklessness.

"You two shut it. We are jumping," Peter commanded, determination flashing in his eyes.
The teenage onlookers, momentarily unnerved, exchanged worried glances. The trio's audacity cast a shadow over their earlier bravado.

"Look, we're off. You're crazy. If you want to kill yourselves, we're off. Come on, lads, these idiots are crazy," the young man declared, leading the retreat. The sceptics descended, leaving behind a trio undeterred by the judgment of their peers.

As the distant figures of the retreating teenagers merged with the horizon, Heytesbury Mill witnessed an audacious act of youthful rebellion, the air pulsating with the unspoken challenge hurled at the very bounds of danger.

The trio stood at the precipice, their youthful bravado warring against the apprehension that gnawed at their resolve. Peter Smith, the self-appointed leader, exuded a confidence that bordered on arrogance, his stature looming over Andy and Johnathon like an ominous shadow.

"We are going to walk the plank, crewmen. You first, Andy, then Johnny, then I," Peter declared, his words echoing off the walls of the ancient Mill.

"Why me first? It's your idea," Andy countered, his voice tinged with uncertainty.

"I am the eldest and am the Captain," Peter asserted, his authority undisputed in the eyes of his companions.

"Andy is right. It's too high, and I don't think we can reach the wall to climb out," Johnathon interjected, his voice a plea for reason amidst the reckless determination.

"You're just a bunch of cowardly custards," Peter scoffed, dismissing their concerns with a wave.

"What if we jump together? The chase looks much too high. But I'd rather climb down if that's alright with you?" Andy suggested, his apprehension palpable.

"No, don't like that," Peter rejected the notion, his resolve unyielding in the face of caution.
As they crept to the edge, a shroud of fear descended, their collective gaze fixed upon the murky depths below. The self-appointed Captain, Peter, stood in the centre, his arms encircling his companions, a facade of courage masking the

uncertainty that lurked within.

"Whoa, that's high. Do you think it's deep?" Andy questioned, his voice trembling with apprehension.

"Yes, it's deep enough. Bet it's cold," Johnathon replied, his voice betraying the unease that gripped them all.

"Still think Andy should go first," Peter insisted, his determination unswayed by the rising tide of doubt.

"You know he can barely swim," Johnathon countered, his plea for reason falling on deaf ears.

"It's not far to the side," Peter countered, his conviction unshakeable amidst the chorus of dissent.

"Peter, I'm telling you, this is a bad idea. Let's climb down," Johnathon implored, his voice tinged with urgency.

"But those bigger boys will think we are cowards and chickens. We are no cowards," Peter retorted, his pride blinding him to the peril ahead.

"You pair of chickens, you call yourselves pirates!" Peters's voice quivered with frustration and fear as the ominous spectre of danger loomed large over their heads.

Peter pushes the pair in,

In the murky depths of the mill chase, chaos erupted as bodies collided with the water's icy embrace. The plunge was unceremonious, a disorienting descent into darkness. Bubbles, limbs, and a bit of blood painted a turbulent picture beneath the surface.

As they surfaced, gasping for breath, the cold shock gripped Johnathon's body. Panic set in as he struggled to regain his bearings in the frigid water.

"ANDY!... ANDY! HELP!" Johnathon's cries cut through the cold air, echoing off the tall brick walls surrounding them.

Frantically treading water, Johnathon reached out for Andy, who, injured and semiconscious, was at the mercy of the icy depths. The cold gnawed at them, fatigue setting in as they fought to stay afloat. Meanwhile, Peter, the instigator of this perilous plunge, observed from the relative safety of the chase wall a mix of fear and voyeur etched on his face.

Peter slipped into the water, unable to resist the darkness beneath the surface. Panic seized him, and in a selfish bid for survival, he attempted to use the other boys as a makeshift platform to reach the wall.

Amidst the chaos, the commotion reached the ears of Old Jed, the seasoned gamekeeper, who rushed to the scene with his loyal collie, Snitch, in tow.

The three boys, now in dire straits, continued to struggle. Losing his grip on the injured Andy, Johnathon felt the icy tendrils of exhaustion and despair. Then, like a lifeline emerging from the abyss, several strong arms reached down from the edge of the wall. A courageous man leapt into the water, seizing Johnathon and pulling him to safety. In a desperate act of bravery, Johnathon pushed Andy upward, allowing the rescuer to lift him to the safety of the wall.

As the scene unfolded, a group of concerned adults rushed forward, draping coats over the unconscious Andy and shivering Johnathon. Snitch, the faithful collie, offered solace in the form of comforting nudges.

The air was thick with tension. The consequences of youthful recklessness lay bare in the pallor of Andy's unconscious form and the tremors wrapping Johnathon's weakened frame. The mill chase, once a place of childish play, now bore witness to the harsh reality of their actions and escape from watery death.

Amidst the aftermath of the perilous plunge, a chorus of

accusatory voices filled the air. The man with the straw boater, stern and concerned, surveyed the scene of near tragedy. "What happened here? You all nearly drowned?" The man's voice echoed with a mixture of anger and genuine worry.

The young man from earlier, still defensive, pointed fingers at the trio of drenched boys. "We told them not to do it and walked off, but we stayed and watched. We knew they weren't stupid enough to do it. But they did."

Old Jed, the seasoned gamekeeper, shook his head in disbelief. "You bloody fools are too small to play in the chase. Grown men have drowned in there."

The blame game unfolded as everyone tried to ascertain the culprit. Andy lay barely conscious, Johnathon coughed up pond water, and Peter, the instigator, trembled with guilt.

"It was Johnny," Peter accused, pointing a shaky finger at Johnathon.

The man's gaze intensified, landing on the pained and confused Johnathon. "You stupid child, you nearly killed your friends."

Old Jed, however, was sceptical. "I don't think that is entirely truthful."

The teenager from earlier, persistent in their accusation, affirmed, "Yes, it is. That one, he pushed them all in."

But Old Jed, a man of keen observation, countered, "I saw one climb down that was Peter. I know Johnathon's father; I don't think he would have pushed his friends in." Looking directly at Peter

The blame shifted, with the man now pointing at Johnathon. "I think it was this one."
Peter eagerly joined in, "He did push us in, called us cowards."

As accusations flew, Old Jed stood firm. "I don't think so."

Amidst the chaos, the man dismissed Old Jed's perspective. "No offence, but you're no spring chicken. How can you see from over there?"

The blame settled on Johnathon, who now faced the consequences of his actions but also the scorn of the adults. The youngster from earlier who told them not to climb even delivered a swift clip to Johnathon's ear.

"Wait till your headmaster hears about this, you little coward," the smartly dressed man declared.

As the apparent victim, Peter, revelling in his role, whispered and exchanged conspiratorial glances with the others when the adults weren't looking.

Old Jed, recognising the gravity of the situation, took charge. "I'll take Johnny home to his dad."

The smart man, addressing the others, declared, "These two, I will drive to the doctor if this one survives his near drowning."

The air hung heavy with condemnation, the consequences of youthful recklessness casting a dark shadow over the trio. The chase, once a place of youthful escapades, now echoed with the weight of their actions. It seemed like the end of summer for these three boys; it was no longer a fun pirate ship of adventure, and now it stood as the threesome nemesis.

***

Under the caress of the morning sun, the quaint village schoolyard bustled with the laughter and chatter of children. Two girls engrossed in a game of Pattycake found themselves at the centre of an unintended spectacle. Behind them, Peter, a boy of mischief and misguided curiosity, attempted to lift one of their dresses, sparking laughter as the girls darted away, leaving him bewildered and frustrated.

As the school bell rang, the rhythmic swing of the school monitor's hand brought the children to attention. At assembly time, they had arrived. The students lined up and filed into the school hall, anticipation lingering like a whispered secret. The neat line of children quietly waited and then rubbed into the school hall, a small room with a raised stage where the teaching staff stood, waiting for the head to start the Assembly. Discipline was expected from the staff as well as the students.

Within the confines of the school hall, the headmaster, a figure of authority and seasoned leadership addressed the gathered students and teachers: his speech, a blend of formality and veiled warnings set the tone for the term.

"The school welcomes Miss Fossett to the teaching staff," the headmaster announced, his voice projecting authority. "Girls, under her guidance, will delve into needlecraft and domestic duties, while Mr. Oliver will oversee the boys in woodcraft."

However, the mood was low as the headmaster delivered unexpected news. "Some sad news for you all," he continued, "Andrew Bryce is convalescing at home. He and two others were playing at Heytesbury Mill a week ago when there was an accident. Hopefully, he will be well enough to attend in November."

The revelation cast shadows on the Assembly, and the children exchanged uncertain glances. The resolute headmaster silenced the murmurs, calling forth two boys, Peter Smith and Johnathon Hodges, to stand in the spotlight. "You two up here now!"

"Quick as a flash, straight as a ruler," the headmaster commanded.

As the two boys assumed their positions, a palpable tension brewed between them. Hate simmered in their exchanged glances, promising a brewing storm.

"Heytesbury Mill is out of bounds. You will die," the headmaster declared sternly. "As these two reprobates nearly demonstrated."

Unexpectedly, a twist unfolded. The headmaster revealed a tale of exceptional bravery, where one accused had displayed courage amidst peril. Initially bearing the weight of accusation, Johnathon smiled as the truth emerged.

"Peter Smith, you have a school certificate of commendation for rescuing your friend," the headmaster declared, applause rippling through the hall.

However, the recognition didn't sit well with Johnathon, whose eyes narrowed in disbelief. The headmaster continued, presenting Peter with a certificate and a book token.

Amidst the applause, Johnathon, now relegated to the role of the accused, faced an altogether different fate. The stern and resolute headmaster called him forward for a public punishment.

"Johnathon Hodges, step forward, raise your hands flat out," the headmaster ordered.
As Johnathon extended his hands, expecting a customary scolding, the headmaster produced a cane. The subsequent

swoosh and strikes echoed in the hall, each blow met with shock and defiance on Johnathon's face.

"For breaking the rules, bullying, and cowardice of the highest order," the headmaster declared with each stroke of the cane.

Swish crack, swish crack, each strike louder than the last; the gathered children watched in morbid curiosity, some gasping at each strike.

In a sudden burst of unexpected rebellion from the brutal injustice, Johnathon's shock transformed into defiance. His gaze shifted to Peter, who, hidden beneath a smirking facade, had played his part in this public spectacle.

In an impulsive surge of anger and frustration, Johnathon drew back his hand. He swung a punch at Peter's face, a defiant act against the unfairness of his punishment. Johnathon's fist struck squarely on Peters's face, and his nose gushed blood. As the blood ran down to Peters's mouth, he licked his lips in genuine joy, and a broad smile cracked.

The headmaster's reaction was immediate. "WHATTTT!!! You, boy, you DESPICABLE BOY!"

In the aftermath, as the assembly hall buzzed with shocked murmurs, Johnathon bolted towards the school door, jumping down from the stage and holding his injured hand, consumed by a mixture of shock and rage. The bright sunlight awaited him outside, starkly contrasting the shadows of injustice within. The headmaster's enraged shouts reverberated behind him, and the air crackled with the weight of defiance and the birth of a schoolyard legend.

Nursing his bleeding face, Peter seized the opportunity to taunt his fellow student further. A triumphant chant echoed through the hall.

"Coward, coward, coward, coward, COWARD." Peter was

RICHARD CAVE

leading the chant.

***

As the village lane echoed with the cruel chant, Johnathon sprinted away, the rhythm of his footfalls drowned out by the haunting echoes of "Coward, coward, coward." Tears streamed down his face, not merely from the pain of his unjust punishment but from the heavy burden of isolation and betrayal.

Seeking solace, he found himself in the embrace of Marlborough Woods. In this verdant sanctuary, the shadows of the trees seemed to dance in sympathy with his turmoil.

Running blindly through the underbrush, he stumbled into ferns, the rough ground offering little comfort. The distant bark of a dog pierced the air, intensifying his fear. Desperation consumed him as he darted behind a tree, trembling.

The barking ceased, replaced by the sudden appearance of Snitch, Old Jed's dog. A mixture of trepidation and relief flooded Johnathon as Snitch approached, barking, then licking away the traces of tears on his cheeks. The once-frightening dog became a source of warmth and companionship as Johnathon walked deeper into the woods.

Seeking solace, he spoke to Snitch as if the loyal canine could comprehend his pain. "It's not fair, Snitch," he whispered, his voice a frail murmur in the vastness of the woods. "Peter just lied, and I did nothing wrong. My friend Andy is dying, and I'm all alone. My father beat me, and I made my mother cry. It's just not fair."

As if understanding the weight of his words, Snitch nuzzled against him, offering a silent but comforting presence. In the tranquil embrace of the woods, Johnathon continued to pour out his heart to the canine confidant.

Old Jed, the wise guardian of these woods, appeared without a sound, settling beside Johnathon. The ageing man listened silently, letting the young boy release the burdens of injustice and despair. Johnathon, his vulnerability exposed, assumed the role of the accused, awaiting judgment.

"Mr. Jed, I did nothing wrong," he uttered, his voice tinged with desperation. "It was Peter who pushed us into the chase. He didn't jump in to save us; he fell in. He's so horrid. I feel bad for Andy. I punched him in the nose as hard as I could. Suppose you will arrest me and turn me into the law?"

Old Jed, a sage amidst the shadows, responded with a hint of playful contemplation. "What say you, Snitch? Shall we tie him up with some baling twine to this tree, or do we hogtie him and drag him all the way to gaol?"

Snitch, with a quizzical look, seemed to consider the absurd proposition. Old Jed's levity lifted Johnathon's fleeting smile, a momentary escape from the gravity of his predicament.
"Well, you are over four feet tall," Old Jed continued, humour woven into his words. "And suppose you go to jail; you are now eight. They could wait for ten years."

"Ten years?" Johnathon questioned, his confusion palpable.

"Till your eighteenth birthday," Old Jed clarified, his words carrying a weight of both jest and solemnity.

"Why?" Johnathon inquired, grappling with the notion.

"That's the legal age for the long drop, a good old-fashioned hanging," Old Jed explained, his face contorting into a playful grimace.

Caught between shock and realisation, Johnathon glanced at the miming spectacle of hanging before him, and then Jed defiantly stuck out his tongue in response.
"Errrrrk!" Old Jed mimicked, adding a touch of theatrical flair. The absurdity of the conversation finally broke through Johnathon's distress, and a genuine, albeit small, laugh

escaped him.

"You forget I was there, and I know it was that Smith boy. He's a wrong 'un and a spoiled proper wrong 'un. I know it was not you," Old Jed reassured him. "Did you punch him?"

"Oh yes, right on the bell," Johnathon proudly admitted, a glimmer of rebellion in his eyes.

"Good, that's pretty good but wrong," Old Jed remarked, shaking his head. "You need to time your actions properly, young 'un. And no, you won't get hung for that. You are no coward."

With a gesture of camaraderie, Old Jed extended a hand to help Johnathon up. He took off his jacket, draping it over Johnathon's shoulders. "Let's get you home. We can pick some flowers and herbs to treat your hand. Snitch likes you; he likes sausages and fox scat – no accounting for Snitch's taste."

Old Jed, Johnathon, and Snitch embarked on their journey, walking towards the Farmhouse. The woods, a silent witness to the injustices and camaraderie of life, stood sentinel as they ventured into the dappled sunlight.

***

Outside the rustic Farmhouse, Johnathon sat on a milk churn, a solitary figure framed by the waning light of day. His eyes reflected anticipation and worry and were fixated on the weathered door. At his feet, Snitch lay asleep, a loyal companion in silent repose.

The door creaked open, and a stern figure emerged. Johnathon's father, Frank, approached with an air of authority, his expression betraying a blend of sternness and concern. The old gamekeeper, hat in hand, appeared behind him, offering a subtle nod of acknowledgement.

Unexpectedly, Frank knelt down and enveloped Johnathon in a tight embrace. For a fleeting moment, the rigid façade of paternal authority gave way to genuine affection. Yet, as abruptly as the embrace began, it ceased, replaced by the stoic bearing that defined Frank Hodges.

"Right, son of mine," Frank began, his voice carrying the weight of paternal responsibility. "Playing by the Mill was wrong, playing on the wheel was wrong, being around that Smith boy is wrong. His father is a wrong 'un, and punching someone is wrong, no matter how justified it feels. We are brought up better than that. Running out of school like a coward is wrong."

The word "coward" hung heavy in the air, and Johnathon, still reeling from the recent ordeal, began to sob. His father continued, each admonishment hitting him like a verbal lash.

"However," Frank continued, a subtle shift in tone indicating a change in the narrative, "Old Jed told me what happened. You're not going back to school, not ever. Your mother and I agree; it's the wrong place for you."

Johnathon's tear-streaked face held a mix of surprise and hope. The unexpected turn in his fate hinges on the following words.

"Instead," Frank declared, "you will become Old Jed's apprentice gamekeeper. You will work for him, and you will give to your mother whatever money you make. As a former schoolmaster at Eton, Old Jed will teach you arithmetic, geography, French, and Latin. And you will behave, boy. This is your last chance."

Johnathon, grappling with a torrent of emotions, managed to express gratitude. "Thank you, Father."

"Don't thank me," Frank sternly replied, the severity returning to his gaze. "Old Jed is going to train you to earn a living. It's going to be tougher than school. Also, you are to keep away from the Smiths and no longer rob Mrs. Warburton. Stop being such a scallywag and make me and your mother proud. Come on, let's go inside for supper. Old Jed will be joining us, so wash up and behave. It's shepherd's pie tonight."

With that, the trio, joined by awakened Snitch, moved inside. Frank's hand ruffling Johnathon's hair marked the transition from an austere father to one with a glimmer of paternal warmth.

As they settled into the Farmhouse, Snitch, ever vigilant, sensed something amiss. The loyal dog whined and ran to the gate, finding it locked. Undeterred, he navigated the farmyard, his keen senses attuned to an anomaly.

A pair of schoolboy legs clad in shorts approached Snitch in the shadows. The child knelt down, beckoning the canine closer. A subtle glint of metal caught the fading light – a lock knife, open, concealed behind the boy's back.

As they settled around the sturdy wooden table, the fragrant aroma of shepherd's pie wafted through the air, promising comfort and a respite from the day's turmoil.

Meanwhile, in the gathering dusk outside, a sinister tableau unfolded. Snitch, the faithful canine companion, wandered unsuspectingly into the clutches of malevolence. The farmyard bore witness to an unspeakable act. Snitch's sudden, agonised yelp pierced the quietude, shattering the serene atmosphere. Sadly, those in the Farmhouse failed to hear Snitch's last cry.

***

The Lower Concourse of Moonraker Flats sprawled under the unforgiving daylight, an urban arena where the concrete jungle clashed with the desperate struggles of its inhabitants. The distant hum of city life formed the dissonant backdrop to a scene unfolding with a foreboding sense.

Daphne emerged from the creaking lift, clutching a hessian bag to her chest like a talisman against the encroaching chaos. The air crackled with tension as she navigated the concrete labyrinth, her vulnerability palpable in the determined grip on her bag.

A gang of pedal bikers, a modern-day manifestation of urban predators, materialised on the scene. Their phones playing grimehouse a symphony of rebellion, as they circled Daphne like sharks scenting blood. The acrid scent of marijuana mingled with the rhythmic beats of the music, casting an ominous veil over the confrontation.

The atmosphere thickened with menace as the bikers closed in, their predatory instincts awakening. Daphne's plea for mercy fell on deaf ears as the gang toyed with her, their bikes dancing perilously close, a macabre game of intimidation.

"You stop that, leave me, God, leave me... I know your mother!" Her voice wavered a frail attempt to assert a semblance of control over the impending storm.
The bikers, however, revelled in their power, their laughter echoing through the desolate concourse. The confrontation escalated a dance of fear and defiance, with Daphne as the unwilling lead.

Suddenly, courage replaced fear, and Daphne swung her bag, a makeshift weapon, a feeble defence against the encroaching darkness. The bikers, momentarily caught off guard, met their match as one tumbled into a heap against a low wall.

But the triumph was short-lived.

A butterfly knife gleamed in the hand of the fallen biker, a sinister punctuation mark to their confrontation. The air thickened with impending violence until a harbinger of justice arrived.

A female police officer, a lone sentinel, emerged to dispel the shadows. Like scattered roaches exposed to the light, the bikers retreated under the officer's authoritative gaze.
"Clear off, you lot! She's an old lady. Do you hear me? PISS OFF!"

Relief washed over Daphne, but a chilling recognition lingered. The leader, astride a stolen bike, bore a malevolent glare. He clutched a stolen relic – the Gold Poppy Brooch, a talisman of guilt for Daphne.

The officer, oblivious to the sinister exchange, approached, demanding answers. Daphne, torn between truth and self-preservation, receded into silence. The leader, executing a cut-throat gesture, disappeared into the urban labyrinth. The female police officer gave her a business card with her name and telephone number, PC Jane Moore.

The bus stop became a refuge for Daphne, tears mingling with shame on her weathered cheeks. Meanwhile, the leader, a phantom on wheels, circled the periphery, leaving laughter in his wake, a dissonant echo of menace lingering in the Lower Concourse's air. Daphne toyed with the card, reading it repeatedly as a tear rolled down her cheek.

***

The summer of 1932 draped Johnny's father's farm in a hazy warmth, a deceptive calm that belied the discord lurking in the shadows. As the sun dipped low, casting elongated shadows across the rustic landscape, Peter Smith, a mischievous figure, coasted up to the hedge near the farm on his bicycle. He peered through the foliage, a voyeur in search of opportunity.

The farmstead stood silent, an idyllic facade hiding the absence of its occupants. Under Old Jed's tutelage at the Lodge, Johnny delved into education. At the same time, Johnny's father, Frank, toiled in the fields, his silhouette a distant figure wielding a scythe against the encroaching grass. The stage was set for mischief.

Unhindered by restraint, Peter approached the Farmhouse. The unlocked door beckoned him into a world not his own. A flicker of rebellion danced in his eyes as he ventured inside, his thieving fingers reaching for a piece of cheese tucked away as his ill-gotten gains.

Intrigued, Peter navigated the labyrinthine Farmhouse, his eyes catching on the telltale signs of a farmer's life – bills and almanacks strewn across a desk, a testament to the struggle for survival. Yet, amidst the mundane, a war relic caught Peter's eye – a trench lighter fashioned from a WW1 .303 brass cartridge. His fingers danced over it, igniting the flame, the mesmerising dance of fire casting shadows on his face.

An inquisitive smile played on Peter's lips as he explored further. A disdainful act followed – a casual wipe of his nose on the arm of a chair, a subtle rebellion against the decorum that adorned the farm. However, his gaze was fixated on the upstairs quarters, where secrets lay dormant.

A school notebook, wrapped in nondescript brown paper, bore the mark of Johnny Hodges, Esquire. Driven by curiosity and a penchant for mischief, Peter liberated the notebook, its Latin studies title promising a forbidden glimpse into an unfamiliar world.

A surge of malevolence seized Peter as he inspected Johnny's haven. A wicked impulse led him to peel back the eiderdown on Johnny's bed, and with a devilish grin, he relieved himself upon it. The act of defiance carried a hidden satisfaction, a mischievous dance with the shadows.

Peter's revelry, however, was cut short. Through the window, the approaching figure of Frank, the patriarch, loomed. Panic seized Peter, and with stealth born of mischief, he fled the scene, a Latin notebook tucked away as a prize in his pocket. The Farmhouse, once a canvas of tranquillity, now bore the subtle scars of a trespasser's intrusion.

***

Fair Oaks, a house steeped in memories, now echoed with the mundane yet necessary task of sorting through Johnny's belongings. The room stripped down to the essentials, bore the indelible mark of a hospital space – a rubber mattress, boxes of memories, and the remnants of a life well-lived.

Judy and Derek, Johnny's kin, were immersed in a family duty, sifting through the tangible fragments of a life reduced to boxes labelled with charitable intentions. Clothes, once worn with pride, now discarded with the weight of loss, bore labels proclaiming OXFAM and MACMILLAN CANCER – an unspoken testament to battles fought and lost.

Into this melancholic tableau walked Daphne, a custodian of cleanliness, pushing a trolley loaded with the tools of her trade. Her arrival added a touch of practicality to the emotional atmosphere as she offered a reassuring acknowledgement of the time needed.
"Not hurrying you, the room is unnecessary till the weekend... for the next guest. So take your time," she spoke, her tone blending understanding and empathy, a nod to the delicate task at hand.

The air thickened with unspoken sorrow as Judy broached a topic that hung in the collective consciousness like a storm cloud. "One of the other nurses said it was your boy David who was assaulted," she remarked, testing the waters of shared grief.
"Danny, his name is Danny. Still in the hospital, he can leave in a couple of days," Daphne clarified, a mother's protective instinct evident beneath her composed outlook.

Grappling with his own turmoil, Derek momentarily let slip a dismissive comment about Danny's perceived nuisance on his bike. "He nearly damaged Vivian, my Volvo. Not cheap to fix that. I pay road tax, don't you know," he uttered, an unintended cruelty.

Judy, a bastion of civility, demanded an apology, a moment of grace in the face of insensitive words. As Derek acquiesced, Daphne stood in the room, a silent witness to the human capacity for empathy and its occasional absence.

Amidst the emotional tapestry, Judy unearthed an old MoD suitcase, a relic of the past bearing the inscription M Hodges. An enigma amid mundanity, it promised a journey into Johnny's history, a discovery waiting to unfold.

Gripped by curiosity, Derek found a locked metal container, its secrets veiled. The pursuit of revelation led him to a quest for a key. The trio embarked on the meticulous task of searching through the refuse sacks – black bags concealing the detritus of life and, perhaps, the key to unlocking a hidden chapter.

Daphne, clad in rubber gloves, ventured into this odyssey of discovery with a hint of disdain for Derek's demeanour. "For the record, I am helping Judy, not you, Mr. Hodges... you're an idiot, and a rude one at that", she declared, her words reflecting an unfiltered truth.

***

Within the sterile confines of the modern NHS hospital, Danny's room became a sanctuary of shared monotony. The flickering light of a television screen illuminated the faces of two friends – Danny, a resilient soul recovering from an assailant's blow, and Andy, his companion in the dreariness of daytime programming.

The news burst forth from the screen, interrupting the dull narrative of soap operas and talk shows. Danny, ever observant, turned his gaze towards Andy, prompting a conversation that would unravel tales of betrayal lurking in the shadows of their shared past.

"Wing Commander, you said something about Old Jed's dog going missing," Danny inquired, his eyes searching for the truth beneath Andy's words.

"Dreadful, it was dreadful. Foxes attacked Snitch, or so Jed said," Andy began, his voice tinged with a weighty sadness. "However, Johnny overheard Jed and Frank one evening, and Johnny would not lie to me."

The atmosphere in the room shifted, the mundane chatter of television giving way to a narrative laced with intrigue and sorrow. The tale unfurled like a forgotten manuscript, revealing a story of companionship tested by an unspeakable act of cruelty.

"What happened?" Danny pressed, sensing the gravity of the revelation to come.

"Sad. Someone had stabbed Snitch to death and beheaded him. Then tossed it onto a fire," Andy narrated, the details hanging heavy in the air. "Jed did not quite recover from that. So, both decided to investigate. I was Little John, and he was Robin Hood."

"Little what?" Danny queried, caught momentarily off guard

by the archaic reference.

"Do keep up, Robin Hood. We had no TV then, like today; we had things called... books," Andy chuckled, a touch of nostalgia colouring his words.

In the hospital room, the news of Snitch's brutal demise opened a portal to a world where the cruel hands of fate tested the bonds of friendship. Danny's room, once a haven for healing, now harboured the echoes of a bygone adventure.

CHAPTER 6

Justice

The summer of 1932 cast its relentless heat upon the quaint village, and as the melody of Noel Coward's "Someday I'll Find You" meandered through the air from an open window, Andy and Johnny both embarked on a curious escapade. The village streets, usually adorned with the laughter of children and the hum of daily life, now echoed with the duo's footsteps, venturing into every nook and cranny in search of a missing companion.

Their quest led them to the war memorial, a silent witness to the passing of time. The sun, unyielding in its midsummer reign, painted the surroundings in hues of gold, yet the adventure had grown tedious. Feeling fatigued, Johnny voiced his doubts about Snitch's demise. He worked the water pump, splashing water into his hand to drink, then wiped his face. Andy rose, and he, too, used the pump.

"I am tired and getting bored. I have not seen any sign of Snitch. I don't believe he's dead," Johnny lamented, eyes scanning the quiet streets.

"But Jed does not lie. You heard him say Snitch was stabbed," Andy reminded, the reality of their canine friend's fate lingering in the air.

The boys sought refuge from the relentless sun, choosing to rest. The scorching summer air carried a hint of uncertainty, a mystery they were determined to unravel.

As Johnny pondered aloud about the unlikely assailant of the gentle Snitch, Andy's mind strayed to a tale shared by Mary Naismith – a tale involving Miss Rutherford, a cauldron, and the peculiar disappearance of other animals in the village.

"Only sheepdog to be herded by sheep. Mary Naismith says that Miss Rutherford has a cauldron out back," Andy mused, the words hanging in the air like an unresolved chord.

"You noticed since we have been looking, we have not seen any other dog or cat. Bit strange," Johnny observed, a spark of realisation igniting in his eyes.

"Do you reckon they are hiding?" Andy wondered, his mind weaving a web of possibilities.

Johnny's gaze shifted towards the village shop, a beacon of potential discovery. With a burst of energy, he sprinted across the quiet road, leaving Andy to follow, burdened by the oppressive heat. Andy crossed the road leisurely, his ginger hair peeking out from beneath his cap, joining Johnny at the sweet shop where a revelation awaited them.

"You found a clue?" Andy inquired, hopeful for a breakthrough.

"Look, on the newspaper stand," Johnny exclaimed, pointing to a handwritten sign below the Wiltshire Times banner.

"Cats and dogs go missing."

The discovery reverberated through the boys, a whisper of ominous events shrouding the seemingly idyllic village. Their covert investigation caught the attention of Mrs Rutherford, who, with a mix of suspicion and jest, warned them against pilfering sweets.

"Ere, what's your game, you two? No, pinching my sweets, that goes for you, Johnny Hodges," Mrs Rutherford chided, her threat laced with a teasing undertone.

"I will get the Constable on you. Now, clear off! A cauldron, I heard you," she added, her laughter trailing off as the boys retreated.

Fleeing towards the direction of the pub, Andy and Johnny sought refuge in a familiar hiding spot, a bush in the garden where secrets and childhood adventures intertwined.
"Oh, what a wheeze she nearly had you. Is it true she is a witch?" Andy pondered, the mystery deepening with every revelation, casting shadows in the summer sun.

Amidst the innocence of childhood adventures, Johnny's keen eyes caught a glimpse of something amiss – a sinister scene unfolding behind the veil of a bush. As if frozen by the weight of impending dread, he guided Andy's gaze towards a haunting tableau.

Peter Smith, a shadow lurking in the periphery of the village's façade, struggled past with a grain sack. A symphony of mewing emanated from within as he unveiled a pair of kittens, their fragile bodies dangling by the scruff of their necks. Once soft and innocent, the mewing morphed into desperate shrieks as Peter swung the sack overhead, each thud against the ground extinguishing the fragile life within.

Andy, stricken with horror, gasped involuntarily. Johnny, acting swiftly, clamped his hand over Andy's mouth, eyes locked on the macabre ballet playing out before them. Once full of life, the kittens are now lifeless in Peter's hands.

In a twisted ritual, Peter, devoid of remorse, opened a coal bunker, a mausoleum for the village's lost souls. The lifeless bodies of dogs and cats were placed neatly onto a morbid pile, a haunting testimony to the darkness concealed within the seemingly tranquil village.
Johnny and Andy cloaked in the shadows, felt their hearts

pound in unison. The air thickened with an unspeakable horror that gripped their very souls. Unseen by Peter, they manoeuvred stealthily from their vantage point, slipping away like phantoms haunted by the ghastly sight.

Yet, as they retreated, a cruel twist of fate left behind a trace – Johnny's cap. Forgotten in haste, it silently witnessed the atrocity, concealing a tape marked with JH's initials within its folds.

Peter, on his return, spies the cap and picks it up,

***

The dimly lit concourse of Coleshill Flats played host to a chilling encounter as the evening cast long shadows across the worn tiles. A solitary figure, Daphne moved with a mixture of apprehension and haste. Her eyes darted nervously, scanning for signs of the menacing bike gang that had become haunting in her daily routine. The council house flats boasted a lift, a stainless steel contraption adorned with textured panels and a central metal bar encompassing its interior.

While most residents of the flats opted for the stairs, those who were infirm or elderly relied on its services. Positioned squarely in the middle, they cautiously extended a brolly or pen to press the filthy buttons for their desired floor.

Inside, the lift's walls were marred by graffiti, a chaotic canvas of messages ranging from racist slurs to hastily scrawled telephone numbers for burner phones. The air was heavy with the stench of urine, a testament to the habits of drug addicts and inebriated individuals who relieved themselves in the corners. Despite the short duration of the ride, occupants couldn't shake off the sense of unease that washed over them as the doors closed and the lift ascended or descended, leaving them feeling vulnerable in its confines.

The lift offered a momentary refuge for Daphne, a brief respite from the unease that clung to the air like a spectre. With a button press, she sought sanctuary on the fourth floor, hoping to escape the lurking shadows 'clutches.

Yet, the lift journey was marred by unexpected interruptions. The doors slid open on the second and third floors, revealing empty spaces that belied the impending threat. Anxiety tightened its grip on Daphne's heart as the door slid open once again on the fourth floor. A moment of relief, however, was fleeting.

A set of hands materialised, grinning faces emerging like

phantoms of mischief. The bike gang leader, an embodiment of menace, stood before her, shattering the illusion of safety. The confined space became a chamber of dread. Daphne instinctively backed into the corner, clutching her bag as a fragile shield against impending harm.

"Hello, sweetie," the bike gang leader sneered, his words dripping with malevolence. Daphne, her voice a plea, begged to be left alone, but her pleas fell on deaf ears. The gang, like a group of cackling hyenas driven by a cruel curiosity, seized her bag, spilling its contents onto the cold floor.

Among the mundane, a packet of prescription drugs lay exposed – Tramadol, a lifeline for Daphne's aching back. The gang leader, revelling in the discovery, proclaimed triumphantly, "Caching, Trammies." He callously pocketed the pills, heedless of Daphne's desperate protests.

The leader lingered as the cronies departed, leaving a trail of violated dignity in their wake. The elevator doors closed, encapsulating Daphne in a confined space with an imminent threat.

Fear painted her face as the bike gang leader confronted her with a stolen possession – a solid gold Poppy brooch. Its significance eluded her, but the gang leader revelled in the potential riches. Accusations of theft hung in the air, and he tore away her name badge, a cruel reminder of vulnerability.
A chilling promise whispered as the doors reopened, releasing the captor back into the shadows. "Be seeing you, Daphne," he taunted, brandishing the name badge as a sinister trophy. The elevator, tainted by the echoes of menace, bore witness to a woman left to grapple with the shadows that now loomed closer than ever. "I know where you work."

***

The air in the Hodges farm kitchen hung thick with the weight of accusation. A policeman's helmet lay ominously on the worn table; beside it, a cup of tea and a pair of leather gloves. The room seemed tense as Constable Dicken sat across from Johnny, flanked by Andy and his father, Frank. Johnny's eyes met his father's piercing gaze while the Constable studied his notes with scepticism.

"So you are telling the Constable and me you have seen Peter kill cats and dogs and store the bodies at the rear of the pub," Frank's voice, gruff and demanding, cut through the charged silence.

"Yes, Dad. Andy and I saw it," Johnny replied, his words hanging like a storm about to break.

Constable Dicken, a no-nonsense figure with an air of authority, leaned forward. "You're not telling me a story, are you? Trying to get Peter into trouble."

"No, Sir, no," Johnny stammered, his words punctuated by a firm shake of Andy's head in agreement.

Constable Dicken continued, his gaze unwavering. "So, according to your statement," he glanced at his notes, "you were playing Robin Hood; that's not important, but you were looking for the lost pets and Snatch."

"Snitch," Johnny corrected, but his interruption only fueled Frank's temper.

"STOP INTERRUPTING THE OFFICER!" Frank bellowed, frustration etched on his face.
Constable Dicken, ever composed, acknowledged the correction.

"It's alright, Frank. Snitch. So, you saw Peter Smith batter a bunch of cats with a sack to death, then store the bodies in a coal shed."

Frank, torn between disbelief and concern, sought clarification. "Johnny, you sure about this? It's quite serious, mistreating animals. Though cats are vermin, are they not, Constable?"

"Protection of Animals Act 1911. They are a grey area," Constable Dicken explained, his stern gaze on Johnny. Turning to Frank, he suggested, "Would you mind driving us all to the pub? Andy, You can go home. I have everything I need from you. Need to speak to Peter's father and get to the bottom of this."

"You know he coddles that boy, Peter," Frank remarked, a hint of frustration in his voice.

"We will sort it out down there. You never know; we might get a free beer out of it,"
Constable Dicken replied, his tone a subtle mix of authority and a touch of dark humour.

***

Under the muted daylight, the village pub stood as a quiet witness to unfolding events. Frank, a weathered figure, leaned casually against his car, fingers fishing for a lighter that wasn't there. A match offered by Constable Dickens materialised in the air, a brief flame flickering in the day's stillness.

"Seem to have lost my lighter," Frank muttered, the words escaping into the village air.

Constable Dickens, a stoic presence, surveyed the scene with a measured gaze. The door swung open, and Billy Smith emerged from the pub, hands drying on a towel, sleeves rolled up, and apron worn casually. Behind the window, the face of Peter lingered, an unwitting observer of the impending encounter.

"How can I help you, gentlemen?" Billy's voice carried a hint of curiosity.

Constable Dickens cut to the chase. "Is that your coal bunker over there?"

A beat of hesitation passed over Billy's features. "Yes, what is it regarding?"

"Never mind that. Can we have a look inside, please?" Constable Dickens's request hung in the air, a veil of mystery shrouding its purpose.

Billy's gaze shifted towards the shed, contemplation etched on his face. "I want to know why."

"It's for the course of some inquiries," Constable Dickens replied, evoking a sense of authority that brooked no argument.
Billy produced a ring of keys from his apron, an everyday item with newfound significance. Constable Dickens examined them, the glint of metal holding potential answers.

"You're the only one with a key, Billy," Constable Dickens observed, seeking confirmation.

Billy nodded. "Yes, it's in my apron all the time."

With that, they set off towards the bunker, leaving Frank to exchange a stern look with Johnny.

"Stay by the car; do as you are told," Frank's command hung in the air, and Johnny, now a silent observer, complied with a nod. The tension lingered, a prelude to what lay hidden in the shadows of the coal bunker.

Johnny stood by the car, eyes fixed on Peter's gaze through the pub window. The stern officer intentionally approached the coal bunker, leaving a palpable tension in the air. Billy, fumbling with his keys, eventually unlocked the bunker door. Armed with a coal shovel, Constable Dickens delved into the shadows within.

In a moment suspended in anticipation, the officer halted his search. The trio—Frank, Billy, and Constable Dickens—turned to Johnny, beckoning him closer. Fear etched on Johnny's face as he reluctantly approached, eyes darting between the stern faces surrounding him. Frank, a pillar of authority, seized Johnny by the collar, delivering sharp slaps as Johnny's gaze reluctantly met the empty coal bunker. No bodies.

Dragged to the car by Frank, Johnny glanced toward Peter, still catching his breath. The ominous smile and a cutthroat gesture sent shivers down Johnny's spine. As Frank bundled him into the car, Peter's cruel victory loomed large.

Behind the wheel, Frank offered Constable Dickens a lift, which he politely declined. The car sped away, carrying a distraught Johnny, tears staining his cheeks. Meanwhile, Constable Dickens lingered in the shadows unseen by the window, listening to the aftermath.

Assuming the Constable had departed, Billy stormed into the

pub, slamming the door behind him. From within, the muffled sounds of chaos echoed.

"Come here, you little bastard! You're lucky I found that carnage before the police did," Billy's voice, a mix of anger and frustration, reverberated. Crashes followed, accompanied by Peter's cries.

As Constable Dickens pulled out his notebook, glanced at his pocket watch, and jotted a note—2:34, Peter stole and killed, NO PROOF—he felt the weight of a dark truth settling.

"Johnny, you poor sod, you were telling the truth," Constable Dickens sighed, a heavy burden on his shoulders.
He looked skyward, seeking forgiveness, grappling with the harsh reality that had unfolded.

***

The hospital room bore the sterile, modern, stark institutional atmosphere of the NHS, a backdrop to the weight of the conversation between Andy and Danny. As Andy paused, his eyes drifted to a cup on the side table, a momentary distraction from the gravity of their discussion.

"I am quite tired now; I will tell you a little bit more," Andy confessed, weariness evident in his tone.

Danny, fueled by curiosity, pressed on. "I have many questions, like how did no one know that Peter was evil?"

Andy, a relic of a simpler time, explained the dynamics of the small village. "Small village, not like today with your phones and gadgets. Small world."

"So once again, Johnny is now a liar. Feel sorry for the kid," Danny remarked, a thread of sympathy woven into his words.

"That was not the worst of it, not the worst of it by far," Andy uttered a sombre note underscoring the gravity of the untold tale—the air thickened with unspoken revelations, leaving a lingering foreboding in the room.

***

An old country garage, once a rustic barn, now served as a mechanic's workshop, weathered and worn by years of use. Positioned prominently out front were two weather-beaten shell petrol pumps, their once vibrant red hues now faded by the relentless sun. A glass optic on each pump allowed a glimpse of the flammable liquid within, offering a means to check for moisture and dirt. Nearby, a pair of red-painted buckets, emblazoned with the word "fire" in white, sat filled with sand and littered with discarded cigarette butts.

Stretching across the yard, a rubber cable was tethered to a pneumatic bell, its purpose of chiming a notification whenever a car traversed its path, signalling the garage attendant to emerge and assist with refuelling. Puddles of water mingled with oil on the concrete floor, creating mesmerising rainbow iridescence under the dim glow of the night sky. The air was thick with the pungent scent of oil and petrol, permeating every corner of the garage.

Adjacent to the workshop stood a modest house where the mechanic resided, its windows darkened as its occupant slept soundly. Secured by an old padlock, the garage's wooden sliding door concealed a stash of small cans containing petrol and kerosene, essential for the day-to-day operations of the workshop.

The night shrouded Warburton's Garage in an eerie silence, broken only by the faint hum of a small solitary light casting long shadows across the forecourt. Moonlight played tricks with the darkness, revealing a figure cloaked in a duffel coat, its hood drawn tightly.

Stealthily, the little fat child navigated the forecourt, a nimble dancer avoiding the rubber bell line at the entrance—his destination: the side where cans of petrol lay in wait. A lock knife made quick work of the lock, and he hefted a heavy petrol can back across the forecourt, careful not to disturb the pneumatic bell line.

Hidden in the ditch, he safeguarded the purloined fuel, his breath heavy with excitement and dread. A couple of large stones found their mark, shattering the glass advertising toppers on the pumps. Mischief danced in the moonlight.

Then, a child's cap landed on the forecourt, taunting punctuation to his nocturnal escapade. Breathing heavily, he ran to the airline, jumping on it with childish exuberance, setting off the forecourt bell. The neighbouring house shrouded in darkness until now, flickered to life.

As the man in pyjamas stumbled onto the court, the shattered glass bit into his slippers. A cap with JH's letters sewn inside caught his attention, illuminated by the moon's glow. Confusion etched on his face, he stood on the forecourt, alone and confused at night, unaware of the orchestrated chaos and the hidden child in the ditch.

***

The soft glow of dawn bathed the farmhouse kitchen as Frank, a seasoned farmer, savoured the last sips of his early morning tea. The thud of his heavy boots echoed through the room as he prepared for the day's farmyard chores. Johnny, his son, lingered over breakfast, aware that the morning tasks awaited him.

Suddenly, the distant hum of a car engine disrupted the tranquil morning. Frank, a furrow forming on his brow, rose from the table, leaving Johnny to clear his plate. Urgent knocks reverberated through the farmhouse, demanding attention.

Frank, the patriarch, swung open the door to confront the intruder, revealing Constable Dickens standing with an air of authority. Frank's stern countenance deepened, arms crossed in displeasure, directing a piercing gaze at Johnny.

"Johnny, where were you last night?" Constable Dickens inquired, his tone carrying a weight of suspicion.

"In bed," Frank responded tersely, defending his son.

"Johnny, answer the question," Constable Dickens pressed, his eyes fixed on the young man.
Johnny, finishing lacing his shoes, looked puzzled. "I went to bed at eight, Dad. What's going on?"

Last night, Warburton's Constable explained that Garage fell victim to a vandal who pilfered a petrol can. "Miss Rutherford's shop, the back of the pub, and a couple of houses were set on fire."

"It wasn't me; I was in bed, wasn't I, Dad?" Johnny protested, desperation evident in his voice.

The Constable emptied a paper bag onto the table, revealing a cap, a lighter, and the scorched remnants of a Latin book. "Latin notebook with your name on it. You're not the criminal mastermind of the century."

Johnny, shock etched on his face, stood shaking with fear.

"Sorry, Frank, but Johnny, get your coat. You are under arrest for theft of petrol, arson, and malicious damage. Both of you need to come with me to the station in Amesbury," Constable Dickens declared.

Johnny ran toward his father, seeking comfort, but Frank pushed him away, torn between shame and anger. He grabbed Johnny's collar as the Constable gathered the damning evidence. Frank looks at his trench lighter, "been looking for that for ages."

***

The side door to the care home swung open with a soft creak, and Daphne Wills stepped out, her vape pen sliding into her hand as she made her way through the gate and onto the street. The Bike Gang Leader was waiting for her like a shadow in the daylight.

Daphne's gaze darted nervously as she spoke.

"Why are you here? People will see."

The leader of the Bike Gang appeared unfazed, a hint of a smirk playing on his lips.

"Wanted to see for myself where you pinched this brooch."

"Please, put it away. Please, I know who you are, your Amelia grandson Stephan," Daphne stated, her anxiety palpable.

The gang leader, seemingly indifferent, continued the conversation.

"Where are my trammies?"

Daphne retrieved a Ziploc bag cunningly hidden among tissues and handed it over. The leader took it casually, discarding the used tissues thoughtlessly on the ground.

Holding up the bag, he inspected the contents—fifteen tramadol.

"My dear Daphne, fifteen is not going quite to cut it. I need more. You know, supply and demand. Market economics."

He tapped her forehead with the bag, causing her to flinch.

"I need thirty for tomorrow, or I ring your boss and tell them what a naughty nursey you are."

Desperation edged into Daphne's voice as she considered her options.

"What if I call the police on you?"

The gang leader's response was chilling, a veiled threat hanging in the air.

"Oh, I will visit Danny in the hospital, Ward E4, Bed 3, and finish the job. Thirty tomorrow."

In the quiet expanse of the Fair Oaks car park, a familiar beige Volvo eased forward, coming to a stop. The bike gang leader, having swiftly departed after encountering Derek, stole a momentary glance at the driver before pedalling away into the distance. The window of the Volvo rolled down, revealing Derek's discerning gaze fixed upon the visibly anxious Daphne.

Derek's concern was palpable as he inquired, "Nurse Daphne, what did that little scumbag want?"
Daphne, caught in the unease of the situation, responded tentatively, "Oh, he was lost, asked me the way."
However, Derek, with a keen eye for deception, was partially convinced. "You sure? I am a justice of the peace, and that little scumbag is a regular visitor to my court."
The Volvo glided into the car park, Derek's words lingering in the air. Daphne left to contemplate the intricate threads of the situation and took a cautious draw from her vape pen, watching Derek vanish into the labyrinth of parked cars.

***

Under the midday sun, the tranquillity of the Hospital Garden of Peace unfolded. A covered bench provided refuge for Danny, wheeled out by the ward sister. An auto-drip bag of morphine hung on the back of his wheelchair. Following suit, Andy, adorned in his electric wheelchair marked with RAF Roundels and the title WINGCO, joined him. The nurse, diligent in her care, fetched a tartan picnic blanket to shield them from a sudden chill.

As the nurse departed, a book in hand, she issued a light warning, "Behave, you two. I'll be back in half an hour and reading over there. Bang on the glass, Wing Commander, if you need help."

The two friends settled in, the serene zen garden offering a brief respite. Andy broke the silence, "Bet you're glad to get out of there, a bit of fresh air."

Danny, tethered to the monotony of hospital life, responded appreciatively, "It's nice. Your visits break up the boredom. Mum can't make it; she's working both our shifts."

Wistfully, Andy advised, "Worrying about work will make you ill."

Danny sighed, "I know. It's getting better, but daytime telly and the constant lights and beeps in the ward drive me insane. And my hair is a mess."

Andy, ever the nonconformist, teased, "Seeing as there's no one about, fancy a little snifter?"

A mischievous wink accompanied the revelation of a hip flask. After hesitating, Danny accepted and took a swig, only to realise it was Lucozade. Laughter ensued, shared between friends.

Their moment of clandestine enjoyment caught the attention

of the vigilant nurse, who hurriedly intervened. "You can put that away NOW! There is no drinking on hospital grounds, and you, Danny, I despair. No more."

Undeterred, Andy dismissed the reprimand with a chuckle, "It's my secret bit of fun, watching them panic and fuss. It's a hoot."

Attempting to shift the focus, Danny requested, "Andy, can you tell me about Johnny meeting Sarah? I'd love to hear."

Andy began to weave the tale with a twinkle in his eye, the small garden providing a sanctuary for stories amid the challenges of the hospital's sterile environment.

CHAPTER 7

Patience

Within the sprawling grounds of Coleshill House, hidden in the embrace of the woods, two figures manoeuvred along a secluded lane. Clad in military fatigues, Johnny and Sarah bore a sidearm at their hips. As they halted to scrutinise the map, Johnny plucked a twig from the ground, deploying it as a makeshift pointer.

"Here's the fork in the road," Johnny indicated.

"And there's the chapel steeple," Sarah confirmed.

Johnny charted their course, "Follow that, through the stream, towards the target."

Abruptly, a piercing whistle shattered the tranquillity, and German soldiers materialised, guns trained on the duo.

"Damn," Sarah muttered.

A Physical Training Instructor (PTI) barked, "Bang, you're dead! Class in around me, at the double!"

Other pairs emerged from the bushes, drawing close to the instructor.

"Well done on getting this far," the PTI acknowledged, "several mistakes, but not bad for your first tactical map reading. Never forget cover and concealment."

Sarah sighed, "We should have hidden in the bushes and did

the map reading there."
The PTI addressed the class, probing for more insights. "Anyone else?"

A student noted, "The map is folded to the page."

Another said, "Hand holding a path to a known landmark."

"Whoa, slow down," the PTI advised. "Never fold the map to the page you're using. Well done on using a twig; fingerprints on the map can be used against you. A path to a known landmark—what does a church have?"

Johnny, light dawning, admitted, "Oh, I forgot. Where there's a steeple, there are people."
"Exactly," the PTI affirmed. "Right, we have a weapons lesson at the main house in five minutes, and it's a six-minute run. What are you waiting for? You're going to be late."
The class sprinted down the path to the main hall as the German guards walked away. During the group, Sarah and Johnny exchanged smiles, a shared triumph amid the challenges of military training.

***

In the dimly lit panelled dining room of Coleshill House, agents in training sat at separate tables, women and men divided, partaking in a meal served with military precision. A coal fire cast a warm glow, but the atmosphere remained disciplined. The staff cleared out, leaving the room to the impending presence of the PTI/Instructor and Mr. Gubbins.

As the double doors swung open, attention shifted to Mr. Gubbins. The room fell silent as the recruits awaited his words.

"As part of your work," Mr. Gubbins began, "some of you are starting to understand it's dangerous. You may have to go into places and areas you normally avoid. We also need to see how resourceful you are."

He continued, explaining the task: pairs would be formed, tasked with visiting a randomly chosen location, sending a postcard to a designated address, and subsequently planning sabotage in a target town. The recruits were to act as married couples, pairs selected by the organisation. Mr. Gubbins concluded with a reminder for the ladies to report back after the mission.

The PTI/Instructor added a touch of humour, "Gentlemen are reminded to behave; ladies will report back on return." He emphasised using false ID papers and a limited budget, warning of the potential consequences if caught.

The staff distributed manila envelopes containing instructions, and Sarah, attempting nonchalance, approached Johnathon. They learned their destination: Penzance, with the target town being Manchester's Gaythorne Gasworks.

"Four days to get to Penzance, Manchester, and back again? That's impossible," Sarah exclaimed.

"We can do it. Have faith. If I have to steal a car, I will,"

Johnathon assured her.

The PTI/Instructor said, "If you steal a car, don't get caught, and ensure it has petrol in the tank. But you know all about stealing petrol..." He winked at Johnathon.

Sarah, puzzled, asked, "What was that about?"

Johnathon replied with a playful smile, "My past haunting me. I'll tell you later, wifey. About time you became an honest woman."

As Sarah playfully punched his chest, Mr. Gubbins observed the pair from the corner of the room.

***

In the quaint village pub, set against the backdrop of November 1941, the air hung heavy with the melodies of "When They Sound The Last All Clear." The establishment buzzed with activity—Peter, now a young man, sat at the bar, nursing a beer poured by his father, Billy. Farmhands gathered, enveloped in a cloud of cigarette smoke, enjoying the beer during the mid-day break.

At a corner table, four spirited Women's Land Army members, known as "Land Girls," added a touch of youthful exuberance to the scene. Sipping ginger ale and sharing laughter, these young women, mostly from upper-class backgrounds, starkly contrasted the rugged masculinity dominating the rest of the establishment. Dressed in dungarees, boots and white blouses, hair tied back, it was an unofficial uniform; they were lodged in the village to help the local farmers.

Peter, captivated by the Land Girls, decided to approach them. Billy, foreseeing trouble, reached out to restrain his son. However, Peter dismissed his father with a swift slap, asserting his independence.

"Peter, no trouble, please. Not like last time," Billy cautioned.

Peter swaggered over to the Land Girls 'table, ignoring his father's advice—the regulars, familiar with such scenes, observed with a shake of their heads. Peter, however, remained undeterred, smiling at the young women who seemed uninterested in his advances.

"Can we help you?" one of the Land Girls asked when Peter loomed over their table, undeterred by their apparent disinterest.

"He's been staring at us all afternoon," remarked another Land Girl named Beryl.

Peter forced himself into the middle seat at their table with a nonchalant demeanour. Unamused, the Land Girls expressed their displeasure. Undeterred, Peter insisted, "You girls need a real man."

Land Girl Pat responded sarcastically, "Well, where is he?"

As laughter erupted among the Land Girls, Peter, persisting in his misguided confidence, responded, "Well, I am right here, girls."

Amused but uneasy, the Land Girls nervously laughed. Unfazed, Peter crossed a line, placing his hands on their knees and making inappropriate remarks. Startled, Beryl knocked over the drinks table and slapped Peter across the face, causing the entire pub to fall silent.

Billy intervened, urging Peter to leave the ladies alone. Ignoring his father's plea, Peter continued his crude advances, escalating the situation. However, his bravado suddenly stopped as he noticed Johnathon Hodges passing by the pub window outside.

Determined to assert dominance, Peter declared, "Here comes the village coward, Johnny Hodges himself. I will teach him what it means to be a real man." Rolling up his sleeves and flexing his knuckles, Peter exited the pub, leaving the Land Girls to watch his departure with relief and curiosity.

Johnathon's footsteps echoed down the village street, the rhythmic tap of his worn shoes on the cobblestone creating a percussive melody. A small suitcase swung lazily in his grip, a companion on the uncertain journey he was about to embark upon. As he approached the village station, grim determination etched across his face, the air grew thick with anticipation. The anxiety of not blowing his cover was palpable.

Just outside the village pub, a tumultuous storm awaited him in the form of Peter Smith. His face bore a glaring hand-shaped welt, a vivid reminder of a recent encounter. As Johnathon passed, Peter intercepted his path like a tempest spoiling for a fight, a dark cloud casting a shadow over the narrow street.

"Excuse me, Peter," Johnathon's calm voice contrasted with the storm around him.

"Where do you think you are going?" Peter's anger was palpable, a seething force ready to unleash.

"That way, please let me be," Johnathon's plea echoed through the tension-laden air.

Peter, fuelled by resentment and disdain, accused, "My dad says you're a coward, dodging Hitler's fight, feigning illness."

"Let me be, and let me get the train," Johnathon implored, seeking an escape from the approaching affray.

But Peter's rage knew no bounds. "You're either a conchy or a coward or both. A coward who hides behind illness while others fight for our country."

Johnathon scanned the pub's window, catching the eyes of a few sympathetic girls, their silent pleas urging him to escape this brewing tempest.

"Why aren't you fighting then? Does that make you a coward?" Johnathon retorted, desperation seeping into his voice.

"I'm in a reserved occupation, essential work. Unlike you, a coward, standing here doing nothing," Peter proclaimed, self-importance dripping from his words.

"Please, let me by," Johnathon implored, attempting to sidestep the looming confrontation.
But Peter's fury knew no bounds. A swift right hook sent Johnathon crashing to the ground. Dazed, he struggled to rise, only to be met with a merciless kick to the ribs. A few Land

girls witnessed the spectacle, fear etched across their faces.

"Fight me, you coward! Come on!" Peter goaded, revelling in his perceived victory.

Blood oozed from Johnathon's mouth as he staggered to his feet, retrieved his suitcase, and stumbled towards the train platform. The pub's entrance swallowed Peter, his triumphant cries lingering in the air.

As Johnathon faded into the distance, battered and bruised, Old Jed emerged from the shadows, his crooked form a silent witness to the village's brutal undercurrents. Snitch, a silent observer, watched with trepidation as Johnathon limped toward the station, leaving behind the tumultuous storm of the village pub.

Johnathon stumbled towards the village train station, a trace of blood staining his face. The daylight cast a harsh glare, revealing the aftermath of the confrontation. His hands moved instinctively to wipe away the evidence, leaving smudges on his face.

Sarah awaited him at the station, a steadfast presence in the tumult. She approached him, a mixture of concern and admiration in her eyes. Taking his hanky, she gently dabbed at the blood, a silent acknowledgement of the violence he had endured.

"You did so well," she murmured, her voice a soothing cadence. "That was brave, what you did."

A weary smile played on Johnathon's lips, the strain of the encounter etched on his features. "With what we have been taught, I could have, you know... but the mission comes first."

Sarah's smile mirrored his, a shared understanding passing between them. Yet, as her gaze shifted over his shoulder towards the pub, a shadow crossed her face, replacing warmth with a steely resolve.

"You could have killed him," she said, her tone turning serious. "He will get his comeuppance. I promise to be there when it happens. He is pure evil... you can smell it on him."

The station platform became a stage for the aftermath of violence, with two figures standing against the backdrop of a village caught in the grip of war.

***

The night clung to the village pub like a shroud, casting shadows on the drunken revelry. The muffled laughter and clinking of glasses seeped through the walls, a symphony of inebriation. Out back, away from the dim glow of the pub, a solitary figure stumbled into view. It was Peter, his silhouette swaying as he approached a wall with unsteady steps.

He began relieving himself in the cover of darkness, blissfully unaware of the storm about to break. A sudden jolt rocked him as a punch landed on his kidneys. His world spun, trousers around his ankles, and in a daze, he turned to face his assailant. A strong hand clamped around his windpipe, crushing the air from his lungs. Then, with a sickening thud, his head met the cold, unforgiving wall.

Hidden in the shadows, the mystery person leaned close, his presence cloaked in darkness. "You ever call him a coward again or touch Johnny," he whispered into Peter's ear, "you won't wake up ever. I will skin you ear to gizzard! He is protected."

As the scene unfolded in the shadows, the back door swung open, bathing the alley in light. A curious pub patron stepped out, catching sight of Peter sprawled on the ground. The mysterious avenger had vanished, leaving only the aftermath of swift justice.

The door creaked open again, and the land girls spilt out, their laughter contrasting the dark events unfolding. They pointed and ridiculed Peter, who, in his semi-conscious state, lay exposed and covered in his own urine. The air was thick with humiliation.

"Oohh, Beryl, is that his thing?" Land Girl Pat teased, drawing laughter from her companions.

"It looks like a penis, but smaller," Beryl retorted, her face reddening at her own boldness.

Constable Dickens emerged from the pub's warmth amid the mockery, a pint in hand. A sly smile played on his lips as he surveyed the scene. Still coming to, Peter found himself half-naked, trousers around his ankles, and Constable Dickens wasted no time.

"Peter Smith, I am arresting you for outraging public decency," he announced, taking a leisurely sip from his pint. The land girls, appreciating the unexpected spectacle, rallied around the constable.

"You're a real hero, Constable," Land Girl Pat quipped, slipping her arm through his.

With a casual wave of his pint, Constable Dickens acknowledged the praise, the hero of the pub's nocturnal theatre.

***

In the sterile confines of the modern NHS hospital room, Danny lay propped against pillows, absorbed in the words of "Life and Times of a Village Bobby." The quiet hum of medical machinery formed an ambient backdrop as he delved into the literary realm of Andy's choice. Meanwhile, Andy, seated in a chair beside the bed, had succumbed to the lull of the hospital atmosphere, his snores punctuating the otherwise muted sounds.

Danny's mother, Daphne, entered the room with a soft smile, her eyes conveying relief and maternal concern. She observed her son engrossed in the book, then turned her attention to the slumbering figure of Andy. A moment of familial warmth filled the air, a respite from the shadows that lingered.

"Hey, Mum, I haven't seen you for a couple of days," Danny greeted, pausing his reading. Have you been covering my shifts?"

Daphne returned the smile, a bittersweet reassurance. "You needn't worry. You get better."

Gesturing towards the oblivious Andy, Danny remarked, "He is fast asleep, deaf as a post, so you will not wake him. Look, he's got me a book to read. It's like James Herriott but about a policeman. Think Andy said it was set in his village."

Seating herself in a chair, Daphne regarded her son with a thoughtful gaze. "Oh, got you some toiletries, pyjamas, and fruit jellies. I know you like them. Need to get your strength up."

"Thanks, Mum. What's that?" Danny inquired, spotting a card among the gifts.

Daphne retrieved the card, adorned with a cheesy cat hanging by a paw on a rope, bearing the words "You've got this." As Danny opened it, a cascade of well-wishes and signatures unfolded.

"Oh, Agnes signed it; there's Mrs Green and my Jeff, mysterious as he had a stroke. Some of the nurses, Miss Fontaine, and one from Mark," Danny narrated with a smile. However, as he continued to read, the atmosphere shifted. His face morphed through a range of emotions—seriousness, frowning, anger—and finally, a glaring look at Daphne.

"What?" she inquired, confusion etched across her face.

"Did you read this at all?" Danny raised the card, his tone laced with accusation.

"No, they gave it to me on the way out. Why?" Daphne replied.

Reading aloud, Danny's voice turned solemn. "Danny, I hope you're feeling better soon, and we're all waiting for you. Tea has never been right since you've been ill. Don't worry about the burglary either; we've chipped in and got you a new laptop. It's not the best, but it will tide you over. All the best, Mark and the night shift."

Sensing the shift in the room, Daphne sat on the edge of the bed, gripping Danny's arm gently. "Dear God, forgive me. Please forgive me, Danny."

"Mum, what the hell has been going on?" Danny demanded.

In the hushed aftermath, Daphne clutched the crucifix on her necklace, thumbing it as tears welled in her eyes. "Oh, Danny, I am in so much trouble."

"Tell me all, and without holding back. I will know. Trust me. Everything."

A frosted window captured her silhouette as Daphne approached the door, shutting out the outside world. Framed in the glass, her face revealed a mixture of sorrow and resolve.

The secrets she carried would soon spill into the open.

CHAPTER 8

Ostracise

The spring sun bathed the quaint village in a gentle warmth, painting a picture-perfect scene. Sarah pedalled her bike into this idyllic haven, seemingly untouched by the shadows of war. Yet, as she approached the village shop, an unexpected frostiness lingered.

A calendar in a shop window displayed the year 1941—and set the stage for a clash of sensibilities. With stern expressions, the shopkeepers stood outside their establishments, casting unwelcoming glances at the approaching Sarah. A collective decision to lock doors reinforced the hostility that lingered.

Undeterred, Sarah leaned her bike against a bollard and approached the last haven, a combination of village shop and post office. However, before she could cross the threshold, Miss Rutherford, the shopkeeper, materialised to block her path, a bastion of disapproval.

"Hello, I am Sarah," she extended a hand for a handshake, met only with icy disregard.

"Hello, Sarah," the greeting hung unanswered, lost in the tension.

"I know who you are, young lady," declared Miss Rutherford, a stern figure "You're with that young man, sinning."

The accusation hung in the air, and Sarah, taken aback, sought clarity. "Sorry, excuse me, sinning? I have no idea what you are talking about. Can I buy my rations?"

Miss Rutherford's disapproving gaze remained unyielding. "We know you are living in sin at Old Jed's place with that young man. Do you not have any shame, out of wedlock and all?"

Sarah, bewildered, responded with defiance. "Sorry, but I don't see what business it is to do with you. Now, can I get my rations?"

With each passing moment, more villagers gathered, their curiosity tinged with hostility. Miss Rutherford, unyielding, continued her moral tirade. "We don't want the likes of you sullying the good name of this village with your harlot ways. Not even had the good sense to see you at church."

The tension escalated as Sarah, resilient yet deeply offended, defended her right to purchase necessities. "Like I said, it's none of your business. Can I buy some of my rations here or not?"

A chorus of judgmental voices from the villagers reinforced Miss Rutherford's stance. "You will not be using the services of this shop. Try the next village down; you have a bike. Use that."

The accusations grew more venomous as villagers labelled Sarah a Jezebel and accused her of consorting with the enemy. Unfazed, Sarah retorted, "I have never been spoken to before in this fashion ever. As for living in sin, it's not the 19th century."

Miss Rutherford, unyielding, continued to square off against Sarah, her arms crossed, a symbol of moral authority. "Vous êtes une vieille bête méchante, espérons que votre prochaine merde est un hérisson" (you evil old hag, hope your next shit is a hedgehog), Sarah remarked in frustration, drawing an unexpected response.

"How dare you speak to me in German, you insolent hussy. You know it's illegal," scolded Miss Rutherford.

"It's French, you uneducated pleb. You're not getting my custom," Sarah asserted.

"You can tell young Johnny that his custom is not welcome here either," declared Miss Rutherford, sealing the fate of Sarah's connection to the village shop.

As Sarah calmly wheeled her bike through the throng, a sense of dignity and defiance emanated. The villagers left behind in their judgmental circle, watched as she departed, a marked outsider in a once-charming village that had revealed its darker underbelly.

Peter Smith lurked in the shadow of the judgmental scene at the village shop, an embodiment of unsavoury intentions. Lecherous eyes followed Sarah as she left the unwelcoming establishment, licking his lips in a display of lascivious desire.

Meanwhile, crossing the road with purposeful strides was Beryl, a Land Girl with a small knapsack slung over her shoulder. Oblivious to the eyes that now fixated on her, she set out on foot toward one of the distant farms, her destination clear, but the danger that trailed her not so.

Behind her, in the eerie quiet that followed Sarah's confrontation, Peter emerged from the shadows. His gaze, previously focused on Sarah, now shifted to Beryl, and an unsettling grin spread across his face. Undeterred by any sense of decency, he followed her, stepping in sync with her strides but maintaining a sinister distance.

Beryl, lost in her own thoughts and the scenic beauty of the village, remained oblivious to the predatory figure tailing her every move. Peter's fixation on his unsuspecting prey intensified, setting the stage for a dark encounter on the outskirts of the village, away from prying eyes and the judgmental whispers that lingered in the air.

***

In the sterile confines of the modern NHS hospital room, the air was tense as family secrets unravelled. Andy, positioned beside the bed, observed the emotional scene between Daphne and her son, Danny. Daphne clung to her son as if seeking refuge from the storm of revelations.

"Wing Commander, how much of that did you hear?" Danny's gaze shifted towards Andy, who admitted to having overheard the entire conversation while feigning sleep.

"I heard it all, every bit," Andy confessed, his eyes reflecting the weight of the shared burdens.

Danny's frustration surfaced as he confronted Andy about the thefts and betrayals. "Not telling me about the burglary, I get. Being threatened to get drugs, I don't get, stealing jewellery out of a dead man's room. I saw you with it. Those poor people, you stole their legacy. How could you?"

Andy, in his wheelchair, interjected, urging Danny to moderate his tone. Now in the spotlight, Daphne clarified that she hadn't stolen the poppy. She began to reveal a pact made with Johnny Hodges, and Andy encouraged her to share the conditions.

"Johnny made me swear to him that when he passed, I was to immediately find the poppy and make sure no one gets it," Daphne disclosed, guided by the urging nod from Andy.

Andy pressed further, asking about the conditions attached to the promise. Daphne hesitated before revealing the specific instructions: she had to send the poppy to the Imperial War Museum in a box sealed with the words "danger" and "toxic" on the outside.

The importance of this revelation became evident as Andy inquired about the reasons. Daphne shared that Sarah, Johnny

Hodges' wife, held a secret within the poppy—a hidden compartment.

"I thought it was Johnny telling me a tall story, but the centre of the poppy has a little... compartment," Daphne explained, her voice carrying the gravity of the revelation.

Danny's curiosity peaked. "Holding what?"

Ever the guide through this labyrinth of secrets, Andy prompted, "Tell him."

With a heavy heart, Daphne delivered the shocking truth. "Sarah kept a pill inside. It was a suicide pill. Cyanide."

"Like James Bond n shit...?" Danny's incredulous reaction hung in the room.

Andy soberly emphasised, "It's lethal in the wrong hands. Lethal."

Daphne, burdened with remorse, acknowledged the severity of the situation. "So sorry, but that boy has got it."

Danny, already grappling with the aftermath of the stabbing, absorbed the gravity of the revelation. "So the guy that stabbed me is walking around with cyanide. The day gets better and better."

Shaking his head, Danny turned to the book in his hands, seeking escape within its pages. "You two just leave me alone for a bit. I need to escape," he declared, turning the page to retreat from the harsh realities surrounding him. Looking for answers in the lines of text and history.

***

The early evening cast a dark hue over Lacock Bridge, where the convergence of a doctor's car and a farmer's tractor formed a makeshift blockade. At each end, a curious crowd had gathered, their hushed whispers mingling with the subdued cries of two Land Army girls seeking solace amidst the grim scene.

On the downriver side, Constable Dickens, the local doctor and a labourer wielding a large billhook huddled together. The focal point of their attention was a stretcher bearing the lifeless form of Beryl. The constable and labourer had their backs turned, granting the doctor the space to conduct his examination.

"Suicide?" Constable Dickens inquired, his voice cutting through the heavy air.

The doctor, his countenance etched with professional gravity, shook his head. "No, not suicide. Despite the appearance, she bashed her head on the rocks and drowned. Oddly enough, there's no water in her lungs, but her work clothes are saturated with blood from before she jumped."

The constable, keenly observant, noted a detail. "Her dungaree straps are undone."

The doctor nodded in acknowledgement. "Well spotted. There's bruising on her throat, a black eye, and something else."

"More bruises," Constable Dickens observed, his gaze drawn to the ominous signs of violence. "Look at the dungarees—a button is missing."

"How did you know that?" The doctor's inquiry hung in the air.

The constable's grim revelation sent shivers through the gathering. "That girl that disappeared earlier this year, near Marlborough."

"Same injuries and a button missing," Constable Dickens confirmed a steely determination in his eyes. "I'll speak to the coroner. It's not suicide, I know that, but I want to catch this man."

The doctor, haunted by the cruelty of the scene, expressed empathy. "Her poor mother and father. A daughter was murdered, but even worse, raped. The shame they have to live with."

"We will catch the bastard, I promise you," Constable Dickens vowed, mindful of the challenges of wartime constraints. "Just understand, with the war, I have limited resources. I had a pint with her a fortnight ago. She had just got engaged."

***

The morning sun cast a soft glow on Coleshill House as recruits gathered by the lake, shrouded in mist that rolled across the glass-like surface. Dressed in military fatigues, they moved collectively, not in an army marching way, towards the jetty that jutted out into the tranquil waters.

A new figure emerged, a small man in Army Physical Training clothes, sporting a long, thin handlebar moustache. His wiry frame bespoke a level of fitness akin to a circus acrobat. An emblem of crossed swords adorned his chest.

"I am Corporal Frank Jackson, Right? It's my job to prepare you for enemy action in the water," the PTI declared, his voice cutting through the morning air. "I presume you can all swim. So when I tell you, I want you to jump in, swim to the rowboat in the middle, and back again. That will be your swim test. Any questions? Right, jump, and it pays to be the first back."

The students eyed the water hesitantly, and as the first person plunged in, the rest followed suit. The shocking cold water elicited gasps, and they raced to the rowboat and back. On the pier, Johnny stood, fear etched on his face.

Beside him, Sarah attempted to coax him into the water. "Come on, Johnny."

Corporal Jackson interrupted, "Miss, if you don't mind getting into the water, thank you."

Sarah jumped in, a momentary squeal escaping her. With rapid breathing, she found composure and glanced back at Johnny before swimming to the boat.

"Right, sonny, we need to know if you can swim here. Can you?" the Corporal addressed Johnny, who looked at the water with fear.

"Sorry, Staff, I had a bad experience in the water as a boy," Johnny confessed.

"Did I order you to give me your life history, son? Get in the water. If you have to walk along the bottom, you fail if you don't get in," the Corporal commanded.

Reluctantly, Johnny approached the edge, but his legs wobbled. Corporal pushes him in without warning, and Johnny floundered with panic.

"If you could be so kind not to drown, sir. I hate paperwork," the Corporal remarked dryly.

The first swimmers returned to the pier, exhausted. One of them grabbed Johnny, holding him up. The Corporal addressed Johnny sternly, "The class will take you as a group to the rowboat and back, but you have a week to learn to swim, or you are gone. Hear that? GONE!"

Sarah, concerned, joined the group in assisting Johnny to the rowboat and back, determined to help him overcome his fear.

***

The pub, cloaked in the warm embrace of flickering firelight, harboured its regulars like a keeper of secrets. The wooden beams creaked in harmony with the hushed conversations, and the tang of Stout lingered in the air. Jed, a fixture in the corner, nursed his drink, a silent observer of the night.

The Landlord, a raconteur in his own right, served drinks and spun tales, adding a layer of charm to the dimly lit establishment. Meanwhile, Peter, his senses dulled by alcohol, found solace at the bar. Amidst this nightly symphony of characters, two regulars, the vet and the teacher, engaged in a spirited debate.

"No, I saw lights by the wood the other night and heard voices. Must have been poachers," the teacher asserted, his voice cutting through the ambient hum.

The vet, ever the voice of reason, said, "But it's not poaching season yet. Why not ask old Jed? He is the gamekeeper."

Catching the wind of the conversation, Old Jed joined in with a gruff interjection, "Ask old Jed about what? It's not poaching time. Nothing you should worry about. That old wood has nothing in it anyhow."

Undeterred, the teacher continued speculating, "Perhaps it's fairies and a witches' coven."

The vet dismissed the notion, "No, it can't be. Miss Rutherford is in bed by nine, or so I am told."

Old Jed offered his own explanation with irritation: "It's nothing like that, probably the home guard doing manoeuvres."

With the liquid courage of inebriation, Peter Smith said, "Well,

I will go have a look tonight."

Old Jed erupted, "You will do nothing of the sort! That's my land. You are not to trespass on it. Do you hear me?"

The vet tried to diffuse the tension, "Jed, calm down. He's just curious. We all are."

"My land doesn't want some hob-footed ingrate traipsing around, upsetting my birds and coppicing," Jed declared with a hint of menace.

Unfazed, Peter Smith asked the seasoned gamekeeper, "Who are you calling a fire grate?"

The air was tense as the pub's regulars were entangled in this dispute, hinting at deeper conflicts within the close-knit community.

Old Jed's rebuke hung in the air, a rough-edged response that cut through the pub's banter like a sharpened blade. The fire crackled, blissfully unaware of the growing tension.

"I said ingrate, not fire grate, you dunce," Jed grumbled, eyeing Peter with disdain and irritation. "Your brother got all the brains. What did you get?"

The teacher, recognising an opportunity to defuse the situation, cautiously interjected, "Jed, you not heard."

"Heard what?" Jed retorted, his gaze fixed on the teacher.

"The whole village knows. The teacher emphasised " the whole village," pointing to the quiet mood that seemed to elude Jed's attention. "You not noticed the black armbands?"

Old Jed's brow furrowed in confusion. "What, his brother? The Navy one?"

Sensing the gravity of the situation, the vet added solemnly, "His convoy was lost two weeks ago."

A shock wave rolled over Jed's weathered features, the news hitting harder than anticipated. The reality of loss sank in, eclipsing the dispute with Peter. Once alive with chatter, the pub fell into a muted hush, the weight of shared sorrow casting a solemn pall over the room.

The tension in the pub escalated as Peter, fueled by anger and wounded pride, moved closer to Old Jed. The vet and the teacher, astute judges of impending conflict, wisely cleared a path, giving the unfolding drama ample space.

"You want to go outside, old man? Teach you some respect. Come on, if you ain't chicken," Peter spat out, his fists clenched, a tempest of rage in his eyes.

Old Jed, a weathered pillar of the village, met Peter's challenge with a calm that belied the turmoil beneath the surface. "You need to calm down, young man. I am old. Hitting an elderly person is not on. I am all frail and such."

Peter, undeterred, continued to flex his fists, the tension in the room escalating with every passing second.

"Go back to your dad. He needs you. Fighting me is not going to help you, now is it?" Jed's voice carried a tone of weary wisdom. "Billy, can you control your child?"

But Peter was deaf to reason, lost in the red mist of his anger. "I am no child. How dare you, Dad, stay out of this."

Billy, sensing the volatile situation, appealed to Jed. "Jed, you know how headstrong he is. I can't control him. Peter, come on. He didn't mean any of it. Here, have a half. Perhaps Jed will buy you a half."

"Nah, I want my ounce of flesh," Peter retorted, his defiance unwavering.

Maintaining his composure, Jed corrected, "It's a pound, you idiot. Billy, call off your boy now, and it will be the end of it."

"Sorry, Jed," Billy sighed, a reluctant acknowledgement of the brewing storm. "He wants to take you outside. Just go out. I want no trouble in here."

"That's it, you old goat. You're getting it in here or out there," Peter threatened, the room held captive by the impending clash.

Jed, shaking his head resignedly, muttered, "Really, just go away... Or just go." The echoes of a brewing storm lingered in the pub, the fragile peace shattered by the inevitability of confrontation.

The pub erupted into chaos as Peter, consumed by rage, started pushing Old Jed backwards. Twice, the forceful shoves made the room tense with anticipation. Suddenly, Jed's weathered hands moved with swift precision. A rabbit punch to Peter's throat left him gasping and vulnerable. With a gentle push, Jed manoeuvred him backwards over Snitch, the faithful companion lying in wait.

Tripping over the dog, Peter fell to the floor, choking and struggling for breath. Jed, with the measured calm of experience, approached. A firm crook pressed into Peter's gut, a flick between the legs, and a hand on his throat – a swift and effective display of Old Jed's prowess.

"I warned you, young man. Now you've gone and embarrassed yourself," Jed remarked as Billy rushed to clean up his son, the aftermath of the confrontation evident. "Told you I was all frail and suchlike."

In a desperate attempt to regain control, Peter pulled a knife from his pocket, swinging it erratically. But before the situation escalated, Old Jed's loyal companion, Snitch, leapt into action. With a savage bite to Peter's forearm, the knife clattered to the floor. Jed continued on his way, disappearing through the door. A sharp whistle and Snitch, ever faithful, followed.

"I'm going to have that old bastard. Going to have him," Peter seethed as he got up from the floor. Unnoticed by the chaos, a dungaree button had fallen from his pocket. Quick to conceal it, he stuffed it back before anyone took notice.

Billy, asserting authority, declared, "You're banned from here, Old Jed. You hear that!" The repercussions of the clash lingered in the air, leaving the pub unsettled in the aftermath of the violent confrontation.

***

Under the silver glow of the full moon, Sarah and Johnny made their way toward the jetty, the lake's calm waters stretching out before them like a vast mirror.

"I couldn't bear it if you left," Sarah confessed softly, her voice carrying the weight of her emotions.

Johnny nodded, the moonlight casting shadows across his troubled expression. "I know. This has been a tough week, but I'm scared of the water," he admitted, vulnerability tinged in his words.

Sarah acknowledged his fear with empathy. "I know. One of the class heard you have nightmares, calling out Andy in your sleep," she revealed, her concern evident.

"Both Andy and I nearly drowned swimming in the mill chase," Johnny recounted, the memories still vivid in his mind.

"Well, you need to learn. How about now?" Sarah proposed, her determination shining through the darkness.

Johnny hesitated, glancing at the imposing manor house behind them. "I don't think the night porter would appreciate us dripping water throughout the house," he replied, his practicality prevailing.

Undeterred, Sarah moved behind Johnny, her actions deliberate and resolute. "Keep your eyes forward," she instructed, her tone leaving no room for argument.

With a boldness that surprised even himself, Johnny listened, and then he peeked as Sarah shed her clothes, the moonlight casting a gentle glow upon her naked form. "Eyes forward, no peeking... take off your clothes. We will leave them here," she commanded, her words, a gentle push toward vulnerability.

Johnny hesitated, uncertainty flickering in his gaze. "But you will see me..." he trailed off, his insecurities laid bare.

"You will not be the first naked man I have seen. I did live in Europe as a child," Sarah reassured him, her voice laced with a hint of amusement.

With a sense of liberation, Johnny shed his clothes, the night air embracing him in its cool embrace. Walking to the jetty's edge, he felt a surge of anticipation mingled with fear. Sarah joined him, her presence a beacon of reassurance in the darkness.

"Deep breath. Shall we? 1, 2, 3, Geronimo!" Sarah exclaimed, her voice filled with exhilaration.

Together, they plunged into the water, Johnny's initial panic subsiding as Sarah's steady hand guided him through the depths. In the tranquil embrace of the lake, they discovered a newfound sense of freedom and connection.

Inside Coleshill Manor House, figures were observing the ad hoc training session.

From the window, Mr. Gubbins, the Corporal, and a mysterious figure observed the scene unfolding by the lake. Sarah's patient guidance contrasted with Johnny's tentative strokes, a testament to their shared journey.

"If that is not an incentive to learn to swim," the Corporal remarked, his voice tinged with admiration.

Mr. Gubbins nodded in agreement. "Well, we need both of them to pass the course. They both have great potential," he acknowledged, pride evident in his tone.

"They will end up falling in love if not careful," the Corporal mused, a hint of amusement colouring his words.

Mr. Gubbins smiled knowingly. "Hope they do. They make a great team, and some romance makes it all worthwhile with all this war nonsense. They've been courting in secret for a couple of months now... I might have pushed it a little," he confessed with a grin.

The mysterious figure rose from their seat, their presence commanding attention. As they stepped into the light, the uniform of a Gestapo officer. He steps forward into the light, revealing him to be Constable Dickens.

"Exactly. Which is why I nominated him for this unit. He and Old Jed know this countryside like nomads in the desert. With Sarah by his side, an unstoppable force," Constable Dickens declared, his words carrying weight and purpose.

"I have a mock interrogation to do with a couple of recruits; it's Syndicate A final week",

As the night unfolded, the currents of destiny intertwined, shaping the lives of those caught in its embrace. In the shadow of war, love and courage emerged as beacons of hope amidst the darkness. Splashes of water and ripples break up the moon's gaze on the water.

***

Danny awoke to the soft glow of morning, the room bathed in a muted light that barely penetrated the drawn curtains. The book lay open on his chest, its pages whispering tales of another era. His gaze shifted to the adjacent bed, where Andy slept, his features softened by the embrace of slumber.

A small wooden table stood by the bedside, and Danny was drawn to a note resting upon it. Simple words etched in familiarity: "See you soon, Mum." A bittersweet reminder of the life he had temporarily left behind.

The door creaked open, and the figure of Miss Fontaine glided into the room. Her presence exuded a comforting warmth as she approached Andy, a fellow traveller on the uncertain road to recovery. A gentle touch adjusted the blanket, and then she turned her attention to Danny.

"See you tomorrow," she offered with a kind smile, her eyes reflecting genuine concern. Andy will come every day till you are better. He cares for you."

A silent acknowledgement passed between them, a shared understanding of the camaraderie that had formed within the sterile walls of the hospital. "Yes, sometimes I think we are his only family," Danny confessed, his voice carrying the weight of introspection. "He probably misses his wife."

Miss Fontaine's eyes softened, sympathy painting her expression. "He never married, which is a shame, as he is such a sweetheart."

"Thank you," Danny replied, a simple acknowledgement laden with unspoken gratitude. Danny's gaze lingered on the open book as she wheeled Andy out of the room.

With a deliberate motion, he reached for the book and began

reading again. The cover, a picturesque portrayal of an English rural village, caught his eye. A jolly policeman, emblematic of an era that had slipped away, looked out from the stylised scene. The title beckoned with nostalgia: A Village Copper, 1931-1971.

As Danny delved into the pages, the stories unfolded like chapters of his own life, each word a bridge between past and present. The village, once dormant in the recesses of memory, now danced vividly within the lines of prose. And within those pages, he found solace—a tether to a world beyond the confines of hospital walls.

***

A small Humpbacked Bridge stood silently in the heart of Marlborough Woods, its ancient stones bearing witness to a dance between light and shadow. The air was crisp as Sarah pedalled back to the lodge, a small case tied securely to her bike's pannier. The woods whispered secrets, but the tranquillity was shattered as Peter emerged, a dark figure against the dappled sunlight.

His eyes, hungry and insolent, traced Sarah's every move. A sudden lurch, and she veered to the side, crashing against the cold stone wall of the bridge. Peter, emboldened, closed the distance.

"Hello, Miss," he drawled, a smirk playing on his lips. Do you need a hand on that bike?"

Sarah recoiled, subtle defiance in her eyes. Peter's fingers, like vipers, danced through her hair, a taunting caress. His voice slithered with suggestive intent.

"If Johnny can't satisfy your needs, how about me?"

A game of shadows and desire unfolded on the bridge. Peter's hand found its way to her breast, and Sarah, a puppeteer in this dark theatre, played along. His arrogance fueled by her feigned compliance, Peter reached for a kiss, intoxicated by his false conquest.

But then, like a tempest unleashed, Sarah's demeanour shifted. In a swift, controlled motion, she gripped his wrist, twisting it until he crumpled in agony. The bike discarded to the road, Sarah stepped forward, her gaze unwavering.

"I expected better of a real man," she taunted, her voice cutting through his cries of pain. Her hand swiftly descended a grip between his legs that left him gasping and humiliated.

Dusting herself off, Sarah reclaimed the bike, her composure unshaken. Control radiated from her every movement. A casual farewell hung in the air as she pedalled away, leaving Peter, nettled and defeated, in her wake.

"Bye, Peter. I have to go—I've got a wedding tomorrow, you understand, you toad. It's where people get married, unlike your mother and father."

As Sarah disappeared into the woods, a scorned Peter crawled out of the nettles, nursing wounds of both physical and bruised pride. Seated on the roadside, he dabbed at his cuts with hanky, vengeful eyes following her retreat.

The stillness was shattered by approaching footsteps on the bridge—a teenage Girl Scout, innocent and unsuspecting, about to cross paths with a man tainted by shadows. Peter, a master of deception, flashed a half-smile, a wolf in sheep's clothing awaiting the next act of his dark drama. Feigned a wounded creature, the girl scout approached; a samaritan bearing nothing but innocence and goodness came to the wolf in sheep's clothing

.

CHAPTER 9

Wedlock

The battered but resilient church stood as a silent witness to a union forged in the crucible of war. Sarah and Andy, dressed in makeshift wedding attire, emerged into the London daylight. Sarah's FANY uniform, worn with pride, bore the scars of resilience. They posed a beacon of happiness amidst the chaos for the church photographer. The surroundings, remnants of a city under siege, framed their unconventional joy.

During the photograph, Sarah clutched a bouquet of flowers, a vibrant contrast to the grim reality of the Blitz. Old Jed, adorned in an Eton School Tie, and Snitch, wearing a garish bow, stood as peculiar witnesses. Mr. Gubbins, a man of influence and secrets, offered his congratulations, a hint of concern etched on his face.

"Congratulations, you two," Mr. Gubbins acknowledged, his eyes carrying the weight of unspoken truths. "Pub round the corner, Mrs. Hodges, there's a sherry waiting for you."

Old Jed, ever the guardian, reminded the newlyweds of their responsibilities. Radiant in her defiance, Sarah thanked him for giving her away in her father's absence.

With a glint of mischief, Mr. Gubbins presented Sarah with a solid gold poppy brooch—a token not just of matrimony but a talisman with hidden worth.

"Very clever, sir," Sarah responded, her words holding a double entendre that only they understood. She kissed Mr Gubbins on the cheek, a rare display of affection.

Johnathon, the stalwart husband, expressed gratitude and concern. "Promise me you will look after her. She is special to me."

As the trio headed for the nearby pub, Snitch, the canine companion, added a touch of irreverence. The bright bow had mysteriously come off, and the dog relieved himself on it with a peculiar sense of timing.

The pub, a haven in uncertain times, welcomed the newlyweds —Stout for Johnathon and sherry for Sarah, a toast to their union amid the cacophony of war.

As they clinked glasses, the air hummed with unspoken vows and the weight of impending separation. In the shadows, Mr. Gubbins observed a silent guardian of secrets, his motives as enigmatic as the war-torn city itself. Glinting in the subdued light, the poppy brooch held the promise of salvation.

The pub, a microcosm of wartime resilience, echoed with laughter and camaraderie. Yet, beneath the surface, an undercurrent of uncertainty pervaded. Sarah and Andy, united in love, faced a future fraught with peril.

The wedding celebration unfolded, a brief respite in a world besieged by conflict. In the heart of London, where the echoes of love collided with the thunderous sounds of war, their union stood as a testament to the indomitable spirit that persisted even in the darkest hours.

***

Fair Oaks Retirement Home, a sanctuary for fading memories and twilight tales, stood silent under the muted English daylight. Daphne, cloaked in weariness, navigated the halls with a trolley laden with the weight of her responsibilities. Her eyes, veiled by the passage of time, betrayed the strain of unseen burdens.

She paused outside a room adorned with a small whiteboard, a feeble attempt to infuse a semblance of homeliness. The name "Mrs Reynolds" gleamed beneath floral stickers, offering a stark contrast to the solemnity of the institution. With practised efficiency, Daphne deposited a yellow plastic bag marked "bio-hazard" onto her cart.

In the silent dance of shadows, she surreptitiously slid a box of Tramadol into the ominous bag, the label a quiet testament to an illicit disposal. As she turned to leave, Miss Fontaine, an embodiment of politeness masking a steely core, intercepted her in the sterile corridor. A clipboard clutched in her hand, a checklist of scrutiny.

"Hello, just checking things off before our next guest. Everything all right?" Miss Fontaine's sing-song voice belied the discerning gaze behind her courteous facade

.

Daphne affirmed the completion of her duties with the practised ease of a charade. Never the vigilant overseer, Miss Fontaine peered into the room, ticking boxes with a clinical detachment that concealed a latent cunning.

"Medicines need accounting for," Miss Fontaine remarked, her eyes narrowing with suspicion.

Daphne, caught in the tangled web of deceit, exhibited the packet and the damning label. The bio-hazard bag, a refuge for secrets meant to be forever buried, is now a canvas for Miss

Fontaine's inquisitive eyes.

"I need to check, please?" Miss Fontaine's annoyance was palpable.

Daphne explained with a rationale wrapped in desperation, "Once in a bio bag, you are not allowed to go back in. Contamination and such. You know the rules regarding body tissue, vomit, and... faecal matter."

Miss Fontaine, momentarily repulsed, grudgingly accepted the explanation. As she walked away, Daphne, the unspoken understanding of a narrowly avoided catastrophe, hung.

However, the reprieve was short-lived. Miss Fontaine, a harbinger of discontent, retraced her steps, her scrutiny unrelenting. The whiteboard, a canvas of names and transient lives, became the focal point of her dissatisfaction.

"It needs cleaning," Miss Fontaine declared, her sing-song voice turning icy.

Daphne pleaded against erasing the final vestiges of existence in invoking a son's superstitions. Miss Fontaine, unmoved by sentiment, admonished them with a curt "Tootle pip!" and vanished down the corridor.

Left alone, Daphne breathed a sigh of relief. Yet, as the shadows converged, Miss Fontaine's footsteps echoed back. Dissatisfied, she returned with a final directive – the whiteboard must be cleaned.

In a quiet act of rebellion, Daphne sprayed bleach onto the sign. The letters dissolved, red ink bleeding like a clandestine confession, blending with the board's green. The act was a silent rebellion against the clinical erasure of lives that once flickered in the shadowed halls of Fair Oaks.

***

The train tracks cut through the heart of the English countryside, bearing witness to an unforeseen tragedy. Constable Dickens, a solitary figure, pushed his bike solemnly, the gravel crunching beneath his worn boots. Ahead, rail workers occupied a desolate scene, their faces etched with shock and dread.

A spectral presence perched on the bank, the engine driver stared into the void. At the same time, his stoker, Charlie, hastened to meet Constable Dickens. A blanket concealed the tragedy sprawled across the tracks, a silent testament to the collision of despair and destiny. A pipe-smoking doctor lingered, shrouded in an air of detached contemplation, as a distant steam train carried oblivious passengers, their gazes fixated on the unfolding spectacle.

The stoker, trembling with the weight of guilt, poured his anguish into the open ears of Constable Dickens. The doctor, a silent arbiter of understanding, acknowledged the pain etched across Charlie's face.

"It's alright, Charlie. It's not your fault," the doctor reassured, the tendrils of smoke from his pipe intertwining with the melancholy in the air.

In the presence of law and medicine, Charlie recounted the haunting moments leading to the tragedy. The wheels of the train ground to a halt, but the spectre of despair had already claimed a life. Constable Dickens, seeking clarity, questioned the circumstances surrounding the incident.

"She deliberately let herself get hit... why? What would make a person do that?" Charlie's words hung in the air, the unspoken echoes of a tormented soul.

As the doctor and constable exchanged glances, a truth unfurled. The victim revealed to be a child, had willingly met her demise on the unforgiving tracks. Constable Dickens, grappling with the harsh reality, steeled himself to uncover the depths of the tragedy.

He approached the lifeless form, gently pulling back the shroud of the blanket. The doctor, a sage witness to the human condition, shared a sombre nod with Constable Dickens, acknowledging the shared burden of comprehending senseless loss.

The girl, a Girl Guide who had crossed paths with Peter earlier, lay battered and broken. Her face bore the scars of an ordeal, her innocence violently stolen. Constable Dickens, now privy to the harrowing details, spoke with sorrow and determination.

"Doctor, I am no expert, but I think she was attacked, then ran onto the tracks deliberately."

The doctor, a repository of countless narratives of despair, added a grim layer to the unfolding tragedy. A badge, sliced away with a knife, revealed the girl's desperate struggle for survival.

"This is the third in the last six months," Constable Dickens declared, his voice echoing with a promise of justice. "When I find the monster who did this, they will hang." The words hung heavy in the air, a vow to unravel the shadows that had claimed one more innocent soul—the sobs of the railwayman echoing along the cut.

***

The room, bathed in the soft glow of daylight, bore the hushed tones of a shared secret. Danny entered with a tray laden with lunch and carefully arranged the contents on the bedside table. Mash and fish in parsley sauce, a modest offering that hinted at a deeper connection between the two men.

"And what do we have here? Mash and fish in parsley sauce," Andy remarked, his eyes twinkling with a wry smile.

Danny, unable to bear the weight of guilt permeating his mother's presence, sought solace in Andy's room. Can I stay for a bit? Can't sit with Mum. Her guilt is burning right through us; can't stand it."

Andy, the pillar of reason, countered, "It's not her fault. She's under a ton of pressure. That boy is evil; he needs dealing with justice of sorts."

As they navigated the delicate intricacies of their predicament, Danny unveiled the grim truth. "She's so scared. We stole some tramadol the other day. He keeps demanding more and more."

Andy, his brows furrowed in concern, shifted the conversation to a more ominous threat. "It's that poppy I'm worried about. It does not bear thinking about if that gets in the wrong hands or a child's."

In the room, where whispers carried the weight of secrets, they grappled with the morality of their actions. "I'm still not sure about it. You said it had a pill in it. I understand why it's there, but in a solid gold brooch?"

Andy, the sage of a bygone era, explained, "They used lipsticks, powder compacts, but we heard the Germans had gotten clever. Who has lipstick in a solid gold container? No one. But a brooch."

The golden escape, shrouded in questions, lingered in Danny's mind. "But gold, what for?"

"Escape. You could pay your passage out of the country or bribe people with it," Andy divulged, his eyes reflecting a tumultuous history.

A sudden knock interrupted the labyrinth of their thoughts, heralding Derek, Johnny's son—a reconciliation hung in the air, adorned with a promise of solace.

"I thought I better apologise to you, Mr. Bryce, for being rude the other day," Derek confessed, his voice tinged with remorse. "Just to let you know, we will invite you to the funeral, and would it be ok to say a few words for Dad?"

As the formality of reconciliation unfolded, Derek's gaze shifted to Danny. "Judy and I are convinced he never served. Would you mind coming with Andy? We have an old bike that needs a bit of oil. You're more than welcome to have it."

The air crackled with an unexpected offer, a glimmer of reprieve for the burdened soul. As Derek extended an olive branch, he revealed a darker truth. "I saw your mother the other day speaking to a character who, let's say, is not a pleasant chap."

A business card, a lifeline in the tangled web of their existence, passed from Derek to Danny. A warning echoed in Derek's parting words, "If something is going on, please let me know."

The door closed, leaving Danny and Andy to wrestle with the shadows of their past. "Suppose you heard all that?" Danny inquired, seeking reassurance in the camaraderie forged amidst the trials of life.

Andy, attuned to the nuances of the world through his hearing aids, replied with a knowing smile. "You can't miss a thing with these."

They decided to redirect the conversation to the sanctuary of Andy's room, where confessions carried the weight of absolution. "Let's talk about something different. How about catching me up with the newlyweds?" Danny suggested a subtle shift toward the mundane, a respite from the relentless march of shadows that trailed their every step.

***

Jed's Lodge, nestled in the embrace of nature, bore witness to a celebration marked by bicycles adorned with tin cans and the infectious joy of Sarah and Johnathon. Ribbons fluttered in the breeze as they reached the entrance. Jed had woven a tapestry of wildflowers, a silent testament to the warmth within.

"Right, old wifey. It's tradition, you know, to carry you across the threshold, so come on then," Johnathon declared with a twinkle in his eye. Sarah, the embodiment of joy and happiness, leapt into his arms. The door creaked shut behind them as they embraced tradition and love.

Inside the Lodge, the air hummed with the anticipation of new beginnings. Still enveloped in the euphoria of marital bliss, Sarah spotted a pristine white envelope on the floor. Curiosity and excitement danced in her eyes as she opened it, envisioning a wedding present.

"Ooh, it might be a wedding present," she mused, her smile radiating infectious delight. However, as her eyes absorbed the contents, a subtle shift occurred. Silence descended, and a shadow of unease crept into her features. With haste, she darted toward the stove, the atmosphere now charged with an unexpected tension.

Johnathon, sensing the abrupt change, seized the envelope and peered inside. Horror etched across his face as he withdrew a single white feather. The weight of its symbolism bore down on them, a feather-light yet ominous sign. The room, once filled with the promise of a shared future, now echoed with unspoken fears.

The Lodge's walls absorbed the unspoken anxiety that pulsed through the room in the dance between light and shadow. The white feather, an unwelcome harbinger, stirred the air with foreboding. The couple, united by love, now faced the unsettling unknown that hovered in the wake of this cryptic message.

As the door to Ed's Lodge stood closed, the white feather whispered secrets, and the once carefree atmosphere transformed into a realm where destiny and darkness intertwined. The tapestry of celebration now woven with threads of uncertainty, Sarah and Johnathon confronted a new chapter marked by the enigmatic presence of a single, haunting feather.

***

Under the sprawling canopy of Jed's managed woods, where nature's breath intertwined with secrets, Peter and his cohorts prowled with an air of trespass. The distant hum of Jed's van faded into the forest's depths, leaving them with a canvas of possibilities.

Marked by scratch scars on his arms and face, Peter led the group through the verdant maze. Guided by a forbidden curiosity, they ventured toward the secluded haven Jed had deemed off-limits. The air carried a hushed tension as if the very woods whispered cautionary tales.

A military camouflage net concealed their destination, a pigeon loft nestled within the forest's heart. Its existence, shrouded in mystery, bore the stamp of meticulous care. With their scrawny elegance, racing pigeons occupied the loft —a secret endeavour flourishing under the watchful gaze of nature. Hidden from the world.

As the trio explored further, they stumbled upon an aviary housing fledgling birds. In the dappled sunlight filtering through the leaves, the existence of this covert avian world unfolded. Pondering the scrawny racing pigeons, a revelation dawned upon Peter.

"Old codger's breeding pigeons. That's how he's making his money," Peter declared, his voice betraying a hint of grudging admiration.

His cohorts, equally perplexed, observed the loft filled with the fluttering symphony of feathers. Pondering the potential of this covert operation, questions simmered in the air like a brewing storm.

"Do you think he's doing this on the black market, the meat?" Peters's friend speculated, his eyes narrowing at the scrawny inhabitants of the loft.

"Well, if he is, he's undercutting my old man," Peter retorted, frustration tainting his tone. His eyes gleamed with a sudden idea, a spark that could kindle trouble.

"Grab those hessian sacks. I have an idea," Peter commanded, his mind weaving a plan to exploit the secret he had stumbled upon in the heart of the woods.

Driven by a reckless blend of greed and malice, Peter withdrew a knife with a glint of malevolence. Once a guardian of secrets, the military camouflage net now succumbed to the sharp blade's intrusion. As strands of fabric fell away like confessions, the hidden world beneath the cover was exposed.

He sauntered through the clearing, his conquest marked by the liberated netting clinging to his clothing. The forest, once a haven of whispers, now echoed with the ominous rustle of feathers. The racing pigeons, betrayed by the sudden exposure, fluttered in disarray.

Like a serpent waiting to unleash its venom, a can of petrol awaited discovery amidst the ferns. Peter, his eyes gleaming with an unsettling blend of satisfaction and mischief, seized the can. A nonchalant flick of a lighter set the end of a cigarette ablaze, casting shadows that danced with sinister delight.

As Peter inhaled the toxic tendrils of smoke, a symphony of avian panic erupted behind him. The once-hidden pigeons, now prisoners of both fear and encroaching flames, flapped desperately against the confinement of their loft.

Laughter, coarse and devoid of empathy, reverberated through the woods. The thugs, like demons relishing chaos, revelled in the discord they had orchestrated. The acrid scent of petrol mingled with the haunting sounds of distressed birds, forming a macabre overture to the impending calamity.

Kindled by recklessness and malice, the flames licked at the edges of the netting. Now an unwitting accomplice, the net fueled the inferno that consumed the sanctuary of Jed's secret. Amidst the chaos, the thugs 'laughter grew, intertwining with the panicked symphony of avian distress.

In the heart of the woods, shadows danced to the unholy rhythm orchestrated by Peter and his henchmen. The fragile balance Jed had maintained, now disrupted, crumbled like burning embers spiralling into the night. The repercussions of this brazen intrusion would cast a pall over the tranquil woods, signalling the emergence of darker shadows yet to come. Peter's face was lit ominously by the orange flames, and he listened to the screams of the birds. He eyed another petrol can entranced. He reached for it,

A cigarette dangled carelessly from his lips, exhaling tendrils of smoke that coiled spiralling. With a sudden snap, the lid surrendered to Peter's persistent assault, catapulting into the air. His knife, discarded in haste, clattered to the ground.
Petrol, the volatile elixir of destruction, splashed onto Peter's arm as if marking him for the chaos he was about to unleash. Ignition seized him like an unholy baptism, flames licking at his sleeve. The sudden inferno painted his face in the spectral hues of malevolence.
The two thugs, loyal but unwilling apprentices to the mischief, reacted instinctively. Their hands danced upon Peter's arm, extinguishing the insidious flames that threatened to consume him. The scent of burnt fabric mingled with the acrid perfume of spilt petrol, a testament to the near-tragedy averted.

**

The winding paths of the village unfolded before Johnathon and Sarah as they cycled through the quaint scenery. His infectious smile revealed a familiarity with the surroundings, a local guide proud to unveil the charms of his home to an eager companion. As they approached a crossroads, Sarah, a playful glint in her eyes, veered off towards the village, defying the expected route. Johnathon waited, the unspoken camaraderie between them tangible.

"You're going the wrong way; it's that way," Johnathon pointed with a grin as Sarah turned back.

"But the sign says..." she began, her smile revealing the delight in her mischief.

"Not that way," Johnathon corrected, a conspiratorial understanding shared between them.

"That way," Sarah chimed in, catching on to the subtle subversion of wartime secrets.

"You and Jed have turned the signs around to confuse the Germans, clever old Johnny. Clever old Jed," she remarked, connecting the dots of their shared deviousness. "I see why you two get on so well."

Johnathon suggested surprising Jed at the pigeon loft, and they initiated a race downhill. Laughter echoed through the air as they pedalled fiercely. At the hill's bottom, their joy was interrupted by an unexpected scent.

"You smell that? It's smoke," Johnathon exclaimed.

Scanning the surroundings, Sarah pointed towards the ominous plumes in the distance. "Over there, smoke."

"No, no, no, no, no," Johnathon muttered, his face tensing with worry. "That's Jed's loft. Come on, hurry."

Their carefree race turned into a desperate dash as the situation's urgency set in. Once a picturesque haven, the loft now held an ominous cloud of concern. Like ephemeral whispers, trails of smoke painted an unsettling narrative against the canvas of the sky. The rustic charm of the loft now echoed with the foreboding drumbeat of unexpected calamity. The sounds of flame and pigeons broke the pastoral scene.

The once serene haven of Jed's pigeon loft now resembled a harrowing scene of destruction. Smoke coiled into the sky like malevolent spirits, mingling with the feathers of once-proud birds that now lay scattered like discarded dreams. The crackling of flames devoured the tranquil air, leaving behind only the acrid scent of burning memories.

Sarah, her eyes wide with disbelief, wandered through the chaos. Once a sanctuary for delicate chicks, the aviary now hosted only devastation. Lifeless bodies of birds, innocent victims of senseless brutality, lay strewn amidst the wreckage. The fragile shells of crushed eggs told a silent tale of shattered hope and unrestrained malice.

Amidst the chaos, Johnathon fought the flames, his frantic efforts a futile attempt to salvage what remained. The dance of orange tongues leapt voraciously, consuming not only wood and feathers but also the essence of Jed's solace.

In the distance, the unmistakable hum of Jed's van grew louder, its arrival heralding a moment of grim revelation. The old man, once a symbol of resilience, now emerged from the vehicle with eyes that mirrored the devastation around him. His birds, his cherished companions, were now reduced to smouldering remnants.

"No, no, no, no, no, no, no, no, my birds, my beautiful birds, why?" Jed's anguished cry echoed through the clearing, reaching the ears of Johnathon and Sarah. Crestfallen and defeated, he moved among the remnants of his avian family, his gaze capturing the horror etched in every feathered carcass.

Johnathon, compelled by anger and sorrow, intended to comfort his mentor. Yet, Sarah, a voice of reason, held him back. "Let him be. He needs to soak it in. He's in shock, too much shock."

The truth of the betrayal hung heavy in the air, and the realisation etched on Johnathon's face. "I know who did it," he declared, eyes scanning their desolation.

He painted a vivid picture of the perpetrators 'callousness, recounting the grim details of the merciless act.

As Johnathon held up the found knife, a grim relic of Peter Smith's malevolence, Jed's eyes narrowed with recognition. "That's the Smiths 'boy's knife. He tried to cut me with it the other night."

Fueled by a quiet rage, Jed issued a directive that cut through the chaos. "Leave your bikes here. Get in the van. We have an appointment to make."

The van, once a vessel of routine journeys, now harboured a sense of purpose born from the embers of betrayal. The trio, bound by a shared mission, left the smouldering ruins behind, setting forth on a path that promised justice and a reckoning for the flames that had devoured more than just a loft of pigeons.

***

Daphne navigated her way up the landing of a run-down block of flats, surrounded by discarded rubbish bags, children's toys, and canine waste. The doors were battered, and some windows were shielded with metal mesh. At the same time, graffiti adorned the walls—far from an appealing neighbourhood. Clutching a scrap of paper bearing an address, Daphne finally reached her destination.

Surprisingly, she found a brand-new, clean door in an unkempt building. The vicinity was unexpectedly adorned with flower boxes and neatly arranged plant pots. Steeling herself, Daphne took a deep breath and tapped the doorbell.

The door creaked open, restrained by a chain, revealing an old frail woman wearing a dress and cardigan she was holding onto a zimmer frame,

"Hello, how can I help you, dear?" Amelia inquired through the slightly ajar door.

With a sense of nervous determination, Daphne replied, "It's about your grandson, Stephan."

Once inside, Daphne surveyed the living room adorned with chintz, porcelain dolls, and doilies. On the electric fireplace, a porcelain dreycart held barrels of beer. Family photos, including images of a young and innocent Stephan, decorated the room. A fresh pot of tea and teacups sat on the coffee table.

Amelia spoke, breaking the silence, "I don't get too many visitors these days, what with my hip and a bit of gout."

"Oh, it's me back that causes me gip. We're having to slow down these days," Daphne replied, attempting to establish a connection.

"You wanted to talk about my grandson. Is he in trouble again?

Had the police around last week," Amelia questioned.

"Yes, he's been bothering my boy and giving me a hard time. Sorry for you to hear that," Daphne confessed.

Amelia, ever the defender of her grandson, chimed in, "He's a bit headstrong, but he's a good lad. Runs a little business doing odd things here and there. He pays for the maintenance of my flat as well. Such a good lad."

"Well, I think he was a little too rough with my Danny," Daphne asserted.

Amelia dismissed it with a nonchalant, "Oh, boys will be boys. You know how they are—a little bit of rough and tumble did no one any harm."

The front door opened, keys jingled, and footsteps echoed in the flat.
"Hey Nan, it's me," Stephan announced as he entered the room.

Amelia redirected him to the front room, where a visitor awaited, prompting Stephan's concern about the visitor being the social worker.

"No swearing in my house," Amelia scolded as Stephan reluctantly entered the room, his demeanour changing to politeness in front of his grandmother.

"Hello, how are you?" Stephan greeted, his smile not quite reaching his eyes.

"I am fine. It's my boy that I am worried about," Daphne responded.

Amelia, sensing tension, intervened, "Right, Stephan, you are to leave her son alone. Heard you were mean to him."

"Nah, Nan, it was a business deal between me and Danny. It got a bit fruity, but business is like that. You know what it's like —no hard feelings," Stephan explained, extending a hand in a feigned gesture of friendship.

Seeing through the charade, Daphne ignored his hand and pushed it away.

Amelia, always the peacemaker, concluded, "There, Stephan, nice and polite. Just business."

As Daphne stood up to leave, Stephan continued to play his part, pretending to be friendly.

"Are you leaving?" Amelia asked as Daphne gathered her belongings.

"Yes, sorry. I have to go. It was a pleasure meeting you," Daphne said, turning and walking out of the flat, the door swinging shut behind her.

"What a strange woman," Amelia remarked.

"Yes, Nana," Stephan concurred.

With a mix of concern and resignation, Amelia reminded him, "You better get more Trammies off her soon. I can't keep lying to the police for you. Drugs are not a good business, even if it does pay for the upkeep."

"Yes, Nan, I have plans for her soon. She will not be in my business plan for long," Stephan asserted.

"Fish fingers and spaghetti for tea, dearest grandson," Amelia said, shifting the conversation to mundane matters.

"I am an honest, hardworking businessman, Nan. Don't you forget it. Yes, five fingers, please," Stephan replied, attempting to maintain an air of innocence

***

The village pub, a seemingly ordinary establishment, stood witness to a clandestine drama unfolding under the watchful eye of Constable Dicken. A black car pulled up, carrying an air of foreboding. Two men, draped in shadows, emerged, their ritualistic cigarette lighting only enhancing the ominous atmosphere. Suited in black, with hat brims hiding their features, they entered the pub like wraiths and looked more like gangsters than police.

In the background, Old Jed, flanked by the ever-loyal Snitch, observed with a quiet intensity. Johnathon and Sarah, perched on a bench, shared a silent vigil, their eyes fixed on the impending chaos.

The tranquillity shattered as raucous noises echoed within the pub—a cacophony of broken glass and raised voices. Constable Dicken emerged, dragging Billy, the Landlord, in tow, his hands bound by cold metal cuffs. The abruptness of his expulsion from the pub painted a grim picture.

Full hessian sacks of pigeons, crude symbols of loss, were flung callously into the waiting car. The suited men handled Billy brutally and quietly, thrusting him into the vehicle. The engine roared to life, drowning the village in its departing rumble.

Approaching Old Jed, Constable Dicken, visibly distressed, removed his helmet and held it under his arm. The old man's eyes sought answers.

"What's going on? It was Peter's tracks we found. His knife and shoe print," Jed questioned, his voice tinged with concern.

"I know it was Peter. I saw his arm, a terrible red burn. I know it was his knife. But Billy, the old fool, confessed to it. The men from the war office wanted someone, anyone. They got Billy, and they're satisfied," Constable Dicken explained with a weariness that age and duty had etched on his face.

The truth, as bitter as the acrid smoke from the ruined loft, unveiled itself. Sarah, ever perceptive, voiced her frustration. "Peter is getting in the way of your work, everyone's work."

His eyes ablaze with righteous fury, Johnathon spoke of the broader consequences. "Do they realise how many lives they put at risk, killing all those birds? I hope he spends a long time in prison. This is not over with Peter. We have no more homing pigeons for our operators in France because of him."

Old Jed, the voice of cautious wisdom, tempered the rising storm. "I hope it is. The foolish man is risking a lot of lives. He is also a danger to the village girls. I am sure he is a deviant."

Sarah, harbouring her own secrets, shifted uncomfortably. She had not divulged the incident on the bridge to Johnathon. The exchange of glances between Jed and Constable Dicken spoke volumes. Johnathon, oblivious, stared at the pub's window, only to find Peter's chilling gaze, accompanied by a throat-slashing gesture—a harbinger of storms yet to come.

***

The care home, a facade of serenity, harboured shadows within its walls. Burdened by the weight of his responsibilities, Danny navigated the muted corridors. His steps echoed the weary rhythm of a man reconciling with the inevitability of another day, sore from his stabbing. He was meant to take it easy, but work and care had a stronger pull.

Entering the staff room, Danny aimed to close the back door. As he approached, a clandestine scene unfolded outside. Daphne, a fragile silhouette, engaged in a covert exchange with an unseen figure. A plastic packet exchanged hands, a transaction cloaked in whispers.

Then, the unknown figure came into view—the leader of the

notorious bike gang, Stephan. His presence cast a foreboding chill. In an act of brutality, he slapped Daphne across the face. The impact reverberated through the silent air, leaving Danny paralysed with fear: a son's helplessness, a spectator to his mother's humiliation. An ice-cold chill went down his spine, his body trembling, his mouth dry. The pain in his side stopped.

Daphne, betrayed and bruised, retreated through the staff door. Danny, torn between a son's instinct to intervene and the stark reality of powerlessness, watched as his mother, once invincible, now crumbled onto a chair. Her face, raw and red, told tales of unspoken torment. Daphne cried, "I should have kept away, I should have never visited that damn woman."

Desperate to offer solace, Danny fetched a tattered towel, soaked it with care, and extended it to his mother. However, pride, wounded as it was, rejected the offered help. Each refusal cut deeper into Danny's soul. Abandoned by his mother's resilience, he sought solace on the back step, a refuge of vulnerability. His mother was staring into the middle distance, devoid of personality, a tear warm and saline rolled down her cheek. The saltiness stung the split on her lip.

Amidst the unseen tragedy, a silent observer stood witness. Andy saw Danny's despair from across the courtyard, the window a barrier. The framed tableau of sorrow, where tears flowed freely and emotions bared themselves in the harsh daylight, was a scene of abject misery.

In the aftermath of this clandestine encounter, Danny wept. Andy, an unwilling spectator to another's pain, grappled with the shadows cast by the harsh sun of reality.

CHAPTER 10

Checkpoint

Wiltshire's idyllic country lanes, bathed in the golden hues of afternoon sunlight, bore witness to the unlikely convergence of worlds. Astride her bicycle, Miss Rutherford pedalled with determination toward the neighbouring village, a mere silhouette against the rustic landscape.

As she crested the hill, the peace was shattered by the abrupt appearance of an army checkpoint. A young sergeant with three stripes on his arm confronted her with an order to halt. The clash of assertive voices filled the air, an incongruity against the serene backdrop.

"Halt! Who goes there!!!!" Sergeants's command echoed across the quiet lane. Immediately jumping into an aggressive pose with rifle thrust forward with bayonet fitted, poised to despatch whoever happened to be in front of it,

"Don't you raise your voice at me, young man," replied Miss Rutherford, her gaze steady, undeterred.

"I said, Halt, don't you understand a simple instruction, woman? " the sergeant insisted, his tone gruff, harsh, and to the point.

"I don't know who raised you. I am a lady; you will refer to me as such," Miss Rutherford asserted with disdain.

"Look at my arm, Miss. Three stripes say I don't have to. Roads closed, turn around, and clear off," the sentry explained, frustration evident in his voice.

Amidst this standoff, a rumble of civilian lorries approached. Unbeknownst to the sentry, soldiers with Royal Engineers cap badges hid behind the canvas cover of the last lorry.

"You are in the way. If you don't go, I have orders to shoot," warned the sergeant, the tension escalating.

"I have, you know. I know the Justice of the Peace. He will hear about it," Miss Rutherford retorted, her resolve unyielding.

"If you don't clear off, you stupid cow, he will hear about it as you will be in front of the coroner on a slab. Now I have orders to shoot. Now piss off," the sentry declared, his patience worn thin.

The gravity of the situation sank in, and fear etched across Miss Rutherford's face. In a swift response to the cocking of the sentry's rifle, she turned her bike around and pedalled off furiously, disappearing from sight. Her legs straining and her back wheel wobbling, her handbag swinging,

A beat passed before the Sergeant, now more at ease, remarked, "It's alright sirs; she has gone now. You can come out."

Familiar faces emerged from the bushes—Jed, the Constable, and Johnathon.

"You're right; she is a snooty old cow," the sergeant quipped, breaking the tension.

"You weren't going to shoot her, were you?" inquired Constable Dickens, seeking reassurance.

"Would the world miss her if I did? You gentlemen, go on your way; you have a job to do," the sergeant said with a wink, acknowledging the peculiar encounter.

As the trio of Jed, the Constable, and Johnathon resumed their journey down the road toward the lorries, the Sergeant watched their figures recede into the folds of the Wiltshire landscape, his duty performed under the watchful gaze of the serene countryside.

***

The smoking area of the care home's garden hosted a poignant reunion under the sun's benevolent gaze. Derek and Judy, siblings tethered by familial history, found themselves seated on a worn bench alongside Andy. The atmosphere bore the subtle weight of memories, a blend of nostalgia and unspoken sorrows.

Beside the door stood an old mountain bike, a relic of better days, a gift from Derek to Danny. The scene unfolded with Danny's curious eyes fixed on the bike, absorbing the camaraderie around him.

Andy initiated a conversation that rippled through the threads of time as they settled. "Your mother had a photo of you kids and Johnny on her bedside table. It was a nice photo."

With eyes alight with reminiscence, Judy acknowledged, "Yes, I have been looking for it. It was our family holiday in France. We went camping for a month."

Derek, drawn into the shared recollections, walked over and joined them. "I remember stealing some wine off the table in that villa. Dad was so cross. Mum thought it was a hoot, as she called it. Loved France."

"It was a weird holiday," Judy reflected. "We went to strange places and stayed in the most wonderful orchards and vineyards."

"Bored in the car, though. Remember, Mum had a ritual in some villages?" Derek nudged the collective memory.

"Oh, I remember. Out of politeness, she said that everyone had to stay in the car, and she would go and speak to a villager or farmer," Judy recalled with a smile.

"Your mother was like magic. She'd go up, say something—what, I don't know—but suddenly, we were part of that French family. They used to take us in and spoil us. Sometimes, though, Mum got sad and would go for long walks on her own," Derek added, his gaze lost in the tapestry of the past.

The revelation about the absence of a map prompted laughter. "Map! I just realised we never had a map! It was infuriating! I had no idea where we were," Judy exclaimed.

"Do you think she knew France much better than she let on? As we had no clue..." Derek pondered a hint of revelation in his eyes.

Andy, the perceptive observer, interjected, "You will figure it out soon. The photo—what do you remember of it?"

"It was before we went to that ruined village. Mum cried, and so did Dad. It was so sad. All the villagers were killed in reprisals after D-Day," Judy shared, the gravity of the memory etched on her face.

Derek, prompted by curiosity, suggested, "Let me Google it on my phone."

Andy interjected with a sombre revelation as Derek immersed himself in his search. "Your mother almost died trying to save Oradour-sur-Glane. in the war."

The words hung in the air, a testament to the unseen layers of their mother's history. The smoking area, now imbued with a tapestry of shared memories and revelations, bore witness to the complexities of familial ties and the echoing whispers of Oradour-sur-Glane.

***

The quaint French village of Oradour-sur-Glane lay shrouded in the cloak of night, a canvas painted in inky hues and punctuated by the muted glow of stars. Silence gripped the cobbled streets, an unspoken agreement that it was time for the villagers to seek refuge in the safety of their homes, for curfew had descended like a heavy curtain.

In the heart of this nocturnal stillness, a solitary figure lingered in the shadows, an elusive spectator of the village's clandestine affairs. The watcher, concealed in the cloak of darkness, observed with an intensity that betrayed a hidden purpose, a mission obscured by the folds of the night.

The silence was soon shattered by the low hum of an approaching German staff car, escorted by the rhythmic purr of a vigilant motorbike outrider. The enemy's intrusion into the village's sacred quietude marked an ominous disruption.

As the car rolled to a stop, a senior SS officer emerged, his uniform adorned with the insignia of authority. The ominous silence was briefly punctuated by the staccato ignition of a cigarette, an ember that mirrored the imminent upheaval. Beside him, the driver, a silent accomplice in the unfolding drama, unfolded a map on the bonnet, a blueprint of intentions etched in cryptic lines.

With a decisive stroke of a red chinagraph pencil, the SS officer marked the village on the map—a sinister declaration of destinies entwined with the ink of malevolence. The village, now etched in scarlet, stood marked for an uncertain fate.

Having etched the ominous map, the officer and his driver, embodiments of impending menace, embarked on their departure, leaving the village in the clutch of the foreboding night. Unbeknownst to them, the vigilant figure in the shadows continued to bear witness, the weight of knowledge etched into their very being.

When the ominous presence was safely beyond the village bounds, the hidden watcher ascended a ladder, a lone sentinel reaching for the heavens. With purposeful determination, a flashlight was unleashed, casting its luminous Morse code against the tapestry of darkness—two flashes, a clandestine signal echoing through the silent village, a harbinger of unseen forces and covert resistance.

The night air hung heavy over the winding road, where shadows played a game with the silhouettes of trees. The hum of a motorcar echoed through the darkness as it navigated a treacherous bend. In the stillness, an eerie scene unfolded—a bicycle lay sprawled across the road, an apparent casualty of the night.

The leading motorbike outrider pulled up abruptly, a harbinger of the following ominous events. A pistol materialised in his grasp, pointed menacingly at the prone figure of a girl. His silent command urged the staff car to halt, its wheels churning to a reluctant stop.

A sudden crack echoed through the night, and the outrider crumpled to the ground, life extinguished in an instant. The girl, seemingly lifeless moments ago, rose with a Stirling machine gun in hand. A shrill whistle pierced the air as if calling forth unseen allies.

From the obscurity of the tree line, a cart materialised, a clandestine barrier against the car's escape. The French Maquis emerged, resolute and driven, their resistance a symphony of vengeance. Gunshots erupted, and chaos enveloped the night.

The staff car, now ensnared in the web of the Maquis, faced an imminent reckoning. They wrested the staff officer from the vehicle, stealing the coveted map, the document that held secrets of profound consequence. A dance of imminent justice unfolded, and the air crackled with tension.

Yet, as fate wove its intricate tapestry, headlights pierced the darkness—a mechanised German infantry unit, a formidable force in relentless pursuit. A brutal firefight ensued, and the clash of ideologies and loyalties was painted against the canvas of the night. The technological might of the German forces against the strong-willed and limited locals an unmatched battle.

Amidst the pandemonium, the girl seized the opportunity to escape into the woods. The staff officer, liberated from his captors, pursued her with determined vengeance. The distant sounds of gunfire gradually faded, leaving the girl in the eerie stillness of the forest.

Running and running, tripping, scraping and dodging brush, through the brush and ferns, her breath laboured and panting, she was fit, but the adrenaline was wearing off, her legs getting heavy; she needed to rest her pursuer. interrupting her peace with the whiz of lead flying past her, smacking limbs and trunks of the arboreal forest,

Beneath the canopy, a fallen tree revealed a natural cave concealed by brush. Here, in the clandestine refuge, the girl unfurled the stolen map. Illuminated by the feeble glow of a match, its revelation unveiled a chilling truth—circles around villages, an ominous declaration etched in German: "Zähler Invasion Frankreich." Notably circled was the village of Oradour-sur-Glane.

In the fragile moment of revelation, the match flickered and died, plunging the cave into darkness. A click of a safety catch resonated by her ear, an ominous prelude to an unforeseen encounter. The German officer loomed, his boots a sombre cadence against the forest floor. In a surreal twist of fate, the lit cigarette offered to the trembling girl cast a spectral glow on the officer's face.

"Ich denke, dass dies das Ende der Straße ist für Sie, meine Dame," he uttered, a chilling finale to a night woven with shadows and secrets. Sarah, shaking with fear, looks up at her captor.

***

The sun bore down on the Lodge, casting long shadows as Johnny toiled amidst the rhythm of sawing limbs. Beads of sweat traced lines down his furrowed brow, his muscles straining against the oppressive heat. His bike leaned against a stack of logs, a testament to the laborious task.

In the distance, a van materialised, its engine humming an unwelcome interruption to Johnny's solitary work. He cast a disgruntled glance over his shoulder, anticipating the intrusion, and behind the wheel was Jed. His hat was wrung between calloused hands; the air buzzed with an unspoken urgency.

Jed's typically silent demeanour now carried a weight, and Johnny, ever observant, sensed an anomaly in the air. Jed's vigilant companion, Snitch, silently witnessed the unfolding events in the van.

"Before you panic, Master Johnny," Jed began, his words hanging in the charged air.

"Panic about what? What's up?" Johnny retorted, his confusion etched on his face.

"Scallywag," Jed replied cryptically, a cloud of secrecy enveloping his words. "Can't tell, but you must drop everything and get in the van... now."

Johnny's irritation simmered, confronted with the enigmatic urgency. "You're frightening me; what's going on? I have no time for whatever this is."

Desperation etched on Jed's face, a rare sight indeed, he implored, "All I know, Master Johnny, is I have to get you in the van. Been told to get you."

Johnny's voice was filled with fear: "For what? I have all this to finish; the war can wait."

"I know nothing. Just get in the BLOODY VAN," Jed pleaded, his urgency escalating. "You don't have much time."

"You're frightening me," Johnny admitted, fingers playing with his wedding ring. Jed's gaze lingered on the symbol of commitment, but no words passed between them.

"I am frightened too," Jed confessed, revealing a revolver. The gravity of the situation hung in the air as Jed pointed to the ring, a silent plea.

Wordlessly, Johnny donned his coat, silently acknowledging the impending gravity. He approached the van, climbed in, and locked eyes with Jed. They shared an understanding—it was not good news.

Jed's van tore through the Wiltshire countryside, the engine's roar punctuating the tense silence. Johnny gazed out the window, watching the landscape blur as uncertainty unfolded beside him. The revolver nestled in Old Jed's lap, catching Johnny's eye, and in a swift motion, he snatched it away, revealing an empty barrel.

"I took 'em out," Old Jed confessed, his eyes reflecting fear and obligation. "Got the password on the telephone this afternoon, told to deliver you somewhere and to use force if necessary."

"What the hell is going on?" Johnny demanded, his frustration mingled with fear.

"I don't bloody know," Jed admitted, a rare vulnerability in his gruff demeanour. "I seriously don't bloody know. I have my suspicions. Just doing as I'm told. Whatever it is, I am scared, alright."

The van raced along rural roads, Jed navigating with a desperation that betrayed his unease. He cut through traffic, skidding around bends, a frantic dance against an unseen adversary.

As dusk settled, the van pulled into a railway bridge culvert, the engine ticking and steaming from its exertion. A black Humber staff car emerged in the growing shadows, headlights flashing in a silent exchange. It pulled up beside Jed's van, marking a clandestine meeting point.

"Looks like you need to get in that," Jed motioned toward the Humber as he spoke.

"What the hell is going on?" Johnny pressed, seeking answers that remained elusive.

"Good luck, Master Johnny. Be safe," Jed wished, a mixture of concern and resignation etched across his face.

Exiting the van, Johnny walked towards the waiting Humber, a silent prayer hanging in the air. The Humber's engine roared to life, propelling Johnny into an unknown realm. Jed left behind, haunted by the weight of the secrets he carried. Sensing the tension, Snitch whimpered and sought solace in Jed's lap.

As the Humber sped away, Jed couldn't shake the feeling that the unfolding events were somehow connected to Sarah. The van's engine hummed in the fading light, and Jed, Snitch by his side, murmured to the faithful companion, "Hey Snitch, I know, I know. He'll be back... I think it has something to do with Sarah. It has to be... Let's go home, eh?"

***

From the outside, the buildings of RAF Tempsford appeared no different from the surrounding farmsteads that dotted the landscape. Weathered timbers and thatched roofs blended seamlessly with the rural scenery, creating an illusion of agricultural normalcy. Rows of crops swayed gently in the breeze, their verdant hues masking the true nature of the facility hidden beneath.

However, beneath this facade lay a hive of activity teeming with urgency and purpose. Hangars that appeared to store farm equipment housed state-of-the-art aircraft ready for night missions deep into enemy territory. Pilots and aircrew, disguised as farmers and labourers, moved about with studied nonchalance, concealing their true identities from prying eyes.

The Humber Staff car sliced through the night, its engine humming clandestinely. Darkness cloaked RAF Tempsford, and the driver extinguished the lights as the vehicle approached farm buildings. The car manoeuvred cautiously towards a barn, slipping into the shadowed refuge. As the barn door slid shut, RAF Crewmen, disguised as farmhands, emerged to assist Johnny, blindfolded and disoriented.

Men in suits and uniformed personnel materialised within the barn's dim interior. The blindfold was lifted, revealing Johnny blinking against the gloom.

"Am I in trouble?" Johnny questioned, searching for familiar faces.

A voice, resonant and authoritative, echoed from the shadows. "No, but dear Sarah is."

"Is that you, Sir?" Johnny asked, seeking clarity.

"We don't have much time, Johnny. Remove all your clothes, including the wedding ring," Mr. Gubbins instructed.

A hint of frustration coloured Johnny's expression as he complied. Led to a table naked, he stood vulnerable as WRAF personnel dressed him in French fashion. The hum of a sewing machine filled the air as they tailored the clothes with meticulous precision.

"Has this something to do with Sarah?" Johnny pressed, yearning for answers.

"Coquelicot," Mr. Gubbins revealed, "that's her codename. Do not call her real name, please."

Confusion and weariness etched Johnny's face. "Sir, I am tired, confused, driven across England by the worst driver in the world. All I want to know is... is Coquelicot alright?"

Acknowledging Johnny's fatigue, Mr. Gubbins motioned for privacy. The RAF Crew and gentlemen retreated to a corner, sharing French cigarettes with the WRAF girls. The room exuded an air of secrecy.

"Your dear Coquelicot has been captured," Mr. Gubbins disclosed upon their return. "We are sending you to France to get her back. She holds information vital to the war effort. It's time to step up."

"Poppy, she loves poppies," Johnny murmured, his thoughts drifting to Sarah.

"Your old friend Jed says your French is very good. He guessed immediately it was Sarah," Mr Gubbins remarked, emphasising the gravity of the situation.

WRAF girls, their eyes concealed by tendrils of smoke, approached with French cigarettes. The clothing, now tailored and smelling distinctly French, completed the transformation. The atmosphere crackled with tension, and as Johnny donned the altered attire, he sensed the weight of a mission that transcended personal boundaries.

***

The cellar of L'Hôtel de Ville in St. Junien bore witness to an abysmal dance of shadows. The air hung heavy with dampness, the only illumination emanating from a solitary light dangling above. A steel bedframe, stripped bare of a mattress, occupied the space alongside a trolley bearing a rubber apron and ominous electrodes. The concrete floor, wet and chilling, hinted at past torments. In the centre of this chamber of despair knelt a figure—a girl in a petticoat.

Sarah's fragile form, once vibrant, now bore the cruel scars of torment. Blood traced a macabre trail from her broken nose, dripping onto the unforgiving floor. Two Nazi guards, stoic sentinels, observed the scene with indifferent eyes. Across from them, an SS officer lounged on a wooden chair, his posture a stark contrast to the brutality unfolding.

The SS officer drew languid drags from his cigarette, savouring the acrid taste that filled the dank air. He spoke with a casual cruelty, relishing in the power he held over the broken figure before him.

"We can keep this going for as long as we want," he taunted, exhaling smoke with disdain. "Your friends are going to be dead soon anyhow, just a matter of when."

Her spirit, seemingly intact despite the physical anguish, Sarah pleaded for mercy. "I know nothing. I am just a seamstress."

The SS officer dismissed her words as lies, recalling the moment he captured her in the woods. A sinister grin etched on his face; he revelled in the apparent victory.

"I know nothing of what you talk about. Please let me go," Sarah implored, her voice a frail whisper.

With a cruel flick of his cigarette, the SS officer directed a shower of sparks towards Sarah. She winced, summoning the strength to lift her gaze. Bruises adorned her face like a grotesque mask, and her eyes, swollen from tears and abuse, conveyed a haunting vulnerability.

The SS officer, displaying a perverse theatricality, pulled out a hip flask and poured brandy into a cup. Taking a leisurely sip, he circled his finger in the air, feigning boredom. A wicked smile played on his lips as he revelled in the twisted dance of suffering, leaving the beleaguered girl to face the grim uncertainty of her fate.

From the outside of the door frame, blue flashes of light and shrieks of pain, the door hiding the depravations and horror inside, between the flashes, the muted laughter of the SS officer.

***

RAF Tempsford lay shrouded in the obsidian cloak of night, a clandestine dance between shadows and secrets. The air crackled with tension as Johnathon, a figure moulded by darkness, waddled with purpose toward the farm buildings, their true nature veiled beneath an artful facade of pastoral innocence. The Lockheed Hudson, an ominous sentinel of the covert operation, loomed on the runway, disguised as just another fixture of the nocturnal landscape.

As Johnathon moved closer, the illusion unravelled—the painted buildings revealed their proper metallic form, and the vehicles shed their rural masquerade—an intricate deception designed to shield the operation from prying eyes. The buildings were painted to look like a farmhouse and barn, and hedgerows and fields were painted over the concrete from the air to look like a normal farm.

Draped in a jumpsuit, a parachute, and a round helmet, Johnathon stood under the ominous shadow of the Hudson. A Parachute Jump Instructor, a spectral figure with wisdom etched into the lines of his face, accompanied him. The runway, not as solid as it seemed, bore the illusion of a hedge painted upon it.

The Parachute Instructor, a veteran of the clandestine arts, pierced the silence, his voice a low growl in the night air. "Have you ever jumped from a Hudson before?"

"No, not jumped from a Hudson," Johnathon replied, his voice a whisper carried away by the night breeze.

"What did you jump from before?" the instructor inquired, peering into the depths of Johnathon's eyes.

"Nothing. This is my first go," Johnathon admitted, a tremor of uncertainty beneath his facade of stoicism.

"Sorry, this will be your first jump?" The instructor's disbelief was palpable, a testament to the gravity of the situation.

"Can't be hard. Just fall; I hope the damn thing opens. You can't miss the ground," Johnathon declared, a nonchalant shrug masking the turmoil within.

The Parachute Instructor turned to Mr. Gubbins, seeking answers in the stoic face of their enigmatic overseer. Mr Gubbins shook his head in silent acknowledgement.

"Sir, you told me he had completed training. What type of agent does training without a jumps course? Well, I be, well, I be. Good luck, son," the instructor muttered, his voice a blend of frustration and resignation.

Assisted by the instructor, Johnathon ascended the short steps to the Hudson, his heartbeat a drumroll of anticipation. Mr. Gubbins, the puppet master pulling unseen strings, offered final instructions. "You will be met by your contact when you land. Taken by the Maquis. Further instructions await with them."

"I will get 'poppy' back, promise," Johnathon vowed, the weight of his words echoing in the obsidian night.

The instructor hopped down, leaving Johnathon alone on the threshold of the unknown. The aircraft, a behemoth in the moonlit night, awaited its passenger. A pact sealed, a dance with destiny set to commence in the clandestine ballet of war and espionage.

**

L'Hôtel de Ville St Junien was a spectral haven of secrets, its corridors echoing the clandestine whispers of wartime intrigue. The cellar door creaked open, shattering the stillness of the night. The SS officer, an embodiment of rigid discipline, snapped to attention, his starched uniform betraying no sign of emotion. A senior Gestapo officer, compact yet exuding an aura of lethal precision, entered the room with the quiet menace of a predator surveying its domain.

His gaze swept over the scene, taking in the kneeling figure of Sarah, drenched and battered. The room reeked of tension, and the puddle beneath Sarah spoke of violence. The Gestapo officer's eyes flicked towards the guards, who released their grip on Sarah's arms at his silent command. A blanket materialised a meagre attempt at comfort for the broken woman at his feet.

Approaching her, the Gestapo officer knelt in the bloodied puddle, unperturbed by the wetness. His leather-gloved hand, an instrument of both authority and cruelty, cradled her injured face. Sarah, barely conscious, attempted to resist, but her efforts manifested as feeble spittle. The Gestapo officer whispered, "I know you can hear me, Geronimo."

Standing abruptly, he confronted the SS officer, a man marked by the turmoil of his own brutality. "She is in my care now. Your amateur attempts at interrogation," the Gestapo officer sneered, disdain etched into his features. "Look at her, unable to stand, let alone speak."

The SS officer, a puppet of Berlin's demands, stammered in justification. "I was trying to find the network. She was not speaking or telling the truth. Time is of the essence here."

The Gestapo officer's voice sliced through the air, a whip

cracking in the darkness. "How can she tell the truth if you break her jaw? Such thuggery brutality. Berlin can wait."

"But..." the SS officer protested, a futile defence against the torrent of rage from his superior.

"SILENCE!" The Gestapo officer's voice thundered. "Or your next order will be at the Eastern Front. I am Berlin." The guard was summoned to escort Sarah away, leaving the two officers alone in the oppressive atmosphere.

"Take off your gloves. Yes, take them off," the Gestapo officer commanded. The SS officer hesitated but complied. The Gestapo officer approached electrodes in hand and placed them against the SS officer's skin. "Here, for demonstration. I will put it on low."

"But, we can show it on the prisoner," the SS officer suggested, desperation lingering in his voice.

"Just amuse me. I still have to make a report." The Gestapo officer's smile betrayed a cruel pleasure as he turned up the voltage, unleashing indescribable pain. The SS officer, writhing in agony, collapsed to the floor, the acrid scent of burning flesh permeating the air.

The Gestapo officer exited the cell, leaving behind the tortured SS officer. Light blue smoke curled upward, a macabre waltz accompanying the man's silent suffering. Amidst Sarah's personal effects lay a solid gold poppy brooch – a relic of her shattered world, now in the possession of a man with a penchant for pain.

The night air hung heavy with the acrid scent of betrayal as the Gestapo Officer emerged from the shadows, stepping over the lifeless bodies of the two German guards, their throats cruelly slit. A haunting tableau of violence marked the cellar door's threshold as blood pooled and seeped under the crack.

From the depths of the darkness, figures materialised – Maquis partisans, their faces etched with the determination of those fighting for liberation. Shedding his oppressive uniform, the Gestapo Officer cast away his jacket, glasses, and hat, revealing a man transformed by circumstance. In a fluid motion, a Maquis fighter tossed a farmer's jacket to him, a camouflage cloak to shield him from the enemy's gaze.

The Maquis cradled the limp form of Sarah, an act of defiance against the brutality she had endured. As they moved through the shadows, the Gestapo Officer revealed his true identity with the utterance of coded words that carried the weight of salvation.

"Hello, dear. I am Geoffrey, code word Coquelicol, and the safe word is Geronimo," he declared, his voice a whisper of reassurance. "Me and the boys are going to get you out of here. You are safe."

Sarah, barely conscious, mumbled in acknowledgement, her response a feeble echo of trust. "Geronimo."

"Me and the boys will get you home, dear. Just in time for tea and toast," Geoffrey promised, the words a beacon of hope in the oppressive darkness. Armed with a fierce determination, the Maquis embarked on their perilous journey, carrying with them the wounded but unbroken spirit of a woman caught in the crossfire of war. The strange Englishman that brought them on this perilous rescue. Sarah is a husk of a girl, fetal and without power, secrets locked in her head.

***

Johnny stood by the aircraft's rear door, his face a blend of determination and anxiety. The loadmaster, a weathered figure, meticulously checked Johnny's parachute equipment and a storage container. As the loadmaster gave a reassuring thumbs up, Johnny grappled with the cacophony assaulting his senses – the metallic scent, the deafening roar, and the turbulence challenging his resolve to rescue Sarah.

A shrill whistle pierced the air from the front of the aircraft, signalling impending action. A seasoned hand at such operations, the loadmaster reached out and swung the door open. With a firm grip, he pulled Johnny towards the yawning expanse. An anxious smile played on Johnny's lips, a nervous attempt to dissuade the inevitable. The unyielding loadmaster checked the static line, the final tether to the world within the aircraft.

Two sharp whistles followed, and Johnny was forcibly propelled into the abyss. "Geronimo," he muttered, a prayer and a rallying cry against the onslaught of the slipstream. Tumbling into the void, he experienced a violent jerk, stealing the air from his lungs before an eerie silence enveloped him.

Amidst the darkness, the moonlight revealed distorted shapes below – a patchwork of woods and fields. The distant flashes of an aerial raid painted a surreal canvas. The realisation struck Johnny that he was descending into hostile territory, the urgency intensifying with each passing moment.

His descent, initially tumultuous, culminated in a landing that mirrored a sack of potatoes hitting the earth. The wind, however, had other plans. It caught his parachute and dragged him until an abrupt stop left him winded. Eyes closed, he braced for the unknown.

Upon opening his eyes, Johnny discovered himself surrounded by armed farmers. In the midst stood a man with an S phone transmitter orchestrating the extraction. With efficiency bordering on choreography, they stripped Johnny of his parachute and outer clothing, revealing a small case, hat, and jacket.

Silently, a pistol changed hands, finding a concealed refuge in Johnny's jacket. No words were exchanged, only purposeful actions in the cloak of darkness. The group, now a clandestine patrol, moved towards the edge of the woods, Johnny's breathing echoing in the quietude. This was no simulation; it was the stark reality of a mission unfolding in the shadows.

***

The rear doors of the nondescript boulangerie van swung open, revealing the clandestine rescue mission in progress. Sarah, once a figure of resilience and tenacity, now limp and doll-like, was passed into the vehicle's recesses, accompanied by Geoffrey, his vigilant eyes fixed on the surroundings, a sterling machine gun clutched in his hands. The night bore witness to their silent exchange, an unspoken understanding of the stakes.

As the van eased into the shadows, the Maquis operatives dispersed in calculated chaos, each slipping away into the cloak of darkness to circumvent the German positions. The van, a fleeting silhouette against the night, continued its journey, weaving through the silent streets of St Junien en route to the sanctuary of the countryside.

The van's tyres whispered against the cobblestones, the only audible sound in the tense silence. Seated within, Sarah embodied a mixture of relief and trepidation, the gravity of the situation etched across her face, falling into unconsciousness and fatigue. Beside her, Geoffrey, the guardian angel with a machine gun, maintained a stoic vigilance, every muscle tuned to the looming dangers.

The town faded behind them, replaced by the sprawling darkness of the countryside. The night held its breath. Secrets whispered in the rustle of leaves as the van navigated through unlit paths, away from the prying eyes of the enemy.

In the confines of the van, Sarah's thoughts were a tumultuous sea – a blend of gratitude for her impending freedom and the uncertainty of what lay ahead. The Maquis, silent shadows in the periphery, executed their manoeuvres with practised ease, a symphony of covert operations playing out under the moonlit sky.

***

The serene atmosphere of a small farm veiled the covert activities unravelling beneath the cloak of night. Hay bales, silhouetted against the timeworn walls of a barn, offered inconspicuous cover. In the darkness, a group of shadowy figures led Johnny towards the barn, where a secret entrance was unveiled as one of the operatives discreetly shifted a hay bale. Silently, they descended into the concealed depths of the barn.

The subterranean refuge revealed itself as they reached the bottom. At a table scattered with maps and equipment, an elderly man, the weight of war etched on his face, smoked a pipe. The seasoned strategist Raymond looked up with a weathered gaze, extending a gruff welcome to the newly arrived operative.

"Call me Raymond. Welcome to HQ. Poppy has been successfully extracted from the town hall tonight. She'll be sheltered in the forest with the British Forces, awaiting transfer tomorrow night. An aircraft will rendezvous for both of you. Keep your name under wraps; it's a matter of life and death. Do you have any questions?"

Johnny, grappling with the surreal turn of events, voiced his uncertainty.

"I'm not sure what I'm doing here."

Raymond, the sage of the resistance, leaned forward, his eyes bearing the wisdom of a seasoned warrior.

"Our intel from the Town Hall indicated Poppy was in dire straits. We need you to make her talk. You share a history with this operator—details I'm not privy to, nor do I need to be."

Johnny's disorientation lingered, compounded by the echoes

of gunfire from his recent descent.

"I saw flashes and fighting as I landed."

"Experienced operatives are engaging the enemy in that very fray. I, on the other hand, landed over a year ago and have exhausted my luck. Your task is critical. Sleep tonight; tomorrow, you work for us. A word of advice—curb the habit of rubbing your ring finger when nervous. Here, you're a solitary man. Such idiosyncrasies can prove fatal. Emulate the locals, their mannerisms, their habits. It might just buy you the time you need. Now, rest."

As Raymond gestured towards a makeshift resting area—a blend of hay and a worn mattress—Johnny absorbed the weight of his mission. The subterranean chamber, a nexus of covert operations, bore witness to the gravity of their cause. In the quiet cocoon of the night, Johnny surrendered to sleep, unknowingly stepping into the vortex of a perilous clandestine world Alien to him.

***

The boulangerie van rolled to a silent stop amidst the dense cover of the woods. Shadows emerged from the inky blackness, figures cloaked in the clandestine attire of the Maquis, bearing arms. Two of them carried a makeshift stretcher, gently placing Sarah, known as Poppy, onto it. With determined yet cautious strides, they ventured deeper into the labyrinth of trees, navigating the obscurity with practised ease.

A small camp materialised within the heart of the woods, concealed by nature's cloak. In the stillness, four figures emerged, adorned in ragged British Military Uniform Battle dress—symbols stripped away, rank and insignia forsaken. Brian Brown, his eyes etched with weariness, drew attention to the limp figure on the stretcher.

"Ere, Boss, look what the animals have done to her."

Major Carstairs, the authoritative figure among them, directed his attention to the wounded Poppy.

"Poor thing. Doc, please sort her out. We need her fit to get out of here."

Doc, the seasoned healer with a past including human and animal patients, responded with a wry smile.

"Yes, boss. Come on, my dear. Fifteen years on Harley Street— you're in good hands."

Brian smirked, "Yes, but you were a vet."

"Warmest finger in London," Doc quipped, presenting his finger with a wink at Sarah.

"Doc, stop frightening the patient," admonished Major Carstairs. The stretcher found its place in a makeshift hide as Doc and an orderly entered, commencing their treatment. Sarah's murmurs, a symphony of fear, resonated within the secluded space. A calming presence, Doc sat beside her, offering a reassuring hand.

In a separate tent, Major Carstairs sought answers from Doc.

"Is she going to be alright to travel?"

Doc, his hands marked by a lifetime of healing, responded with a gravity that bespoke the severity of Poppy's condition.

"If Geoffrey had been an hour later, this would have been a seance. Nearly every bone broken, electrocution burns. I would be surprised if she ever has children."

The unexpected saviour, Geoffrey, entered the scene, now adorned in battledress. His voice held a touch of relief.

"She's looking a lot better than when I found her. Well done, Doc. Thought we lost her."

The revelation caught Major Carstairs and Doc off guard. Geoffrey approached Sarah, placing a significant gold brooch in her hand and offering words of encouragement.

"Good luck charm, is it, young lady? You hold onto that."

***

The French valley sprawled before Johnny and his Maquis Group, a patchwork of rural landscapes and woods. Fifteen rugged men, seasoned by the harsh realities of their surroundings, traversed the varied terrain in silence, a silent march guided by the expertise of those intimately acquainted with the land.

As they reached the treeline, Johnny, the Englishman amidst these hardened fighters, halted the procession. His eyes scanned the seemingly tranquil landscape, his instincts tingling with a warning that eluded his comrades.

"Why'd you stop? It's clear, look..." The Maquis Leader urged, his impatience evident.

Johnny, however, stood his ground, eyes fixed on the nuances of nature that escaped the casual observer.

"No, it's not. Look," Johnny countered, pointing out the subtleties that betrayed the illusion of serenity. "The cows are down there, gathering. To the left, no birds. Over the hedge, birds are starting to roost."

A dismissive scoff from the Maquis Leader followed, his confidence in the familiar surroundings clouding his judgment.

"And so, we go," he declared.

But Johnny, the foreigner in this familiar landscape, saw the anomalies for what they were—a foreboding sign in the natural order.

"Cows are inquisitive. They'll go and look at what's different in the field. And the birds should be roosting in the trees above. Something's not quite right, trust me," Johnny warned, his conviction met with disdain.

"You English, you are a lâche," the Maquis Leader sneered, branding Johnny a coward.

"Lâche, coward?" Johnny echoed, the accusation met with a challenge in his eyes.

Undeterred, the Maquis Leader signaled his men to move forward, marching abreast in an extended line. Johnny, however, lingered, a silent witness to the unfolding events.

The arrogant Maquis Commander swaggered into the middle of the field, his gaze returning to Johnny with a triumphant shrug—an "I told you so" arrogance. In that moment, a sudden impact against his shoulder sent him sprawling in pain, the sharp crack of a hidden machine gun echoing through the valley.

Chaos ensued as some of the Maquis fighters assumed firing positions, only to be pinned down by the relentless hail of bullets from the concealed machine gun. Johnny, wide-eyed and on edge, sought refuge behind a log. His escort mirrored his uncertainty, unsure of the next move in this unexpected battleground.

***

The French rural road, veiled in the soft glow of daylight, witnessed a desperate exodus. The Citroen U23, laden with brave fighters and their precious cargo, meandered through the labyrinthine lanes. Sarah lay on a stretcher inside, the medic and his comrades tending to her battered form.

Geoffrey steered the truck with determined urgency, a soldier at his side navigating the winding path. A small French car, leading the way, carried resistance fighters on the tense journey. Sarah, lost in delirium, repeated the word "our" like a haunting mantra, her mind a battleground of confusion and pain.

As the convoy approached a bend, the distant staccato of machine gun fire echoed through the air. Doc, the medic, acknowledged the ominous sound, recognising the dire straits of their comrades.

"Bloody hell, sounds like the other guys are in a right pickle," Doc remarked, a note of concern in his voice.

Geoffrey, leaning halfway out of his window, relayed the decision to press on. "We will carry on and pray no one has heard it. We need her alive back in London as soon as possible."

A thumbs-up from Doc signalled to understand, and the journey continued. Doc sought to comfort the delirious Sarah, assuring her they were nearing safety. However, her mind remained ensnared by a singular word, "our."

Abruptly, a familiar adversary emerged—the German Staff Car, menacingly trailing the underpowered truck. The SS Officer bandaged and visibly weakened, leaned out the window, firing his Luger at the retreating vehicle.

As the makeshift airfield drew near, Doc unleashed a barrage of gunfire from the back of the truck, attempting to stave off the relentless pursuit. Sarah, now fully awake and screaming, felt the hot metal of spent rounds hitting her face. Undeterred, Doc, with a large knife in hand, attempted to cut the restraining straps on her stretcher.

"Hello, my pretty. I am Doc. I am with the British Army," he spoke with a mix of reassurance and determination. "Even though officially we are not here, we are taking you home. Let us do our job, eh? Who dares wins."

Sarah, her mouth and jaw swollen, eyes filled with tears, struggled to communicate. "Oura, Oura," she repeated, desperate to convey something crucial. Ignoring her, Doc resumed firing, hot brass raining down on her.

The truck's rear tyre exploded, deepening into a bank and hedge. The engine stalled, leaving them vulnerable. Stunned and with a damaged weapon, Doc struggled to regain his composure. A bullet pierced the bulkhead, striking the driver, who slumped over the steering wheel.

Undeterred by the chaos, a small French car executed a daring manoeuvre, confronting the German Staff Car head-on. The staff car, with a passenger wielding an MP 40, retaliated, riddling the car with bullets. An anticlimactic descent into a ditch followed, but the SS Officer and his companion pressed forward, closing in for the final confrontation.

***

The French valley, once tranquil, now echoed with the harsh symphony of warfare. Johnny, alongside his French comrades, found themselves in a relentless crossfire. Pinned down by the ruthless German machine gun, Johnny's mind raced for an escape plan.

Crawling towards what seemed like a stream, he soon realised it was a sewage ditch—brackish water mixed with slurry, a vile concoction of the farmland. Undeterred, Johnny gestured to his escort, who, understanding the desperate move, crossed himself before following Johnny into the foul darkness.

As they submerged themselves in the stinking water, the sewage ditch provided an unexpected refuge, allowing them to flank the German machine gun. Amid the relentless gunfire, tragedy struck. Johnny's escort, climbing up prematurely, fell victim to enemy fire, fatally wounded. Johnny seized the fallen rifle, pushing forward through the murky depths.

Gagging and covered in filth, Johnny pressed on, propelled by a fierce determination to alter the course of the battle. Meanwhile, frustrated by the Englishman's apparent absence, the Maquis leader rallied his remaining fighters. The unrelenting German machine gun repeatedly thwarted their attempts to advance.

In pain, the Maquis leader crawled to a vantage point and surveyed the battlefield with a spyglass in hand. The source of their torment became clear—an enemy machine gun mounted on a motorbike and sidecar. The situation seemed dire until a muddy figure, concealed head to toe, raised a rifle to fire.

Click.

Realising the weapon was malfunctioning, the German machine gunner engaged in a brutal hand-to-hand struggle.

The muddy figure, better trained, ruthlessly plunged the bayonet into the German's neck, ending the conflict with a grim finality.

As the French fighters slowly rose, the muddy figure emerged from the sidecar, wiping filth from his face. To their surprise, it was Johnny.

"Sacre Bleu, it's you, Englishman!" exclaimed the Maquis leader, patting Johnny on the back and regretting it instantly as he tried to wipe away the muck.

Johnny focused on the ongoing gunfire and silenced them with a gesture. "You hear that? It's the sound of gunfire. That's Poppy. I need to get to her now. Can you ride a bike with that arm?"

The leader listened, nodding in acknowledgement. Despite his mud-covered appearance, Johnny was the beacon of hope they needed in the chaos of war.

***

The French rural road bore the scars of conflict as the SS officer, hands bandaged and grimacing in pain, approached the truck. With a visceral pull, he removed the dressing from his wounds, revealing burned and blistered skin. His hands, damaged but determined, extracted a pistol from its leather holster.

Accompanied by two men, they approached the truck cautiously. The SS officer, glancing at the seemingly lifeless Sarah and the bodies of Doc and Geoffrey, kicked Geoffrey's lifeless form—a recognition of the man who had electrocuted him earlier. Suddenly, Doc and Geoffrey sprang to life, dispatching the guards with lethal precision. The SS officer, momentarily stunned, found himself face to face with the knife-wielding Sarah.

With a swift motion, Sarah grabbed the SS officer's chin, exposing his vulnerable neck. The knife descended, extinguishing the light in his eyes as he crumpled to the ground. Sarah, depleted from the ordeal, collapsed, dry heaving. Doc and Geoffrey rushed to her side, carefully prying the knife from her trembling hand.

In the distance, the sound of an approaching plane grew louder. The SAS team focused on their rescue and barely noticed the French Maquis resistance arriving on German motorbikes, one displaying the Free French Army cross. The tension dissipated as they joined forces, aiding Sarah and retrieving the fallen German officer's belongings.

The Lysander plane touched down, its engine still running as they struggled to lift Sarah onto the stretcher. A surprise awaited them as a dirty, smelly figure squeezed into the plane beside her—a mysterious addition to their ragtag group.

Once a battleground, the landscape now witnessed an unlikely alliance, united by the shadows of betrayal and the pursuit of survival. The plane's engine roared, carrying them away from the scene of chaos, leaving the rural road to the ghosts of conflict and the men who for a brief moment kept the wolf from the door.
The aircraft flew into the enveloping dusk.

In the belly of the Lysander aircraft, the evening sky enveloped Sarah in blankets, her trembling form cradled by Johnny. The roar of the plane's engines filled the compartment, but a sudden jolt shattered the rhythmic hum.

"WE HAVE A GERMAN FIGHTER ON OUR TAIL! HOLD ON, WE WILL GET YOU TO BLIGHTY," the pilot's voice echoed, urgency piercing through the cacophony. Bullets hammered the aircraft; each hit sent shudders through its frame. Despite the onslaught, the determined pilots fought to reach the safety of England.

The navigator fell, a life snuffed out by the relentless hail of bullets. The wounded but resolute pilot steered the aircraft toward the English coastline. Johnny, realising the dire situation, reached through to grasp the control column, supporting the injured pilot in their desperate bid for survival.

As the Lysander descended, the white cliffs and a stretch of beach came into view beyond the cockpit. The battered and wounded plane approached the grassy fields atop the cliffs, guided by fading hope. Just as it seemed they might escape the clutches of the German fighter, flak exploded in the sky, sealing their fate.

The fatal blow struck the pilot, ending his struggle. The German fighter retreated, leaving the Lysander hurtling toward the unforgiving sea. Johnny, summoning every ounce of strength, managed to level the plane momentarily. Turning to Sarah, he understood the inevitable.

"WE ARE GOING TO HAVE TO SWIM!" he shouted over the chaos.

"GErrriiimoo," Sarah responded, her weakened voice carrying determination.

"THAT'S RIGHT, GERONIMO!"

The Lysander crashed into the sea, swallowed by the relentless waves. In the darkness, the once thunderous noise was replaced by the haunting sounds of the ocean. Smashing against the thin frame of the aircraft, water washing over the glass seeking any opening so the maelstrom can swallow,

In the inky waters of the English Channel, Johnny, bearing Sarah's weight, swam determinedly toward the distant beach.

Their bodies, numbed by the freezing water, pressed on through the night. The crashing waves echoed the relentless trials they faced.

As they approached the shingle, exhaustion set in, and Johnny's strength waned. In the dim light, the cold reality of barbed wire awaited them. Undeterred, Johnny manoeuvred through the obstacles, dragging Sarah towards the elusive safety of the shore.

A rowboat with two sailors emerged from the shadows. One aimed a rifle at the struggling figures, while the other illuminated the scene with a flickering torch. On the beach, soldiers, alerted by the commotion, hurried towards them, rifles aimed.

"HALT! WHO GOES THERE?" barked an English soldier, his voice cutting through the night.

Johnny, gasping for breath, managed a whisper, "WHITE 1212 POPPY SCALLYWAG."

"TELL ME WHO YOU ARE, OR WE FIRE!" demanded the soldier.

"Hold it; calm down, lads. They're civilians," intervened an English officer, recognising the dire situation.

Still clutching the shivering Sarah, Johnny uttered, "Cold, so cold."

The officer, grasping the urgency, ordered his men to get on the telephone exchange and call "Whitehall 1212 Poppy Scallywag." Blankets were draped over the exhausted duo as they were ushered away from the water's edge.

"My god, they're escapees. Look at this poor woman. She's been tortured," the officer murmured. Soldiers scrambled to assist Johnny and Sarah, their bodies near the brink of hypothermia.

Shedding his coat, the English officer covered Sarah while Johnny, worn and battered, clung to her. As they were carried away from the beach, Sarah's hand clutched tightly to the gold brooch—their emblem of endurance and survival.

***

In the tranquil afternoon garden, Andy shared a tale that unfolded like an ancient manuscript, each word etching a secret history onto the ears of his captive audience—Judy, Derek, and Danny. Their faces bore expressions ranging from scepticism to disbelief, their minds grappling with a narrative that seemed more fiction than fact.

Derek, eyebrows furrowed, questioned the authenticity of the revelations. "This is unbelievable. I'm not sure if I quite believe it, Judy?"

Judy, with a measured scepticism, sought clarification. "Mum and Dad in occupied France; if their mission was so secret, how do you know all this?"

Andy, gazing into the distant folds of memory, explained calmly. "Don't forget, I was close friends, almost your Dad's brother before the war. I pieced together what happened from them, and another told me what happened."

"Another? I don't understand," Derek confessed, his confusion mirrored in his furrowed brow.

"Danny, I am tired; it's getting cold. May you?" Andy requested, the fatigue evident in his voice. Danny nodded, understanding, and wheeled Andy into the warmth of the home, leaving Derek and Judy in contemplative silence.

As Danny attended to Andy, the shadows of the past lingered in the air. Derek, undeterred, continued to grapple with the revelations. "This is boys' own Andy McNab stuff. Mum and Dad, spies in France—I don't understand."

Judy's mind, wrestling with the implications, voiced a thought that echoed a lingering doubt. "What if what the wing commander says is true? He has all his faculties. Why would he lie?"

Meanwhile, in the confines of the room, Danny assisted Andy, adjusting blankets and ensuring his comfort. In a quiet moment, Andy's gaze fell upon a black and white photo, a relic of a bygone era. The framed image held the essence of a clandestine mission—four figures frozen in time: Andy, Johnny, Sarah, and Mr. Gubbins.

"Could you pass that photo over, please?" Andy requested, his eyes fixed on the tableau frozen in silver and grey.

Danny, picking up the picture, looked at it before passing it over to Andy. The veteran's smile, a mixture of warmth and melancholy, touched his eyes as he gently rubbed the glass as if caressing the memory of someone dearly missed.

"Oh, oh, Andy, I did not realise," Danny spoke with a sudden realisation.

"No one did then; it was illegal," Andy replied, his voice carrying the weight of a clandestine past.

Danny's eyes fixed on the photo, and he understood. "You're not looking at Johnny or Sarah, but that man next to you."

"We called him Mr. Gubbins. That was not his real name; he used that name to grease the wheels with paperwork. Men from the Ministry seeing that name signed on paperwork moved mountains," Andy revealed, the weight of history etched in his features.

"You cared for him. It was him who told you what happened to Sarah and Johnny," Danny surmised.

Andy smiled at Danny, silently acknowledging the unspoken bond they shared. Reaching out, Andy held Danny's hand with a gentleness that transcended words.

"Wingco, I never realised; you hid it so well," Danny murmured, his voice carrying a newfound understanding of the man behind the stoic facade.

***

In the eerie stillness of the night, Andy lay in bed, the soft embrace of weekend leave wrapping around him. The distant echoes of war seemed to pause, allowing a fleeting moment of respite. However, the tranquillity shattered abruptly, fractured by the unmistakable sounds of a car engine, slamming doors, and hurried footsteps on the drive.

Rushing downstairs, Andy's eyes widened as the door swung open, revealing a scene that would etch itself into the fabric of his memory. Johnathon, his comrade in arms, stood at the threshold, cradling Sarah. The living room awaited them as a temporary sanctuary, and Andy could sense the weight of unspoken stories etched into their battered forms.

Sarah lay on the sofa, a portrait of suffering—her face swollen, bruised, cuts tracing a map of agony on her skin. Emaciated and fragile, she bore the scars of an ordeal that defied comprehension. Johnathon followed, a mirror image of anguish, his body a canvas of wounds, though not as severe as Sarah's.

Andy, a silent witness to their arrival, stood there, stunned by the brutal reality. The room held a heavy silence, punctuated only by the laboured breaths of the wounded.

The man in the suit, Mr. Gubbins, looked at Andy. "Flight Lieutenant Bryce, you are not to tell a soul what you see here tonight, do you understand?"

An army major, stern and unyielding, reinforced the command. "That is a direct order. You are not to tell anyone about it. Do you understand?"

Andy, torn between duty and humanity, struggled to

comprehend the gravity of the situation. "No, but look at her and him."

The army major, unmoved, delivered a chilling ultimatum. "Do you want to spend the rest of the war alone in the glasshouse?"

"No, no sir, but look at her. Do you want me to fetch the doctor? Johnny needs a brandy, I need a brandy," Andy pleaded, his concern overriding the orders.

Mr. Gubbins intervened, revealing a veiled truth. "Flight Lieutenant Bryce, if you are pushed into what happened to Mr. and Mrs. Hodges, she was caught in the blitz with a blast. She was sent to the countryside to convalesce, understood?"

Andy nodded, brandy bottle in hand, offering solace that seemed insufficient in the face of their ordeal. "Here is my secretary's number. Call me if anything happens. Anything, no matter how small or innocuous it seems. Good man. Johnny promises never to leave the house until she is well. Here are some extra ration cards. Look after them like they are your own."

As the weight of responsibility settled, Andy's eyes locked onto Mr. Gubbins for a moment too long. There was an unspoken exchange, a fleeting connection that transcended the given orders.

"Good man. Jed will be here in the morning to make arrangements with you," Mr. Gubbins stated, the echoes of secrecy resonating in the room. The door closed behind them, leaving Andy with the silent testimony of war's merciless grip on those who bore its scars.

***

The underpass, a gloomy passage etched into the heart of the council estate, became a desolate canvas as the evening descended. Daphne, wearied from her shift, approached the dimly lit entrance. A moment of hesitation gripped her, her gaze sweeping down the length of the underpass. The weight of the cross around her neck, a silent talisman, offered a brief pause of reassurance.

With a breath, Daphne stepped into the underpass, her pace quickening. The narrow walls loomed around her, a labyrinth of concrete shadows. Her cautious eyes scanned the surroundings, a subtle tension in her movements betraying the underlying unease.

At the end of the passage, a left turn beckoned. She navigated the corner, disappearing from sight. The silence was palpable before erupting into a cacophony of muffled cries and desperate shouts. The air crackled with tension as Daphne's hand, fingers tightly clutching the cross, emerged and fell limply onto the cold pavement.

The tragedy held its breath, a fleeting moment frozen in time. Unaware of the tragedy unfolding steps away, a passerby approached with a pushchair. The mundane collided with the macabre as the woman's eyes widened at the sight before her. Panic set in, and a phone emerged, a lifeline in the face of horror.

In the fading light, the underpass concealed its secrets, the convergence of shadows marking the abrupt end to an ordinary evening. Daphne's silent scream echoed through the cold, unforgiving walls, leaving a chilling imprint on the underpass—a place where shadows whispered tales of the unforeseen. The brightly coloured graffiti mocked the silence.

***

The wail of sirens punctuated the evening air as a police car pulled up outside Fair Oaks Retirement Home. As he passed through the dimly lit corridor, Danny felt a sudden chill crawl up his spine. The uniforms approached, and he instinctively opened the door, the weight of their presence sinking into his bones. A conversation ensued, words exchanged in muted tones, and Danny, overwhelmed, crumpled against the wall, the shock etched on his face like a haunting portrait.

As the police car eased out of the driveway, it carried with it a broken man, leaving behind the oppressive stillness of Fair Oaks.

***

Inside the intensive care ward, the sterile environment crackled with the dissonance of medical machinery. The police, silent sentinels at the door, awaited a glimpse into the grim tableau that awaited them.

Daphne lay on the bed, a spectral figure marred by the brutality she had endured. Her face, once a testament to the passage of time, now bore the cruel marks of violence—swollen, bleeding, and adorned with cuts. Tubes and wires tethered her to life, a fragile thread in the face of a merciless assault.

Danny entered, his steps tentative, the echo of his shoes lost in the chorus of beeping machines. He approached Daphne, her frail form a stark contrast to the vibrant spirit he had known. Bravery etched across his face, he pressed a tender kiss to her forehead. The sound of machines reached a crescendo, a dissonant symphony echoing the chaos within him. As tears streamed down his face, he covered his ears, seeking solace in the temporary silence he imposed.

Beyond the glass window, PC Jane Moore observed Danny, a solitary figure navigating the depths of despair. She dabbed her eye with a handkerchief, a futile attempt to stave off the shared grief that permeated the room. The nurse, a guardian of the afflicted, approached her.

"Is she going to make it?" the police officer inquired, her voice hushedly.

"The next couple of hours will tell," the nurse replied, her gaze fixed on Daphne's fragile form. "Severely beaten."

The police officer's thoughts drifted to the malevolent force behind this brutality. "Who would do such a thing to a lovely lady like Daphne?"

The nurse, ever the bearer of grim truths, mentioned the tramazine packets, their emptiness echoing a sinister tale. The officer's furrowed brow betrayed a mix of frustration and determination.

"Trammies? What was she doing with Trammies?" the officer questioned.

"She will not be able to tell you for a long while, even if she survives the night," the nurse said.

The officer, her suspicions veiled, declared a shift in the investigation. "We are treating this as a mugging. We need to step this up to attempted murder. Poor Danny—they tried to murder him too."

"They?" the nurse inquired.

"I have my suspicions," the officer admitted. "But the slippery bastard always seems to get away or have an alibi. I'll wait with Danny, whether he needs me or not." The lines of her face revealed a resolve to unveil the shadows that lingered on the streets that night. The sodium streets seem dim with the city's collective shame.

***

The quaint cottage stood silent under the muted daylight, a seemingly serene tableau that belied the turbulence within. A curious spectre of the village, Miss Rutherford traversed the cobblestone path, the air heavy with unspoken tension. A distant murmur of discontent whispered through the air, drawing her attention like a moth to a flame.

As she approached the cottage's weathered windows, the screams and shouts crescendoed from within. Intrigued and apprehensive, Miss Rutherford crept closer, her curiosity wresting control from the caution that pricked at her senses. Peering through the window's timeworn panes, the grim tableau unfolded before her eyes.

Sarah, ensconced in the bed, became a canvas of despair, her frail form marred by a tapestry of cuts and bruises. The shadows of a sinister ballet danced across her skin, each mark an indelible record of a torment not meant for the light of day. Beside her, Johnathon, sleeves rolled up, seemed a reluctant actor in this macabre drama, his presence a testament to a struggle etched into the lines of his face.

A sudden interruption shattered the eerie tableau as Miss Rutherford grappled with the scene before her. Old Jed, weathered and grizzled, emerged from around the cottage corner, a shotgun cradled in his arms like an extension of his wrath.

"Oi, you old witch, clear off! Go on, clear off, sticking your nose where it doesn't belong," Old Jed barked, his voice a raspy growl echoing through the air.

Startled, Miss Rutherford recoiled, a fleeting witness banished by the gatekeeper of this hidden tragedy. Emerging from the doorway, Andy sought to challenge her intrusion, but she vanished like a weasel, leaving only the echo of her hurried footsteps.

The silence followed was pregnant with unspoken truths, the cottage witnessing a secret tale of pain and survival. The spectre of Miss Rutherford's fleeting presence lingered as a ghostly reminder of the shadows that clung to the cottage walls, concealing a narrative not meant for casual observers.

Andy remembered his implicit instructions, retrieved the card from his pocket, and hurried to Jed's telephone to call Whitehall.

It was not long before the weasel interference surfaced. It started off with one or two villagers, till a large group formed, held off by Jed, a Lynch mob of sorts.

A brewing storm of anger and discontent raged outside the humble abode, a congregation of judgmental eyes fixated on the cottage like vultures circling their prey. Old Jed, weathered and resolute, stood guard with a shotgun, a solitary sentinel against the impending tempest of retribution.

Andy, a solitary figure in the sea of animosity, walked into this maelstrom. The village constable, Dickens, approached Old Jed with a familiarity born of shared histories, addressing him with a coarse affection.

"Jed, you scallywag," Constable Dickens greeted his tone a peculiar blend of camaraderie and authority.

"Sorry, pardon?" Old Jed responded confusion etched on his furrowed brow.

"Scallywag. Is this to do with it?" Constable Dickens queried, a silent understanding passing between them.

Old Jed nodded gravely, acknowledging the storm within the cottage's walls. He steeled himself for the task at hand, a lone guardian against the rising tide of condemnation.

"Ladies and gentlemen, you are to leave here immediately!" Constable Dickens proclaimed, his voice cutting through the gathering murmur.

Yet, the crowd's indignation swelled, fueled by the whispers of accusations against Johnathon, the alleged wife-beater and war dodger. Peter Smith, a fiery voice in this chorus of judgment, bellowed accusations, demanding a twisted form of justice.

In this tumult, a military truck rumbled in, bearing two Royal Military Police (RMPs) who descended purposefully. Constable Dickens welcomed their intervention, a beacon of order in the encroaching chaos.

The lead RMP, a no-nonsense figure, approached Constable Dickens. "Hello, sir. Been sent from the camp. We understand there is an urgent situation going on."

The constable, burdened by the weight of his responsibilities, briefed the RMP about the urgency and the need for immediate intervention.

"My CO sent me, and he says to treat them like I would the King. We'll get them to safety," the RMP assured, exuding an air of military authority.

As the RMPs took charge, the constable pointed out Peter Smith, a venomous figure in the crowd. The lead RMP, armed with a pickaxe handle, confronted Peter, swiftly diffusing the brewing confrontation with a forceful blow to Peter's midriff.

Meanwhile, Andy seized the opportunity to usher Johnathon and Sarah into the military truck. Urgency hung in the air as the truck raced away, leaving behind the turmoil of the crowd and the impending storm.

Yet, justice is a fleeting concept, easily overshadowed by the relentless pursuit of revenge. Unbeknownst to the fleeing trio, Peter Smith, consumed by a vindictive rage, seized Old Jed's van, initiating a perilous quest that would shatter the semblance of escape. The echoes of vengeance reverberated as the chase unfolded, an ominous prelude to the trials awaiting them on the road to sanctuary.

The stolen van hurtled through the dimly lit countryside, its engine roaring with the fury of Peter Smith's vengeful pursuit. Inside the military truck, the trio—Andy, Johnathon, and the unconscious Sarah—clung to the hope of escape, unaware of the impending calamity.

In the inky darkness, Peter, a harbinger of malevolence, closed the gap between the stolen van and the army truck. The pursuit reached a fever pitch, a dance of shadows on the desolate road, each twist and turn escalating the tension. Peter clipped the rear wheel of the army truck, causing it to twist side-on.

Then, in a heart-stopping moment, the military truck careened off the road, crashing into an unforgiving abyss. The impact reverberated through the vehicle, flinging its occupants into a chaotic disarray of limbs and pain.

Andy, Johnathon, and Sarah, once cocooned in the fragile safety of the truck, now found themselves entangled in a twisted metal wreckage. Sarah, still unconscious, bore the brunt of the collision, her fate hanging precariously in the balance.

The RMP, their stoic guardians, were not spared. The driver, entrusted with safeguarding those under their charge, was now a casualty of the relentless pursuit. Injured and incapacitated, the RMP shared in the toll exacted by the vendetta that unfolded on the darkened road.

Amidst the wreckage, a silent tableau of pain and desperation, Peter emerged unscathed. The embodiment of malevolence, he left the scene with a sinister satisfaction, disappearing into the shadows like a ghoul. He clasped in his hand an RMP cap badge.

For Andy, Johnathon, and the unconscious Sarah, the crash marked the intersection of escape and entrapment. In the cold aftermath of the collision, the night bore witness to a tableau of suffering, the cost of a vendetta that refused to be extinguished.

The simple country hospital room, bathed in the dim glow of morning light, bore witness to a fragile awakening. Sarah, her body still weak from the clutches of a month-long coma, opened her eyes to a world that had changed, a world still shrouded in the mysteries of her own convalescence.

Johnathon, the arbiter of relief etched on his face, rushed to her side as she gestured for a notepad. Capital letters formed words from the pencil transcending the silent realm she found herself in: "Oradour-sur-Glane, to be destroyed in the event of an invasion."

The weight of those words hung in the air, a revelation that whispered of shadows lurking in the corners of a war-torn past. His eyes reflecting the gravity of the revelation, Johnathon stood on the precipice of a truth that beckoned with both dread and duty.

"Oh my, oh no, Sarah, my dear Sarah," he uttered, grappling with the weight of the knowledge that now bound them.

In a mute exchange, Sarah, her voice a casualty of the ordeal, conveyed her urgency through written words. "How long sleep?"

"Over a month, Sarah. French resistance and special air

services rescued you. I flew over to help repatriate you," Johnathon shared, the lines on his face etched with the struggle of emotions.

Exhausted, Sarah succumbed to sleep again, leaving Johnathon alone with the shadows that danced in the room's corners. Unbeknownst to both, an unseen observer stood in the recesses, a presence woven into the fabric of covert operations and clandestine truths—Mr. Gubbins.

"Well done, Johnny. That was hard to do. We will let the doctors tell her. Your job now is to go to the Hyde Park Hotel. You've been seconded to the SAS. A man named Yuri will fund you. Hunt these kraut bastards down. Never come home till you do," Mr. Gubbins declared, his voice a directive shrouded in the urgency of wartime secrets.

"Sarah?" Johnathon's voice wavered, tethered between duty and the yearning for the woman he loved.

"I think she shouldn't know about Dynamo. The doctors or I will tell her," Mr. Gubbins responded, his gaze holding a weight of unspoken truths.

"Can you make sure Peter goes to prison for what he did and look after my wife?" Johnathon implored, his desperation echoing in the stark hospital room.

"He is missing at the moment. Hyde Park Hotel, Yuri. Get yourself there, and remember, don't come home till you get them all," Mr Gubbins commanded, the shadows of war and retribution stretching beyond the confines of the hospital room into a world where duty and sacrifice danced in the silence between whispers.

CHAPTER 11

Volunteer

The soft glow of daylight seeped through the curtains, casting a sombre atmosphere in the retirement home. Andy, a custodian of long-buried truths, began to unravel a tale that would redefine the family's understanding of their parents.

"Your mum and dad never went back home ever again," Andy's gravelly voice resonated in the room, each word etching the weight of hidden burdens and the harsh judgments of a village clouded by wartime misconceptions.

Derek, grappling with scepticism, confronted the narrative. "Now, this is the ramblings of an old man with dementia. This can't be all true, seriously?"

In defence of Andy's credibility, Danny, the attentive nurse, interjected. "Sorry, Mr. Hodges, but Andy does not have any dementia. He is still as sharp as a pin. He's telling the truth."

Undeterred by disbelief, Derek continued to challenge the revelations. "What do you know? Just a poxy nurse. Dad's body has not got buried yet. I have been told he was a malingerer, coward, wife-beater, and crook. He was none of those things. He was kind and considerate and never raised a hand in anger to anyone. Then you come out with stories of derring-do, the SAS, and spies, and rescue in France. My head is spinning."

In an attempt to bridge the gap between reality and revelation, Danny gently pressed on. "Sorry, but you are not listening to what is being said. Bless your mum; I looked after her and loved brushing her hair. Did you know she spoke fluent French?"

Judy caught between the known and the unknown, injected a note of disbelief. "Mum never spoke French at home. I know she went to a posh school, but none of the family heard her speak French."

His revelations continued to unfurl, challenging the family's preconceptions and plunging them into a web of espionage and wartime intrigue.

Andy, the keeper of long-buried secrets, continued with a quiet resolve. "I have. One of the other people here had a stroke, and his relatives came over from France. Your mum translated for the nurses. Spoke it like a local."

Danny, the nurse caught in the crossfire of family secrets, hesitated before unveiling another layer of their mother's clandestine life. "She had mail from the special forces club in London. I saw it accidentally. She asked me not to tell anyone. She was very serious about it. She gave my mum special instructions."

Grappling with the staggering implications, Derek voiced the incredulity of the family. "You are telling me mum was a spy?"

Still tethered to the image of her mother as a secretary, Judy sought refuge in denial. "What are you all talking about? Mum retired as a civil servant. Think about it, Judy. What if she never left that world at the end of the war?"

Derek, pushing for clarity, questioned Andy about their father's involvement. "So how was Dad involved?"

Andy, a repository of wartime truths, sought to dispel misconceptions. "Your dad was not a coward, nor a pacifist, nor did he have asthma. He was one of Churchill's men, a secret army of landowners, gamekeepers, and farmers who could live off the land for long periods."

Judy, grappling with the contradiction of her father's failed medicals, questioned further. "But he failed his medicals. Was this so he could join this secret army?"

The weight of revelations settled heavily in the room as Andy continued to lay bare the truth, his words weaving a tapestry of espionage and wartime exploits.

"Correct," Andy affirmed, his gaze piercing through the layers of disbelief. "To the world, he was a failure, but to military intelligence, he was a godsend. Fit, intelligent, able to live off the land, good with a rifle, poacher, and small-time thief. All the attributes Churchill needed... When he and I went to Lords to enlist, they had already enlisted him, but he did not know it then. They faked him being a failure. It hurt him that."

Derek, struggling to reconcile the image of his father with the newfound truth, interjected, "But Dad joined the Dad's army, you know, Home Guard."

"He had no idea until he was sent on his signals course," Andy clarified, his words resonating with the weight of untold history. "But he was redirected to a spy training camp, where he was trained as a spy and saboteur, using his unique skills. Danny, don't let us hold you back. Go see your mum."

Now a participant in the unveiling drama, Derek acknowledged Danny's presence. "Sorry, Danny. We will look after the Wingco. You see your mum. You should not be here at work. Go, we've got it."

Danny left the room, propelled by a mix of urgency and

newfound purpose. As he half-ran to the door, he cast a backward glance. Derek responded with a thumbs-up and a wink—uncharacteristic camaraderie amid unfolding truths. Meanwhile, Judy, processing the revelations, strove Andy's hand and adjusted his blanket, seeking a silent connection amidst the tumultuous revelations.

Judy, grappling with the sudden revelation of her father's concealed heroism, voiced the anguish that the family had unknowingly carried for years.

"But Dad spent the entire war branded a coward, thief, and wife-beater. It must have been hell for him," she lamented, her words echoing the weight of a tarnished reputation.

Andy, a repository of long-guarded secrets, replied with empathy, "It took me ages to get it out of him, but Old Jed was one, and so was the constable. Churchill recruited them to cause problems with the Germans if we got invaded. Your Dad, Constable Dickens, and Old Jed were a little unit to deal with that."

Still absorbing the staggering revelations, Derek inquired about the origin of his parent's love story, shedding light on a romance obscured by the shadows of war.

"Your mum and he were at the same training school. They both fell in love and got married," Andy recounted. "I did a bit of digging, and the unit your Dad joined was called the Auxiliaries. For a while, the SOE and Auxiliaries trained together. That's where he met your mum. They both arrived at the post office at the same time. I know that part; he knew she was the one straight away."

Judy, touched by the romantic intricacies woven amidst the chaos of war, sought to understand her mother's post-war journey.

"How romantic! What happened to Mum after?" she inquired, her voice tinged with curiosity and emotion.

Andy continued the narrative, "She had to stay in England as D-Day had already happened, but her local knowledge helped. The SOE was disbanded, and she went to work for the War Ministry."

Judy, envisioning her mother's silent struggles, empathised, "Knowing Mum, the guilt of not getting the information out must have been hard to bear."

Andy, now revealing Derek's father's post-war exploits, disclosed, "I did see your Dad in uniform after D-Day. He joined the SAS in the search for war criminals. When he came back after the war, he mentioned nothing. He asked me to keep it all hush-hush and cloak and dagger. See, your Dad was a real hero. He was not ashamed of his service; he just knew he had to keep it secret. Your Mum supported him."

Judy, recognising the untold sacrifices her parents endured, acknowledged, "She must have lost a lot of friends during that time."

"A team went out to find the perpetrators of war crimes, the murders of SOE agents, and the resistance. Your Dad was on that team," Andy affirmed, unearthing another layer of the concealed history.

Derek, reeling from the staggering revelations, reflected on a childhood visit to a French village and its newfound significance.

"Well, the village we visited in France as children—was that the one she tried to save?" he questioned, seeking confirmation.

Andy's response was delivered with a heavy truth, "Your Mum

ended up in a coma for two weeks. Not in time to tell anyone. By the time she recovered, the Germans had massacred over 647 men, women, and children."

Derek, Judy, and Andy reflected on the weight of a long, concealed history settling upon them. Fueled by a renewed sense of justice, Derek wanted to confront the past.

"My god, poor old Mum, those poor people," Derek mourned, grappling with the profound ramifications of the untold story.

"So it was not a holiday. It was a pilgrimage or memorial. Poor old Mum, the burden. The trip must have been closed. We, as kids, did not understand," Judy remarked, her words capturing the complex emotions surrounding the family's past.

"Oh, I'd like to have a word with that bastard, Peter," Derek declared, his tone tinged with simmering anger as the layers of the past unfolded.
Amidst the weighty revelations, Andy, the keeper of hidden truths, suddenly burst into laughter laced with a sense of ironic closure.

"He's dead," Andy stated, his amusement ringing. He cast a conspiratorial glance around the group, emphasising the gravity of the shared secret.

"He's dead," he reiterated, the repetition echoing the finality of the past. Catching onto the cryptic exchange, Derek sought more details about the demise of a figure intertwined with the shadows of their history.

"When was this? Hope it was slow and painful," Derek inquired, his tone reflecting a lingering resentment.

"It must have been when you were kids. He was found in his pub," Andy disclosed, the words carrying a note of poetic justice. The revelation of Peter's demise was bittersweet, closing a chapter in a narrative rife with secrets and untold stories.

CHAPTER 12

Maternal

Danny sat devotedly by his mother's side in the quiet confines of the hospital room, where the sterile scent of antiseptic hung in the air. His phone, drained of life, lay forgotten, and a sense of monotony crept in. Seeking solace in his small day bag, he retrieved a book gifted by the enigmatic Wingco – the Biography of a Village Copper.

His fingers carefully traced the worn edges of the book as he opened it to a well-worn page marked by a frayed bookmark. Amid the narrative, a vivid tale unfolded.

"Danny, feeling the weight of his own memories, spoke softly, addressing his slumbering mother.

"I know you're asleep, Mum. Let me share this with you."

The words flowed as he immersed himself in the story, transporting both himself and his mother to the heat of the summer of 1966 when the village copper delved into the investigation of a chilling murder.

***

A blue and white police car stood sentinel outside the village Post Office. A small crowd gathered, hushed whispers circulating. Inspector Dickens, visibly aged but retaining an air of authority, stepped out of another police car, leather briefcase in hand. Jed and Snitch, weathered by time, observed from the sidelines. Jed leaned on a stick, a copy of the Racing Post peeking from his pocket.

"Hello, sir. It's inside—the remains," the constable greeted.

"No, the body is inside. Anyone else been here?" Inspector Dickens inquired.

"Just the local doctor. He said to send for you, sir, but I can handle these remains—sorry, body," the constable replied.

"You're doing a good job. Let me handle this for now," Dickens reassured, patting the constable's shoulder before entering the shop. The door closed behind him.

Inspector Dickens strolled toward the till, its tray absent. Miss Rutherford lay on the floor, evidence of strangulation stark on her bruised neck. Throughout, he fidgeted with a lemon drop in its wrapper. The doctor, an elderly figure with a walking stick, observed a sorrowful expression.

"She looks so tiny, so frail. She used to scare us as kids. She could be someone's granny," Dickens mused.

"So sad. It's a robbery," the doctor remarked.

"Anything else taken?" Dickens inquired.

"Look at her hat. She never took it off. The hat pin is missing," the doctor pointed out.

"I hope to God it's not the same pervert. Please tell me no,"

Dickens muttered.

"I had to check. Her shoes had come off, her underwear was missing, and she had been..." the doctor hesitated, choking up. Dickens offered a hip flask.

"Have a snifter. I thought this nonsense was over. Whoever it is, they're asserting their power," Dickens stated, the doctor shuffling uncomfortably.

"We need to warn the village. Poor Gladys. Look at her, a little old woman. There is no family either, just a cat. The wife and I will look after it now," the doctor suggested.

Dickens looked up, smiling.

"Gladys, fancy that. In thirty years, I never knew her name. She was terrifying when I was a kid," Dickens confessed, kneeling down to straighten her hat. He looked very sad.

"Miss Rutherford, Gladys, I will get whoever did this to you. I promise," Dickens vowed, standing up and walking to the door. He carefully placed the lemon drop back with the other sweets, turned, looked back at the body, shook his head, and then put on his police cap, his face a thundercloud.

***

The night enveloped the quiet village train station, its silence broken only by the haunting whistle of a departing steam train. From the carriage emerged a lone figure—a young lady adorned in a mini dress, a coat adorned with buttons, and a hat. Her small suitcase clutched tightly; she surveyed the empty platform. Checking the timetable against her wristwatch, a shiver coursed through her, prompting her to drape a small shawl around her shoulders.

Finding no solace in an open waiting room, she sought refuge in the small car park. A glance at the out-of-order phone box dashed any hopes of shelter. Unperturbed, her gaze shifted to the street, where a Morris Minor pulled beside her.

The driver, concealed from view, conversed with the young lady.

"Is there a taxi or a pub nearby? It's freezing, and the next train is two hours away. Caught the wrong one... such a ninny," she lamented.

"No taxis, love, and the pub is closed," the driver replied.

"Darn, I'm in such a bind. I had to change at Andover and got on the wrong train," she explained.

"Andover's not far. I can give you a lift," the driver offered.

"I don't have any money, really can't be a bind," she admitted.

"You sound very posh if you don't mind me saying," the driver observed.

"I am at Cheltenham Ladies College, well, leaving for University, Magdalen College," she revealed.

"Put your case in the rear; I'll give you a lift to Andover," the driver kindly suggested.

"Will you, man? That is so righteous!" she exclaimed.

She got into the car, revealing an unnoticed taxi and its driver engrossed in a newspaper as it drove off.

Dianne found herself in the confined space of the car, the soft murmur of the radio creating an atmosphere of chilled relaxation. Seeking warmth, she pulled out a cigarette, lit it, and handed it over to the unseen driver.

As the car glided past Peter's pub, its lights aglow, Dianne couldn't help but comment, "Hey Daddio, the lights were on."

The driver, still unseen, remained indifferent to her remark. Undeterred, she playfully questioned, "Are you on the make with me?"

Again, her query met with silence. The car continued its journey, leaving the village behind and passing the road sign indicating Andover to the left.

Curiosity tugged at Dianne, and she inquired, "You know a shortcut, as it was a left back there."

The driver's cigarette had been extinguished. Seizing the opportunity, she leaned across, her cleavage catching the dim light. She skillfully rekindled the cigarette, illuminating the driver's face—it was Peter Smith. A sly smile crept across his face as he touched her knee.

"Not cool, not cool," Dianne uttered, her discomfort evident.

The Morris Minor cut through the darkness of the rural lane, its engine humming softly. Abruptly, the car slammed its brakes, causing a jittery motion as though a struggle unfolded within. Amidst the night, a woman's screams pierced the air, sending an unsettling silence in their wake.

***

The early morning sun painted the sky with hues of pink and orange as Danny perched on the high ledge of the hospital multistory car park. The city below was beginning to stir, with the distant sounds of ambulances marking the start of a new day. With the Crime book in hand, Danny was absorbed in its pages, finding solace in the quiet moments atop the building.

As the door creaked open, footsteps approached, and a female police officer, PC Jane Moore, made her way toward Danny.

"Hey, Danny," she called out.

Danny raised his book in greeting. "I'm not jumping, not like that. I just came up for some peace and to read my book."

PC Jane Moore understood and approached him. "I know, Danny. I can see that."

"Did someone call to say you had a jumper?" Danny inquired.

"Yes, you'd be surprised how many have bought their ticket off the world up here. I don't like heights," she admitted.

"It's just quiet, you know? You can see the whole city; people can't hurt you here. I can just read my book," Danny explained.

Curious, PC Jane Moore asked, "What's it about?"

Danny showed her the cover. "It's about a village constable looking for a serial killer. It's a true story, but they didn't have bad people like today. Today, people are more vicious, ya know what I'm saying."

He carefully placed a bookmark in the book and closed it with reverence.

"Like the people that hurt your mum?" PC Jane Moore guessed.

Danny nodded. "Yes. Do you have any idea who it was?"

"We have a strong person in mind. His family has an alibi for him, and his gang were all good little boys at home," she explained.

"Mum... Mum was in a bit of bother with him," Danny admitted.

"Yes, trammies," PC Jane Moore confirmed.

"You know!" Danny was surprised.

"We suspected it for a while. Don't worry; your mum is not in any trouble. She was under immense pressure," PC Jane Moore assured.

"But you will have to interview her," Danny noted.

"Well, that will have to wait. Going to have to wait after her stroke," she replied.

"Nah, she was beaten up. She did not have a stroke," Danny corrected her.

PC Jane Moore's expression shifted, realising the misunderstanding. "Danny, how long have you been up here? She had a stroke an hour ago. No one told you."

"For Christ's sake! Why did you not lead with that?" Danny exclaimed. Clutching his stab wound, he carefully climbed down onto the car park tarmac and quickly barged past the police officer, who followed in haste.

***

As the morris minor resumed its journey, it moved steadily toward the woods, its lights extinguishing into the encompassing shadows. Slowing to a creep, it entered a secluded wood car park, vanishing into obscurity. The only discernible light emanated from the driver's side—a solitary cigarette glowing in the darkness.

The silence of Jed's woods was occasionally punctuated by the rustling of leaves and the distant hoot of an owl. In the heart of the darkness, Jed, weathered and grizzled, sat perched on a fallen bough, his shotgun resting beside him. Snitch, his loyal canine companion, lay in a peaceful slumber at his feet, unaware of the impending disturbance.

Suddenly, Snitch jolted awake, his senses attuned to something unseen. Jed, stirred by the dog's abrupt awakening, directed his gaze toward the direction Snitch was fixated on. The subtle sounds of a car navigating through the obsidian night reached their ears, accompanied by the rhythmic snapping of twigs. A door creaked open, releasing muffled voices into the night.

Jed rose, a slower ascent than in his younger years, traversing the darkness toward the source of the commotion. In the shadows, he discerned a figure hastily pulling up trousers and darting toward a parked car. Snitch, responding instinctively, bounded towards the vehicle. But as the dog approached, a heartless kick from the figure, revealed to be Peter, sent Snitch yelping and limping.

Jed, closing the distance as the car sped away, caught a fleeting glimpse of Peter's retreating form and the familiar car. The whimpering and limping Snitch confirmed the cruelty inflicted upon him. Focused and determined, Jed moved toward the injured dog.

Drawing closer, Jed discovered a tragic scene in the moonlit underbrush—a lifeless Dianne lay there, her eyes red and puffy, fixated on the vast expanse of the night sky. Kneeling beside her, Jed sought her fading pulse, the warmth dissipating as she grew colder and bluer. A profound realisation struck—a large button from her coat was missing.

In a blend of grief and urgency, Jed staggered back, unintentionally catching his foot on a gnarled root. As he looked down, he discovered not only Snitch's wounded form but also Dianne's lifeless foot. His gaze travelled upward, meeting her vacant eyes. With a heavy heart, Jed, burdened by the weight of the night, began the arduous journey home, Snitch limping loyally at his side. The need for a phone or a car propelled him toward the village green, where the dim glow of a telephone kiosk offered a glimmer of hope in the enveloping darkness.

***

The room was cloaked in the hushed stillness of the night. Johnny and Sarah lay nestled in the embrace of their bed, entwined in the arms of sleep. The rhythmic ticking of the clock echoed through the room, a silent lullaby in the darkness.

Abruptly, the tranquillity was shattered by the persistent ring of the telephone. A disoriented Johnny fumbled in the dark, his hand reaching out to grasp the intrusive device. Now illuminated by the soft glow of a bedside lamp, Sarah observed Johnny's struggle.

"Sarah, it's 3 in the bloody morning. Who is it?" she inquired, her voice tinged with annoyance.

Johnny, still half-submerged in the realm of sleep, listened intently to the voice on the other end. "Yes, yes, Sarah, quiet, I can't hear... Hello, is that you, Jed? You okay? Did you find a body in the woods? Do you think it's who? Seriously, are you drunk?... Okay, well, call the police next. Hurry up."

The conversation concluded. Johnny replaced the phone on the cradle, sinking back into the bed. Sarah, now wide awake, sought an explanation. "Who was that?"

"It's Jed," Johnny replied, his voice heavy with the weight of the revelation. "Jed was looking for poachers and witnessed a murder in his wood. He's calling the police now."

"A murder?" Sarah's eyes widened with disbelief.

Johnny continued, "He found a girl's body and someone driving off. He says it was that arse, Peter. Said he's calling the police, then getting his shotgun to shoot the bastard."

The gravity of the situation sank in, and they both looked

up, exchanging a shared concern. Sarah, fueled by a sense of urgency, got out of bed. "You go see him, stop before he does anything stupid. It's an hour and a half away. So, you go see him. I will give Dickens a call."

Johnny, a bit stunned, was spurred into action. "C'mon, chop chop. Get your clothes on. You should be gone by now."

As Sarah dialled Chief Inspector Dickens, their bedroom became a hub of activity, a quiet storm brewing in the nocturnal tranquillity.

With a determined purpose, Sarah reached into the bedside cabinet, her hand navigating the contents until it found the familiar shape of a Rolodex. The plastic wheel clicked softly as she turned it, swiftly zeroing in on the letter D. Her fingertip paused momentarily before landing on the desired contact.

"Dickens," she mumbled, finding the name she sought. A brief nod of satisfaction followed as she gripped the telephone receiver.

"Ah, Dickens, there you are," Sarah spoke into the phone, her tone a mix of urgency and authority. With a firm hold on the conversation about to unfold, she began dialling the number, a lifeline in the dark hours of the night.

***

The night was draped in shadows, shrouded in an unsettling stillness as Jed staggered towards his Lodge, his breath a desperate rasp in the crisp air. His once agile form now moved with a hesitant slowness, a testament to the passage of time. Behind him limped Snitch, a loyal companion marred by a similar weariness. Together, they raced towards the sanctuary of the Lodge, their urgency palpable.

Jed fumbled for the key in the dim light, hidden cunningly in the letterbox. A piece of string offered a lifeline to the key, and with a quick, practised motion, he pulled it free and unlocked the door. The wooden portal swung open, swallowing them into the shelter within. Snitch paused, casting a backward glance, a low growl emanating from his throat. The door closed with a decisive thud.

Outside, an empty Morris Minor sat on the road, a silent witness to the unfolding drama. From within the Lodge, a cacophony erupted – shouts, glass shattering, and the ominous banging of a struggle. Snitch's voice cut through the chaos, barking and growling, then reduced to a whimper. A sharp thump echoed, followed by Snitch's plaintive whimpers.

Jed's anguished cries mingled with the sounds of a beating. The door burst open, revealing a dishevelled Jed cradling the lifeless form of Snitch. They stumbled down the garden path, a tragic tableau of loyalty and brutality. And then, as if summoned by the malevolence, Peter emerged, wielding a fire iron. The blows rained down on Snitch, extinguishing the flicker of life that remained, and then turned towards Jed.

The garden path now bore witness to death, the bodies of Jed and Snitch sprawled in silent testimony. With a chilling detachment, Peter reached down, plucking Snitch's name tag as a macabre trophy. Once proudly adorning Jed's trousers, the

Eton tie was callously yanked off. Walking away, Peter headed towards the house, a fuel can in hand. He poured its contents at the entrance, the liquid glinting eerily in the moonlight.

With a deliberate motion, he ignited the fuel, the flames licking at the entrance, devouring the evidence of the gruesome act. Peter stood, a silhouette against the growing inferno, watching as the fire danced and roared, a perverse satisfaction etched across his face. The Lodge, once a sanctuary, now became a funeral pyre, engulfed in the relentless embrace of the consuming fire.

The night it held its secrets, the crackling of flames and the fading echoes of despair echoing through the stillness. The Lodge, now a charred monument to betrayal, stood as a testament to the darkness within.

***

Danny bursts into the room breathlessly, PC Moore trailing behind. He clutches his side in pain, and the officer hesitates at the door, respecting the personal space. Daphne lies in the hospital bed, hooked up to a drip, her face swollen from the recent beating. Despite the pain, she tries to communicate with Danny, slurring her words.

Danny moves to her side, settling into a chair. His fingers gently sweep the hair from her eyes, and she intensely gazes at him. He takes her limp hand into his, holding it tenderly. A feeble attempt at a smile plays on her lips, and a single tear escapes Danny's eye.

As her breathing becomes shallower, the pulse oximeter drops to 82, accompanied by a warning buzzer. Recognising the sound, Danny kisses her on the forehead. He then reaches for a crucifix, placing it on her lips as she attempts to kiss it.

Daphne passes away peacefully, and Danny, overcome with grief, embraces his mother. The police officer lingers, pushed aside by a ward nurse who rushes in. The nurse gives a glance to the shocked policewoman before closing the door. The sound of rain falls on the window, the rivulets matching the tears on Danny's face, like the city beyond is crying in harmony.

Alone with the lifeless body, Danny holds his mother, inconsolable. The nurse, having shut the door on the policewoman, exchanges a look with her. The policewoman pulls the radio to her lips.

"station, can you inform CID that the mugging last night is now a murder? Also, I haven't told the son about his flat being burned out by arsonists last night. It doesnt rain but it pours."

***

The morning sun painted the rural road with hues of warmth as Johnny approached Jed's Lodge with a purposeful drive. The air carried an unsettling quiet, broken only by the distant hum of a fire engine and the melancholic chimes of bells. Smoke hung heavy in the air, a foreboding curtain that concealed the unfolding tragedy.

As Johnny neared the scene, the fire glow flickered on the horizon, casting an ominous glow. His footsteps quickened, urgency etched across his face. A fire engine stood amidst the chaos, its hoses battling the remnants of the inferno. A police car, a silent sentinel, marked the gravity of the situation.

Pulling up, Johnny leapt from his vehicle and sprinted towards the Lodge. A stern-faced police officer intercepted him, attempting to bar his way. Ignoring the obstruction, Johnny cast a quick glance at the path where a tarp concealed two lifeless forms. His heart pounded as he pushed past the policeman, determination etched on his face.

Two firemen, valiant but futile in their attempt to hinder him, tried to block Johnny's path. Undeterred, he pressed forward, his desperate journey culminating in a heart-wrenching discovery. Falling to his knees, he peeled back the tarp, revealing Jed and Snitch, frozen in a final, protective embrace.

Firefighters halted the advancing policeman, allowing Johnny to grieve openly. His mentor and dear friend lay before him, victim to a senseless act of violence. The weight of loss pressed upon Johnny, leaving him shattered and inconsolable.

Another police car arrived, and Chief Constable Dickens, a figure of authority, rushed to Johnny's side. His attempt to console met with Johnny's steely determination.

Johnny, eyes fixed on the fallen duo, declared, "I know who did it. Give me ten minutes head start."

Concern etched on his face;Chief Constable Dickens urged Johnny to reconsider. "You're not in that world anymore. Think of Sarah and the children."

But Johnny's resolve remained unshaken. "I want that bastard."

To divert Johnny's focus, Constable Dickens said, " I have one question. Jed and Snitch always seemed to be around. How old was Snitch? Must have been ancient."

Johnny, pointing towards an oak tree adorned with four wooden headstones, replied with a sombre smile, "He was like a father to me, the best man I've ever worked for. Shit at naming dogs."

A bittersweet laughter passed between them, ending in a heartfelt embrace. Constable Dickens, acknowledging the pain, shifted the conversation to a grim reality.

"I have to go. There's another body. I could use your tracking skills. It's a young girl who has yet to start university. Jed saw who did it. I'm not asking you; I'm telling you to help."

Johnny, stopping in his tracks, looked up at Constable Dickens. "He's not wearing his Eton Tie. Sarah and I got him a new one when his last one fell apart. And Snitch, his brass name tag is missing."

Constable Dickens exhaled, biting his lip, his gaze drifting to the horizon. Behind him, the house continued to blaze, sparks swirling like phantom embers in the tragic aftermath.

***

The morning air hung heavy with tension as a police car stood sentinel against the backdrop of a solemn wood. Constable Dickens and Johnny, surrounded by a roped-off area, prepared for a grim revelation. Other police officers maintained a cordon, their presence a stoic acknowledgement of the gravity of the situation.

Constable Dickens broke the silence, his voice carrying a weight of responsibility. "You ready?"

Johnny, a civilian with a determination etched on his face, replied, "As I ever will be."

The Constable gestured toward the wooded area. "She is."

"QUIET!" Johnny interjected, rebuking the officer for disrupting the sanctity of the moment. "Sorry, I need to see and hear it for the first time."

With deliberate steps, Johnathon approached the tree line. A pocket knife emerged, and he cut a long stick, his gaze fixed on the Constable. He ventured into the woods, methodically searching, his keen eyes scanning the ground, trees, stems, and mud. In due time, he discovered Dianne's lifeless form. An impenetrable mask of emotion concealed any reaction as he looked about and walked back to Constable Dickens.

"My boys did not get too far. We are still waiting for the doctor," the Constable informed him.

"The car drove in. She was knocked out, dragged out the door, and then to the bush, where he raped her. She must have woken up, as there was disturbed mud made with heels —those shoes had gone. Then, carried on. Something must have disturbed him, as he left handprints in the mud, possibly pulling his trousers up. Then, strangled her. Her top button is missing. Then he gets in the car and escapes," Johnny recounted, his voice steady, recounting the horrors etched in the disturbed earth.

"Anything else?" inquired Constable Dickens.

Johnny, his eyes reflecting a sombre familiarity with tragedy, remarked, "You've seen this before."

"What makes you say that?" questioned the Constable.

"Well, the button on her coat is missing, and Jed's tie and dog brass are missing," Johnny pointed out.

"I've been chasing this bastard for years. The Chief Constable says it's not a priority, but he is an idiot. He takes a memento, a little keepsake," Constable Dickens confessed.

"Peter used to bully others at school when he won. He would steal or take something of theirs," Johnny shared, drawing connections between past patterns and present horrors.

"Peter Smith. He always has an alibi. He's clever and astute," remarked Constable Dickens.

"You have to play by the rules. I am trained to break them. You need to let me help you. Just one thing," Johnny emphasised.

"Yes?" queried Constable Dickens.

"Keep Sarah out of this, for her sake," Johnny pleaded, a protective instinct woven into his solemn request.

***

The hospital corridor stretched before Danny, its dim lighting casting shadows on scattered, worn chairs. Hunched over, he clutched his knees, his face etched with unmistakable distress. In the background, PC Jane Moore observed the scene, a silent witness to the emotional turmoil. A distant sound echoed through the corridor—a lift bell signalling someone's arrival. The officer nodded as the newcomer stepped out, their brown brogues and chino trousers revealing a figure heading toward Danny.

Approaching quietly, Derek stood before Danny, who looked up at him with questioning eyes.

"Danny, I am so sorry for you, Danny," Derek expressed his condolences.

"Why are you here?" Danny asked, his tone laden with confusion and sorrow.

"It seems you have no family. The nursing home contacted me after the police spoke to them," Derek explained, trying to offer some semblance of understanding.

"You did not know my mum that well," Danny retorted, a hint of scepticism in his voice.

"That's true," Derek admitted, "but speaking to my wife this morning, we feel you need a lot of help."

"I don't need no help. Mum's gone; that is it. I will go back this morning, and I will take over the flat once the funeral is over. I need no looking after, not a child," Danny asserted, his words a defence against the vulnerability threatening to surface.

Despite his resistance, Derek placed a comforting hand on Danny's shoulder. Danny shrugged it off, but Derek persisted.

The police officer approached, kneeling in front of Danny. While Derek's hand remained on Danny's shoulder, the officer reached out, gently stroking his cheek before placing her hand on him. Danny, caught in this unexpected show of empathy, felt mixed emotions.

"There is some bad news," Derek reluctantly disclosed.

The police officer continued, "Your flat was completely burnt out last night, arson. You have nowhere to live."

Derek added, "I rang the council, and they can't find you any emergency accommodation. You have no family."

In a surprising turn, PC Moore gave a solution: "Derek and his wife have offered a room for you to stay in until it's all sorted."

As Derek nodded, smiling with genuine concern, he added, "It would be our pleasure to have you under our roof. Let's get you out of this horrible place; you need some rest."

Danny rose from his seat, following the trio toward the lift. However, he abruptly broke away, returning to the chairs to retrieve the book he had been reading. It had become his sole possession in the wake of the recent upheaval. With the book in hand, he rejoined the supportive company inside the lift, uncertain of the solace or challenges ahead.

***

The village pub stood as a weathered outpost against quaint serenity. A Dreyman worked diligently, delivering barrels of beer to replenish the spirits within. The typical bustle of a pub's loading routine unfolded, Yet, Peter, the proprietor, stood aloof, an unlit cigarette dangling from his lips as he observed the labour without assistance.

In this tranquil tableau, the day took an unexpected turn. A police car slid into view, the gravel crunching beneath its tyres. Chief Inspector Dickens emerged, his gaze fixed on Peter. He strode purposefully towards the smoking landlord, his presence a harbinger of unwelcome news.

"Right where you were last night?" Constable Dickens demanded, his voice carrying the weight of authority.

Peter's response was laced with insolence, "What's it to do with you?"

"Last night, Jed and his dog were murdered," Constable Dickens delivered the news with a sombre directness.

The retort that escaped Peter's lips was as callous as the act he dismissed, "How do you murder a dog? You sentimental prick."

Constable Dickens's indignant response, his patience tested, "Who the hell do you think you are talking to?"

Peter, unyielding, spat back, "You, you useless tosser."

The nearby Dreyman, during his beer delivery, overheard the exchange, a shock of disbelief crossing his features as he glimpsed Peter's audacity.

"Hey, get back to work, you," Peter barked at the Dreyman, diverting attention from his confrontation with the law.

The relentless questioning continued, "Where were you last night?" Constable Dickens pressed on, determined to unearth the truth.

With a casual arrogance, Peter responded, "Well, I was at the Lodge."

"Jed's lodge?" the Constable sought clarification.

"No, the Masonic lodge. Ring any of them; they'll tell you I was there," Peter asserted, a smug assurance permeating his words.

Constable Dickens, taken aback by the revelation, probed further, "You're telling me you're a Mason?"

"Not telling you anything, Constable," Peter deflected, his disdain for authority evident. His lack of sympathy reached a new low as he callously added, "To be honest, if you ask me, that prick groundskeeper had it coming."

The atmosphere, once charged with the mundane tasks of the village, now crackled with tension and suspicion.

Johnny moved with a calculated stealth in the shadowed recesses at the rear of the village pub, away from the heated exchange between Chief Inspector Dickens and the uncooperative Peter. His figure blended seamlessly with the surroundings, a silhouette navigating the periphery.

The side door, an unassuming portal to the secrets held within, confronted Johnny. He eyed the locked barrier with a measured gaze, assessing the challenge ahead. A subtle smile played on his lips as he retrieved a lockpick kit from the folds of his jacket, an instrument of finesse in the hands of a skilled infiltrator.

Kneeling on the worn floor, Johnny's focus narrowed to the intricate dance between metal and mechanism. The lockpick glided with practised precision, its dance an unspoken conversation between the intruder and the barrier that sought to impede him. As Johnny effortlessly picked the lock, the subtle clicks and hushed whispers of tumblers falling into place resonated in the still air.

Johnny rose as the door yielded to his expertise, dusting off the imaginary residue of his clandestine endeavours. The faintest hint of a victorious smirk played on his lips, a testament to his proficiency in shadows. The threshold crossed, Johnny slipped into the pub, his entry unnoticed amidst the chaos at the front.

Once a bustling hub of community life, the village pub now stood in silence, a dormant witness to the unfolding drama. Empty chairs perched on tables, and cloths shrouded the pumps, rendering the place a ghostly echo of its former conviviality. Electric lights hung dormant from the ceiling, casting a dim glow over the flagstone floor beneath Johnny's stealthy steps.

Slipping into the shadows, Johnny's gaze fell upon the wooden steps leading to the top floor. The absence of ambient light heightened his senses as he silently removed his shoes, tying the laces together and draping them over his neck. Barefoot, he ascended the creaking steps with the agility of a seasoned intruder.

Peering through the upstairs window, Johnny observed the scene below. The Chief Inspector had successfully ensnared Peter in a distracting conversation. With the coast seemingly straightforward, Johnny continued his ascent, reaching the top floor with calculated ease. The empty pub below, a tableau of abandonment, lent an eerie backdrop to his clandestine mission.

Peters's room awaited, and Johnny approached the locked door with a practised touch. The latch yielded to his deft hands, and he slipped into the room, leaving the door ajar for a hasty exit if needed.

A thorough search ensued, but the room revealed no immediate secrets. Johnny's attention shifted to the dresser, where he discovered a deceptive second drawer. A tap on its back section unveiled a hidden compartment, concealing a trove of money and aged erotica. His investigative instincts heightened.

A biscuit tin nestled within the hidden recess drew Johnny's interest. Placing it on the bed, he uncovered an unsettling collection—a mishmash of ladies' underwear, some soiled, alongside an assortment of buttons, brooches, a hat pin, and a girl guide badge. Aware of the ticking clock, Johnny swiftly sketched the items on paper, capturing the evidence in a crude illustration.

Time pressed on, and Johnny, determined and methodical, cleared the bed. As he left the room, he knelt again to relock the door, unaware of the silent presence behind him. The bathroom door, unnoticed until now, swung open, revealing a young woman clad in nothing but a bath towel and another draped over her head.

Cigarette burns and bruises adorned her fragile form, a silent testament to unspeakable horrors. Johnny, catching sight of her, pressed a finger to his lips, urging her into quiet submission. The unspoken exchange conveyed urgency and caution as both figures stood at the precipice of a truth that lingered.

Amidst the heated exchange between Chief Inspector Dickens and Peter, the village pub held its breath, the façade of tranquillity shattered by a sudden, shrill female scream echoing from the upper floor. Peter's gaze shot upward, his features contorted with surprise and alarm. The Dreyman, previously absorbed in his duties, abruptly abandoned his post and hurriedly descended into the cellar, a bewildered expression on his face.

Peter stormed through the front door with a decisive pivot, propelled by an instinctive urgency that overpowered any resistance he may have harboured. The Chief Inspector, registering the abrupt disruption, looked upward, his brow furrowing in suspicion. Shaking his head, he abandoned the argument with Peter and darted around the pub, racing towards the back in response to the unsettling cry that pierced the air.

The pub, once a haven of quietude, now crackled with an unspoken tension. The abrupt disturbance propelled the unfolding narrative into unforeseen territory, leaving the characters between the known and the mysterious. The Chief Inspector's pursuit of the scream's source marked a divergence in the unfolding drama, leading towards uncharted territories hidden within the depths of the village pub.

In the dim-lit chaos of the village pub, Johnny descended the stairs, his senses heightened by the situation's urgency. However, an unexpected obstacle appeared in the form of the Dreyman, emerging from the cellar door and blocking Johnny's path. Quickly, Johnny altered his course, rushing towards the back door. The Dreyman, a formidable force, intercepted him, a collision of strength and desperation.

The struggle unfolded with primal intensity. Drawing on his training, Johnny broke free from the strongman's grip, a dance of evasion and counteraction. He threw the Dreyman against the wall deftly, seizing control of the situation. A precise knee to the kidneys left the strongman momentarily incapacitated. Amidst the tumult, a girl in a towel descended the stairs, her eyes wide with fear and fascination.

However, the chaos escalated further as Peter, unseen until now, delivered a stunning blow to Johnny's head with a cricket bat. Stunned, Johnny stumbled towards the back door, vulnerable to Peter's ensuing assault. The brutality of the punches left Johnny reeling, struggling to maintain composure.

The girl, witnessing the violence, rushed forward in a desperate attempt to intervene. Peter, blinded by rage, prepared to strike her. A moment of hesitation, a glance towards the Dreyman who bore witness, provided a brief respite. In that crucial moment, Johnny seized the opportunity to burst through the back door, escaping the relentless onslaught.

Peter, thwarted in his pursuit, rushed to the door, only to be confronted by the unexpected arrival of Chief Inspector Dickens. The bumbling authority figure, oblivious to the chaos within, questioned the unfolding scene. Brandishing his truncheon, Constable Dickens demanded an explanation.

"Get out of the way! Just caught some bloke trying to steal from me," Peter spat out, attempting to deflect attention.

The Chief Inspector, unaware of the true nature of the situation, urged Peter to provide a description. Meanwhile, the girl with the towel seized the chance to escape, racing back up the stairs. Constable Dickens, catching sight of her bruised form, confronted the disturbing reality hidden beneath the surface of the seemingly ordinary pub.

As the tension reached its zenith, Johnny seized the opportunity. Glancing at his unwitting ally blocking the doorway, he sprinted to the awaiting police car. Climbing into the back, he hid from view, a fugitive taking refuge in the shadows as the village pub unravelled in the face of hidden truths and escalating violence.

As the police car cruised along the road, Chief Inspector Dickens broke the silence, questioning the outcome of the chaotic scene at the village pub.

"Hope you got something after all that. Where did that girl come from?" he inquired, his tone a mix of curiosity and exasperation.

"Oh, I got something alright," Johnny responded cryptically, passing over a sheet of paper. The Chief Inspector pulled the car to the side of the road, unfolding the paper as Johnny moved to the front seat.

Opening the brass rubbing paper, Chief Inspector Dickens stared in shock at the rubbings. His hand trembled as he pointed to the individual impressions.

"God, oh my god, look here," he gasped.

Now in the front seat, Johnny observed the Chief Inspector's reaction. The rubbings held a weight of revelation, a sinister truth etched in the imprints.

"found underwear and pornography as well," Johnny added, his voice measured.

The Chief Inspector, still processing the revelation, identified specific rubbings. "This one, Girl Guide, raped. She is the only one to have gotten away. She killed herself. This one here, dungaree buttons. You recognise the hat pin?" he explained.

Johnny leaned in, examining the paper closely. "Miss Rutherford herself. That's her hat pin. She always wore that."

The Chief Inspector folded the paper, placing it solemnly in his pocket. The weight of concealed truths lingered in the air.

"We told the public that Miss Rutherford slipped and fell and broke her neck... In reality, this monster broke in, raped, and killed her, and stole a large amount of cash from the safe," the Chief Inspector revealed a sombre acknowledgement of a past shrouded in deception.

"There was a lot of money in there as well," Johnny added, the gravity of the crimes unfolding.

"No woman is safe with that deviant about, no woman," the Chief Inspector declared, his words carrying the weight of a pledge to justice.

Johnny, still grappling with the horrors exposed, redirected the conversation. "Who was that girl in there? She was covered in bruises and what looked like fag burns."

Constable Dickens shook his head, glancing at Johnny. "First, we must clean you up and get you to the doctor. Sarah will kill me if you go home looking like that. Let's say you were mugged, file a report."

As the police car resumed its journey, the shadows of a dark past lingered, leaving Johnny and the Chief Inspector on a path to uncovering the truth beneath the seemingly peaceful village's veneer.

***

In the heart of the 1960s police headquarters, the atmosphere hung heavy with the scent of bureaucracy, old files, and the lingering haze of half-smoked cigarettes. The ceaseless clatter of typewriters and the ambient murmur of detectives piecing together cases created a backdrop of a bygone era.

Chief Inspector Dickens occupied the corner office, where a bowl of lemon drops sat inconspicuously amidst the organised chaos of papers and ashtrays. Hunched over a typewriter, he battled with misspelt words, correcting errors with white snopake. The room, a microcosm of the era, captured the mundane yet relentless essence of police work.

A shadow materialised over Chief Inspector Dickens' desk, prompting him to look up and remove his glasses. The Chief Constable loomed, a palpable air of discontent clinging to his presence.

"I hear you may have solved the Wiltshire strangler case," remarked Chief Constable Waterstone.

"Yes, been at that case for years, normally three or four a year," replied Constable Dickens.

"I hear that some of these women may have been very loose with men, you know, asking for it, you know, bawdy women," remarked Chief Constable Waterstone.

"I don't think they wanted to be raped and strangled, and we have a couple of teenagers, one schoolgirl, and an elderly lady. All are matching the same MO," countered Constable Dickens.

"But you have a prime suspect," the Chief Constable pointed out.

"Yes, quite exciting. We know that whoever it is has been

taking items as trophies or souvenirs," explained Constable Dickens.

"These souvenirs were taken from the bodies of the victims, correct? Then why do I have one of my lodge telling me you said it was him," inquired Chief Constable Waterstone.

"One of your lodge?" questioned Constable Dickens.

In the dimly lit office, the Chief Constable began absentmindedly fiddling with the gold ring adorning his hand, its surface engraved with the masonic square and compass—a subtle emblem of his affiliations.

"Yes, Brother Smith was at the lodge the night of the murder of Mr. John Edward Blythe," Chief Constable Waterstone stated, his tone carrying an air of authority. He continued, scrutinizing Constable Dickens with a piercing gaze, "Did you find any souvenirs in the illegal search you conducted with a civilian?"

Constable Dickens, caught off guard, stammered, "Er, sir?"

"I am ordering you to drop all lines of inquiry with Mr. Peter Smith. Also, the use of former members of what I suspect to be Intelligence services does not bode well for your career," the Chief Constable asserted, his words hanging heavily in the air.

"But, sir, we found those items in the house of Peter Smith, and sod my career," Constable Dickens protested, a sense of urgency in his voice.

The Chief Constable leaned back, his gaze unwavering, "After reading your report, it quite clearly states that an Eton Tie and a dog collar tag were stolen. If your theory was correct, your civilian friend would have found the tie and dog tag. Is that not correct?"

"Sir!" Constable Dickens exclaimed, a mixture of frustration and desperation etched on his face.

In the hushed tension of the office, Constable Dickens erupted, his fury manifesting in the slam of his desk. He glared at the Chief Constable, defiance burning in his eyes.

"It's an order; drop that line of inquiry now. I am your superior officer; don't push it. Now, stand down. You are not far off your pension. Do you want to jeopardise that now? For your interests, stand down..." The Chief Constable's words echoed through the quieted office, an unspoken threat lingering in the air.

Constable Dickens, seething, uttered a terse "Sir." The Chief Constable calmly walked out a self-satisfied smile on his lips. The office held its breath, officers stealing glances at the scene, uncertainty lingering in the atmosphere.

As the Chief Constable left, Constable Dickens reached for a lemon drop, the crinkling of the wrapper punctuating the heavy silence. Deep in thought, he picked up the phone and dialled a lengthy number, a call burdened with reluctance.

"Jones Laundry Services, what order was your item under?" came from the other end.

Cautiously, Constable Dickens covered the microphone and his mouth, scanning the room to ensure no one witnessed the clandestine call. "Mr. Scallywag," he replied.

"Please hold... connecting you now," the operator chimed in.

With an audible click, the line connected, and Constable Dickens took a breath before speaking into the phone. "Hello, boss. I have a problem. People are in danger."

He pressed the cradle button three times, a signal ingrained in clandestine communication, and waited for the callback. The operator's voice broke the silence, "Bluebell Pub, outside, 1 hour. Wear civilian clothes."

Putting the phone down, Constable Dickens grabbed a handful of lemon drops from his pocket, a tangible manifestation of his unsettling journey into the shadows. As he left, the weight of an impending rendezvous pressed upon him.

The Bluebell Pub in Salisbury cast a quaint charm, its wooden bench outside as an unassuming meeting place. Constable Dickens clad in his suit with a trilby perched on his head, sat untouched with a folded copy of that day's Times in his right hand.

Approaching with a measured pace, Mr. Gubbins, now aged and slowed by the passage of time, took a seat and observed Constable Dickens.

"You need to relax a little more. I have taken up embroidery; semi-retirement is not what it seems," Mr. Gubbins remarked, his weathered face reflecting the experiences of a bygone era.

Constable Dickens, though, was focused. "Thought you would be a cricketer or fly-fishing type of man."

"Cricket's full of cheats; it's boring, and I feel sorry for the fish. How can I help you?" Mr Gubbins replied, his demeanour a blend of casualness and sagacity.

"Well, been on a case since I was a constable. It's been eating me up; it was my first murder and many more after. I know who is doing it," Constable Dickens confessed, a weight lifted in sharing his burden.

"Peter Smith, from your old village," Mr. Gubbins deduced, showcasing an understanding based on years of experience.

"Nothing escapes you," Constable Dickens marvelled.

"Yes, including using a mutual friend to find evidence," Mr. Gubbins acknowledged with a knowing smile.

"How the hell do you know that?" Constable Dickens inquired, a mix of surprise and curiosity in his voice.

"I am or was in the intelligence game. A police report of a mugging involving Johnathon Hodges came across my desk. I was not best pleased," Mr Gubbins explained, shedding light on his connection to covert operations.

"He found evidence, strong evidence, but the Chief dismissed it all, him and those damn Masons," Constable Dickens lamented, frustration etched on his face.

"I am on the square. I am one, too. The rest of the grand lodge looks down unfavourably on police corruption. That is in the process of being sorted. Have faith. Please," Mr. Gubbins reassured, his words carrying the weight of experience and a promise for justice.

Constable Dickens handed over the Times, a sense of urgency in his eyes. Nestled within was a manila envelope, concealing the weighty case report on the Wiltshire strangler – a compilation of information that had haunted him for years.

"You can have this for a couple of days. I want to catch this bastard before he kills another innocent girl," Constable Dickens declared, his determination palpable.

"I will see it gets put back in the files at your station as soon as I can," Mr. Gubbins assured, a calm confidence radiating from his aged features.

"You don't have access," Constable Dickens pointed out, surprised.

"I have one or two other employees that may be at your station," Mr Gubbins cryptically revealing a smile on his lips. The shock on Constable Dickens' face did not go unnoticed.

"Are you going to give me one of your lemon drops in your left pocket?" Mr. Gubbins asked, a playful glint in his eyes.

Constable Dickens obliged, handing over a lemon drop. Mr. Gubbins, with a nod of thanks, got up and strolled away. The constable patted his left pocket, a smile breaking across his face – a fleeting moment of levity in a serious pursuit.

***

The burnt-out shell of what was once Daphne's home loomed in front of Derek and Danny. They carried empty plastic boxes and cautiously approached the aftermath of extensive fire damage. A futile hope lingered in the air—perhaps something had survived the flames and water's destructive dance. Derek gently encouraged Danny to enter first, acknowledging the moment's gravity.

Inside, shock and silence enveloped them. The walls, once vibrant with life, were now charred and wet. The stairs, compromised by the fire, stood as a haunting reminder of the chaos unfolding. Danny made his way to the living room, an air of solemnity surrounding him. Derek, attempting to break the heavy silence, began sorting through items. Danny, in response, nodded or shook his head, deciding the fate of each artefact.

A glint of light caught Danny's eye amidst the scorched remnants. Derek retrieved a picture frame with a press cutting and handed it to him. A smile crossed his face as Danny cleaned the soot off the glass.

"Me mum as a little girl, she was on the Windrush—the photo, it's her," Danny shared, pointing to the image. It depicted a frightened little girl held in the arms of a British policeman, tears streaming down her face.

Derek expressed sympathy, "Poor little thing, travelling all that way to this miserable, cold, wet country."

Danny recounted his mother's story, "She said she was crying because she lost her mother's St. Christopher she was wearing. Thought she would be in trouble."

"St. Christopher, the patron saint of travellers," Derek noted.

Danny continued, "Yes, the policeman in the photo gave her his crucifix, which I have in my pocket. She said it brought her good luck."

Sensing the moment's weight, Derek put his arm around Danny. "She did have good luck; she had you for a son."

The room echoed with Danny's self-doubt. "Am I good luck? This is all my fault."

Derek vehemently rejected the notion, "Please, no more talking like that. It's that scumbag out there that has done this. Not you."

" You say so," Danny conceded, surveying the room's remnants.

"I do bloody well say so. My dad survived the war with less; you can, too," Derek affirmed.

Amid the despair, Danny carefully placed the picture frame and photograph in the plastic "keep" bucket—a small act of preservation in the face of overwhelming destruction.

***

Salisbury Victorian Terrace stood silent under the cloak of night as a police car eased to a halt on the suburban street. Constable Dickens emerged, his presence casting a shadow against the dimly lit surroundings. The row of Victorian terraced houses loomed, their facades carrying the weight of history.

Approaching one particular house, he reached for the doorknob and gently pushed the door open. The glow of the streetlights seeped into the front hallway, revealing a glimpse of the modest interior. A soft hum emanated from the television in the front room, where the theme music of Coronation Street filled the air with its familiar melody, unusually resonant.

Constable Dickens stepped across the threshold, the creaking floorboards beneath his weight adding to the hushed ambience. The lights in the front room cast a warm glow, starkly contrasting the darkened exterior. The constable closed the door behind him, the faint echoes of the Coronation Street theme persisting as he ventured further into the house. The night held its secrets,

He entered his home with the weariness that only years of enforcing the law could bring. The living room, bathed in the soft glow of twilight, carried the remnants of familial warmth. As he hung his hat on the peg and placed his keys in the fruit bowl, a comforting purr signalled the arrival of his feline companion.

"Hello, Fusspot. Fancy some cream or fish? Let's check the kitchen," murmured Constable Dickens, his voice a low hum in the quietude.

Passing the stairs, a cacophony disrupted the solitude. The

intrusive blare of a television advertisement clashed with the oppressive silence, intensifying the constable's unease.

"Mary?... I am home. Have you plated my dinner?" His queries echoed through the halls, met only by the relentless buzz of the TV. Passing a family photo on the wall, the bright smiles of his wife and daughter hinted at an ominous reality.

"Mary, Susan? MARY SUSAN, ANSWER ME?" Constable Dickens called out once more, desperation colouring his voice. The silence that greeted him in the dimly lit kitchen heightened the suspense.

He turned on the lights, still cradling Fusspot. A haunting scene unfolded – two figures tied to chairs. Mary, bearing the marks of violence, sat next to Susan, their eyes reflecting fear.

Suddenly, the constable's grip on Fusspot slackened as shock seized him. A dark figure, Peter Smith, occupied the room, cruelly manipulating Susan and tearing a CND badge from her breast.

In this chilling moment, the boundaries between duty and personal anguish blurred. Constable Dickens faced a stark confrontation that would test his resolve and the very fabric of justice itself. A policeman's worst fear, the horror of the job, found its way into his home, family and peace. His voice sliced through the tension as he confronted the vile scene.
"Get your hands off her, you bastard!" he bellowed, his eyes ablaze with a righteous fury.

The night air was thick with tension, and the police car rolled to the end of the street. The constable at the wheel glimpsed the Chief's forgotten briefcase and hesitated. A moment later, he made a decision, steering the vehicle back towards Constable Dickens' house.

As the car stopped, a sudden eruption shattered the stillness.

The front of Constable Dickens' house burst outward, a violent explosion tearing through the Victorian terrace. Debris rained down, casting a ghostly pall over the scene. The shocked officer stared in horror at the devastation, his open mouth a silent witness to the unexpected cataclysm.

Amidst the chaos, a startled cat darted into the street, its eyes wide with fright. A shadow lingered at the edge of the disaster – Peter Smith, watching the havoc unfold with a malevolent satisfaction. The night had taken a sinister turn, and the consequences were etched across the shattered facade of Constable Dickens' once-quiet home.

***

The graveyard lay quiet, bathed in the gentle glow of a sombre afternoon sun. Three simple wooden crosses adorned with the names Trevor Dickens, Susan Dickens, and Mary Dickens stood sentinel over three empty graves. The remnants of a recent service lingered, populated mostly by police officers in their crisply pressed uniforms. A fleeting presence, the vicar nodded in acknowledgement before disappearing into the distance.

As the residual crowd dispersed, two figures lingered behind. Mr Gubbins, a stoic veteran, approached the graves, each step weighted with a gravity of its own. He bent, the soil in his hands cascading onto the vacant resting places. A paper bag emerged from his pocket and carelessly dropped into the late Constable Dickens' open grave. Lemon drops spilt out, a poignant gesture in the face of tragedy.

Johnathon, a stalwart companion, observed Mr Gubbins with a hint of sarcasm. "Never thought you were the sentimental type."

Sarah, another onlooker, couldn't shake the sorrow from her expression. "Boss, this is so sad."

"The papers are reporting it as a simple gas explosion," Mr Gubbins remarked, brushing the dirt from his knees.

Johnathon scoffed, "You think otherwise? Something else? You know."

"We found something at the house when retrieving the bodies," Mr Gubbins admitted, a discomfort shadowing his eyes.

"They are dead, they can't hear you. Dead is dead, the end," Johathon declared, a voice hardened by the realities of life.

"You sound like Old Jed. Speaking of old Jed, this is all linked, has to be," Mr Gubbins cryptically suggested.

Sarah, impatient with mysteries, demanded, "What really happened? Stop being so annoyingly spook-like and tell us. I have enough of this at the office."

"We know that the civil rights groups in Northern Ireland are going paramilitary," Mr Gubbins began, revealing a layer of the intricate puzzle.

"That's one of my cases. They need money, ammunition, arms, and explosives. We captured a big shipment a couple of months ago – old War Office stock," Sarah interjected, connecting the dots.

"Well, we found some remains of plastic explosive and part of a time pencil at this family's house. I am convinced he and his family were murdered," Mr Gubbins disclosed, his gaze fixated on the graves.

"Time pencils, like what Johnny and I used in the war?" Sarah inquired, recognizing the weight of the revelation.

"Exactly. Not modern stuff, but old stuff. No one makes it anymore. Most of it was disposed of," Mr Gubbins clarified, unleashing a flood of memories.

"We had that stuff in the stay-behind bunkers, but it was all decommissioned," Johathon recalled, a trace of uncertainty in his voice. "But was it? No one kept records. Where were you when the auxiliary disbanded?"

"I was in Germany looking for war criminals with the Special Air Services," Johathon replied, his mind retracing decades.

"I was recovering at Stoke Mandeville Hospital at the time. It took a year to learn to walk again," Sarah added, the specter of the past lingering.

"So, was your bunker decommissioned or not?" Mr Gubbins pressed, unearthing a hidden truth.

"Jed. Jed would have said, the stupid old goat maintained it, didn't he?" Johathon mused, grappling with the uncertainty.

"What killed this family, I am sure, came out of that bunker. Damned sure it is. It was no gas explosion. Plus, his daughter was missing clothing items," Mr Gubbins stated, the weight of his conviction palpable.

"It explains where these arms we captured in Belfast have come from. Clothing missing? What do you mean?" Sarah probed, her investigative instincts kicking in.

Johnathon, grimly connecting the dots, asked the crucial question. "Who could have known or stolen from it and killed the Constable? Did you say clothing? Knickers?"

Mr. Gubbins nodded sadly, his gaze shifting to Susan's grave. "Well, I think you and the Constable spooked someone when you did your little act of burglary."

Sarah, now confused, sought clarification. "Burglary? I thought you were not active, Johnny. You promised me. Whose house did you go into?"

Johnathon, with a sense of certainty, revealed the dark truth. "Peter Smith. Rapist, strangler, and murderer. He has been taking trophies as well. We know he killed old Jed..."

Sarah's hand collided with Johathon's cheek in a resounding slap that cut through the graveyard's hushed atmosphere. The sting of the impact echoed in the solemn surroundings as Sarah unleashed her fury.

"HOW DARE YOU LIE TO ME!" she exclaimed, her voice sharp

and filled with betrayal. The onlookers, scattered mourners in the distance, discreetly averted their gaze, recognising that this was no ordinary domestic dispute.

"He is the one who beat you to a pulp; that was no mugging; you lied to me... are we next? We have to think of our children!" Sarah's words carried anger, fear, and concern for their family's safety.

Unable to meet her eyes, Johnathon looked down at the ground with a heavy heart. "Sorry, we cannot be selfish," he admitted, his voice tinged with regret. "We need to think of the children that live near that monster. No woman or girl is safe with him around."

In a moment of shared understanding, Sarah looked up at Johathon and embraced him. Softly whispering, she reassured him, "You are a good man."

Turning her attention to Mr. Gubbins, Sarah sought answers and guidance. Her eyes locked onto the seasoned intelligence operative, awaiting his counsel in this dark revelation.

Mr. Gubbins, with a gravity befitting the situation, disclosed their next steps. "I am meeting with the Crown Court on Monday alongside the French Court. Due to the secrecy of this, we can't have members of the public knowing about the stay-behinds, assassination lists, and the links to supplying paramilitary groups. He will have to be tried in absentia, a full D notice as well. We have to follow the letter of the law. I think you and the children need a little holiday near Wiltshire, a working holiday."

The weight of the situation hung in the air as the trio grappled with the harsh reality that justice, in this instance, would be pursued in shadows and secrecy.

CHAPTER 13

Rage

The sun hung high in the sky, casting shadows across the tranquil garden park as Danny reluctantly followed behind Andy's electric wheelchair. His steps were heavy, and a cloud of sadness enveloped him. Unkempt and lacking his usual pride, Danny's appearance betrayed the tumultuous storm within.

Andy, determined to enjoy their time outdoors, urged Danny forward, a temporary escape from the confines of the nursing home.

"Lift your feet up, lad," Andy called out.

Danny, lost in his thoughts, mumbled, "What was that, Wing Commander?"

"I said lift your blooming feet up, m'lad," Andy reiterated.

The world seemed to have crumbled around Danny, and he found little solace in the simple joys of a walk in the park. His dishevelled appearance reflected the chaos that had become his life.

Andy, however, abruptly paused the wheelchair, turning back to Danny with a peculiar gesture—his hands forming a makeshift temple under his chin, a decision reached.
"Boohoo, boo bloody hoo," Andy declared, the unexpected bluntness leaving Danny stunned. He stopped walking, confusion etched across his face.

"You WHAT!" Danny exclaimed.

"I said BOO BLOODY HOO," Andy repeated, unyielding.

"Are you taking the piss?" Danny demanded.

"WHINING AND CRYING are not going to HELP you," Andy asserted, undeterred.
"I am not whining and crying. How dare you? Take that back!" Danny retorted, his frustration mounting.

"Youth of today have no bloody backbone. Oooh, my mum's dead, got nowhere to live, I am a poof, and I am so lonely. Oooh, pity me. So bloody what!" Andy mocked.

"You're starting to grate on me, old man," Danny admitted.

"You have done nothing but whine since being stabbed. You are weak and nothing but a crybaby coward, moping about like a wet weekend in Paris," Andy continued, delivering harsh truths that cut through Danny's emotional defences.

"How dare you! What would you know about it? WHAT!" Danny cried, tears streaming down his face. Andy's unexpected tirade had shattered the facade of friendship.

"You would have died in the first wave of the War. You have a distinct LACK OF MORAL FIBRE!!! You sicken me, you wannabe nurse fairy," Andy spat.

"I HAVE LOST MY MUM! Sod you. Take yourself back to the home," Danny shouted.
"Even your mum did not know you were a homosexual, poor excuse for a man," Andy taunted.

Fueled by anger, Danny turned back to Andy and approached the wheelchair. He grabbed the old man by his collar, his hand poised to strike, but he restrained himself.

"HIT ME, YOU QUEER BASTARD! HIT ME!" Andy goaded.

Danny swung his fist forward, only to have Andy deftly evade the blow. Stunned, Danny looked at Andy, who was grinning.

"Oh, phew, that took some effort, Danny, me lad. How does that feel?" Andy asked.

"I am shaking. My head is spinning," Danny confessed, his body trembling.

"See, you have what it takes to fight back," Andy reassured him.

"You set me up, you old bastard," Danny accused.

"Less of the old," Andy quipped.

"I wanted to hurt you. So sorry, Andy," Danny admitted, collapsing to the ground, his body shaking uncontrollably.

"Don't be. I want YOU to defend yourself for when the time comes, not if but when," Andy declared as he offered guidance to the shaken Danny.

As the adrenaline coursed through Danny's veins, he struggled to comprehend the emotional maelstrom he had just experienced.

"Can't stop the shaking," Danny uttered.

"That's adrenaline, son. It will be over soon. And boy, the comedown will be bad if you're not used to it," Andy explained.

"Did you mean that gay stuff?" Danny inquired.

"Of course not. The only person who didn't know you were gay was your mum. You were just her sweet little boy. Everyone but her knew," Andy clarified.

"Why did you make me so angry, enough to hit you? Why?" Danny questioned.

"Because I am permitting you to get that bastard that killed your mother. He keeps escaping the law. Just don't get caught,"

Andy advised.

"Don't get caught. I don't care if I do," Danny asserted.

"I care if you do. If you're banged up, who will I watch Countdown with?" Andy joked.
"You cheat anyway," Danny retorted.
"What do you mean cheat, you cheeky little sod? You punch like a sissy. Cancelling Countdown, gonna be Rocky instead," Andy teased as the two friends left the park, their banter echoing through the air.

***

Under the cloak of night, the Liverpool Docks stood silent and mysterious. A tiny Ford Anglia navigated the shadows, its lights extinguished as Sarah, the driver smoothly engaged the handbrake. Johnny took a strip of packing tape in the passenger seat and covered the courtesy light, stealing a fleeting peck on Sarah's cheek. Dressed in dark boiler suits and watch caps, the pair merged seamlessly with the darkness.

Closing the car doors was a deliberate, noiseless act, part of their meticulously planned covert operation. Johnny, ever watchful, scanned the surroundings to ensure their activities remained unseen.

Approaching the fence, they noticed the glint of barbed wire overhead. Undeterred, they draped a thick blanket over it. Sarah, ever vigilant, manipulated the chain link. At the same time, Johnny, resourceful as ever, pulled a rope through the fence, securing it to muffle any potential clinks. Gracefully scaling the fence, Sarah anchored herself with the rope cleat, allowing Johnny to follow suit. Their movements were a synchronised dance, a testament to their history of collaboration.

In a hushed whisper, Johnny remarked, "Just like old times."

Silhouetted against the night, they traversed the yard, exploiting the cover of darkness on their way to the export goods yard. In the distance, stevedores and workers took a break, perched on boxes, enjoying sandwiches, tea, and cigarettes during the early morning reprieve.

Sarah and Johnathon located the boxes of interest, expertly undoing wire clasps with a cutter. Within, cardboard boxes marked "War Office" with serial numbers awaited their exploration. Sarah opened one, revealing time pencils. A glance passed between them, Johnny nodding in approval.

Another packet, marked "Gun Cotton Pads," drew Sarah's attention, but Johnny intervened with caution.

"Stop. These are over twenty years old and very unstable. Let me deal with them," he whispered.

A large glass syringe filled with a yellow liquid emerged from Johnny's pocket. He injected it through the packet, neutralising the explosive pads with precision.

"This will make the explosive neutral. The time pencils I can't touch—too dangerous," he explained.

Digging deeper, Sarah discovered wax paper square blocks —plastic explosives. She pocketed one after scrutinising the label, showing it to Johnny.

"This is the auxiliary stock. We used this at the training school," she said.

Johnny noticed the newspaper used as packing material. Unravelling one, he found it to be the Wiltshire Times.

"Well, there's proof it is Peter," he remarked.
"Yes, the same paper where he lives. But it does not tie him to this shipment," Sarah replied, focusing on the evidence.

A subtle smile played on Johnathon's lips as he turned the page, revealing the front page with a delivery mark in pencil— the name of Peter's pub.

***

The sun cast a warm glow over the canal path as Danny, clad in his care assistant uniform, accompanied Andy on an afternoon stroll. Andy, nestled comfortably in his motorised wheelchair, chatted animatedly while Danny walked alongside. In Andy's hand, a bread bag lay ready for feeding the ducks and swans that populated the serene waterway.

As they meandered along the canal's edge, the gentle breeze carried the laughter of children and the occasional quack of a duck. Danny and Andy were enveloped by a sudden chill while passing beneath a bridge. Danny's eyes caught sight of a "For Sale" sign planted on the path ahead. Without hesitation, he hastened forward, bending to retrieve the sign so Andy could continue unhindered.

The air was crisp with the promise of spring, and the tranquillity of the afternoon stroll belied the mysteries that awaited them around the bend.

As Danny stooped to retrieve the sign, a sudden, brutal force slammed into his back, knocking the wind from his lungs. His body convulsed in pain as he crumpled to the ground, unable to utter a sound. The world spun around him, his vision blurred with agony as he struggled to comprehend what had just happened. Unable to move, unable to call for help, he lay there, vulnerable and at the mercy of unseen assailants.

Danny lay on the ground, his voice stifled by shock and pain as a barrage of boots and kicks rained down upon his body. Each blow seemed to paralyse him further, rendering him immobile and at the mercy of the relentless assault. Through blurred vision, he caught sight of mountain bike wheels in motion, followed by the sickening thud of his bike hitting the ground.

Meanwhile, Andy remained in his chair, a defiant figure amidst the chaos. With his stick in hand, he fought against the baying gang, pushing them away as they closed in on him. But the odds were against him, and soon, one of the assailants ripped his medals from his chest, adding insult to injury. The air filled with shouts and jeers as they continued to taunt and strike him.

Despite his bravery, Andy couldn't suppress the fear rising within him. With hands raised in a feeble attempt to shield himself, he braced for each blow, his resolve tested by the relentless assault. As Danny lay winded on the ground, Stephan Greenes 'sneering face sent a chill down his spine. The chaos around him seemed to intensify as Andy, gripped by terror, attempted to manoeuvre his wheelchair away. But Stephan Greenes approached with chilling composure, calmly redirecting the joystick control, sending Andy's chair perilously close to the canal's edge.

In slow motion, Danny watched in horror as the wheelchair teetered on the brink. Andy's desperate cry for help pierced the air, echoing off the surrounding walls. Then, with a sickening splash, the chair plunged into the murky water. Andy was still strapped in, thrashing and struggling against the inevitable descent.

The gang, revelling in their cruelty, pulled out their phones to capture the scene, their laughter mingling with Andy's frantic splashing. With a callous disregard for human life, they swiftly departed, leaving Danny alone and battered, crawling weakly towards the water's edge, his body a canvas of pain and blood.

With trembling hands, Danny reached out as he watched his friend sink beneath the surface, bubbles trailing in his wake. In a final act of contempt, Stephan Greenes tossed a poppy brooch to the ground before Danny, crushing it beneath his heel. Overwhelmed by anguish and despair, Danny succumbed to darkness, his consciousness slipping away as he lay beside the unforgiving waters of the canal.

***

Sarah and Johnny arrived at the car park atop Boxhill in Surrey, their Ford Anglia settling into a quiet spot. They stepped out cautiously, scanning their surroundings for any signs of surveillance. Making their way to a secluded bench, they decided on the serenity of the observation area, providing a momentary respite.

Their solitude was interrupted by the arrival of another figure – Andy, an old school friend of Johnny's. Johnny's face lit up with recognition, a warm smile spreading across his features.

Feeling a sense of déjà vu, Sarah pieced together the puzzle before her.

"I knew it. I just knew it, Andy. You're with MI5, aren't you?" she exclaimed.

Johnny said, "You disappeared after the war, old friend."

"And yet, you were never too far away," Sarah added. "I thought I saw you lurking around my workplace. Can't miss that red hair anywhere."

Andy, with a calm character, confirmed Sarah's suspicions. "I'm a regional liaison with cover. I happened to be stationed at Salisbury Police Station. For the police, I'm just a civil servant, working quietly in the background. The less they know..."

Sarah's attention shifted, "So, you're aware of Constable Dickens then?"
Andy nodded solemnly. "Yes, it's quite sad. I've postponed my retirement until his replacement arrives."

Johnny steered the conversation towards more pressing matters. "Let's cut to the chase. We've got evidence linking Peter Smith to supplying weapons and ammunition to the IRA."
"And there's something else about Peter," Andy interjected.

"He's a psychopath, a truly honest psychopath. Inspector Dickens had him in his sights. But the police masons covered for him, including the Chief Inspector. It cost Dickens his life, as you're aware."

Sarah handed over the plastic explosive and the newspaper evidence to Andy, acknowledging its importance for the trial in absentia.

As the conversation veered towards lighter topics, Johnny inquired about Andy's plans for retirement.

Andy pondered momentarily before replying, "Hmm, write a book. I'll use my dog's name for security. A book about a country copper."

Johnny chuckled, "You're going to use the name Hermitage as an author?"

Andy nodded with pride, "Hermitage Banks, indeed I am."

***

Danny sat in the wheelchair, battered and bruised, beside Derek's beloved Volvo in the multistory car park of the hospital. His face, hidden beneath the hood of his hoodie, bore the evidence of a recent altercation, every mark a testament to the violence he had endured.

Derek approached, concern etched on his face as he reached out to assist Danny into the car. But all he received in return was a sombre shrug from Danny, his eyes clouded with pain and exhaustion.

"Home then, get you some rest," Derek offered, his voice laced with worry.

But Danny's request caught him off guard. "Can we go to the care home first, please?" he asked, his tone tinged with urgency.

Derek hesitated, glancing at his watch. "You sure? We have a meeting with the police this afternoon," he reminded Danny.

"Yes, sure. Care home first," Danny insisted, his voice steady despite the turmoil.

Derek frowned, unconvinced by Danny's resolve. "Well, I think it's too soon, but you're adamant that you need some form of closure," he conceded reluctantly.

"I was not just his bloody nurse or carer; he was my friend. I need to do something," Danny asserted, his voice trembling with emotion.

Derek sighed, resigning himself to Danny's wishes. "Well, OK, you're the boss. But for the record, I think it's a bad idea. A bad idea."

With a heavy heart, Derek slipped on his driving gloves, the leather creaking softly as he started the car and pulled away from the car park. The engine roared to life, drowning out the silence between them as they embarked on a journey fraught with uncertainty and pain.

***

The evening cast a subdued hue over the scene in Andy's house's dimly lit living room. Clad in his pyjamas, slippers, and robe, Andy sat by the table, his gaze fixed on the silent television screen. The faint glow of the set illuminated his features, revealing lines of weariness etched into his face.

With a sense of urgency, Andy gripped the phone tightly in his hand, his voice low as he spoke into the receiver.

"Yes, Johnny, have some news," he murmured, his tone grave. "Another young girl has been snatched from a caravan park...years old...yes, Wiltshire... it's not on the news...but I think it's him...he lost surveillance last night up in the Wirral. We think he travelled south...yes...the boys looked at the stuff... I can't say too much on an open line, but it's the same...court proceedings with the UK and France start tomorrow in his absence...he has a legal team for his defence."

With a heavy sigh, Andy replaced the phone on the receiver and leaned back in his chair, exhaustion weighing heavily upon him.

A voice broke the silence, drawing Andy's attention. Mr Quentin Tavistock, a figure of authority and respect, sat opposite Andy, dressed in matching pyjamas. His presence brought a sense of gravity to the room, his words laden with significance.

"How did he take it?" Mr Tavistock inquired softly, his eyes fixed on Andy.

"You know, Quentin," Andy replied wearily, "he just wants to bury the man, just bury him, sod the court."

Mr. Tavistock nodded in understanding. "It has to be all legal," he reminded Andy gently.
"I know, we know about breaking the law," Andy conceded, his

voice tinged with resignation.

With a gesture of sympathy, Mr Tavistock reached out. He placed a hand on Andy's, the weight of his touch conveying reassurance and solidarity.

"You are a good man, Andy," he affirmed quietly. "A good man. That scumbag that killed Mr Dickens and all those girls will face the justice of sorts."

In the quiet of the room, the weight of their shared burden hung heavy in the air, a testament to the darkness that lurked beyond the safety of Andy's home. And as the evening pressed on, they both knew their fight for justice was far from over.

***

Danny and Derek entered the dimly lit room of the Wing Commander's quarters, greeted by a sense of coldness and desolation. The atmosphere was heavy with memories of days gone by, evidenced by the array of pictures and knickknacks adorning the space – relics of a bygone era, relics of war.

Cardboard boxes lay scattered across the bed, filled to the brim with the Wing Commander's belongings – clothes, trinkets, and memories bundled together in a haphazard jumble. Danny carefully placed a "Countryside Copper" book into one of the boxes, and a token of friendship returned.

"Thanks, dear friend, just returning it," he muttered quietly, his voice tinged with sadness.
Meanwhile, Derek's curiosity got the better of him as he noticed something peculiar in another box. With a half-smile, he retrieved a familiar book " –Countryside Copper" by Hermitage Banks.

"Look in this box," Derek exclaimed, his excitement palpable. "He has a half dozen of those books."

As Danny's eyes scanned the contents of the box, a mixture of surprise and intrigue flickered across his face. But before he could comment, their conversation was interrupted by the arrival of Miss Fontaine, the nursing staff member tasked with clearing the room.

"Hello, hello," Miss Fontaine said, her voice sharp and businesslike. "We are waiting for the bin men to clear this away."

Danny's brow furrowed in disapproval. "Sorry, but he is dead, and you have the bin men in to clear the room. That's disrespectful," he retorted, his tone firm.

But Miss Fontaine remained unmoved, focusing solely on the

task at hand. "Danny, we have a new guest tomorrow that needs this room. Stop being so sensitive," she replied curtly.

Derek, however, was quick to come to Danny's defence, his words laced with indignation. "I see, Miss Fontaine, that your sensitivity and care show no bounds," he remarked, his voice dripping with sarcasm.

Miss Fontaine brushed off their concerns with a dismissive wave of her hand. "Be as that may, this is a business, not a charity. This stuff has to go," she declared, her tone final.

But Derek had other plans. "We will take it, we will take it all, and preserve the memory of a war hero. Like these books," he asserted, holding up the copies of "Countryside Copper" for emphasis.

Miss Fontaine's expression softened slightly as she revealed a piece of the Wing Commander's past – a story of rejection and resilience. "Oh, so you act like a friend, but you don't know about his books," she remarked, her tone tinged with bitterness. "Hmm, he wrote those when he retired. He is Hermitage Banks and made some money out of it as well. He stopped writing when his long-term partner, an old retired Home Office civil servant, died."

Derek's eyes widened in surprise, his perception of the Wing Commander shifting instantly. "So, he has no family?" he inquired, his voice filled with sympathy.

Miss Fontaine shook her head sadly. "His family disowned him when they discovered he was gay. He came out in...one of the first. It was taboo at the time," she explained, her words heavy with judgment.

The revelation left Danny feeling sadness, anger, and a newfound kinship. "Miss Fontaine, I still work here, do I not?" he interjected, his voice steady.

"Yes, Danny, you do," Miss Fontaine conceded, her tone

begrudging.

Danny took a deep breath, steeling himself for what he would reveal. "Well, I am gay," he declared, his words hanging in the air, uncertain of the reaction to come.

But Derek's response was swift and unwavering. "I know you are, son. Proud of you," he affirmed, his hand resting reassuringly on Danny's shoulder.

Danny felt relieved as he processed Derek's words, a newfound sense of acceptance and belonging filling the room. "You called me son. Do you mean that?" he asked, his voice tentative.

"Of course I do. I am not a dinosaur yet," Derek replied with a chuckle, his tone warm and genuine. "I happen to like the Village People..."

As the echoes of their laughter filled the room, Danny and Derek shared a moment of connection, bound together by their past struggles and triumphs. In the face of adversity, they found solace in each other's company, forging a bond that transcended the boundaries of time and space.

***

Derek and Judy were drawn closer together, the gravity of Andy's past revelations sinking in with every word he uttered.

"You don't think, Judy, you know that holiday," Derek inquired, his voice heavy with curiosity and concern.

Judy, her mind flickering with memories, responded, "It could be a coincidence, but we were thrown out of a pub on a family holiday in Dad's old village."

Derek, spurred by a sudden realisation, pulled out his phone, fingers tapping away in search of something meaningful. Andy continued his tale, sharing a narrative connecting the dots of a past they had long tried to bury.

"There was only one pub, and Peter took over his dad's," Derek said as he handed his phone to Judy.

Derek urged her to explore the information he had uncovered. "Googled it. This came up: 'Murder of Publican Peter Smith, stabbed to death in the pub.' Ah, there's a press cutting. Says suspicions are of a motorbiker leaving the pub in haste. The motorbiker attempted to rob Peter Smith and escaped on his motorbike. Police are appealing for witnesses...'"

Derek paused, grappling with a sudden revelation. "Chief Constable Dickens. No, that can't be the same village, Bobby?"

Derek pondered aloud, "Wonder if Mum knew he had been murdered?"

Judy, her thoughts racing, considered the implications. "Mum must have known, and Dad?"

Judy, her eyes seeking answers, questioned, "Are you suggesting?"

Derek interjected, voicing the unspoken query, "That Dad and Mum had something to do with his murder?" The revelation hung in the air, casting a shadow over the unsuspecting family as they grappled with the possibility that their parents' wartime deeds had left a haunting legacy. He sat back and watched the memory play out like it was yesterday.

***

Under the bright summer sun, a Ford Anglia rolled into the pub's car park, filled with the Hodges family. Eager children burst out, their excitement palpable. Sarah and Johnathon, however, approached the entrance with a mixture of anticipation and hesitation.

In the pub's cosy interior, Derek and Judy, radiating youthful energy, quickly chose a table by the window. Johnny settled in with his children in another corner. Across the room, a man in a suit buried himself in the day's edition of The Times, his face hidden. Beside him, another gentleman savoured a glass of brandy, partially obscured.

Sarah engaged a diligent barmaid who was meticulously drying glasses at the bar.
With politeness, Sarah said, "Could we have three lime cordials and a stout for him, please?"

The barmaid, displaying curiosity, asked, "Visiting, are we?"

Reflectively, Sarah responded, "Yes, you could say that. Revisiting old haunts, laying to rest some old ghosts."

The barmaid, now thoughtful, commented, "You and your husband seem kind of familiar."
Opening up, Sarah shared, "My husband grew up here in the village. I met him at the start of the war, not far from here."

Curious, the barmaid noted, "You seem so familiar too."

Sharing more of their story, Sarah continued, "My husband, Johnny—the larger one over there with the kids—we left quite suddenly. Spent some time at the lodge, near the woods."

Nostalgically, the barmaid recalled, "Old Jed's place. I loved him, a nice, kind man, and his old, mangy dog. That dog never left his side, not once."

Sentimental, Sarah added, "He looked after me when I was very sick and took Johnny on as an apprentice."

Gently, the barmaid mentioned, "You know, how can I put it? He's no longer with us."

Nodding, Sarah acknowledged, "That's one of the old ghosts I'm here to lay."

In a warning tone, the barmaid said, "Word of gentle advice: when the landlord comes in, don't mention any of this, please. He has a foul temper."

Glancing around to ensure the landlord wasn't within earshot, the barmaid gingerly set the bar towel down. Anxiety etched her features, her hands bearing the marks of relentless wringing, now red and raw.

"He's not a nice man, a bit of a crook," she confided, voice hushed. "I think he knows more about Old Jed than he's letting on. That's as much as I can say or dare."
Detecting an air of fear, Sarah inquired, "You're scared of him?"
Nodding hesitantly, the barmaid replied, "You should be, too. He's not nice, and don't let your little girl wander off by herself in here... please."

With a wary glance, the barmaid placed a tray carrying lime cordials and a stout on the counter. Sarah picked up the tray and made her way over to the family table.

Johnathon noticed the troubled expression on Sarah's face as she returned to their table. He couldn't help but inquire, "You look like you've seen a ghost."

Deep in thought, Sarah replied, "I know that girl from somewhere. She's scared of the landlord and has bruises on her arms. Look at how she walks—it's like she's expecting something to happen any minute."

Concern etched on his features, Johnathon offered, "Do you want me to speak to her? She's practically walking on eggshells. I think it's the same girl I saw last here."

Asserting her capability, Sarah said, "I've got this. Best take this tray back."

Making her way to the bar, Sarah noted the barmaid with her back turned. Deliberately dropping the tray onto the bar, she startled the barmaid, who jumped and turned. A silent confirmation passed between Sarah and Johnathon, solidifying their suspicions.

The barmaid, recovering from the bang, exclaimed, "Oh, you gave me such a fright!"
Sarah quickly apologised, saying, "Sorry, I am very clumsy."

The barmaid, visibly nervous, shared, "Me too. Hope his lordship doesn't hear it; he's out back."

Sarah suggested, "Let's talk girl to girl. You're scared of him." She glanced back at Johnathon, who signalled reassurance with an OK sign.

The barmaid, caught off guard, questioned, "What makes you say that?"

With empathy in her eyes, Sarah disclosed, "I have my experience of being scared, abused, even tortured."

Observing the barmaid's demeanour change, Sarah gently held her and then offered a handkerchief. "Not from your husband over there? He looks kind; swear I have seen him before."

Looking down in shame, the barmaid said, "No, during the war —long story. I am more concerned about you. Have you lived here long?"

Opening up, the barmaid shared, "I am a stepchild. My mum married him. I hated him from the off. There were rumours in the village that he married my mother for her money."

Expressing sympathy, Sarah said, "I'm Sorry to hear that. I will ask you a direct question: Is your stepfather, by any chance, called Peter?"

The revelation struck the barmaid, who gasped, "My God, you know him. He's out back, you know what he's like. I think you best leave. He's a bastard. Not nice around women, thinks he's a charmer... which he ain't."
Determined, Sarah asked, "Does he do things with you that you're ashamed about? You can nod. I am going to help you."

The reticent barmaid slowly nodded, a tear trailing down her cheek. She appeared breathless and suddenly looked more vulnerable and weak.

"Most of the girls in the village will not talk about it, but there are rumours he had his wicked way with some of the village girls. Some have left," she confided, her voice barely above a whisper. "Old Jed knew something, and one night he came storming in here and threatened Peter... A couple of nights later, Old Jed and his dog were murdered, you know..."

Glancing cautiously around her, the barmaid leaned in close to Sarah. "My mum one night got drunk and took too many pills. Police were called; they said it was an unfortunate accident. She later died in the hospital, but to this day, I think he killed her. She never had pills before."

Sarah's expression softened with sympathy. "Gosh, you poor thing. Why have you not left, gone your own way?"

"He keeps my wages for my rent, and it's a roof. I have no money and no relatives. My Aunt in Coleshill passed away. I used to visit as a little girl at her post office," the barmaid explained.

Realising the gravity of the situation, Sarah summoned her

husband. "Excuse me, Johnny, could you please come over here?"

Johnny stood up and made his way to the bar, perplexed by Sarah's request.

"Johnny, this lovely lady used to live at the Post Office in Coleshill during the war," Sarah introduced, a spark of recognition lighting up in Johnathon's eyes.

Johnathon's confusion turned to realisation, and a warm smile crept onto his face as he looked at the barmaid. "I bought you a bag of toffees... Amelia, isn't it?"

Amelia, the barmaid, responded with a nostalgic grin. "Thought I recognised you two. You both came on the same day. I must have been tiny then. You bought me sweets."

"He didn't have enough change, so I gave him the rest. Then I had to marry him," Sarah teased, putting her arm around Johnathon.

"Biggest mistake of my life... only joking," Johnathon chuckled. "Sarah says you're having problems."

Amelia glanced over at Sarah, who nodded reassuringly. Sarah reached for Amelia's arm, gently patting it. Slowly lifting the cuff, Amelia revealed a multitude of hidden bruises. She looked at Johnny with shame.

"Are there any more like that?" Johnny asked with concern, his eyes fixed on Amelia. Amelia, tears streaming down her face, nodded silently.

Johnathon's direct inquiry left Amelia startled. Her eyes widened in disbelief at the unanticipated question. Seeking solace, she glanced at Sarah, who offered a subtle nod, signalling that it was okay to answer. Amelia, flustered and embarrassed, quickly nodded in affirmation.

Maintaining a composed demeanour, Johnathon continued,

"Can you clean her up, please?" Sarah guided Amelia through the bar hatch to the saloon area. She wiped Amelia's face with a hanky, gently applied makeup, and comforted her.

Meanwhile, Johnathon spotted a pack of playing cards on a nearby table. Picking them up, he strolled over to the corner where the man with the newspaper was seated. Their conversation unfolded unheard by others. Afterwards, Johnathon returned to the family table, the weight of the situation evident in his eyes.

With a calm and reassuring tone, Johnathon addressed Judy and Derek, "This nice lady is going to teach you how to play a game. If you hear any shouting, the game is to play hide and seek in our car. But you must play snap first. The first one to snap and then hide in the car when shouting wins. You OK with that, Amelia?"

Amelia nods in agreement, adopting a protective demeanour for the children's sake. She looks at Johnathon, a silent acknowledgement of her readiness, and joins the children to play snap. Oblivious to the unfolding tension, the children engage in the game. At the same time, Amelia, though concealing her own turmoil, begins to feel a sense of safety.

Peter barges into the bar area, his eyes locking on Sarah and Johnathon. Recognising the familiar faces, his temper flares, and he storms towards them with violent intent. Sensing the threat, Sarah and Johnathon move quickly to block the door, preventing Peter from reaching Amelia, who fled outside.

The children, alarmed by the sudden tension, run out of the pub door toward the car, thinking it's all part of the game. Their innocent cries and shock reveal the unintended impact of the escalating situation on their young minds. Amelia, now outside, becomes their unintentional leader in this impromptu escape.

The pub car park was filled with the echoes of turmoil as children, still teary-eyed and confused, followed Amelia's instructions, running toward the waiting car. Their cries echoed in the air, creating a poignant backdrop to the chaotic scene. Uncertain about the right moment to re-enter, Amelia hesitated at the pub door, her emotions in turmoil and the disconcerting sounds of shattering glass emanating from within.

Sarah and Johnathon tried to comfort the distressed children while rushing toward the car. In the backseat, their tears mingled with the palpable tension.

"I left my handbag; I need to retrieve it. Johnny, stay here," Sarah said, a hint of concern in her voice.

Leaning over, Johnathon gripped her hand, his worry evident. "Be careful, take every precaution. He's a caged tiger."

"This is not my first encounter with a tiger," Sarah determinedly replied.
"Well, it's going to be his first."

With that, Sarah entered the pub, and Amelia followed closely, protectively holding her arm.

**

In the murky depths of the alley behind the nightclub, the pulsating rhythm of music echoed off the walls, mingling with the laughter of Sally and her friends as they stumbled out into the night. Their laughter was buoyant, fueled by alcohol and excitement, despite the chill in the air that nipped at their scantily clad forms.

In this nocturnal scene, Stephan rode his bike, accompanied by a watchful friend on another bike. His presence was like a shadow moving through the darkness, his eyes sharp and calculating as he approached Sally and her friends.

"Here is a bag of five. Tenner, this will do the biz for you girls," Stephan announced, his voice slick with confidence.

Sally raised an eyebrow, her scepticism evident. "Tenner? That's cheap for a bag of five," she remarked, her tone teasing.

Stephan smirked, his charm oozing with every word. "Tenner each, fifty quid. Hurry up, the old bill is about," he urged, a sense of urgency creeping into his voice.

Without hesitation, Sally collected the money from her friends and handed it to Stephan. He snatched the money eagerly, passing it to his companion without a second thought.

"Stick them under your tongue when you go inside. If you want any more or anything stronger... or my company," Stephan added with a wink, his gaze lingering on Sally suggestively. "My burner number is on the back of that bus stop. Just call it, and we'll call back. Nice doing business with yer."

Sally chuckled, a hint of mockery in her voice. "Yes, thanks, stud," she replied, her tone playful.

As Stephan cycled into the night, Sally and her friends exchanged amused glances. "Call me if you want a good time," one of the girls joked, her laughter echoing in the alley. "Looks like he stopped off his paper round to do some happy pills."

Sally shushed her friend, a nervous glance cast over her shoulder. "He'll hear you," she whispered, her voice tinged with apprehension.

Sure enough, Stephan had overheard their conversation. He spat on the ground with a contemptuous snarl before pedalling away with his companion in tow.

"Aww, scared studly off," one of the girls taunted, her laughter ringing into the night. "I'm too much of a girl for him."

With a final burst of laughter, Sally and her friends pushed their way to the front of the queue, flirting shamelessly with the bouncers as they disappeared into the neon-lit interior of the nightclub.

***

Feeling a sense of urgency and a need to ensure their safety, Johnathon decided to take matters into his own hands. Exiting the car, he noticed an open window in the bedroom. Without hesitation, he ascended the drainpipe, disappearing into the window with a silent, stealthy manoeuvre concealed from the children's watchful eyes.

In the dimly lit pub, the aftermath of chaos was evident – shattered glass strewn across the floor. A palpable tension hung in the air. Holding a broken shotgun, Peter appeared, fumbling with the stock and attempting to load it, his frustration adding to the charged atmosphere.

***

The early morning hours cast a hushed atmosphere in Derek's dimly lit kitchen. Clad in a dressing gown, Danny could not sleep, his restless energy drawing him to the kitchen. With a sigh, he opened the fridge door, the soft glow illuminating the room as he reached for a carton of milk. Pouring himself a glass, he settled at the breakfast bar, the cool liquid offering a momentary distraction from his thoughts.

As he took a sip, a faint buzzing sound drew his attention to the couch, where Derek's mobile phone lay. Seven missed calls from Judy flashed on the screen, a sense of urgency emanating from the device.

Before Danny could react, the shrill ring of the main house telephone shattered the silence, accompanied by noises from upstairs and the clatter of a phone hitting the floor. In a flurry of movement, Derek descended the stairs, hastily pulling on trousers and shoes.

"Oh, did I wake you? It's an emergency! You, you're a nurse, put some clothes on quickly. HURRY!" Derek exclaimed, his urgency palpable as he tossed Danny the mobile phone.

Danny caught it instinctively, his mind racing as he hurriedly shut the fridge door with a slam and rushed upstairs to dress. Meanwhile, Derek hastily opened the clamshell mobile phone and dialled Judy's number.

"Judy, Judy, I know, I know. Stay there, call an ambulance, call a bloody ambulance. Me and Danny will be over. He's a nurse... I know he's not a nurse, but he's medical!" Derek's voice crackled with urgency as he relayed instructions to Judy on the other end of the line.

As Derek's wife, Paula, descended the stairs in a daze, Derek's attention turned to her. "Go back to bed! I will sort this," he ordered tersely, his voice cutting through the confusion.

Danny determinedly descended the stairs, dressed in a

tracksuit and trainers. Paula blocked his path, but Derek wasted no time urging her aside. "Bloody move, let the boy through!" he barked, his frustration evident.

Danny and Derek rushed out the front door together, the urgency propelling them forward. In haste, Derek bypassed his usual rituals, jumping into the car and speeding without hesitation. As they tore down the driveway, Derek's frustration boiled over, his anger directed at the situation unfolding before them.

"Stupid, stupid girl," Derek muttered, his fist pounding the steering wheel in frustration.
"Derek, what's going on? You're frightening me!" Danny exclaimed, his voice tinged with concern.

"It's Sal, Sally. The one permanently attached to that mobile phone," Derek replied grimly, focusing solely on the road ahead.

"Is she in trouble?" Danny pressed, his mind racing with possibilities.

"She's had a bloody overdose," Derek answered, the gravity of the situation weighing heavily upon them both.

***

Amelia, seeking refuge, dashed into the bar area, clutching the phone. As she lifted the receiver, the realisation of a deadline sent a shiver down her spine. Half-hiding behind a shelf, she watched in fear as Sarah walked, seemingly unfazed, directly toward the enraged landlord.

With a shotgun, Peter sidled up to Sarah, his breath invasive. Calmly, she pushed the barrel of the broken weapon to the side, undeterred.

"We can do this right now, just you and me while your coward is in the car," Peter sneered, licking her face with a sinister grin. His glare shifted to the terrified Amelia in the corner.

"You, girl, you're next! I'll have both of you at the same time."

Closing the gun together, ready to fire, Peter's threats hung in the air. However, Sarah remained unyielding, firmly in control of the precarious situation.

Sarah looks over the men at the corner table,

"Monsieur, voici les messieurs en question, je peux confirmer que c'est Peter Smith (Sir this is the gentlemen in question I can confirm this is Peter Smith)"

The Gentlemen in the corner both nod their heads.
Sarah looks back at Peter and walks up to him, almost face to face. She is strong,

"I have a number for you, 647. "

Confused, Peter questions Sarah, "64 what? "

Sarah looks him in the eye and cooly and succinctly tells him, "You killed 647 men, women and children. During the war, when you put me in a coma, I could not pass on the message that an entire French village was destined to be wiped out; your ignorance killed those people, and then you murdered

Old Jed and snitch, Set fire to the lodge, Countless rapes, murders round the villages, and you have been abusing your stepdaughter.

Sarah's gaze bore into Peter, her eyes reflecting a mix of sorrow and resolute determination. She held up a faded press cutting, a relic from a dark chapter in their shared history — a gas explosion that had claimed the lives of a police officer and his family. Despite the gravity of the tragedy, Peter callously dismissed it with a heartless laugh.

"You not only orchestrated the destruction of a secret wartime pigeon messaging service, but your actions have caused immeasurable suffering. You are a coward, a murderer, an abuser, a thief. Your existence has left a trail of destruction, and you deserve to face the consequences."

In response, Peter's callous smirk and crossed arms betrayed a defiant and unrepentant soul. His arrogance seemed impenetrable, shielded from the weight of his sins. Sarah, fueled by a potent mix of anger and a steadfast commitment to justice, stood her ground. It was a moment of reckoning, where the truth confronted the embodiment of evil.

Peter then runs his hand down Sarah's face, then to her top; there is a button on one side that he starts playing with.

Amelia stood tall, her eyes burning with a newfound strength that had emerged from her painful past. The weight of her history, once a burden, had transformed into a source of resilience, and she spoke with unwavering determination.

Amelia's spirit remained unbroken in the face of Peter Smith's callous words. The memories of her mother's tragic fate and the years of enduring abuse fueled a fire within her, propelling her to confront the malevolent force that had cast its shadow over her life.

"You took my mother's life, but you won't break me," Amelia declared, her voice resonating with a newfound resolve.

The cruelty and twisted actions that had defined her past would no longer dictate her future. She had found her voice, which echoed with a promise to expose the truth.

Peter Smith scoffed, attempting to dismiss her words, but Amelia pressed on. Empowered by the strength she had discovered within herself, she confronted him with a fearless gaze.

"You can't silence me anymore," she asserted, the echoes of fear dissipating with every word. "Your reign of terror ends here. I'll be a voice for those who suffered in silence and ensure you face the consequences for every life you've ruined. You know, when I went north to see relatives, I had an abortion in some seedy house in Birmingham. I was sick for months. But you did not care. ."

As Amelia spoke, the shadows of fear began to retreat from her spirit. The negativity that had surrounded her transformed into a joyous crescendo of empowerment. She stood firm, ready to face the challenges ahead, determined to bring justice not only for herself but for all the victims who had endured Peter Smith's malevolence.

Amelia's courageous stand against Peter Smith left her emotionally drained and physically weakened. The weight of years of abuse and the revelation of her mother's fate had taken its toll on her resilient spirit. Amelia's strength wavered as the echoes of her powerful words lingered in the air, and her trembling legs gave way beneath her.

With a profound sigh, Amelia crumpled to the ground, her body succumbing to the accumulated exhaustion of years spent enduring the darkness that Peter had wrought upon her life. Fueled by newfound determination, the once indomitable force now lay vulnerable and shattered.

Her chest heaved with sobs as the emotional floodgates opened, releasing the pent-up anguish she had carried for so long. The weight of the past pressed down on her, and the shadows that had haunted her retreated only to be replaced by the stark reality of her pain.

In that moment of vulnerability, as Amelia collapsed in the corner, racked with emotion, crying and curled up in the fetal position, the gentleman in the corner, still reading the Times, put his paper down carefully. He folded it, his figure in shadow, and then got up, putting on his hat and gloves. He strolled behind Peter, who remained unaware of his presence. Simultaneously, the other gentleman calmly rose to follow Mr. Gubbins.

As the characters closed in around Peter, their collective actions became a silent symphony of support for Amelia, a testament to the strength that emerged from shared resilience and a determination to confront the shadows of the past.

Amelia's voice trembled as she unleashed the torrent of pain and anger that had been buried within her for years. The room fell silent, and Mr. Gubbins spoke gently, understanding the gravity of her emotions.

"Amelia, I can sense the agony you've been carrying. It's time to free yourself from this torment. Close your eyes, put your hands over your ears, and let it all out. You're stronger than you think, and facing these demons will free you. Trust me."

Amelia hesitated momentarily, her tears mixing with the anguish in her heart. She took a deep breath, closed her eyes, and covered her ears as if shielding herself from the haunting memories. In the quiet of that room, she released the pain, the frustration, and the nightmares that had haunted her for far too long.

As Amelia poured out her story, the gentlemen in the corner,

Sarah and Johnny, stood in solemn silence, acknowledging the weight of her words. Mr. Gubbins, a figure of quiet strength, waited patiently for the release to unfold. The room became a sanctuary, witnessing Amelia's cathartic journey.

Amid her agony, Amelia felt a strange sense of relief. She had faced the monster of her past and spoken the unspeakable; with each word, she severed the chains that bound her. The darkness that shrouded her soul dissipated, making way for a glimmer of light.
When she finished, her body trembled with the exertion of releasing years of pain.

Mr. Gubbins, offering a kind smile, spoke softly, "Amelia, you've taken the first step toward healing. Now, close your eyes, put your hands over your ears, and do it yourself. Once you do that, you will be free forever. Trust me."

Mr Gubbins 'visitor produced a sheaf of papers from his pocket. With a deliberate gesture, he let them fall to the floor at Peter's feet, the pages adorned with elegant French script. The scattering papers lay there, an unspoken challenge echoing in the room.

Peter Smith, visibly agitated, couldn't contain his frustration.

"Who the hell do you think you are, and what's this rubbish?" he spat out.

Maintaining a stern gaze, the visitor responded, "Read it, Peter. It's a record of your sins, meticulously documented by those who suffered because of you."

Reluctantly, Peter picked up the papers, his eyes scanning the foreign words. As he read, his face contorted with rage and realisation. The script detailed the atrocities he had committed during the war and the pain he had inflicted on innocent lives.

"This is unreadable! Lies! Some fancy French nonsense won't judge me, whatever it says," Peter retorted, his voice filled with defiance.

Maintaining a calm air, the visitor countered, with a heavy French accent, "The truth transcends language, Monsieur. Your past has caught up with you, and justice demands it's due."

As Peter grappled with the damning revelations before him, the weight of accountability began to settle on his shoulders. The room, once a haven for his malevolence, now bore witness to the unveiling of his dark history. Ignorance of the French word Mort made his arrogance abrupt; if he had understood it, he might have presented a character more scared.

In the dimly lit room, an air of finality settled over the atmosphere as justice loomed large. A firm grip ensnared Peter's neck, and a Fairbairn Sykes commando knife pressed against his carotid artery. Johnny, standing behind him, manipulated the knife with a controlled and deliberate force. The room held its breath, a grim tableau of retribution.

Sarah and the two gentlemen strategically moved to shield Amelia from the impending spectacle, sparing her the grisly sight unfolding behind them.

In a surprising display of skill, Johnny fiercely struggled with Peter. The latter, taken aback by Johnny's proficiency in hand-to-hand combat, found himself overpowered. Johnny, now in control, positioned the knife at Peter's carotid artery, a symbol of the impending justice.

Mr Gubbins, a harbinger of the long-awaited reckoning, spoke with cold finality,

"Compliments of the Secret Intelligence Service and the French government. Also, from the families of all those girls and children you raped and murdered."

He glanced at the Frenchman, who nodded solemnly. The Frenchman placed a black cap on his head, and Johnny, with a measured intent, began the slow and painful descent of the knife.

"In my pocket, you bastard is a signed death warrant. You have been sentenced to death by both governments. You are going to die like you lived—a coward," Mr Gubbins declared with a seething resolve.

With a solemn expression, the French judge uttered the final words, "Que Dieu ait pitié de votre âme (May God have mercy on your soul)." The room bore witness to the culmination of justice, a bittersweet resolution for the countless lives marred by Peter's malevolence.

The room fell silent as Peter's lifeless body lay on the ground, the weight of justice finally catching up to him. His eyes, once filled with arrogance, now stared into the abyss, haunted by the damning finality of the word "coward."

Mr Gubbins and the French Judge approached the lifeless form, treating it with an odd mix of solemnity and closure. They covered Peter's remains with a tablecloth, a symbolic gesture to shroud his crimes and atrocities from the world.

The French Judge, a man burdened by the weight of the law and justice, took a moment for prayer. The air seemed to carry the weight of his words as he signed the sheaf of papers with a pen, breaking its nib symbolically.

Merci, Monsieur Adieu.

With that, the French Judge extended his hand to Mr Gubbins, a silent acknowledgement of shared justice served. The room held a lingering air of resolution, a closure for the victims and a testament to the unyielding pursuit of justice, no matter how delayed.

Johnny extended a tin box towards Mr Gubbins, a grim repository of Peter's sinister trophies – a chilling reminder of his crimes. Inside were a tie, a dog tag, lemon drops, a CND badge, a hat pin, a Girl Guide badge, and other morbid mementoes collected from the scenes of rape and murder.

Mr Gubbins took a deep breath, acknowledging the weight of the evidence within the tin. He addressed Sarah, his tone a mix of assurance and encouragement.

"Sarah, go be with your beautiful family. Forget all this; forget the war. Andrew and I will deal with this. For Johnny and you, the war is now over."

The tin box served as a macabre testament to the horrors they faced, and now it was in the hands of those who would ensure justice and closure for the victims. The room, still heavy with the gravity of recent events, seemed to exhale as Sarah hesitated momentarily before leaving, seeking solace with her family.

Amelia, her face etched with tear streaks, approached Mr Gubbins slowly, her face reflecting visible shock.

"Is he dead?" she questioned.

"I hope so, do hope so," Mr Gubbins replied.

Sarah returned to Mr Gubbins, swiftly ran, embraced him, and kissed his cheek.
"Johnny and I..." she started to say.

"I know, I know. This man was a vile creature; the committee decided he had to go. The French Government insisted on it," Mr Gubbins explained.

"French Government?" Amelia sought clarification.

"His evil actions during the war, his prison record, and the murder of Major Jed signed his death warrant. He was tried in absentia. He was to be arrested and deported to France today, but coming in with that shotgun, he decided for us. I am shocked to hear what that monster did to you," Mr Gubbins elaborated.

Sarah walked up to Amelia, hugged her, and exited the pub. The sound of a car reversing quickly and gears crunching reached their ears.

"What do I do now?" Amelia questioned, her voice quivering.

"Well, that's up to you, dear. Here is an envelope with £300 for resettlement, a train warrant, and a passenger cruise ticket with your passport can be arranged. You can go anywhere in the world you like. Your Aunt and I were good friends, and she often discussed moving to Australia. There is a man named Andrew; he will come in a minute. He is a good friend and will care for you," Mr Gubbins advised.

"What do I do with him, though?" Amelia inquired, her eyes reflecting a mix of fear and uncertainty.

"Don't worry about the body. Tell people it was a guy on a motorbike that robbed the till. There is an unmarked grave for him at Dartmoor Prison; he deserves no mercy on his wretched soul. No one alive here will miss him. We can't have the British public knowing about this; there will be an uproar," Mr Gubbins assured her, trying to provide some semblance of reassurance during the chaos.

***

The nightclub's pulsating energy had long faded into the early morning hours, replaced by the stark reality of flashing blue lights and the hushed whispers of paramedics attending to Sally. Derek's car screeched to a halt on the double yellow lines, his urgency evident as he leapt out, followed closely by Danny. A police officer approached his authoritative presence, momentarily halting Derek's movements.

"Hello, Magistrate, what are you doing here?" the officer inquired, his tone respectful yet tinged with curiosity.

"That's my niece. How is she doing?" Derek's voice carried a note of concern as he brushed past the officer, his gaze fixed on Sally's form on the gurney.

As Derek and the police officer conversed, Danny made his way to the side of the ambulance, where Sally's friends huddled together under silver Mylar blankets. The scene was tense, the air thick with worry as they awaited news of their friend's condition.

Meanwhile, Derek peered into the ambulance, his heart sinking at the sight of Sally lying semi-conscious, hooked up to oxygen and a drip. The police officer provided a brief explanation of the situation, detailing the drugs involved and the paramedics 'actions.

Acknowledging the officer's words with a terse nod, Derek climbed into the ambulance, taking Sally's hand in his own. His touch was gentle as he adjusted the blanket around her, his concern palpable in the dimly lit space.

"Thank you for your help, but do me one thing," Derek said, his voice firm as he addressed the officer. "Find who did this to her."

The officer nodded in understanding, a sense of determination evident in his response. "Yes, sir. Yes, sir."

Meanwhile, Danny engaged Sally's friends in conversation, his cool, calm yet determined as he sought information. The girls, though apprehensive, offered insights into the drug scene, detailing the process of arranging a meeting with their dealer.

As one of the girls, Jilly, led Danny aside, their conversation became clandestine. She revealed the method of contacting the dealer, discreetly pointing out a list of numbers on the wall of a nearby recycling bin.

"Take the bloody cigarette; pretend you don't want the police seeing," Jilly urged, her urgency underscoring the seriousness of their situation.

Danny accepted the cigarette with a nod, his mind racing with the implications of their discovery. "Clever," he remarked, a note of admiration in his voice.

As Jilly returned to the group, Danny remained rooted to the spot, his thoughts consumed by the dangerous game they were now embroiled in.

CHAPTER 14

Victim

PC Jane Moore's knock on the door of Amelia Greene's residence echoed through the modest hallway, heralding the arrival of an unwelcome visitor. As the door creaked open, revealing the figure of Stephan Greene's grandmother, Amelia, her facade was one of both hospitality and guardedness.

"Not going to take up too much time," PC Jane Moore began, her tone brisk and businesslike. "Have you seen Stephan?"

Amelia's response was warm, her invitation inside a testament to her hospitality. "He has gone to work, Dear. Cup of tea and a biscuit?"

But PC Moore declined the offer, her urgency apparent. "No to the tea. I am in a hurry. Where is he, then? His work?"

Amelia's memory faltered momentarily. "Oh, you know, dear. I can't quite recall... Is he in trouble? Such a sweet boy looks after his nana."

With a dismissive shake of her head, PC Moore pressed on. "No, I just want to speak to him."

"Well, he's running his business. Probably at the garages," Amelia offered, her concern for Stephan evident. "I have a garage he uses. The house number is on that. Are you sure you don't want a cup of tea? I have some Earl Grey."

But PC Moore was resolute in her mission. "No thanks, but if you see him, tell him I need to speak to him."

"He is a good boy, no trouble at all," Amelia defended, her protective instincts flaring. "Why do you have to pick on him so much? He is good to his nana."

Yet a steely resolve lurked beneath Amelia's grandmotherly facade, a hint of the authentic Amelia Greene. As PC Moore's gaze swept the room, she caught sight of a photograph—a pub, with Amelia depicted grimacing outside.

Suddenly, the atmosphere shifted, Amelia's persona transforming into something harder-edged and more resilient. "Well, you must be tough to survive; you know the score."

Ignoring the subtle threat in Amelia's words, PC Moore pressed on, her gaze lingering on the photograph. "This you, pregnant?"

Amelia's response was tinged with sorrow and pride. "Yes, Stephan's father."

"He's not around anymore?" PC Moore inquired, her curiosity piqued.

"Nah, he died in Australia, left me with Stephan, his child. Brought him up myself back here," Amelia explained, her voice tinged with regret and determination.

"Was his dad a crook too?" PC Moore's question was direct, her suspicion evident.
Amelia's kind granny routine was not working for her.

Amelia's reaction was swift and fierce. "Take that back! How dare you! He was a good kid despite him being an illegitimate bastard."

But PC Moore was unfazed, her words cutting. "They say evil skips a generation... You see your Grandson, tell him I want to see him. You have a day, or I will kick the door in shortly. You might want to ensure you have plenty of tea for then."

With a final, contemptuous look, PC Moore exited the flat, leaving Amelia alone with her thoughts. Retrieving a burner phone from her knitting bag, Amelia dialled a number, her voice cold and determined.

"Stephan, the police have been around. She's coming to your lockup now. I think she knows. How do I know? Yes, she's coming now. We'll deal with her, make her disappear, and love you too. Bangers and mash for looking after your nana."

***

In the quiet of Derek's kitchen, Danny sat hunched over a cluttered table, his gaze fixed on some diaries and constable books. His mind seemed distant, lost in a labyrinth of thoughts and unanswered questions.

As the front door swung open, Derek entered, shedding his driving cap and slipping off his gloves. His movements were deliberate as he approached Danny, sitting beside him at the table.

"You alright, son?" Derek's voice was gentle, tinged with concern.

Danny's response was laden with fatigue and worry. "Yes, I could not sleep last night. How is Sally?"

"She is in ICU at the moment," Derek replied solemnly. "Her friends were admitted as well for observation."

Danny's eyes betrayed his helplessness. "When I saw her in the ambulance, I felt helpless. Could not do nothing."

"We both did," Derek acknowledged, his voice heavy with shared anguish. "But she knew you were there. Take comfort in that."

The weight of anger hung heavy in the air as Danny voiced his frustrations. "Are you not angry?"

"Extremely," Derek admitted, his tone measured. But shouting and hollering and slamming doors will not help. It's just noise."

The conversation shifted to darker territories, Danny's voice laced with bitterness. "He killed my mum, then killed Andy and nearly killed Sally with his drugs."

Derek's response was tinged with resignation. "The police are looking into it. They need evidence. He always has a cast-iron alibi and is very good at this. He will be caught."

Danny's frustration boiled over as he lamented the justice system's shortcomings. "Yes, then let out again due to some smarmy lawyer and the courts which don't care... You are a magistrate, but you must agree it's very biased."

Derek's agreement was tinged with weariness. "Yes, I know. I have tried locking that excuse for a human being for most of his life... What have you got here?"

Danny's attention shifted back to the diaries and books before him. "I have been up all night because I went through Andy's stuff in the garage: Andy's book, a rough manuscript for volume two, and a couple of diaries."

"Research?" Derek inquired, his curiosity piqued.

"Well, the constable books are not fiction," Danny explained, his voice tinged with intrigue. "They are based on a real constable, A Trevor Dickens, who was in a gas explosion with his family. Very sad. But Andy's diary says it was a real explosion done by a serial killer called Peter Smith."

Danny paused for a moment, his voice heavy with significance. So, I looked into him online. He has a birth certificate in England and a death certificate in France as a French civilian... Executed for war crimes and multiple murders."

Derek's brow furrowed in confusion. "That is strange, I grant you that. But why are you bringing this up?"

"This is the bit I am getting my head around," Danny explained, his voice tinged with urgency. "She had a boy, who later had a son. Stephan Greene. They came back to the UK on his first birthday."

As Danny delved deeper into his revelations, Derek's expression grew increasingly incredulous. "It's been a long night. I am tired, and this makes no sense at all. You're saying my mum and dad arrested him."

"Yes," Danny affirmed, his tone resolute. "Your Mum was working with Andy at MI5, and your dad was retired from SAS. Not only that, Peter Smith was supplying explosives to the IRA. The same explosives used to kill that policeman's family."

"They say evil skips a generation," Derek muttered, his thoughts swirling with the weight of revelation.

"It's all linked," Danny concluded, his voice heavy with conviction. "It's all bloody linked."

Derek's mind raced with the implications of Danny's discoveries, grappling with the enormity of the revelations. "What would Dad do? What would Dad do?"

Danny's response was chilling in its certainty. "Your Dad would have killed Stephan a long time ago, that I am sure."

"You are talking about murder, conspiracy to murder. That's highly illegal," Derek cautioned, his voice tinged with apprehension.

"Well, I know how to get to him before he strikes again," Danny declared, his resolve unwavering. "Sally's friend gave me the means to contact him for drugs."

***

The Chatham Main Line, typically a bustling transportation artery, now lay shrouded in an eerie stillness. Police tape cordoned off the area, and a TV helicopter buzzed overhead, its whirring blades slicing through the tense atmosphere. Along the road adjacent to the tracks, a convoy of police and ambulance vehicles stood sentinel, their presence a grim testament to the gravity of the situation.

In the distance, a train sat idle, its driver and guard huddled on the sidings with paramedics attending to them. The train driver, his face etched with panic, clutched an oxygen mask, the victim of a paralysing panic attack induced by the harrowing events that had unfolded.

Amidst this chaos, a British Transport Police Inspector trudged along the track, flanked by the line foreman who led the way. The inspector donned blue plastic booties, a futile attempt to shield his shoes from the grim reality that awaited him.

The inspector's gaze fell upon a chilling sight as they approached the crime scene. Sprawled upon the tracks lay the lifeless body of a police officer, her form battered and bruised, stripped of dignity and clothing. The absence of her radio and camera hinted at a sinister sequence of events that had unfolded.

"Oh god, she's one of us," the inspector murmured, his voice laced with anguish.
A forensic team hovered nearby, their meticulous work underway. One of them, a solemn figure clad in protective gear, approached the inspector with grim news.

"We found her warrant card," the forensic officer reported. "PC Jane Moore. We can't match the face due to the injuries."

The inspector's mind raced with a torrent of questions,

grappling to make sense of the senseless violence that had befallen one of their own. "What the hell was she doing here? Does her station know?"

The forensic officer shook his head, his expression grave. "We have been discreet thus far. We have not told anyone she's a serving police officer."

"We need to notify her family," the inspector declared, his voice heavy with the weight of responsibility. "I best call her station."

During this tragedy, amidst the chaos and confusion, a harsh truth loomed—the thin blue line had been breached, and a dedicated officer had paid the ultimate price in service to her duty. And as the investigation unfolded, the shadow of darkness descending upon the Chatham Main Line threatened to engulf all who dared to seek justice.

***

Another city, not far from London,

The Volvo rumbled through the deserted streets, raindrops cascading down its windshield like tears shed by a mournful sky. The nightclub loomed ahead, a shadowy monolith shrouded in the cloak of night, its once vibrant facade now dulled by the relentless downpour.

Behind the wheel, Derek gripped the steering wheel with a sense of grim determination, his jaw set in a steely resolve. Beside him sat Danny, his features etched with a mix of apprehension and purpose, his gaze fixed on the dimly lit alleyways that flanked the building.

As they rounded the nightclub's rear, the streetlights' glow cast eerie shadows across the slick pavement. The air hung heavy with the scent of rain-soaked asphalt, a tangible reminder of the vigilante mood that enveloped them in the twilight at the end of the day and the night economy.

With a subtle nod from Derek, Danny reached for his mobile phone, his fingers deftly navigating the device's screen despite the dim illumination. As they crept past the bins that lined the alley, Danny raised the phone, capturing several photographs of the graffiti-strewn wall with practised precision.

Each snapshot captured a moment frozen in time, a silent testament to their clandestine mission. And as they slipped away into the night, the echoes of their presence lingered in the rain-soaked streets, a whispered promise of secrets yet to be unveiled.

***

In the dimly lit TV room of Fair Oaks, Danny moved with purpose, his steps measured and deliberate. The soft hum of the television filled the air, its glow casting flickering shadows across the worn carpet. The senior nurse, a beacon of authority, momentarily vacated the room, leaving Danny to carry out his clandestine mission.

As he traversed the room, Danny's gaze swept over the residents, each one a silent testament to the passage of time. Some sat lost in their own world, their eyes clouded with forgetfulness. In contrast, others retained a semblance of lucidity, their expressions flickering with fleeting moments of recognition.

With practised ease, Danny navigated the delicate dance of deception, his hands deftly retrieving tramadol pills from willing participants. The exchange was silent, each transaction a silent pact sealed with a knowing glance.

But amidst the quiet hum of activity, a weathered hand grasped Danny's, its grip firm and unwavering. Turning to face the source, Danny was confronted by Frank Jackson, a stalwart among the residents, his eyes brimming with a mix of resolve and concern.

"Ere lad," Frank's voice cut through the stillness, his words laced with a sense of urgency, "I know you are going after the bastard that got Andy."

Danny nodded a shared pact, the shared purpose that bound them together. Frank's words hung heavy in the air, a stark reminder of the dangers that lurked in the shadows.

"This is the last time we will do this for you," Frank continued, his tone tinged with a sense of finality. And another: do not get bloody caught. We have no idea what it is, but make sure you are back next week." Frank drops a pile of pills into Danny's hand; Danny looks about the room. The patients that are asleep are faking it; some are smiling, and one gave him a thumbs up,

Danny's jaw tightened, a silent vow forming in the depths of his soul. He understood the gravity of their actions and the risks they took to pursue justice. But for Danny, the stakes were higher than ever, his resolve unyielding in the face of adversity.

"I won't," Danny replied, his voice a solemn oath, "this is for Mum and Andy, not for me."
Frank released his grip with a nod of understanding, allowing Danny to continue his mission. As Danny exited, the weight of their collective burden hung heavy on his shoulders, a constant reminder of the sacrifices made in the name of justice. And as he stepped back into the world beyond Fair Oaks, Danny knew that he carried with him the hopes and dreams of those who could not fight for themselves.

"I watched Johnny learn to swim; it's for him too" Frank pulls up his sleeve, a tattoo of crossed swords on his wrist.

Danny turns, and at the doorway is Josephine; she smiles, "Get the bastard". Danny walks up, and Josephine whispers, "This is a civil service retirement home for MI5. Did you not know?"
Danny: "Sorry?"

Josephine walks off and waves, "Get the bastard. These old spooks want you to, and this young spook wants you too."

***

In the dim glow of the kitchen, Danny sat hunched over his laptop, his eyes fixed intently on the screen. The soft illumination cast shadows across his face, accentuating the lines of concentration on his brow. On the screen, a demonstration of palming and sleight of hand unfolded, the magician's fingers moving with fluid precision as he manipulated a small pea.

Danny mimicked the movements with a furrowed brow, his fingers dancing across the table's surface with practised precision. But despite his efforts, the pea remained stubbornly visible, betraying his lack of finesse.

Derek entered the room, his presence a silent interruption to Danny's concentration. Leaning against the doorframe, he watched with amusement and scepticism as his nephew struggled with his newfound skill.

"You need to get better at that," Derek remarked, his tone laced with gentle teasing. "I can still see it."

Danny sighed in frustration, his shoulders sagging with the weight of disappointment. "I am trying, really I am," he replied, his voice tinged with frustration.

Derek offered a sympathetic smile, his eyes crinkling at the corners. "Well, I am off picking up Judy and taking her to see Sally," he announced, his tone shifting to reassurance. "She is sitting up now; they are taking the tube out today. You best have that sorted by the time I get back."

With a nod of agreement, Danny returned his focus to the screen, his determination renewed. As Derek exited the room, the sound of his footsteps fading into the distance, Danny's fingers resumed their dance, the pea becoming a silent accomplice in his quest for mastery.

***

Amelia sat in the dimly lit living room, the glow of the TV casting flickering shadows across the worn furniture. As the evening news began, her attention was drawn to the screen, where a passive-faced newsreader delivered the latest report.

"Today, a police spokesman has confirmed the body found on the Chatham Rail link is that of Police Constable Jane Moore," the newsreader announced, his voice echoing in the quiet room. "The circumstances of the death have yet to be released, but it is believed that she took her own life in suspicious circumstances. The police have appealed for any wit—"

The words faded into the background as a sense of dread washed over Amelia. Without hesitation, she reached for her burner phone, fingers trembling as she dialled a familiar number.

"Stephan, what have you gone and done," she muttered, her voice tight with concern.

"Told you not to get caught... Do not 'oh Nan' me... I told you to get rid of her, meaning she disappeared... She escaped! She had handcuffs with her!"

As she spoke, a mixture of frustration and fear laced her words, the weight of the situation bearing down on her. She listened intently to the response on the other end of the line, her brow furrowing with each passing moment.

"Well, you've done it now," she continued, her voice rising slightly. "What... No... Alright, you were here all night, fish fingers for tea as usual... And you came with me to bingo... The girls will back me up. They love you, Stephan..."

Her words trailed off as she listened to the voice on the other end, her mind racing with possibilities. With a deep sigh, she shook her head, a sense of resignation settling over her.

"Well, if you get stopped and at the police station, call me 'Nana' on the phone, and I will know," she instructed, her tone firm. "You're a liability at times..."

As she ended the call, a sense of unease lingered in the air, the weight of uncertainty pressing down her shoulders. With a heavy heart, she leaned back in her chair, the flickering light of the TV casting long shadows across the room as she contemplated the tangled web of lies and deceit that had woven itself around her family.

***

Derek's house, Danny's eyes were fixed on the television screen, the same news report playing repeatedly. Danny's heart sank as the image of PC Jane Moore and her fiancée flashed across the screen.

"They have killed her, I know it," Danny muttered into his phone, his voice trembling with a mixture of grief and rage. "She's dead, Derek... You go back to Sally, but I must sort it out now."

With a heavy heart, he ended the call and stared at the items spread out before him on the table – a packet of tramadol and a gold poppy brooch. His hands shook as he picked up the brooch, turning it over in his fingers.

"What did you say about this brooch used by the SOE to carry a pill?" he murmured, his mind racing with possibilities.

Danny's fingers fumbled with the brooch, twisting and turning it for answers. With a sudden burst of determination, he focused on the ruby gem in the middle, his fingers working to pry it loose. A small white pill encased in a yellowing gelatin container rolled onto the table as the gem finally gave way.

For a moment, Danny was frozen in disbelief, the weight of his discovery settling heavily upon him. He backed away from the table, his eyes fixed on the pill and tramadol before him, the reality of his situation sinking in.

Uncertain of his next move, he paced back and forth in the kitchen, his mind racing about what to do next. With a sudden surge of fear, he realised the danger of his discovery and its implications.

Approaching the table cautiously, Danny retrieved a pair of tongs and rubber marigolds from the sink, his movements deliberate and cautious. With bated breath, he carefully picked up the cyanide pill, his heart pounding in his chest.

As he held the deadly pill between the tongs, Danny took a deep breath, steeling himself for what lay ahead. With a sense of grim determination, he prepared to dispose of the lethal substance, knowing that the path he was embarking on was fraught with danger and uncertainty.

***

Under the grey sky of the daytime, Derek's car rolled along the road, its interior enveloped in a silence that mirrored the atmosphere's heaviness. Judy sat in the passenger seat, tears streaming down her cheeks as she stared blankly out the window, lost in anguish. The absence of music from the radio and Derek's red, puffy eyes spoke volumes about the weight of their shared sorrow.

As the car neared Judy's house, Derek stopped it in the driveway, but neither moved. Judy's voice broke the oppressive silence, her words choked with emotion.

"Twenty per cent... How do they know twenty per cent?" she cried out, her anguish pouring forth. "Will she have to learn to walk again? Do I have to take her to the toilet? What the hell do I do?"

Derek's gaze shifted to Judy, his hands gripping the steering wheel tightly as he struggled to contain his emotions.

"You're a great mum, Judy," he reassured her, his voice hoarse with emotion. "A great mum. It's not your fault. Maybe she will recover."

But Judy's despair was palpable as she shook her head in disbelief. "She will not," she murmured, her voice trembling with despair. "Twenty per cent brain damage... She will have to learn to talk and walk... I will have to bathe her... She's years old, and now I am her mother, her nurse."

The weight of Judy's grief bore down on Derek as he listened, his heart breaking for her. As Judy's punches landed on him, he remained stoic, absorbing her pain without flinching.

"I want my bloody daughter back," Judy cried out, her voice filled with anguish. "The drugs took her away from me."

With a heavy heart, Derek unclipped his seat belt and reached out to Judy, pulling her into his arms as she shook with sobs. Together, they wept, the rain on the car windows concealing their shared sorrow from the outside world.

***

In the dimly lit kitchen of Derek's house, Danny sat at the table, his eyes fixed on the array of tablets before him. A pile of tramadol pills lay on one side, while a single cyanide tablet sat ominously on the other. His gaze remained transfixed, lost in a tumult of thoughts and emotions.

Unnoticed by Danny, the door creaked open, and Derek entered the room. Without a word, he pulled out a chair and sat opposite his troubled friend. Together, they sat silently, their eyes drawn to the paraphernalia of misery before them.

Danny broke the silence, placing a series of newspaper printouts on the table. Headlines screamed tales of violence, tragedy, and despair: "Teenager stabbed in hate crime," "Arson at flats," "Woman killed in mugging," "Elderly WW2 RAF Hero drowns in Canal Mugging," "Girl overdoses on MDMA GHB drug at Nightclub," "Drugs epidemic on estate," "Police no-go zone," "WPC suicide inquiry," "Crime Wave has to Stop."

Derek's eyes, red and weary, scanned the headlines, his heart heavy with the weight of the world's suffering. He reached out, his finger resting on the word "Stop" on the headline that Danny had indicated.

In that simple gesture, a silent understanding passed between them. Derek lowered his head in shame, then lifted it again to meet Danny's gaze, his eyes conveying a tacit acknowledgement of their shared responsibility. Permission had been granted—a silent agreement forged in the crucible of their collective pain. Now, the work has to begin.

***

Inside the bustling Mecca Bingo Hall, the air was thick with the anticipation of potential winnings. Paula and Judy stood at the bar, their voices drowned out by the lively chatter of other patrons. They reached their designated table with drinks in hand, clutching oversized bingo books and pens.

As the bingo caller's voice echoed through the hall, summoning players to their tables, Paula and Judy settled into their seats, their facade of enjoyment painted on. They exchanged knowing glances, their eyes scanning the room until they locked onto a familiar figure across the hall.

Amelia, accompanied by her entourage of bingo aficionados, was engrossed in the game. Her presence commanded attention, her swagger exuding confidence and authority. Judy discreetly reached for her mobile phone, her fingers swiftly typing a message on the WhatsApp group chat: "playing."

With their eyes fixed on Amelia, Paula and Judy remained vigilant, observing her every move with curiosity and suspicion. They knew every detail mattered in this den of chance and uncertainty, where fortunes could change instantly.

***

On a sodium-lit street outside the nightclub, Derek sat in his car, bathed in the glow of the dashboard lights. His eyes focused intently on the task as he meticulously jotted down a telephone number in a weathered notepad. Once satisfied, he tucked the notepad away and manoeuvred his car around the corner, finding a discreet parking spot.

With urgency, Derek retrieved a nondescript cardboard box from the backseat. Swiftly unwrapping it, he revealed a pristine mobile phone box, its contents untouched. Carefully, he extracted the phone, deftly inserting the SIM card and battery before powering it on. Referencing the number he had just recorded, Derek composed a message. He hit send, the tension palpable as he awaited a response.

A notification chimed in, causing Derek to startle in his seat. The message displayed a cryptic instruction: "Cemetery gate twenty minutes, 20 quid for tammies, for hard." The situation's urgency weighed heavily on him as he fired up the engine and set off towards the outskirts of town.

As Derek approached the cemetery, the ominous silhouette of gang members on motorbikes loomed in the distance, converging on the same destination. Parking discreetly at a safe distance, he killed the engine. He extinguished the lights, sinking low in his seat as he observed the cemetery gates with trepidation.

Heart pounding, Derek watched anxiously as Stephan and his cohorts arrived for the illicit exchange, the air thick with the anticipation of danger and deceit. Every moment was fraught with peril in this shadowy underworld of illegal transactions. Derek found himself teetering on the edge of a dangerous precipice.

***

Under the shroud of darkness, Danny moved stealthily through the dilapidated flats, cloaked in black attire that blended seamlessly with the night. His steps were deliberate, each footfall calculated to avoid any unwanted attention. With a sense of purpose, he ascended to the floor where only Amelia's flat remained inhabited, the rest succumbing to neglect and decay. Or fear of being next to criminal royalty.

As he traversed the desolate hallway, Danny's phone buzzed with an incoming message on WhatsApp. He paused momentarily, glancing at the screen before resuming his journey. Drawing closer to the edge of the building, he surveyed the balcony below, noting the gaping holes in the brick lattice. Danny leapt across the void without hesitation, his movements swift and sure despite the treacherous terrain below.

Unbeknownst to him, a mysterious figure shrouded in darkness observed his daring leap from the nearby walkway. Clad in a dark suit, the watcher remained concealed within the shadows, an enigmatic presence amidst the night.

Having successfully traversed the gap, Danny climbed up and over the balcony wall with practised ease, repeating the same daring feat to reach Amelia's balcony above. He tested the sliding patio door cautiously, finding it unlocked. Silently slipping inside, Danny found himself in Stephan's unkempt bedroom, a shrine to the gangsta lifestyle adorned with posters and paraphernalia.

Amongst the clutter, Danny's keen eyes fell upon a nightstand, its surface cluttered with remnants of illicit indulgence. Carefully prying open a small tin box adorned with marijuana leaves, he uncovered a cache of ten tramadol pills. Swiftly pocketing the contraband, Danny replaced them with an identical number of counterfeit pills, his actions methodical and precise.

Before departing, Danny donned a plasterer's facemask and blue nitrile gloves, leaving no trace of his presence behind. With his mission accomplished, he retreated into the night, leaving only shadows and silence in his wake.

Around him, people observe his every action, from doors, windows, and cars unseen by anyone else. Talking to each other via radio. From a distance, invisible.

***

The subdued atmosphere of the graveyard enveloped Danny and Derek as they stood amidst the aftermath of the dual funeral for Andy and Johnny. British Legion standard bearers, their task complete, meticulously folded away the flags while mourners quietly dispersed. Among them, a man clad in dark trousers and a blazer adorned with the RAF colours lingered nearby, his presence evoking a sense of solemnity. Nearby, another figure, solitary and stoic in a beige beret, bore the insignia of the SAS, accompanied by comrades sporting spirit of freedom badges from the SOE.

As the care home minibus departed, Danny and Derek, both impeccably dressed, walked in subdued silence down the path, followed closely by Judy and Paula, who engaged in conversation behind them. Derek's blazer bore the weight of his father's medals, including the French Croix de Guerre, a poignant reminder of his family's legacy of service.

"It seems fitting," Derek remarked softly, breaking the heavy silence in the air, "that they are buried together on the same day."

"They were friends until the end," Danny concurred, his voice tinged with melancholy.

"I wish I had known Andy better," Derek confessed, a note of regret in his tone. "He often kept to himself when we visited."

"I know," Danny replied sympathetically. "Your mum, Johnny, and he were like a trio of mischief-makers."

"They must have been a handful," Derek mused, a wistful smile on his lips.

"The care home feels quieter now," Danny observed, his gaze drifting towards the horizon.

"It's a shame Sally couldn't be here," Derek lamented. "She

adored her granddad, always getting into mischief together."

"Him and his secrets," Danny remarked, a hint of amusement in his voice.

"Well, you'd best be nice to Judy and me," Derek interjected, a mischievous glint in his eye as he produced an envelope from his pocket.

Danny's eyes widened in surprise as he accepted the envelope, his curiosity piqued.

"What's this?"

"Something good has come out of all this," Derek declared with a smile.

Judy approached her presence with comforting reassurance. "Take it, son," she urged, linking her arm with Danny's.

Danny nodded, his mind reeling with disbelief as he opened the envelope to reveal its contents. Inside lay a substantial sum of money, a testament to Andy's generosity and foresight.

"It's a trust fund for nursing college," Derek explained, pride evident in his voice. "Judy and I are the trustees."

"Andy left it for you," Judy added, her tone warm and encouraging. "All we ask is that you use it to pursue your dreams."

A moment of quiet reflection passed before a gentleman approached, his bearing both authoritative and enigmatic.

"Excuse me, Judy," the man addressed her, his gaze fixed on Danny. "May I borrow the young man for a moment?"

Danny followed the mysterious figure to a nearby bench, and his curiosity was piqued as they both took a seat.

"You're the police," Danny observed astutely, his eyes narrowing with suspicion.

"Ah, very astute," the man acknowledged with a nod. "I am of sorts. My father left you a sum of money for nursing college."

Danny's brow furrowed in confusion. "I never asked for it. I didn't even know he was wealthy."

"Relax, young man," the man reassured him. "I'm not interested in the money. However, your recent actions have not gone unnoticed."

Danny's heart quickened with apprehension. "What do you mean?"

"When my father was murdered, I tasked a surveillance team with finding his killer," the man explained. "Your intervention provided the resolution we needed."

Realisation dawned on Danny as the gravity of the situation sank in. "You mean Stephan?"

"Exactly," the man confirmed. "He met his end from a Tramadol overdose, a fitting demise for a cockroach of his calibre. We know you laced his tramadol with cyanide."

His gran, a particularly nasty piece of work herself, found him; we bugged her phone. It turns out she was the lynchpin or, as the boys in the office call her, the Godmother. Poor joke, I know, but true. She ordered your mother's murder, My father's, and a talented police officer."

Danny's mind raced as he absorbed the implications of his actions. "Murder..."

The man held out a phone, its screen displaying a chilling video. "We found this on Stephan's phone and other incriminating evidence. Your involvement in these crimes cannot be ignored. Some of these videos are of you being stabbed and beaten, your Mum, god rest her soul, and ... dad. PC Moore"

Danny's stomach churned with nausea as he watched the harrowing footage unfold before him.

"But fear not," the man continued, his tone reassuring. "I'm not here to arrest you. I'm offering you a job. Bravo for using the cyanide pill from her brooch."

"Your Dad, Andy books inspired me. His friend Johnny was, to everyone, a coward, but he was a hero; Sarah was a hero too; the books taught me courage through adversity; when Sally nearly died, all I could think of was the hundreds of others around the city he could have killed. I had to do something, anything. I had to do the right thing. I could not live with my shame of not fighting back any further, " Andy sobbed.

"Which is why we are offering you a job, to continue that cause."

Danny's eyes widened in disbelief, his world spinning with newfound possibilities. The conversation between Danny and the enigmatic figure remained shrouded in secrecy, their futures intertwined in the shadowy realm of law and justice. Then, the lament of the last post from a bugle added a haunting air to the funeral.

***

Amelia sat alone in her quiet flat, the world's weight bearing on her fragile shoulders. Footage of her solitary figure, interspersed with scenes of the gang members each facing the consequences of their crimes, flickered across the television screen. The atmosphere was heavy with anticipation, a palpable tension hanging in the air like a suffocating blanket. The news media flooded the airwaves with her photo, Stephan, and the dawn raids on the gang.

, A pot of fresh tea steaming by her chair. Expectant.

In her trembling hand, she clutched a letter, its official seals bearing the weight of authority and judgment. With trembling fingers, she traced the words inscribed upon it:

"Dear Miss Amelia Shrank, you were allowed to seek a new life in Australia to become a good citizen. You ignored the events of July 16th and the grant the UK government gave you. Use this moment to renounce your Grandson's life of crime and give up all those who took part in this scheme. The abhorrent sins of your Stepfather have followed you, and you have been found in contempt of court on July 16th, 1967. We are watching you, waiting, and one day, we will collect you for the evil precipitated by yourself and your Grandson. Signed, "The court of human justice."

As the letter slipped from her grasp, it fluttered to the floor, a damning testament to her guilt and shame. Drool pooled on her lifeless body, sprawled across the floor with vomit smeared on her chin, a large glass of gin, and empty packets of tramadol scattered around her like macabre confetti.

The door erupts as the police dressed like beetles swarm the flat, weapons raised. Red laser dots danced around Amelia's lifeless form.

In the doorway, a solitary figure emerged from the shadows.

Mr. Simeon Tavistock, his expression unreadable, bent down to retrieve the letter from the floor. He tucked it into his pocket with solemn reverence, a silent witness to the tragic demise before him.

Without a word, Mr. Tavistock turned and slowly walked out of the room, leaving a scene of desolation and despair. Outside, approaching footsteps echoed in the hallway, followed by the unmistakable presence of law enforcement.

More police entered the flat, their expressions grim as they surveyed the scene before them. In Stephan's room, they discovered the remnants of a police officer's radio and camera, a silent testament to the darkness that had consumed them all.

The search became less gentle as every item in the flat was smashed; Amelia's favourite pottery of the drey cart broke on the fireplace, an officer boot walks over the photo of her and her brother hitting it, the picture of her in younger days, in dungarees, with a CND badge, and a brownie badge, and hairpin, A police officer finds a box, under her bed, with buttons, coins, rings, an RAF blazer badge, Daphnes works badge, and PC Moore collar numbers.

CHAPTER 15

Revelation

The large SUV rumbled to a halt amidst the dense woods near Salisbury, its occupants—Derek, Judy, Sally, and Danny—eager to uncover the hidden secrets. Judy sat beside Sally, who was in an altered state, her oxygen mask a stark reminder of her frailty. Meanwhile, Derek and Judy stepped out, armed with a map and a mobile phone, their eyes scanning the surroundings for any sign of their elusive destination. Danny stayed behind with Sally, nursing his new sister.

In the distance, a woodsman appeared by a pickup truck, his rugged appearance a testament to a life spent amidst the wilderness. Derek and Judy approached him with a makeshift map, their curiosity piqued.

"Are you here for the bunker as well?" the woodsman inquired, his tone tinged with intrigue.

Judy explained their purpose, seeking information about their parents' wartime residence. The woodsman nodded knowingly, regaling them with tales of the old Gamekeeper lodge and cottage, both of which had succumbed to flames in the aftermath of World War II.

As they ventured deeper into the woods, the woodsman recounted the tragic fate of the Gamekeeper, a victim of arson, and his loyal dog, both beaten to death in a senseless act of violence. Derek and Judy pressed on despite the pallid atmosphere, their determination unyielding.

Amidst the trees, the woodsman revealed the existence of a secret underground bunker, unknown until recent years. He guided them to a concealed entrance, warning of the potential hazards.

Descending into the depths of the bunker, Derek and Judy's hearts raced with anticipation. In the dim light, they searched for clues that might shed light on their parents' clandestine past.

Suddenly, Derek's voice broke the silence, a note of urgency in his tone. "Judy, do you think...?"

Judy's eyes widened in realisation as Derek's words hung in the air. Could it be possible? Were they about to uncover the truth behind their parents' wartime exploits?

The woodsman, intrigued by their reaction, climbed back up the ladder to join them, his curiosity piqued by their sudden revelation.

With trembling hands, Derek reached for his mobile phone, his excitement palpable.

"Danny, it's all true!" he exclaimed, unable to contain his elation. "Mum and Dad were bloody war heroes!" He turned his camera phone to a tree nearby; carved in the trunk,

Johnny & Sarah

Judy's heart swelled with pride as she looked upon her brother, a sense of closure washing over her. "Bless them," she whispered,
With a newfound sense of purpose, Derek and Judy emerged from the depths of the bunker, their minds ablaze with possibilities. Together, they would honour their parents' memory and ensure their sacrifices were never forgotten.

CHAPTER 16

France Rememberance

In the quaint village of Oradour-sur-Glane, Derek and Judy stood amidst the ruins, their figures starkly contrasting with the devastation surrounding them. Behind them, Sally sat in her wheelchair, her presence a silent testament to family bonds. Danny stood behind in a suit, looking thoughtful, wearing a Queen Alexandra's Royal Army Nursing Corps Tie.

As they placed a wreath on the ground, a wartime wedding photo of Johnny and Sarah, their love immortalised in sepia tones. A small wooden cross bore the inscription, "Mum, Dad," a poignant reminder of the lives lost to war.

Suddenly, the suited figure of Mr. Simeon Tavistock appeared, his presence both enigmatic and imposing. Without a word, he placed two wreaths adorned with the SOE cap badge and a SAS Wreath with Blue poppies before silently retreating into the shadows.

At that moment, Derek and Judy felt a sense of closure, their journey coming full circle as they paid tribute to their parents' legacy. As they turned to leave, their hearts heavy with emotion, they knew that their loved ones would never be forgotten, their memory living on in the hearts of those they left behind.

"Bless them, bless them... they are all reunited now, I hope. Mum, dad, friends," Judy murmured, emotions swelling within her. She played wistfully on her keepsake from Mum, a gold poppy with a ruby inset.

The End.

Printed in Great Britain
by Amazon